FUTURE LEGEND

Just then I spy a light growin' deeper in the cave. A
white light, and brighter than any star. Before I
could point it out to Lee, that light shooted from the
dark and pass right through me with a flash of cold.
Then come another light, and another yet. Each one
colder and brighter than the one previous, and comin'
faster and faster, 'til it 'pears the cave brightly lit
and the lights they flickerin' a little. It were so damn
cold that the rainwater have froze in my hair, and I
were half-blinded on top of that, but I could have
swore I seen somethin' inside the light. And when
the cold begin to heaten up, the light to dwindle, I
made out the shape of a woman . . .

"Listen," she say. "You know where I come from?"
And Lee say, No, but he's been a'wonderin'. "The
future," she tell him. "Almost a hundred years from
now. And I come all that way to see you, Lee
Christmas . . ."

—From "Aymara"
by Lucius Shepard

TIME TRAVELERS

From ISAAC ASIMOV'S SCIENCE FICTION MAGAZINE

Edited by Gardner Dozois

ACE BOOKS, NEW YORK

TIME TRAVELERS

An Ace Book/published by arrangement with
Davis Publications, Inc.

PRINTING HISTORY
Ace edition / March 1989

ISBN: 0-441-80935-9

Ace Books are published by The Berkley Publishing Group,
200 Madison Avenue, New York, New York 10016.
The name ''ACE'' and the ''A'' logo are trademarks
belonging to Charter Communications, Inc.

10 9 8 7 6 5 4 3 2 1

ACKNOWLEDGMENTS

The editor woud like to thank the following people for their help and support: George Scithers and Shawna McCarthy, for having the good taste to buy most of this material in the first place; Sheila Williams, who has labored behind the scenes on *IAsfm* for many years and played a part in the decision-making process involved in the buying of some of these stories; Susan Casper, who did much of the thankless scut-work involved in preparing the manuscript; Tina Lee and Charles Ardai, who did much of the basic research needed; Cynthia Manson, who set up this deal; Florence B. Eichin, who cleared the permissions; and especially to my own editor on this project, Susan Allison.

CONTENTS

AIR RAID

John Varley

"Air Raid" was purchased by George Scithers, and appeared in the very first issue of IAsfm. *Another story by Varley, "Good-Bye, Robinson Crusoe," was one of the featured novelettes in our premier issue, so Varley was asked to come up with a pseudonym for "Air Raid"—there being an old prejudice against two stories by the same author appearing in the same issue— and it finally appeared under the name "Herb Boehm." This pseudonym did not remain secret for long, however, and "Air Raid" went on to become one of the year's most popular stories, appearing in Best of the Year anthologies and on award ballots. It remains a jazzy and jolting story that goes straight for the jugular.*

John Varley appeared on the SF scene in 1975, and by the end of 1976—in what was a meteoric rise to prominence even for a field known for meteoric rises— was already being recognized as one of the hottest new writers of the seventies. His books include the novels Ophiuchi Hotline, Titan, Wizard, *and* Demon, *and the collections* The Persistence of Vision, The Barbie Mur-

ders, *and* Picnic on Nearside. *His most recent book is
the collection* Blue Champagne. *He has won two Nebula and two Hugo Awards for his short fiction.*

I was jerked awake by the silent alarm vibrating my skull.
It won't shut down until you sit up, so I did. All around me in
the darkened bunkroom the Snatch Team members were sleeping singly and in pairs. I yawned, scratched my ribs, and
patted Gene's hairy flank. He turned over. So much for a
romantic send-off.

Rubbing sleep from my eyes, I reached to the floor for my
leg, strapped it on and plugged it in. Then I was running
down the rows of bunks toward Ops.

The situation board glowed in the gloom. Sun-Belt Airlines
Flight 128, Miami to New York, September 15, 1979. We'd
been looking for that one for three years. I should have been
happy, but who can afford it when you wake up?

Liza Boston muttered past me on the way to Prep. I
muttered back, and followed. The lights came on around the
mirrors, and I groped my way to one of them. Behind us,
three more people staggered in. I sat down, plugged in, and at
last I could lean back and close my eyes.

They didn't stay closed for long. Rush! I sat up straight as
the sludge I use for blood was replaced with supercharged
go-juice. I looked around me and got a series of idiot grins.
There was Liza, and Pinky and Dave. Against the far wall
Cristabel was already turning slowly in front of the airbrush,
getting a caucasian paint job. It looked like a good team.

I opened the drawer and started preliminary work on my
face. It's a bigger job every time. Transfusion or no, I looked
like death. The right ear was completely gone now. I could
no longer close my lips; the gums were permanently bared. A
week earlier, a finger had fallen off in my sleep. And what's
it to you, bugger?

While I worked, one of the screens around the mirror glowed. A smiling young woman, blonde, high brow, round face. Close enough. The crawl line read *Mary Katrina Sondergard, born Trenton, New Jersey, age in 1979: 25.* Baby, this is your lucky day.

The computer melted the skin away from her face to show me the bone structure, rotated it, gave me cross-sections. I studied the similarities with my own skull, noted the differences. Not bad, and better than some I'd been given.

I assembled a set of dentures that included the slight gap in the upper incisors. Putty filled out my cheeks. Contact lenses fell from the dispenser and I popped them in. Nose plugs widened my nostrils. No need for ears; they'd be covered by the wig. I pulled a blank plastiflesh mask over my face and had to pause while it melted in. It took only a minute to mold it to perfection. I smiled at myself. How nice to have lips.

The delivery slot clunked and dropped a blonde wig and a pink outfit into my lap. The wig was hot from the styler. I put it on, then the pantyhose.

"Mandy? Did you get the profile on Sondergard?" I didn't look up; I recognized the voice.

"Roger."

"We've located her near the airport. We can slip you in before take-off, so you'll be the joker."

I groaned, and looked up at the face on the screen. Elfreda Baltimore-Louisville, Director of Operational Teams: lifeless face and tiny slits for eyes. What can you do when all the muscles are dead?

"Okay." You take what you get.

She switched off, and I spent the next two minutes trying to get dressed while keeping my eyes on the screens. I memorized names and faces of crew members plus the few facts known about them. Then I hurried out and caught up with the others. Elapsed time from first alarm: twelve minutes and seven seconds. We'd better get moving.

"Goddam Sun-Belt," Cristabel groused, hitching at her bra.

"At least they got rid of the high heels," Dave pointed

out. A year earlier we would have been teetering down the aisles on three-inch platforms. We all wore short pink shifts with blue and white stripes diagonally across the front, and carried matching shoulder bags. I fussed trying to get the ridiculous pillbox cap pinned on.

We jogged into the dark Operations Control Room and lined up at the gate. Things were out of our hands now. Until the gate was ready, we could only wait.

I was first, a few feet away from the portal. I turned away from it; it gives me vertigo. I focused instead on the gnomes sitting at their consoles, bathed in yellow lights from their screens. None of them looked back at me. They don't like us much. I don't like them, either. Withered, emaciated, all of them. Our fat legs and butts and breasts are a reproach to them, a reminder that Snatchers eat five times their ration to stay presentable for the masquerade. Meantime we continue to rot. One day I'll be sitting at a console. One day I'll be *built in* to a console, with all my guts on the outside and nothing left of my body but stink. The hell with them.

I buried my gun under a clutter of tissues and lipsticks in my purse. Elfreda was looking at me.

"Where is she?" I asked.

"Motel room. She was alone from 10 PM to noon on flight day."

Departure time was 1:15. She cut it close and would be in a hurry. Good.

"Can you catch her in the bathroom? Best of all, in the tub?"

"We're working on it." She sketched a smile with a fingertip drawn over lifeless lips. She knew how I liked to operate, but she was telling me I'd take what I got. It never hurts to ask. People are at their most defenseless stretched out and up to their necks in water.

"Go!" Elfreda shouted. I stepped through, and things started to go wrong.

I was faced the wrong way, stepping *out* of the bathroom door and facing the bedroom. I turned and spotted Mary Katrina Sondergard through the haze of the gate. There was no way I could reach her without stepping back through. I couldn't even shoot without hitting someone on the other side.

Sondergard was at the mirror, the worst possible place. Few people recognize themselves quickly, but she'd been looking right at herself. She saw me and her eyes widened. I stepped to the side, out of her sight.

"What the hell is . . . hey? Who the hell . . ." I noted the voice, which can be the trickiest thing to get right.

I figured she'd be more curious than afraid. My guess was right. She came out of the bathroom, passing through the gate as if it wasn't there, which it wasn't, since it only has one side. She had a towel wrapped around her.

"Jesus Christ! What are you doing in my—" Words fail you at a time like that. She knew she ought to say something, but what? *Excuse me, haven't I seen you in the mirror?*

I put on my best stew smile and held out my hand.

"Pardon the intrusion. I can explain everything. You see, I'm—" I hit her on the side of the head and she staggered and went down hard. Her towel fell to the floor. "—working my way through college." She started to get up, so I caught her under the chin with my artificial knee. She stayed down.

"Standard fuggin' *oil*!" I hissed, rubbing my injured knuckles. But there was no time. I knelt beside her, checked her pulse. She'd be okay, but I think I loosened some front teeth. I paused a moment. Lord, to look like that with no makeup, no prosthetics! She nearly broke my heart.

I grabbed her under the knees and wrestled her to the gate. She was a sack of limp noodles. Somebody reached through, grabbed her feet, and pulled. *So long, love! How would you like to go on a long voyage?*

I sat on her rented bed to get my breath. There were car keys and cigarettes in her purse, genuine tobacco, worth its weight in blood. I lit six of them, figuring I had five minutes of my very own. The room filled with sweet smoke. They don't make 'em like that anymore.

The Hertz sedan was in the motel parking lot. I got in and headed for the airport. I breathed deeply of the air, rich in hydrocarbons. I could see for hundreds of yards into the distance. The perspective nearly made me dizzy, but I live for those moments. There's no way to explain what it's like in the pre-meck world. The sun was a fierce yellow ball through the haze.

The other stews were boarding. Some of them knew Sondergard so I didn't say much, pleading a hangover. That went over well, with a lot of knowing laughs and sly remarks. Evidently it wasn't out of character. We boarded the 707 and got ready for the goats to arrive.

It looked good. The four commandos on the other side were identical twins for the women I was working with. There was nothing to do but be a stewardess until departure time. I hoped there would be no more glitches. Inverting a gate for a joker run into a motel room was one thing, but in a 707 at twenty thousand feet . . .

The plane was nearly full when the woman that Pinky would impersonate sealed the forward door. We taxied to the end of the runway, then we were airborne. I started taking orders for drinks in first.

The goats were the usual lot, for 1979. Fat and sassy, all of them, and as unaware of living in a paradise as a fish is of the sea. _What would you think, ladies and gents, of a trip to the future? No? I can't say I'm surprised. What if I told you this plane is going to—_

My alarm beeped as we reached cruising altitude. I consulted the indicator under my Lady Bulova and glanced at one of the restroom doors. I felt a vibration pass through the plane. _Damn it, not so soon._

The gate was in there. I came out quickly, and motioned for Diana Gleason—Dave's pigeon—to come to the front.

"Take a look at this," I said with a disgusted look. She started to enter the restroom, stopped when she saw the green glow. I planted a boot on her fanny and shoved. Perfect. Dave would have a chance to hear her voice before popping in. Though she'd be doing little but screaming when she got a look around . . .

Dave came through the gate, adjusting his silly little hat. Diana must have struggled.

"Be disgusted," I whispered.

"What a mess," he said as he came out of the restroom. It was a fair imitation of Diana's tone, though he'd missed the accent. It wouldn't matter much longer.

"What is it?" It was one of the stews from tourist. We stepped aside so she could get a look, and Dave shoved her through. Pinky popped out very quickly.

"We're minus on minutes," Pinky said. "We lost five on the other side."

"Five?" Dave-Diana squeaked. I felt the same way. We had a hundred and three passengers to process.

"Yeah. They lost contact after you pushed my pigeon through. It took that long to re-align."

You get used to that. Time runs at different rates on each side of the gate, though it's always sequential, past to future. Once we'd started the snatch with me entering Sondergard's room, there was no way to go back any earlier on either side. Here, in 1979, we had a rigid ninety-four minutes to get everything done. On the other side, the gate could never be maintained longer than three hours.

"When you left, how long was it since the alarm went in?"

"Twenty-eight minutes."

It didn't sound good. It would take at least two hours just customizing the wimps. Assuming there was no more slippage on 79-time, we might just make it. But there's *always* slippage. I shuddered, thinking about riding it in.

"No time for any more games, then," I said. "Pink, you go back to tourist and call both of the other girls up here. Tell 'em to come one at a time, and tell 'em we've got a problem. You know the bit."

"Biting back the tears. Got you." She hurried aft. In no time the first one showed up. Her friendly Sun-Belt Airlines smile was stamped on her face, but her stomach would be churning. *Oh God, this is it!*

I took her by the elbow and pulled her behind the curtains in front. She was breathing hard.

"Welcome to the twilight zone," I said, and put the gun to her head. She slumped, and I caught her. Pinky and Dave helped me shove her through the gate.

"Fug! The rotting thing's flickering."

Pinky was right. A very ominous sign. But the green glow stabilized as we watched, with who-knows-how-much slippage on the other side. Cristabel ducked through.

"We're plus thirty-three," she said. There was no sense talking about what we were all thinking: things were going badly.

"Back to tourist," I said. "Be brave, smile at everyone, but make it just a little bit too good, got it?"

"Check," Cristabel said.

We processed the other quickly, with no incident. Then there was no time to talk about anything. In eighty-nine minutes Flight 128 was going to be spread all over a mountain whether we were finished or not.

Dave went into the cockpit to keep the flight crew out of our hair. Me and Pinky were supposed to take care of first class, then back up Cristabel and Liza in tourist. We used the standard "coffee, tea, or milk" gambit, relying on our speed and their inertia.

I leaned over the first two seats on the left.

"Are you enjoying your flight?" Pop, pop. Two squeezes on the trigger, close to the heads and out of sight of the rest of the goats.

"Hi, folks. I'm Mandy. Fly me." Pop, pop.

Halfway to the galley, a few people were watching us curiously. But people don't make a fuss until they have a lot more to go on. One goat in the back row stood up, and I let him have it. By now there were only eight left awake. I abandoned the smile and squeezed off four quick shots. Pinky took care of the rest. We hurried through the curtains, just in time.

There was an uproar building in the back of tourist, with about sixty percent of the goats already processed. Cristabel glanced at me, and I nodded.

"Okay, folks," she bawled. "I want you to be quiet. Calm down and listen up. *You*, fathead, *pipe down* before I cram my foot up your ass sideways."

The shock of hearing her talk like that was enough to buy us a little time, anyway. We had formed a skirmish line across the width of the plane, guns out, steadied on seat backs, aimed at the milling, befuddled group of thirty goats.

The guns are enough to awe all but the most foolhardy. In essence, a standard-issue stunner is just a plastic rod with two grids about six inches apart. There's not enough metal in it to set off a hijack alarm. And to people from the Stone Age to about 2190 it doesn't look any more like a weapon than a ballpoint pen. So Equipment Section jazzes them up in a plastic shell to real Buck Rogers blasters, with a dozen knobs and lights that flash and a barrel like the snout of a hog. Hardly anyone ever walks into one.

"We are in great danger, and time is short. You must all do exactly as I tell you, and you will be safe."

You can't give them time to think, you have to rely on your status as the Voice of Authority. The situation is just *not* going to make sense to them, no matter how you explain it.

"Just a minute, I think you owe us—"

An airborne lawyer. I made a snap decision, thumbed the fireworks switch on my gun, and shot him.

The gun made a sound like a flying saucer with hemorrhoids, spit sparks and little jets of flame, and extended a green laser finger to his forehead. He dropped.

All pure kark, of course. But it sure is impressive.

And it's damn risky, too. I had to choose between a panic if the fathead got them to thinking, and a possible panic from the flash of the gun. But when a 20th gets to talking about his "rights" and what he is "owed," things can get out of hand. It's infectious.

It worked. There was a lot of shouting, people ducking behind seats, but no rush. We could have handled it, but we needed some of them conscious if we were ever going to finish the Snatch.

"Get up. Get *up*, you *slugs!*" Cristabel yelled. "He's

stunned, nothing worse. But I'll *kill* the next one who gets out of line. Now *get to your feet* and do what I tell you. *Children first! Hurry,* as fast as you can, to the front of the plane. Do what the stewardess tells you. Come on, kids, *move!"*

I ran back into first class just ahead of the kids, turned at the open restroom door, and got on my knees.

They were petrified. There were five of them—crying, some of them, which always chokes me up—looking left and right at dead people in the first class seats, stumbling, near panic.

"Come on, kids," I called to them, giving my special smile. "Your parents will be along in just a minute. Everything's going to be all right, I promise you. Come on."

I got three of them through. The fourth balked. She was determined not to go through that door. She spread her legs and arms and I couldn't push her through. I will *not* hit a child, never. She raked her nails over my face. My wig came off, and she gaped at my bare head. I shoved her through.

Number five was sitting in the aisle, bawling. He was maybe seven. I ran back and picked him up, hugged him and kissed him, and tossed him through. God, I needed a rest, but I was needed in tourist.

"You, you, you, and you. Okay, you too. Help him, will you?" Pinky had a practiced eye for the ones that wouldn't be any use to anyone, even themselves. We herded them toward the front of the plane, then deployed ourselves along the left side where we could cover the workers. It didn't take long to prod them into action. We had them dragging the limp bodies forward as fast as they could go. Me and Cristabel were in tourist, with the others up front.

Adrenalin was being catabolized in my body now; the rush of action left me and I started to feel very tired. There's an unavoidable feeling of sympathy for the poor dumb goats that starts to get me about this stage of the game. Sure, they were better off, sure they were going to die if we didn't get them off the plane. But when they saw the other side they were going to have a hard time believing it.

The first ones were returning for a second load, stunned at

what they'd just seen: dozens of people being put into a cubicle that was crowded when it was empty. One college student looked like he'd been hit in the stomach. He stopped by me and his eyes pleaded.

"Look, I want to *help* you people, just . . . what's going *on*? Is this some new kind of rescue? I mean, are we going to crash—"

I switched my gun to prod and brushed it across his cheek. He gasped, and fell back.

"Shut your fuggin' mouth and get moving, or I'll kill you." It would be hours before his jaw was in shape to ask any more stupid questions.

We cleared tourist and moved up. A couple of the work gang were pretty damn pooped by then. Muscles like horses, all of them, but they can hardly run up a flight of stairs. We let some of them go through, including a couple that were at least fifty years old. *Je*-zuz. Fifty! We got down to a core of four men and two women who seemed strong, and worked them until they nearly dropped. But we processed everyone in twenty-five minutes.

The portapak came through as we were stripping off our clothes. Cristabel knocked on the door to the cockpit and Dave came out, already naked. A bad sign.

"I had to cork 'em," he said. "Bleeding Captain just *had* to make his Grand March through the plane. I tried *every*thing."

Sometimes you have to do it. The plane was on autopilot, as it normally would be at this time. But if any of us did anything detrimental to the craft, changed the fixed course of events in any way, that would be it. All that work for nothing, and Flight 128 inaccessible to us for all Time. I don't know sludge about time theory, but I know the practical angles. We can do things in the past only at times and in places where it won't make any difference. We have to cover our tracks. There's flexibility; once a Snatcher left her gun behind and it went in with the plane. Nobody found it, or if they did, they didn't have the smoggiest idea of what it was, so we were okay.

Flight 128 was mechanical failure. That's the best kind; it

means we don't have to keep the pilot unaware of the situation in the cabin right down to ground level. We can cork him and fly the plane, since there's nothing he could have done to save the flight anyway. A pilot-error smash is almost impossible to Snatch. We mostly work mid-airs, bombs, and structural failures. If there's even one survivor, we can't touch it. It would not fit the fabric of space-time, which is immutable (though it can stretch a little), and we'd all just fade away and appear back in the ready-room.

My head was hurting. I wanted that portapak very badly.

"Who has the most hours on a 707?" Pinky did, so I sent her to the cabin, along with Dave, who could do the pilot's voice for air traffic control. You have to have a believable record in the flight recorder, too. They trailed two long tubes from the portapak, and the rest of us hooked in up close. We stood there, each of us smoking a fistful of cigarettes, wanting to finish them but hoping there wouldn't be time. The gate had vanished as soon as we tossed our clothes and the flight crew through.

But we didn't worry long. There's other nice things about Snatching, but nothing to compare with the rush of plugging into a portapak. The wake-up transfusion is nothing but fresh blood, rich in oxygen and sugars. What we were getting now was an insane brew of concentrated adrenaline, super-saturated hemoglobin, methedrine, white lightning, TNT, and Kickapoo joyjuice. It was like a firecracker in your heart; a boot in the box that rattled your sox.

"I'm growing hair on my chest," Cristabel said solemnly. Everyone giggled.

"Would someone hand me my eyeballs?"

"The blue ones, or the red ones?"

"I think my ass just fell off."

We'd heard them all before, but we howled anyway. We were strong, *strong,* and for one golden moment we had no worries. Everything was hilarious. I could have torn sheet metal with my eyelashes.

But you get hyper on that mix. When the gage didn't show,

and didn't show, and *didn't sweetjeez show* we all started milling. This bird wasn't going to fly all that much longer.

Then it did show, and we turned on. The first of the wimps came through, dressed in the clothes taken from a passenger it had been picked to resemble.

"Two thirty-five elapsed upside time," Cristabel announced. "Je-zuz."

It is a deadening routine. You grab the harness around the wimp's shoulders and drag it along the aisle, after consulting the seat number painted on its forehead. The paint would last three minutes. You seat it, strap it in, break open the harness and carry it back to toss through the gate as you grab the next one. You have to take it for granted they've done the work right on the other side: fillings in the teeth, fingerprints, the right match in height and weight and hair color. Most of those things don't matter much, especially on Flight 128, which was a crash-and-burn. There would be bits and pieces, and burned to a crisp at that. But you can't take chances. Those rescue workers are pretty thorough on the parts they *do* find; the dental work and fingerprints especially are important.

I hate wimps. I really hate 'em. Every time I grab the harness of one of them, if it's a child, I wonder if it's Alice. *Are you my kid, you vegetable, you slug, you slimy worm?* I joined the Snatchers right after the brain bugs ate the life out of my baby's head. I couldn't stand to think she was the last generation, that the last humans there would ever be would live with nothing in their heads, medically dead by standards that prevailed even in 1979, with computers working their muscles to keep them in tone. You grow up, reach puberty still fertile—one in a thousand—rush to get pregnant in your first heat. Then you find out your mom or pop passed on a chronic disease bound right into the genes, and none of your kids will be immune. I *knew* about the para-leprosy; I grew up with my toes rotting away. But this was too much. What do you do?

Only one in ten of the wimps had a customized face. It takes time and a lot of skill to build a new face that will stand up to a doctor's autopsy. The rest came pre-mutilated. We've got millions of them; it's not hard to find a good match in the body. Most of them would stay breathing, too dumb to stop, until they went in with the plane.

The plane jerked, hard. I glanced at my watch. Five minutes to impact. We should have time. I was on my last wimp. I could hear Dave frantically calling the ground. A bomb came through the gate, and I tossed it into the cockpit. Pinky turned on the pressure sensor on the bomb and came running out, followed by Dave. Liza was already through. I grabbed the limp dolls in stewardess costume and tossed them to the floor. The engine fell off and a piece of it came through the cabin. We started to depressurize. The bomb blew away part of the cockpit (the ground crash crew would read it—we hoped—that part of the engine came through and killed the crew: no more words from the pilot on the flight recorder) and we turned, slowly, left and down. I was lifted toward the hole in the side of the plane, but I managed to hold onto a seat. Cristabel wasn't so lucky. She was blown backwards.

We started to rise slightly, losing speed. Suddenly it was uphill from where Cristabel was lying in the aisle. Blood oozed from her temple. I glanced back; everyone was gone, and three pink-suited wimps were piled on the floor. The plane began to stall, to nose down, and my feet left the floor.

"Come on, Bel!" I screamed. That gate was only three feet away from me, but I began pulling myself along to where she floated. The plane bumped, and she hit the floor. Incredibly, it seemed to wake her up. She started to swim toward me, and I grabbed her hand as the floor came up to slam us again. We crawled as the plane went through its final death agony, and we came to the door. The gate was gone.

There wasn't anything to say. We were going in. It's hard enough to keep the gate in place on a plane that's moving in a straight line. When a bird gets to corkscrewing and coming apart, the math is fearsome. So I've been told.

I embraced Cristabel and held her bloodied head. She was groggy, but managed to smile and shrug. You take what you get. I hurried into the restroom and got both of us down on the floor. Back to the forward bulkhead, Cristabel between my legs, back to front. Just like in training. We pressed our feet against the other wall. I hugged her tightly and cried on her shoulder.

And it was there. A green glow to my left. I threw myself toward it, dragging Cristabel, keeping low as two wimps were thrown headfirst through the gate above our heads. Hands grabbed and pulled us through. I clawed my way a good five yards along the floor. You can leave a leg on the other side and I didn't have one to spare.

I sat up as they were carrying Cristabel to Medical. I patted her arm as she went by on the stretcher, but she was passed out. I wouldn't have minded passing out myself.

For a while, you can't believe it all really happened. Sometimes it turns out it *didn't* happen. You come back and find out all the goats in the holding pen have softly and suddenly vanished away because the continuum won't tolerate the changes and paradoxes you've put into it. The people you've worked so hard to rescue are spread like tomato surprise all over some goddam hillside in Carolina and all you've got left is a bunch of ruined wimps and an exhausted Snatch Team. But not this time. I could see the goats milling around in the holding pen, naked and more bewildered than ever. And just starting to be *really* afraid.

Elfreda touched me as I passed her. She nodded, which meant well-done in her limited repertoire of gestures. I shrugged, wondering if I cared, but the surplus adrenaline was still in my veins and I found myself grinning at her. I nodded back.

Gene was standing by the holding pen. I went to him, hugged him. I felt the juices start to flow. *Damn it, let's squander a little ration and have us a good time*.

Someone was beating on the sterile glass wall of the pen. She shouted, mouthing angry words at us. *Why? What have you done to us?* It was Mary Sondergard. She implored her bald, one-legged twin to make her understand. She thought she had problems. God, was she pretty. I hated her guts.

Gene pulled me away from the wall. My hands hurt, and I'd broken off all my fake nails without scratching the glass.

She was sitting on the floor now, sobbing. I heard the voice of the briefing officer on the outside speaker.

". . . Centauri 3 is hospitable, with an Earth-like climate. By that, I mean *your* Earth, not what it has become. You'll see more of that later. The trip will take five years, shiptime. Upon landfall, you will be entitled to one horse, a plow, three axes, two hundred kilos of seed grain . . ."

I leaned against Gene's shoulder. At their lowest ebb, this very moment, they were so much better than us. I had maybe ten years, half of that as a basketcase. They are our best, our very brightest hope. Everything is up to them.

". . . that no one will be forced to go. We wish to point out again, not for the last time, that you would all be dead without our intervention. There are things you should know, however. You cannot breathe our air. If you remain on Earth, you can never leave this building. We are not like you. We are the result of a genetic winnowing, a mutation process. We are the survivors, but our enemies have evolved along with us. They are winning. You, however, are immune to the diseases that afflict us . . ."

I winced, and turned away.

". . . the other hand, if you emigrate you will be given a chance at a new life. It won't be easy, but as Americans you should be proud of your pioneer heritage. Your ancestors survived, and so will you. It can be a rewarding experience, and I urge you . . ."

Sure. Gene and I looked at each other and laughed. *Listen to this, folks. Five percent of you will suffer nervous breakdowns in the next few days, and never leave. About the same number will commit suicide, here and on the way. When you get there, sixty to seventy percent will die in the first three years. You will die in childbirth, be eaten by animals, bury two out of three of your babies, starve slowly when the rains don't come. If you live, it will be to break your back behind a plow, sunup to dusk. New Earth is Heaven, folks!*

God, how I wish I could go with them.

THE SMALL STONES
OF TU FU

Brian W. Aldiss

"The Small Stones of Tu Fu" was purchased by George Scithers, and appeared in the March-April 1978 issue of IAsfm (we were bi-monthly then), with an illustration by George Barr. A quiet story, it won no awards and attracted no particular attention, but it remains one of the most subtle, erudite, and delightful tales that IAsfm has ever published, a celebration of the human spirit as well as a journey through the vast expanses of time.

One of the true giants of the field, Brian W. Aldiss has been publishing science fiction for more than a quarter of a century, and has more than two dozen books to his credit. His classic novel The Long After-noon of Earth *won a Hugo Award in 1962, "The Saliva Tree" won a Nebula Award in 1965, and his novel* Starship *won the Prix Jules Verne in 1977. He took another Hugo Award in 1987 for his critical study of science fiction,* Trillion Year Spree, *written with David Wingrove. His other books include the acclaimed* Helliconia *trilogy—*Helliconia Spring, Helliconia Sum-mer, Helliconia Winter—*The Malacia Tapestry, An Is-*

17

land Called Moreau, Frankenstein Unbound, *and* Crypt-
ozoic. *His latest book is the collection* Seasons in Flight.
He lives in Oxford, England.

———————

On the 20th day of the Fifth Month of Year V of Ta-li
(which would be May in A.D. 770, according to the Old
Christian calendar), I was taking a voyage down the Yangtse
River with the aged poet Tu Fu.

Tu Fu was withered even then. Yet his words, and the
spaces between his words, will never wither. As a person, Tu
Fu was the most civilised and amusing man I ever met, which
explains my long stay in that epoch. Ever since then, I have
wondered whether the art of being amusing, with its implied
detachment from self, is not one of the most undervalued
requisites of human civilization. In many epochs, being amusing is equated with triviality. The human race rarely understood what was important; but Tu Fu understood.

Although the sage was ill, and little more than a bag of
bones, he desired to visit White King again before he died.

"Though I fear that the mere apparition of my skinny self
at a place named White King," he said, "may be sufficient
for that apparition, the White Knight, to make his last move
on me."

It is true that white is the Chinese colour of mourning, but I
wondered if a pun could prod the spirits into action; were they
so sensitive to words?

"What can a spirit digest but words?" Tu Fu replied. "I
don't entertain the idea that spirits can eat or drink—though
one hears of them whining at keyholes. They are forced to
lead a tediously spiritual life." He chuckled.

This was even pronounced with spirit, for poor Tu Fu had
recently been forced to give up drinking. When I mentioned
that sort of spirit, he said, "Yes, I linger on life's balcony, ill
and alone, and must not drink for fear I fall off."

Here again, I sensed that his remark was detached and not self-pitying, as some might construe it; his compassion was with all who aged and who faced death before they were ready—although, as Tu Fu himself remarked, "If we were not forced to go until we were ready, the world would be mountain-deep with the ill-prepared." I could but laugh at his turn of phrase.

When the Yangtse boat drew in to the jetty at White King, I helped the old man ashore. This was what we had come to see: the great white stones which progressed out of the swirling river and climbed its shores, the last of the contingent standing grandly in the soil of a tilled field.

I marvelled at the energy Tu Fu displayed. Most of the other passengers flocked round a refreshment vendor who set up his pitch upon the shingle, or else climbed a belvedere to view the landscape at ease. The aged poet insisted on walking among the monoliths.

"When I first visited this district as a young scholar, many years ago," said Tu Fu, as we stood looking up at the great bulk towering over us, "I was naturally curious as to the origin of these stones. I sought out the clerk in the district office and enquired of him. He said, 'The god called the Great Archer shot the stones out of the sky. That is one explanation. They were set there by a great king to commemorate the fact that the waters of the Yangtse flow East. That is another explanation. They were purely accidental. That is a third explanation.' So I asked him which of these explanations he personally subscribed to, and he replied, 'Why, young fellow, I wisely subscribe to all three, and shall continue to do so until more plausible explanations are offered.' Can you imagine a situation in which caution and credulity, *coupled with extreme scepticism,* were more nicely combined?" We both laughed.

"I'm sure your clerk went far."

"No doubt. He had moved to the adjacent room even before I left his office. For a long while, I used to wonder about his statement that a great king had commemorated the fact that the Yangtse waters flowed East; I could only banish the idiocy from my mind by writing a poem about it."

I laughed. Remembrance dawned. I quoted it to him.

> "I need no knot in my robe
> To remember the Lady Li's kisses;
> Small kings commemorate rivers
> And are themselves forgotten."

"There is real pleasure in poetry," responded Tu Fu, "when spoken so beautifully and remembered so appositely. But you had to be prompted."

"I was prompt to deliver, sir."

We walked about the monoliths, watching the waters swirl and curdle and fawn round the base of a giant stone as they made their way through the gorges of the Yangtse down to the ocean. Tu Fu said that he believed the monoliths to be a memorial set there by Chu-Ko Liang, demonstrating a famous tactical disposition by which he had won many battles during the wars of the Three Kingdoms.

"Are your reflections profound at moments like this?" Tu Fu asked, after a pause, and I reflected how rare it was to find a man, whether young or old, who was genuinely interested in the thoughts of others.

"What with the solidity of the stone and the ceaseless mobility of the water, I feel they should be profound. Instead, my mind is obstinately blank."

"Come, come," he said chidingly, "the river is moving too fast for you to expect any reflection. Now if it were still water . . ."

"It is still water even when it is moving fast, sir."

"There I must give you best, or give you up. But, pray, look at the gravels here and tell me what you observe. I am interested to know if we see the same things."

Something in his manner told me that more was expected of me than jokes. I looked along the shore, where stones of all kinds were distributed, from sand and grits to stones the size of a man's head, according to the disposition of current and tide.

"I confess I see nothing striking. The scene is a familiar one, although I have never been here before. You might come upon a little beach like this on any tidal river, or along the coasts by the Yellow Sea."

Looking at him in puzzlement, I saw he was staring out across the flood, although he had confessed he saw little in the distance nowadays. Because I sensed the knowledge stirring in him, my role of innocent had to be played more determinedly than ever.

"Many thousands of people come to this spot every year," he said. "They come to marvel at Chu-Ko Liang's giant stones, which are popularly known as 'The Eight Formations,' by the way. Of course, what is big is indeed marvellous, and the act of marvelling is very satisfying to the emotions, provided one is not called upon to do it every day of the year. But I marvel now, as I did when I first found myself on this spot, at a different thing. I marvel at the stones on the shore."

A light breeze was blowing, and for a moment I held in my nostrils the whiff of something appetising, a crab-and-ginger soup perhaps, warming at the food-vendor's fire further down the beach, where our boat was moored. Greed awoke a faint impatience in me, so that I thought, before humans are old, they should pamper their poor dear bodies, for the substance wastes away before the spirit, and was vexed to imagine that I had guessed what Tu Fu was going to say before he spoke. I was sorry to think that he might confess to being impressed by mere numbers. But his next remark surprised me.

"We marvel at the giant stones because they are unaccountable. We should rather marvel at the little ones because they are accountable. Let us walk upon them." I fell in with him and we paced over them: first a troublesome bank of grit, which grew larger on the seaward side of the bank. Then a patch of almost bare sand. Then, abruptly, shoals of pebbles, the individual members of which grew larger until we were confronted with a pile of lumpy stones which Tu Fu did not attempt to negotiate. We went round it, to find ourselves on more sand, followed by well-rounded stones all the size of a man's clenched fist. And they in turn gave way to more grit. Our discomfort in walking—which Tu Fu overcame in part by resting an arm on my arm—was increased by the fact that these divisions of stones were made not only laterally along the beach but vertically up the beach, the demarcations in the latter division being frequently marked by lines of seaweed or of minute white shells of dead crustaceans.

"Enough, if not more than enough," said Tu Fu. "Now do you see what is unusual about the beach?"

"I confess I find it a tiresomely *usual* beach," I replied, masking my thoughts.

"You observe how all the stones are heaped according to their size."

"That too is usual, sir. You will ask me to marvel next that students in classrooms appear to be graded according to size."

"Ha!" He stood and peered up at me, grinning and stroking his long white beard. "But we agree that students are graded according to the wishes of the teacher. Now, according to whose wishes are all these millions upon millions of pebbles graded?"

"Wishes don't enter into it. The action of the water is sufficient, the action of the water, working ceaselessly and randomly. The playing, one may say, of the inorganic organ."

Tu Fu coughed and wiped the spittle from his thin lips.

"Although you claim to be born in the remote future, which I confess seems to me unnatural, you are familiar with the workings of this natural world. So, like most people, you see nothing marvellous in the stones hereabouts. Supposing you were born—" he paused and looked about him and upwards, as far as the infirmity of his years would allow—"supposing you were born upon the moon, which some sages claim is a dead world, bereft of life, women, and wine. . . . If you then flew to this world and, in girdling it, observed everywhere stones, arranged in sizes as these are here. Wherever you travelled, by the coasts of any sea, you saw that the stones of the world had been arranged in sizes. What then would you think?''

I hesitated—Tu Fu was too near for comfort.

''I believe my thoughts would turn to crab-and-ginger soup, sir.''

''No, they would not, not if you came from the moon, which is singularly devoid of crab-and-ginger soup, if reports speak true. You would be forced to the conclusion, the inevitable conclusion, that the stones of this world were being graded, like your scholars, by a superior intelligence.'' He turned the collar of his padded coat up against the breeze, which was freshening. ''You would come to believe that that Intelligence was obsessive, that its mind was terrible indeed, filled only with the idea—not of language, which is human—but of number, which is inhuman. You would understand of that Intelligence that it was under an interdict to wander the world measuring and weighing every one of a myriad myriad single stones, sorting them all into heaps according to dimension. Meaningless heaps, heaps without even particular decorative merit. The farther you travelled, the more heaps you saw—the myriad heaps, each containing myriads of stones— the more alarmed you would become. And what would you conclude in the end?''

Laughing with some anger, I said, ''That it was better to stay at home.''

''Possibly. You would also conclude that it was *no use* staying at home. Because the Intelligence that haunted the earth was interested only in stones; that you would perceive. From which it would follow that the Intelligence would be hostile to anything else and, in particular, would be hostile to anything which disturbed its handiwork.''

''Such as human kind?''

''Precisely.'' He pointed up the strand, where our fellow-voyagers were sitting on the shingle, or kicking it about, while their children were pushing stones into piles or flinging them into the Yangtse. ''The Intelligence—diligent, obsessive, methodical to a degree—would come in no time to be

especially weary of human kind, who were busy turning what
is ordered into what is random.''

Thinking that he was beginning to become alarmed by his
own fancy, I said, ''It is a good subject for a poem, perhaps,
but nothing more. Let us return to the boat. I see the sailors
are going aboard.''

We walked along the beach, taking care not to disturb the
stones. Tu Fu coughed as he walked.

''So you believe that what I say about the Intelligence that
haunts the earth is nothing more than a fit subject for a
poem?'' he said. He stooped slowly to pick up a stone, fitting
his other hand in the small of his back in order to regain an
upright posture. We both stood and looked at it as it lay in Tu
Fu's withered palm. No man had a name for its precise shape,
or even for the fugitive tints of cream and white and black
that marked it out as different from all its neighbours. Tu Fu
stared down at it and improvised an epigram.

> ''The stone in my hand hides
> A secret natural history:
> Climates and times unknown,
> A river unseen.''

I held my hand out. ''You don't know it, but you have
released that stone from the bondage of space and time. May
I keep it?''

As he passed it over, and we stepped towards the refreshment vendor, Tu Fu said, more lightly, ''We take foul medi-
cines to improve our health; so we must entertain foul thoughts
on occasion, to strengthen wisdom. Can you nourish no belief
in my Intelligence—you, who claim to be born in some
remote future—which loves stones but hates human kind? Do
I claim too much to ask you to suppose for a moment that I
might be correct in my supposition . . .'' Evidently his thought
wandered slightly, for he then said, after a pause, ''Is it
within the power of one man to divine the secret nature of the
world, or is even the whisper of that wish a supreme egotism,
punishable by a visitation from the White Knight?''

"Permit me to get you a bowl of soup, sir."

The vendor provided us with two mats to lay over the shingle. We unrolled them and sat to drink our crab-and-ginger soup. As he supped, with the drooling noises of an old man, the sage gazed far away down the restless river, where lantern sails moved distantly towards the sea, yellow on the yellow skyline. His previously cheerful, even playful, mood had slipped from him; I could perceive that, at his advanced age, even the yellow distance might be a reminder to him—perhaps as much reassuring as painful—that he soon must himself journey to a great distance. I recited his epigram to myself. "Climates and times unknown, A river unseen."

Children played round us. Their parents, moving slowly up the gangplank on to the vessel, called to them. "Did you like the giant stones, venerable master?" one of the boys asked Tu Fu cheekily.

"I like them better than the battles they commemorate," replied Tu Fu. He stretched out a papery hand, and patted the boy's shoulder before the latter ran after his father. I had remarked before the way in which the aged long to touch the young.

We also climbed the gangplank. It was a manifest effort for Tu Fu.

Dark clouds were moving from the interior, dappling the landscape with moving shadow. I took Tu Fu below, to rest in a little cabin we had hired for the journey. He sat on the bare bench, in stoical fashion, breathing flutteringly, while I thought of the battle to which he referred, which I had paused to witness some centuries earlier.

Just above our heads, the bare feet of the crew pattered on the deck. There was a prolonged creaking as the gangplank was hoisted, followed by the rattle of the sail unfolding. The wind caught the boat, every plank of which responded to that exhalation, and we started to glide forward with the Yangtse's great stone-shaping course towards the sea. A harmony of motion caused the whole ship to come alive, every separate part of it rubbing against every other, as in the internal workings of a human when it runs.

I turned to Tu Fu. His eyes went blank, his jaw fell open. One hand moved to clutch his beard and then fell away. He toppled forward—I managed to catch him before he struck the floor. In my arms, he seemed to weigh nothing. A muttered word broke from him, then a heavy shuddering sigh.

The White Knight had come, Tu Fu's spirit was gone. I laid him upon the bench, looking down at his revered form with compassion. Then I climbed upon deck.

There the crowd of travellers was standing at the starboard side, watching the tawny coast roll by, and crying out with some excitement. But they fell silent, facing me attentively when I called to them.

"Friends," I shouted. "The great and beloved poet Tu Fu is dead."

A first sprinkle of rain fell from the west, and the sun became hidden by cloud.

Swimming strongly on my way back to what the sage called the remote future, my form began to flow and change according to time pressure. Sometimes my essence was like steam, sometimes like a mountain. Always I clung to the stone I had taken from Tu Fu's hand.

Back. Finally I was back. Back was an enormous expanse yet but a corner. All human kind had long departed. All life had disappeared. Only the great organ of the inorganic still played. There I could sit on my world-embracing beach, eternally arranging and grading pebble after pebble. From fine grit to great boulders, they could all be sorted as I desired. In that occupation, I fulfilled the pleasures of infinity, for it was inexhaustible.

But the small stone of Tu Fu I kept apart. Of all beings ever to exist upon the bounteous face of this world, Tu Fu had been nearest to me—I say 'had been,' but he forever *is*, and I return to visit him when I will. For it was he who came nearest to understanding my existence by pure divination.

Even his comprehension failed. He needed to take his perceptions a stage further and see how those same natural forces which create stones also create human beings. Far from it—I regard them with the same affection as I do the smallest pebble.

Why, take this little pebble at my side! I never saw a pebble like that before. The tint of this facet, here—isn't that unique?

I have a special bank on which to store it, somewhere over the other side of the world. Only the little stone of Tu Fu shall not be stored away; small kings commemorate rivers, and this stone shall commemorate the immortal river of Tu Fu's thought.

TIME AND HAGAKURE

Steven Utley

"Time and Hagakure" was purchased by George Scithers, and appeared in the Winter 1977 issue of IAsfm *(we were quarterly then), with a cover and interior illustrations by Frank Kelly Freas. A study of a man caught, quite literally, between two worlds, it bristles with vivid images, and strange—and poignant—juxtapositions.*

Steven Utley's fiction has appeared in The Magazine of Fantasy & Science Fiction, Universe, Galaxy, Amazing, Vertex, Stellar, Shayol, *and elsewhere. He is the co-editor, with Geo. W. Proctor, of the anthology* Lone Star Universe, *the first—and possibly the only—anthology of SF stories by Texans. Born in Smyrna, Tennessee, Utley now lives in Austin, Texas.*

Inoue stepped into his apartment, closed the door and found himself on a sparsely wooded hillside. Not far from where he stood, a shaggy titan scratched its haunch and belched awesomely. Storm clouds were gathering in the sky overhead.

Inoue groped his way along the wall until he bumped into a chair. He eased himself down into it. From a table beside the chair, he plucked a photograph and held it as though it were a talisman. The phantom Megatherium went down on all fours and began tearing at the earth with its long, curved claws. Ghost lightning flashed on the horizon.

Control, Inoue told himself. He forced himself to concentrate on the picture, a curling yellow snapshot of a woman whose face reflected years of strain, whose eyes had once seen the sun touch the earth. Opaque eyes; blind, burnt eyes.

Across the room, the enormous ground sloth mooed softly, then shimmered and dissolved. The Pleistocene thunderheads swirled away.

Inoue studied cracks in the dirty plaster ceiling. Good, he thought, good. Don't let it run away with you. You have to be able to control it for a while closer each time. Relax. Relax.

He settled into the cushions and closed his eyes. He could feel the power coiled within, tensed to strike at him if he let it, tensed and ready to do his bidding if he made it.

He took a deep breath, and he began.

The floor disappears as Tadashi starts to swing his legs over the edge of the cot. He stares down through the sky. Far below, silhouetted against a bright sea, the dark gnats of many airplanes swirl about angrily. As he watches, one of the gnats flares up like a match and drops toward the ocean, trailing a fine ribbon of burning gasoline and oily smoke. Tadashi pulls his legs back and huddles upon the cot. A wailing noise fills his ears.

"Lieutenant!"

He starts and looks up from the air battle. At the far edge of the sky, where the horizon merges with the wall of the hut, stands a glowering giant, fists on hips.

"What's the matter with you?" the giant demands. "Can't you hear the sirens?"

Tadashi shakes his head helplessly. His gaze returns to the dogfight. Two more airplanes are going down. The sea ripples, then yields to the familiar wooden planks. The airplanes vanish, swallowed up in the chinks between the planks. Tadashi rubs his eyes.

"Are you all right?" the giant says in a more solicitous tone.

"I . . . Captain Tsuyuki?"

"Of course! Aren't you well, Lieutenant?"

Tadashi puts his feet on the floor and is relieved to feel fine splinters tickling his soles. He rises and sways unsteadily, his head suddenly light, his stomach buoyant. "I'll be all right, sir. I was—the siren! Bombers!"

"They're going for the Yokosuka-Tokyo area," says the captain as Tadashi snatches up his jacket and boots. "The mechanics are warming up the planes. Get into the air immediately!"

Tadashi crams his feet into the boots and clomps past Captain Tsuyuki.

Inoue became aware of the pain mounting behind his eyes and cursed softly as he slipped away from Lieutenant Tadashi Okido. He slumped in his chair, massaging his temples, then got up and went to the window. Outside, the lights of Tokyo held back the night.

When, in the forty-third year of his life, the power had first manifested itself, had begun running amok inside his head, Inoue's Tokyo—dirty, overcrowded, very dangerous Tokyo— started to hold new terrors for him. Thuggee stranglers stalked their victims through the corridors of his apartment complex. Barbarian hordes rode down out of the sky to lay waste to crude towns and villages that lay superimposed upon the dreary confusion of the metropolis. Assyrian, Roman, and Aztec priests wandered past the shrines of the city, and sun-blackened slaves labored to erect pyramids. Waves of mounted knights broke under black rains of arrows from long bows. Volcanoes loomed over the skyline and blew themselves to atoms. Prehistoric glaciers crunched along the highway to Kyoto, and monster-infested coal forests reclaimed boulevards.

Three hundred million years of ghosts filled his head and spilled out into his world.

He returned to his chair and picked up the photograph again and stared into the woman's eyes, the blind, burnt eyes, the eyes seared, ruined, made useless, that time when the sun had come down to engulf Nagasaki.

It had been in the fifth month of his affliction that she came to him the first time. Bent over the lathe, he had glanced up to discover a small garden where the north wall of his tool and die shop was supposed to be. The woman stood there, looking younger than he could recall having ever seen her in life. But he knew her. He had some of the ancient photographs, pictures of her in her bridal attire and drab wartime kimono.

Her gaze was fixed on a point behind and slightly above his head. Awe and terror were creeping into her expression, and a brilliant light made her seem as pale as paraffin. She opened her small mouth and uttered a soundless scream. Her hands rose to her face to claw at her eyes. She fell prone, still screaming, still silent.

Crouched over his lathe, Inoue had reached out for her and caught just a word.

He had seen her several times more in the weeks and months that followed. The scene was always the same; once, though, an enormous iguanodon wandered past, unmindful of the furies raging all around it, unmindful of the stricken woman. Each time, Inoue tried to reach her, to hold tight to her. Each time, he caught only the single word.

Inoue folded his hand over the photograph and forced himself to concentrate and slipped away murmuring the word, the name, *Tadashi, Tadashi* . . .

Tadashi is wedging himself into the cockpit of his airplane. Jerking his fur-lined flying helmet down over his close-cropped skull. Waving the ground crew out of the way. Rolling forward, gaining speed. Up. Up. Retract the landing gear.

Up. **listen** Up. Three thousand feet and climbing. Young Shiizaki, Tadashi's new wingman, is a poor pilot whose ship makes known its resentment of his heavy hand. Tadashi grimaces in annoyance and signals Shiizaki to remain in position. Seven thousand feet and climbing. **listen to me** Eight thousand feet. Nine. There is a stab of pain between Tadashi's eyes. **please listen to me** He blinks it away.

It had taken Inoue another year to locate the man Tadashi. The stream of Time was a twisting, treacherous one. Inoue cast himself into those waters and discovered what it was to have been a mastodon asphyxiating in a tar pool. He experienced the terror and agony of a Russian officer being torn to pieces by mutinous soldiers. He was a Cro-Magnon woman succumbing to hunger and cold. He bore children. He raped and was raped. He decapitated a man. He was drawn and quartered. He knew moments of peace. He ate strange foods and spoke odd languages. He made love with a filthy Saxon woman and with a rancid Spanish nobleman. He cast himself into the waters of Time again and again, and he felt himself drawn closer to his objective every sixth or seventh attempt, and then, finally, at last—

Tadashi is wedging himself into the cockpit of his airplane. Jerking his fur-lined flying helmet down over his close-cropped skull. Waving the ground crew out of the way. Rolling forward, gaining speed. Up. Up. Away.

Tadashi cruises at seventeen thousand feet, tense behind the controls of the obsolete Zero-Sen fighter. The almost-daily air raids, the seemingly interminable howling of the sirens, the endless mad scrambles to waiting planes, are taking their toll. He had been having difficulty keeping his food down lately, and food is hardly so abundant anymore that it can be wasted in such a manner. His head hurts intermittently. He has been making too many mistakes in the air, overshooting targets, firing his guns too soon or too late and, always, for too long. Ammunition thrown away, wasted in ineffectual feints at the enemy bombers' shiny aluminum bellies.

Gone is the sure, deadly aim, gone the lightning-quick reflexes that made him an ace over the Phillipines. He will, he knows, make the final mistake very soon now, and then a Hellcat or a Mustang will blow him out of the air. A precious airplane lost, thrown away in a moment of inattention or confusion.

And what of your wife? Tadashi frowns behind his goggles and reproaches himself. He will only hasten his own end if he permits his mind to wander thus.

He is, he tells himself, a warrior. If he dies, he will die a warrior's death and ascend to Yasukuni Shrine. He will sell his life dearly, for that is his duty and his honor. *Hagakure,* the Bushido code, is too deeply engrained in him. He cannot imagine alternatives to that code— "A Samurai lives in such a way that he will always be prepared to die" —or to the Emperor's precepts to all soldiers and sailors of Japan: ". . . be resolved that duty is heavier than a mountain, while death is lighter than a feather."

Tadashi catches the flash of sunlight on unpainted aluminum in the distance. He wags his wings to attract Shiizaki's attention and points, then has to bank sharply as Shiizaki, craning his neck to search for the enemy formation, lets his plane swerve toward Tadashi's. Tadashi waves his clumsy wingman back into position and mentally curses both the lack of radios, which have been removed to lighten the Zero-Sens, and the scarcity of fully trained flyers. He opens the throttle and begins closing the gap between himself and the bombers.

In the space of a year, the Americans' B-29's have flattened virtually the whole of Japanese industry, have severely decimated populations in the major cities, have brought his homeland to its knees. The B-29's are gigantic aircraft, by far the largest he has ever seen. Their size notwithstanding, they are almost as fast as his interceptor, well armed and strong, altogether insuperable machines. Some of them have been brought down, but not many, not enough, and, for the most part, the behemoths seem discouragingly unconcerned with both fighters and flak.

Tadashi feels his guts drawing up into a tight, hard knot as he begins his approach. *Perhaps this is the day,* a part of him whispers, and he clamps his teeth on his lower lip, trying to repress the murmur of panic. The rearmost B-29 in the formation swells in his gunsight. He thumbs off the safety switch, checks his range-finder and opens fire. Tracers simultaneously spit from the bomber's tail guns. There is the whine of a ricochet. Tadashi flinches, scowls, completes his firing pass, kicks the rudder to the left to check on Shiizaki.

Stitched by tracers, Shiizaki's Zero-Sen sweeps past the B-29, turns on its side and explodes.

you must listen to me think of her the war will soon be over and she will need you in the hard times to follow go back and land and call her to you without delay please please listen to me

Tadashi grimly drops into position behind a second bomber. But the American plane suddenly shimmers and dances in the sky before him, refusing to stay neatly framed in the gunsight. His eyes throb, his head hurts. The Zero-Sen wobbles sickeningly as his hand slips on the control stick. **I CAN SAVE US ALL IF YOU WILL LISTEN TO ME** and for just a moment he is deaf to the roar and vibration of his plane, removed, face to oddly familiar face with a middle-aged man whose furrowed brow glistens with perspiration, whose eyes are screwed tight with some great effort. Tadashi gives a cry of alarm, and the man appears to gasp and then smiles. The face shatters into scintillae of light. His bride reclines with him in semi-gloom, her skin slick with post-coital perspiration, her delicate fingers tracing patterns on his shoulder and breast as she whispers endearments, *I love you, Tadashi, I shall always love and honor you, stay with me, stay with me, with me, we shall have fine, brave sons and graceful daughters.* He blinks, perplexed, filled with longing, and opens his mouth to speak to her. The soothing liquid flow of her voice is rudely terminated by the sound of canopy glass shattering. A sliver gashes his cheek. He wrenches himself away from his wedding night and finds himself bearing down on the B-29. He cannot remember how to fire his guns.

I don't need to shoot, he thinks. The moisture is gone from his mouth. I don't need to shoot.

break away I've seen you do this many times too many times I am tired sickened by the violence I've seen going mad because of what happened what is going to happen at Nagasaki there is no way to stop the ghosts except by coming to you making you break off this futile engagement Japan is doomed nothing you can do now can change that you can only return to your base and save yourself your wife me

Tadashi shakes his head savagely and gropes for the throttle. Finds it. Opens it to overboost. no no no *no no* NO NO, a scream behind his eyes, the words tumbling out, running together, *nonono,* and the Zero-Sen leaps forward.

Inoue moaned, drew himself into a ball, quivered in his chair, sweat popping from every pore, fingers digging into scalp, teeth grinding together.

Then he realized that he had crumpled the photograph. He smoothed it out, whimpering softly to himself. A brittle corner had broken off. He found the wedge-shaped chip of paper in his lap and placed it on the table.

I can do it, he thought, I've made little ripples in Time, I've made him feel my presence, made him see, hear, feel things. I've broken through to him at last, he understands now, he's going to listen this time. I'm going to save us all.

But his headache was worse now. He put the picture into the pocket of his shirt and tiredly rubbed his face for a moment before getting up to go to the window again. He took the picture from his pocket and carefully cupped it in his hand. He regarded the dead eyes sadly.

He had tried, so many times, to reach her and warn her away from the doomed city. Had tried and failed: only that moment of her terror in the garden was open to him.

He had tried to return to the day, early that last month of the war, when Lieutenant Tadashi Okido had sent his young bride to stay with his uncle in Nagasaki. Had tried and failed: only an hour of another, later day in the lieutenant's life was open to him.

He had been trying for weeks to cut short the lieutenant's mission of interception.

He was being driven mad in a Tokyo overrun with phantoms which he alone could see, and Lieutenant Tadashi Okido was his one hope. The Samurai Tadashi, who had to be made, somehow, convinced, somehow, to return to the airfield and call his wife away from Nagasaki.

Tadashi, who, in sending her to that place, had unknowingly cursed Inoue with the power.

This time, Inoue thought, this time it must not happen as it did.

LISTEN TO ME YOU MUSTN'T DIE HERE AND NOW YOU MUST LIVE LONG ENOUGH TO SAVE YOUR WIFE AND MY SANITY YOU OWE IT TO US TO LIVE LISTEN ALL THE REMAINING YEARS OF HER LIFE WILL BE A TORMENT WITHOUT YOU AND Tadashi shakes his head savagely and gropes for **MY LIFE HAS BECOME HELL BECAUSE OF YOU** the throttle **YOU AND YOU ALONE** finds it **CAN SAVE US** opens it to **PLEASE LISTEN** opens it to **LISTEN** opens it to overboost, and the Zero-Sen leaps forward to plow through the bomber's tail assembly. The shivering fighter's starboard wing buckles like pasteboard and disintegrates. The cowling shoots away as the radial engine begins disgorging pistons. The Japanese and American planes fall away from each other, fall away spinning, throwing off pieces of themselves.

damn you

A large pterodactyl soared past the window. Sobbing with frustration, Inoue pressed his fist against the grimy pane. Go away, Go away. Go away.

He looked at the photograph in his hand, and he said to the woman with the ruined eyes, I found him, I spoke to him, told him, showed him what was at stake. I invaded the past, I altered it a very little, but why doesn't he listen? Why does he keep doing it? What's wrong with him? Why can't I make him understand?

And he cried out, "Mother, doesn't he even *care?*"

Slammed and held by centrifugal force against the wall of the cockpit, Tadashi dazedly listens to his wife's pleas and feels her hands rove down over his body, and he tells her that he loves her, has loved her from the moment he first glimpsed her in her father's house, will love her always, and he tells her that their children, yes, their children will be fine, beautiful children, and he bids her goodbye, knowing she is proud of him now and will follow his example should the need to do so arise, for he is a warrior, with a wife worthy of a warrior, he has abided by the dictates of *Hagakure* and is assured of his place of honor at Yasukuni Shrine, and it is intensely hot and bright in the cockpit, there are screams which may be his own, but he is resolved that duty is heavier than a mountain, while death is li—

THE COMEDIAN

Tim Sullivan

"The Comedian" was purchased by George Scithers toward the end of his reign as editor, and appeared in the June 1982 issue of IAsfm, *with an illustration by Ron Logan. Bittersweet, poignant, and suspenseful, "The Comedian" went on to be one of the year's most popular stories. Certainly it features one of the genre's oddest protagonists—a very sympathetically portrayed kidnapper of young children. . . .*

Tim Sullivan's fiction appears with some regularity in Isaac Asimov's Science Fiction Magazine, *as well as in* The Twilight Zone Magazine, Chrysalis, New Dimensions, *and elsewhere. He reviews regularly for* The Washington Post Book World, U.S.A. Today, Short Form, *and elsewhere, and contributed many of the horror movie reviews for the recent* Penguin Encyclopedia of Horror and the Supernatural. *His most recent novel is* Destiny's End. *Upcoming are an original horror anthology he's editing, called* Tropical Chills, *and a new novel, entitled* The Parasite Wars. *Born in Bangor, Maine, Sullivan now lives in Los Angeles.*

Yogi Bear wore a wanted poster on his paunch.

"They'll never see that kid alive again," a passing woman said.

The kidnapper's heart fluttered like a hummingbird's wings. There were two pictures of a little boy named Paul Simpson on the poster, and an offer of one hundred thousand dollars to anyone with information leading to his return. But Paul Simpson's rich parents wouldn't have any better luck than those of the other five children the kidnapper had taken. He had not abducted them for money.

Glancing at the woman, he was relieved to see that she wasn't speaking to him. The giant Yogi–teddy bear standing in front of the toy store had momentarily attracted her attention, just as it had attracted his. Now she rejoined the mall's milling shoppers, Jordache jeans jiggling in a way the kidnapper knew he should have found enticing. She had probably filed Paul's disappearance with countless other urban horror stories.

The kidnapper could have told her this one was different.

He remembered abducting little Paulie . . . and other kids, too . . . they had struggled, and then became weak . . . and then . . . He couldn't remember anything else. God, how he needed a drink.

He wiped his sweating face, bristles scratching his hand, and tried to think. His head began to ache, and saliva dribbled out of the side of his mouth. To make matters worse, his clothes were rumpled and he smelled like a goat. Better clean up his act, or he would get caught.

Shaking his head, he walked away from the toy store. Laughter and bright, multiple-color images soon distracted him. It was a display of TVs. A comedian mugged out of half a dozen screens.

Ordinary as this was, it disturbed the kidnapper. He stopped to listen to the guy's *shtik*. The timing and delivery seemed adequate, and the material was all right, but there was still something wrong. The longer he watched, the more it troubled him. It was as though he were a dog on a leash, tugging to free himself from the powerful hands that held him back. . . .

But this wasn't his master.

His head starting to ache again, he turned and walked away. Why had the comedian affected him so deeply? He couldn't come up with a reason, and the pain was so bad that he didn't want to think about it.

He passed a florist's and a clothing store, stopped in front of a video games arcade. He would try here first; parents frequently left their children in such places with a handful of quarters, going off under the illusion their kids were safe.

Such complacency angered the kidnapper. Every day, parents endangered their own children. If they gave him no opportunity to steal their children, maybe he'd be freed . . . or maybe he'd be killed so he wouldn't tell what he knew.

But what did he know?

"Diversions," he said, reading aloud the arcade's sign, "Video Games, Electronic Games, Pinball."

It was a dimly lit place, the better to show off the games' bright graphics. Whining, jangling, booming effects slashed the inside of his skull. He was in lousy shape. Just walking through the mall had tired him. He was trembling, short of breath, his knees rubbery, and he had a headache that never seemed to go away. A junk food diet and a drinking problem didn't help, but he really didn't give a damn about his health anymore. He didn't care about anything except getting the job done. If he was going to be shut up for good once it was over, well . . . at least it would be over.

If he wasn't killed, the police would catch him. Then there would be a trial, and he'd spend the rest of his days in a prison, or a madhouse . . . or be executed.

No chance of a normal life again. Christ, he couldn't even remember his own name.

He knew he shouldn't be thinking about what would happen to him. He was just asking for a headache. Besides, he had to keep moving. Otherwise, the cops would get him before he got the last two kids.

Fishing in his pocket for a quarter, he started playing a Missile Command game. He failed to save the earth, a lurid color field remaining after the holocaust.

"I won't be long, honey," he heard a woman say to her daughter as he stared at the blasted landscape. "If anyone bothers you, tell the man behind the counter." Purse swinging, she hurried out.

The little girl stood alone in the clamor of the arcade, wide eyes staring up at the adults and teenagers towering above her. She was no more than seven or eight years old, brown hair, green eyes. She wore a light blue T-shirt that said "I'm Huggable." Clutching her quarters, she bit her bottom lip and surveyed the rows of machines. Several were vacant, and she soon settled on Space Invaders. An empty wooden box helped her reach the controls.

As her quarter clinked into the coin slot, the kidnapper stole up behind her. He casually looked up and down the aisle, as though trying to decide which game to play next. No one paid any attention to him.

He felt under his windbreaker for the tranquilizer gun, turning back toward the little girl. He slowly raised his hand to clap over her mouth. But she was no longer zapping marauding aliens. She stared at his reflection in the smudged glass of the screen.

"Child molester!" she screamed, turning to glare up at him. *"Pervert!"*

The piping voice clamped onto his skull like an alligator's jaws. He slapped his hands over his temples, people turning to stare at him.

"Hey man," the counter man shouted, "you touch that kid, your ass is in jail!"

"I . . ." The kidnapper could barely speak, his throat dry and constricted. ". . . I thought she was my daughter."

"You did not!" The little girl set her jaw defiantly. "You were gonna molest me! My mommy told me to watch out for you!"

"Get outta here," the counter man said.

The kidnapper backed away. He turned and walked stiffly by the planters filled with ferns and the wooden benches, crossing to the other side of the mall. His face was hot and his head throbbed. He hoped to God the guy wouldn't call the cops.

Outside the mall's main entrance, he was grateful to be away from the noise. He was falling apart; only adrenaline kept him going now. The midday sun made his eyes water, tears flowing into the sweat that stained his clothes. He noticed a lamppost with a lettered F sign and wondered where he'd left the goddam van.

Come to think of it, he'd parked under a C sign. He spotted it and started walking toward it. As he cut between two cars, he came upon a kid playing with a yo-yo.

The kidnapper looked around. Nobody was in any of the cars near the little boy. The shimmering parking lot was still.

"Every cloud has a silver lining," he said.

"Huh?" The kid looked up at him. He snapped the yo-yo up and caught it. The kidnapper saw that it was emblazoned with Superman's insignia.

"I'm just looking for my kids," the kidnapper said. "I think they're around here someplace."

The little boy looked sad: "I haven't seen anybody."

"Well, they must be inside the van," the kidnapper said, sensing that it might not be necessary to use the tranquilizer gun just yet. "We've got a lot of stuff to play with in there."

"Really?" Squinting into the sun as he looked up, the kid looked like a little freckled monkey.

"Come take a look. They're right over here." The kidnapper started towards the C sign. Hesitating a moment, the boy ran after him.

The red van gleamed brightly in the sun. As they neared it, the kidnapper felt terrible guilt for stealing another child. But what choice did he have? He was only an instrument, a tool . . . and he had never hurt any of the children.

"Here we are, buddy," he said, unlocking the back doors of the van. "What did you say your name is?"

"Jimmy," the little boy replied. "Where are the kids?"

"Right in here, Jimmy." The kidnapper threw open the back doors of the van. "See."

Six kids sat on benches within the dark enclosure, three on either side. Between them danced a man, puffing out his cheeks and making his jaw stick out like Popeye. He was transparent in places, sparkling here and there, and zigzag lines of color distorted his shape for a second.

"What time is it?" the comedian asked in a funny voice.

The kidnapper drew the tranquilizer gun from under his jacket and fired a dart. Jimmy's little body stiffened, and his cry was drowned out by the comedian's raucous reply to his own question: *"It's Howdy Doody time!"*

The kidnapper clapped his hand over Jimmy's mouth, tossing the tranquilizer gun inside the van. Jimmy struggled ineffectually as he was lifted up and carried inside, too. The kidnapper hunkered over the child's body inside the dark, cramped space, holding him tightly until he weakened and became still.

None of the other children appeared to notice the abduction, nor did they notice when the kidnapper placed Jimmy on the bench beside a little black girl.

Jumping out of the van and slamming the doors shut, the kidnapper went around to the driver's side, let himself into the broiling cab, and turned the ignition key. He turned on the air conditioner while he waited for the idle to smooth out.

Just as he started to back out of the parking space, a police car pulled into the lot. He slammed on the brakes and ducked down in the seat as the cop drove behind him, praying to Christ the arcade counter man hadn't reported him. In the rearview mirror, he watched the cop pull in front of the mall and go inside. Then he slowly backed out and eased onto U.S. 1. The wheel was slippery in his sweating hands.

"Close one, dummy."

The kidnapper looked at the comedian, a fuzzy image of Bozo the Clown now, seated on the passenger's side.

"You . . ." The kidnapper remembered now. The comedian made him take the children. It had almost come back to

him in the mall . . . the giant teddy bear . . . the TV store
. . . but his struggle to regain his memory had hurt his head.
". . . you . . ."

". . . are mah sunshine," the comedian sang in a nasal
twang, "mah only sunshine. You make me spirit those kids
a-way."

"That's not funny."

"Everybody's a critic."

"Tell me what you're doing this for."

"But you know too much already. Yeah, I think you need
a refresher course in forgetting."

"No, please, I . . ."

"Say what, you crazy nut? Gonna be a good boy from here
on in, or do I have to send you back to Never-Never Land?'"

"If you do that, who'll drive?" The kidnapper could see
the scenery rushing by through the comedian's unfocused
image. "You aren't substantial."

"Of course I'm not substantial, dummy. I'm Bozo the
Clown, not Edwin Newman. But don't worry, you'll still be
in the driver's seat. Sort of on automatic pilot."

"Won't that be dangerous?"

The comedian chuckled like Curly of the Three Stooges,
his body becoming rotund, and topped with a stubbly crew
cut. "Nah, you do better that way."

"Please," the kidnapper said, starting to sob. "I'm burnt
out. Don't do it to me anymore."

"Well, gee," the comedian said, turning into Jack Benny.
The kidnapper wept. "Why are you doing this? What do
you want from me?"

"Oh, Rochester, where's my violin?" Benny said, resting
his fingertips gently against his cheek. "I don't have any
choice, either, ya know. It's no fun watching you drool all
over yourself, but I've got to be careful."

Frustrated, the kidnapper swerved to avoid a speeding Datsun.
Its driver honked at him as though he had been at fault.

"Well, gee," the comedian said, "it looks like the old
Maxwell's got life in her yet. But, ya know, I really think
you'd drive better if you didn't have anything on your mind."

Gotta keep him from putting me under, the kidnapper thought. I know I can remember everything, starting with my name. I just need a little time. But the shimmering, imperfect image of Jack Benny was looking at him thoughtfully. "I really think you need some rest, kidnapper. Ya see, tomorrow is a big day for you."

"Somebody controls you," the kidnapper said. "Somebody controls you, just like you're controlling me. Who is it?"

"I've got a secret." The comedian straightened his bow tie, the very picture of Garry Moore. "Can you guess who's pulling my strings?"

"Couldn't be anyone on Earth . . . the technology's too advanced. Aliens?"

"Mork from Ork?" Robin Williams asked with an impish grin. "Or John Q from outer space?" Where Robin Williams had been, the plump face of Jonathan Winters grimaced at the kidnapper.

"Why not? You must have intercepted our TV signals, and . . ."

"Nah," Maxwell Smart replied. "Would you believe videotapes from Sri Lanka?"

"Then you *are* manipulated by aliens."

"In a pig's eye."

"Then you must come from the future."

"What time is it, dummy?" Buffalo Bob demanded.

"Huh? No, please, I . . ."

"It's Howdy Doody time!"

Speckled light. Dark motes. Fade to black.

Drunk as a skunk, the kidnapper slowly climbed the stairs, holding on to a metal railing. He was headed toward the third-floor walkup he'd rented for the week. He just needed a place to crash for the night, a place where nobody would bother him.

But what was he doing days? He'd left his regular job to work on a special mission here, hadn't he? Couldn't think about that now, though. Too tired.

Unlocking the door, he entered the tiny efficiency apartment and snapped on the air conditioner set in the room's single window.

"The Beach," he said, his voice croaking from disuse. "Miami Beach." He threw his windbreaker on the floor.

Long shadows were cast on the sand below. In the shards of late afternoon sun between them, a few working girls were still basking, taking it easy before they readied themselves to earn their nightly bread in the restaurants or hotels, or on the street. Soon the little patches of warmth they had staked out would be lost in darkness.

The kidnapper went to the tiny refrigerator in the corner and took a cold beer, downing it in two long mouthfuls. Then he stretched out fully clothed on the lumpy mattress. He didn't look forward to sleeping, exhausted as he was. When he dreamed, he often had nightmares about children shambling like tiny "Living Dead" creatures out of a George Romero movie.

"George Romero," he muttered, wondering if the name was a key to his past. He thought about it, but nothing came to mind. He was too tired to concentrate, anyhow. He felt that he had suffered unbearable tension today, though he couldn't remember why. Now he was drained, empty as an old Coke bottle. What had he done to make himself feel so rotten?

He closed his eyes to the waning light, falling into a nightmare of children with glazed eyes marching into the bloody jaws of a hideous, laughing clown.

He awakened in the dark. He hurt all over, and his sheets were soaked in spite of the air conditioner. He shook like a newborn mouse.

Rising, he massaged his temples before getting a fresh beer. He started to snap on the little Sony TV on the shelf over the fridge, but something made him stop. TV was bad for him; he would play the radio instead.

Sweetly flowing saxophone music filled the cramped room. He went into the bathroom, shucking his clothes and stepping into the shower. The cold water woke him and soothed him at the same time. The aching wasn't so bad after a few minutes.

He turned off the shower, got out, and toweled himself dry. Then he applied shaving cream to his chin and started scraping off the several days of stubble on his mustached face.

The music stopped, replaced by the sound of teletype machines. The news. As he shaved, the kidnapper grew depressed at the ominous parade of economic problems, social unrest, and the acrimonious breakdown of the summit at Oslo.

Local news was no better, a petty catalogue of drug busts, burglaries, and murders. And then something made him put down his razor before he was through shaving.

"Police believe they know who's been kidnapping children around South Florida this past week. An apparent abduction attempt at North Miami's Woodlake Mall yesterday afternoon failed, but a second child was taken in the parking lot. Joe Ciano, manager of a game room in the mall, was able to give a detailed description of the apparent kidnapper, matching the description of a missing person. Chris Reilly, an employee of the State of Florida's Endangered Species Program, left his job at Everglades National Park late last Monday afternoon without a word of explanation. Reilly drove away in a red 1973 Dodge van, and hasn't reported in or called in since."

"Chris Reilly," the kidnapper said, staring at his reflection in the mirror. "Chris Reilly . . ."

"Reilly," the radio announcer went on in his cheerful voice, "is thirty-five years old, has dark hair, dark eyes, and a mustache. He's five feet eleven inches tall, and weighs one hundred eighty-five pounds. The suspect is armed with a tranquilizer gun that shoots darts filled with procaine, a drug used to subdue wild animals for scientific study. He is apparently tranquilizing his young victims prior to abduction. Authorities believe Reilly may be suffering a nervous breakdown due to a divorce earlier this year.

"If you see a man driving a red Dodge van, license number SHM-393, please report his whereabouts to the police.

"The Hallandale city council today voted to . . ."

Yes, it was all true . . . except for the motive. Janet had left him in February, but he had become used to living alone since then. . . . Monday, he'd been out in the canoe looking for a young alligator to tag. After drugging it, he was supposed to slip a numbered aluminum band over its snout, so the Department could follow its migrations as it grew older.

He'd never found his 'gator. Instead, this three-dimensional image had flickered into existence right over the canoe in the air, chortling like the Great Gildersleeve. The image was kind of faint, but the voice was clear. Even though Gildersleeve faded in and out, the apparition had done something to Chris's mind.

Ever since then, whenever he wanted to put Chris to sleep, he just said: *"It's Howdy Doody time!"*

"The comedian," Chris said. He had made Chris look for children to abduct. Whenever Chris tried to remember why he was the kidnapper—or when he didn't work at it hard enough—his head started splitting like it had been smacked with a baseball bat. And the comedian could make him forget. . . .

How many children had he taken? First there was a little blonde girl in Flamingo. Then the little black boy, Thomas. And then Susie. Chris counted seven, altogether.

The comedian wanted eight. Four of each sex. Chris was supposed to take one more, a girl. Good God, what did the comedian have in mind for those babies down in the van?

"I gotta call the cops," he said. There were clean clothes in the closet. The comedian had let him buy them and the other things he needed after he had taken all of his money out of the bank on Monday. He slid into a fresh pair of jeans and a blue work shirt. There was no phone in his room, so he would have to get to the pay phone in the parking lot downstairs. He was working on the bottom button of the shirt when a Diamondback crawled inside his brain and bit down hard, its venom paralyzing him.

"Going someplace, dummy?"

Don Rickles stood between him and the door. "Are you stupid, or does your mother dress you that way?"

Chris lurched toward him. The pain in his head drew a

bloody film over his eyes. He almost fell, but managed to hold on to the dresser as his knees buckled.

"The children," he gasped, struggling to catch his breath.

"Hang on to your lid, kid," the comedian said, wagging his finger like Kay Kayser, "here we go again."

"No!" Chris screamed. "I won't let you take them!" He reeled toward the door again, passing through the image this time. The hairs on his arms stood up. He shoved open the door, the pain singing inside his skull like a billion crickets. Supporting himself on the railing, he scrambled down to the landing. His legs were silly putty, but he managed to stay on his feet somehow. Then he was at the second-floor landing. He half crawled the rest of the way down, and then he was staggering across the parking lot. The pain had become refined, exquisite in its agony. He refused to surrender to it. His strength was his identity. He was Chris Reilly, a decent human being, and he would not give the children to the comedian.

Stay away from the van, he told himself. Stay out in the open. He doesn't like to show himself. You might make it that way.

He saw the flimsy shelter of a pay phone ahead, a glowing shrine in the early-morning darkness. Then he was clutching at the receiver, reaching in his jeans for a quarter.

"No," he moaned. "Oh, God, no." No change in the pockets. Freshly laundered pants. He slumped against the metal shelf under the phone, hearing the busy signal as the receiver dropped. It struck his leg and dangled a few inches above the ground.

"All right. All right, already." Bespectacled and redheaded, the comedian stood on the shelf inside the little phone shelter. He leaned against the oblong box of the phone, a foot-high Woody Allen. "I'm proud of you. You're a hero. Practically a John Wayne. So stop whimpering; you're embarrassing me."

The pain subsided. Chris leaned against the booth, trembling and out of breath.

"I'm like death, taxes, and mothers-in-law," the comedian said. "You can't get away from me."

"Why?" Chris was just waiting for the comedian to ask him what time it was, wearily reciting the usual litany of questions. "Where did you come from? Who sent you?"

"Well, you guessed it before. I'm a projection from the future. I'm on a loop stretching from my time back to yours. Your brainwaves are my anchor in your time."

"A loop?" Chris struggled to understand. "What kind of loop?"

"It's kind of hard to explain, but the loop is tightening all the time. I first focused in on its outermost periphery, homing in on a pattern featuring beta waves with an interaction of alpha and theta—human, in other words. You."

"A random choice?"

"Yeah, but for what it's worth, you seem to be a bright guy."

"Thanks, but it's a wonder I can think at all after what you've put me through."

"It had to be done."

"Yeah, right. I'm standing here talking to Woody Allen, right? I'm crazy. Maybe I really did abduct a bunch of kids. Maybe I even meant to molest them . . . or even kill them."

"Kill them? With kindness, maybe. We can't pass a Burger King without you running in to pick up a snack for the little monsters. Never have I seen such a boy scout. The way you put away the beer, I didn't figure you for Jimmy Stewart in *Mr. Smith Goes to Washington*."

"The beer . . ." Chris could still taste it. "Why'd you let me drink so much?"

"At first it helped keep you in line, but after a while it just numbed out your brain—helped break down the conditioning."

"I've always had a weakness for drinking. My wife . . ."

"Look at you, ready to confess all your sins. If everyone had half your guilt, it never would have happened."

"*What* never would have happened?"

Archie Bunker blotted out Woody Allen. He patted his

potbelly and took a drag from his cigar. "The Big One, meathead. Double-ya Double-ya Three."

"A nuclear war . . . ?"

"Oh, whoop-de-doo. You sure do catch on quick. Just like the rest of them dingbats back in your time, blowing everything to hell just to show who was the biggest jerk."

"You mean it's gonna happen?" Chris asked. "It's really gonna happen?"

"The biggest cookout in history, meathead, only the marshmallows and weenies got a funny glow."

"Oh, God . . . the world . . . civilization."

"Most of it. Libraries destroyed, stored information frazzled by the blasts' pulses—we did find some old videotapes in Sri Lanka. Some egghead was studyin' comedy. But you know somethin'? We loined a lot about youse from them tapes. Too bad ya didn't use 'em to tape shut ya leaders' yaps."

"How can you joke about it?" Chris cried out, scared and enraged. "What's wrong with your head?"

"You think this one's bad," Groucho Marx said, "you shoulda seen the other one."

"What?"

"That's right. Gene damage. No relation to Gene Kelly, or Gene Autry, either. And nobody up ahead knows what to do about it. It's hard to take two aspirins and go to bed if you don't have arms and legs."

"Oh, Christ . . . the children. . . ."

"Say, you really *are* quick on the draw, Tex. We need a few kids to start a new gene pool. Who knows, maybe we can get a healthy breed of human going again if we work at it a little."

The sodium vapor lights began to wink out along Collins Avenue. Pink streaks of dawn touched the clouds over the ocean. Chris stared at the dull afterglow of the lamps, wondering if he could believe the comedian. "Why did you put me in that comatose state?" he demanded.

"Because there isn't much time," Groucho said. "Sort of like playing 'You Bet Your Life.' I had no idea you'd say the secret woid, but you did. Now I don't have the time to wrestle with you anymore. I have to trust you . . . I'm just glad you're not a used-car salesman.

"Look, Chris, haven't you noticed that I'm getting clearer all the time?"

Chris stared at the stooped figure in a tuxedo as Groucho paced across the aluminum shelf. The image was sharper than it had been yesterday in the van. Compared to its clarity in the canoe a week ago, it looked almost solid. "Yeah, I see."

"It's because we're getting closer to the disjunctive node."

"Disjunctive node?"

"Right, that's what causes the time loop. We can project across time around the node, closing in on it all the time. Our past, your future, it's really all the same. Waves and particles come and go around it anomalously, but it takes a helluva lot of power—and it's only going to be open for a few seconds."

"What happens when it opens?"

Groucho sucked on his cigar until the coal glowed red hot, demonstrating the growing brightness of his image as they drew closer to the disjunctive node. "Then matter can be pulled through into the future."

"The kids!"

"You got it." Groucho exhaled a cloud of smoke. "That's how we're gonna get 'em outta here."

Chris laughed aloud, the incongruously happy sound echoing through the still parking lot. But a germ of suspicion still infected him. "Why didn't you just tell me all this in the first place?"

W. C. Fields stared at him as though he were an insect. "There's a sucker born every minute, Christopher, my lad, but I couldn't be sure you weren't the exception." He consulted his pocket watch. "Precious little time to persuade you of the nobility inherent in my masterful plan. Considerably less time to dawdle now. My trusty timepiece indicates that there is slightly less than one hour before the aforementioned disjunctive node opens."

"An hour?"

"Fifty-six minutes, eighteen seconds, by my reckoning."

Fields snapped the watch shut, dangled it by its fob, and dropped it neatly into its pocket. "I suggest we get started."

Chris started toward the van, and then stopped dead in his tracks. "How do I know you're telling the truth?"

"You don't, my inquisitive companion. You don't. You are, however, hopelessly embroiled in this imbroglio, and there are only minutes remaining. Can you afford to risk inaction?"

Chris thought it over. If the comedian was lying, there was nothing to lose by going along with him now. The police would surely catch up with him today. And if it was true . . . if the comedian had really come to save the children . . . and the entire human race in the bargain . . .

"Okay," he said. "Kids will be on their way to school soon, so maybe we—oh, shit, I don't have my keys."

"They'll be necessary only to open these formidable metal doors, my dear Christopher. We can hardly venture forth in a vehicle the authorities are searching for."

"But how do we . . . ?"

"Find the node? My inquisitive innocent, I am being drawn to the node as the loop tightens. Indeed, I cannot avoid it." He waved his cane in a northerly direction. "Just up the beach."

"Good." Chris ran up to get his keys, feeling the adrenaline surge. When he got back downstairs, the comedian had turned into a darkly handsome young man wearing a suit twenty years out of fashion.

"Lenny Bruce!" Chris said. "You were always one of my favorites."

"*Now* he stops to admire my stuff," the comedian said. "I just needed something a little less conspicuous."

"What if we can't get another kid before it's time?" Chris said, unlocking the back.

"One of the girls will have to take an extra boyfriend, which might start the first war up ahead." The comedian smiled as the doors opened. "Come on out, kids. It's time to get a little exercise."

The children stirred and began to jump silently onto the

asphalt, one by one. "Jackie, Thomas, Michael, Cherie, Jimmy, Susie, and . . . Paulie."

"Paulie." Chris remembered the poster on Yogi Bear's paunch, and the agonizing struggle to regain his identity. "Comedian, you play rough."

"There's a lot at stake." Lenny Bruce almost looked real now, except for an occasional ghostly line wavering around him. "Let's get going."

The children in tow, they started up Collins Avenue. A jogger passed, eyeing them curiously. The sun was a brilliant disc reflected on the water as a rippling orange bar.

"Forty-five minutes," the comedian said.

They walked faster. The sun was warm and Chris was glad he wasn't wearing his windbreaker. Then he remembered that he had worn it only to hide the dart gun. "The gun," he said, turning to go back and get it.

"Forget it, jerk-off," Bruce said. "No time."

"Right." Traffic was picking up, and Chris noticed school buses and cars with children in them. Then a police car passed by, freezing his heart. The cop looked at them, and then drove on.

"Jesus," Chris breathed. "Jesus, Mary, and Joseph."

"They don't expect to see two men," the comedian said.

"It's still a miracle he didn't stop me," Chris said. "These city cops."

"The boys in blue. Miami's finest. Mean, just like most people in your time," Bruce said. "I guess there was just no way out of blowing the whole place to hell."

"Yeah," Chris said, hearing an angry horn blow on the street. "We all sensed it was going to happen sooner or later. Nobody knew how to stop it, though."

"Assholes."

They kept walking. Chris wanted desperately to find one last little girl. Perhaps his conditioning hadn't completely worn off. "How much time is left?"

"Twenty-eight minutes." The comedian turned to the children. "How ya doin', kids?"

"Fine," Jackie said. Jackie Tiger was a Miccosuccee Indian girl. Chris had loved her dark, liquid eyes and black hair from the first. He and Janet had never had any children; that was one reason their marriage hadn't lasted. And now he was bonded to the comedian, with seven children to protect from a world gone mad.

A middle-aged couple passed them, smiling at the children. Both wore Bermuda shorts in the already considerable heat.

"Say good morning kids," the comedian said.

"Good morning," the children all sang in unison.

"You've still got them under your thumb," Chris said. "Will they be zombies like this in the future?"

"Are you serious? Look, this is one time when the end justifies the means, believe me. But they'll be free up ahead. We've got a pretty nice place set up for them, in fact."

"Utopia?"

"No such thing." Lenny gestured around them. "But better than this toilet any day. Keep walking. We've only got fifteen more minutes."

Chris walked as quickly as the children's shorter legs would permit. He began to count the seconds. Sixty, one hundred, two hundred, three hundred.

"Ten minutes," the comedian said.

They were almost jogging now. The comedian looked just like a living, breathing, three-dimensional human being, the reincarnation of Lenny Bruce, come to see the unhappy world end.

"Look." Chris saw a group of kids waiting at a bus stop. One was off by herself a few yards, examining an ant hill. She was a little East-Asian girl.

"Perfect!" the comedian said. "Such a gene pool we'll have if you can nab her."

"Have the kids tell her they're walking to school," Chris said. "Make them ask her if she wants to go with them."

"All right, but if it doesn't work right off, you gotta grab her. Okay?"

"Okay."

"Kids," the comedian said. "See that little girl over there? I think she's really nice, don't you? Why don't you ask her if she wants to walk to school with us? Make sure you tell her about all the fun we have.''

The children giggled. Chris and the comedian passed the little girl and hesitated while the question was put to her by Paulie, the others joining in persuasively from time to time in their high voices.

Another police car drove by.

''Jesus,'' Chris muttered

''What's your name?'' Susie asked the little girl.

''Premika.''

''Are you from around here?'' Jimmy asked, spinning his yo-yo.

''No, I'm from Thailand.''

This seemed to confuse the children. Jackie said, ''Do you want to walk to school with us or not?'' as though she were growing impatient.

Premika looked at Chris and the comedian. ''Who are those men?'' she asked in her lilting accent.

''Nobody,'' Michael said. ''Just two men.''

Premika shook her head emphatically. She would not go.

The bus pulled up to the curb, and the children lined up as the driver opened the door. Premika was separated from the others by the comedian's seven children.

''Move!'' the comedian said.

Premika was looking worriedly at the bus. Chris lunged and scooped her up, turning to run with her kicking and screaming in his arms. The other children ran behind.

''Four minutes!'' the comedian shouted.

''Put me down!'' Premika screamed. ''Put me down!'' Then she started babbling in Thai, alternately wailing and shrieking. Her sneakers drummed at Chris's thigh as he clapped a hand over her mouth.

The bus driver laid on his horn, and the children at the bus stop were shouting excitedly.

''It's just ahead,'' the comedian said. ''You can make it, Chris.''

But Chris's lungs were already aching, and his heart felt as though it had doubled in size. He kept running, though, feeling Premika's warm tears run over his fingers, mingling with his sweat. She bit his hand, but he didn't let go, even when blood started running down his wrist.

Sirens wailed somewhere behind them.

"Hurry up, kids!" Lenny shouted. "It's not much farther."

Premika was whimpering now, nearly fainted. But Chris didn't lighten his grip. She could have been faking, waiting for a chance to break free.

"This way!" The comedian led them onto a public beach.

Chris saw Haulover Pier cutting through the glittering waves ahead, his calves aching from running in the sand while carrying Premika. His breath came in strangled gasps, and his arms felt as though they would fall off. But he couldn't quit, not now.

The sirens drew closer. Rubber screeched. Car doors slammed. A man shouted through a bullhorn: "Give it up, Christopher Reilly. You can't go any farther."

As if to prove it, a security guard ran toward Chris from the far end of the pier. Chris turned to see half a dozen cops sprinting over the sand, pistols drawn.

"No," Chris said. "Not this close."

Early sunbathers watched apprehensively, catching Chris's eyes as he desperately searched for a way to keep going.

"Let the children go, Mr. Reilly. It's gonna be all right. Just let the kids go."

As though in response, the children gathered closer about Chris, Premika, and the comedian.

The policemen leveled their pistols, clutching them in both hands, legs spread.

Chris started to cry. He let the confused Premika down, and she stood in the sand with the other children, looking curiously up at her kidnapper.

"Sir," the policeman said to the comedian, "please come with us first, then you, Mr. Reilly."

The comedian stepped obediently forward, and turned into Charlie Chaplin. The policemen gaped as he twirled his cane.

Baggy pants fluttering, Chaplin turned back to the children, shoulders wiggling with silent mirth, white teeth flashing below his mustache.

''Is it too late?'' Chris whispered, not wanting to believe it.

Chaplin looked at him and winked. And winked out.

The beach was silent, but for the sea breeze.

A new sun rose in the west.

Chris remembered the radio report about the failed summit at Oslo. The war had come at last.

Rippling flame surged towards the beach. Hotels, condominiums, towers crumbled like sand castles. Whirling at the shockwave's advancing rim was a scintillant point.

The children shrank around Chris. He spread his arms to hug them tight.

A policeman dropped his gun as the point came toward him, and then all the cops and bathers were crushed into the heaving sand.

Just before the shock wave reached them, Chris and the comedian's kids were sheltered within the disjunctive node, a whorl of perfect light.

And then they were gone.

TWILIGHT TIME

Lewis Shiner

"Twilight Time" was purchased by Shawna McCarthy, and appeared in the April 1984 issue of IAsfm, *with an illustration by Ron Lindahn. Hard-hitting and powerful, "Twilight Time" sweeps us along with it on a journey to a past decade that might not be* quite *the way you remember it—with good reason.*

Lewis Shiner is widely regarded as one of the most exciting new writers of the eighties. His stories have appeared in Isaac Asimov's Science Fiction Magazine, The Magazine of Fantasy & Science Fiction, Omni, Oui, Shayol, Wild Card, The Twilight Zone Magazine, *and elsewhere. His first novel,* Frontera, *appeared in 1984 to good critical response. His most recent book is* Deserted Cities of the Heart, *and he is currently working on a new novel entitled* Slam. *Shiner lives in Austin, Texas, with his wife, Edith.*

I

The part of the machine they strapped me to looked too much like an electric chair. A sudden, violent urge to resist came over me as the two proctors buckled me down and fastened the electrodes to my scalp.

Not that it would have done me much good. The machine and I were in a steel cage and the cage was in the middle of a maximum-security prison.

"Okay?" Thornberg asked me. His thinning hair was damp with sweat and a patch of it glistened on his forehead.

"Sure," I said. "Why not?"

He turned some switches. I couldn't hear anything happen, but then, this wasn't *I Was A Teenage Frankenstein* and sparks weren't supposed to be climbing the bars of the cage.

Then a jolt of power hit me and I couldn't even open my mouth to tell Thornberg to cut the thing off. My eyes filmed over and I started to see images in the mist. A distant, calmer part of my brain realized that Thornberg had cut in the encephalograph tapes.

We'd been working on them for weeks, refining the images detail by detail, and now all the pieces came together. Not just the steep hills and narrow streets of the town, not just the gym and the crepe-paper streamers and Buddy Holly singing, but the whole era, the flying saucer movies, the cars like rocket ships, rolled up blue jeans and flannel shirts and PF Flyer tennis shoes, yo-yos, the candy wagon at noon recess, William Lundigan and Tom Corbett and Johnny Horton. They all melted together, the world events and the TV shows, the facts and the fiction and the imaginings, and for just one second they made a coherent, tangible universe.

And then I kicked and threw out my arms because I was falling.

II

I fell the way I did in dreams, trying to jerk myself awake, but the fall went on and on. I opened my eyes and saw a quiet blue, as if the sky had turned to water and I was drifting down through it. I hit on my hands and knees and felt the dirt under my fingers turn hard and grainy, felt the sun burn into my back.

Off to the left sat a line of low, gray-green hills. The ground where I crouched was covered with tough bull-head weeds and the sky overhead was the clear, hot blue of an Arizona summer.

The San Carlos Mountains, I thought. He did it. I'm back.

From the angle of the sun it looked to be late afternoon. I'd landed outside the city, as planned, to avoid materializing inside a crowd or a solid wall.

I sucked the good clean air into my lungs and danced a couple of steps across the sand. All I wanted was to get into town and make sure the rest of it was there, that it was all really happening.

I found the highway a few hundred yards to the south. LeeAnn was a tight feeling in my chest as I headed for town at a fast walk.

My eyes were so full of the mountains and the open sky that I didn't notice the thing in the road until I was almost on top of it.

The pavement was not just broken, but scarred, cut by a huge, melted trench. Something had boiled the asphalt up in two knee-high waves and left it frozen in mid-air. The sand around it looked like a giant tire track in icy mud, a jagged surface of glassy whites and browns.

The strangest part was that for a couple of seconds I didn't realize that anything was wrong. My memories had become such a hash that the San Carlos Reservation had turned into a desert from a Sunday afternoon *Science Fiction Theater* and any minute I expected to see Caltiki or a giant scorpion come over the nearest rise.

I knelt to touch the asphalt ridge. Nothing in the real 1961, the one in the history books, could do this to a road.

A distant rumbling made me look up. A truck was coming out of the east, and it was swollen with all the outlandish bumps and curves of the middle fifties. I jogged toward it, waving one arm, and it pulled up beside me.

The driver was an aging Apache in faded jeans and a T-shirt. *"Ya-ta-hey,* friend," he said. "Goin' in to Globe?"

"Yeah," I said, out of breath. "But I need to tell you. The road's . . . torn up, just ahead."

"Got the road again, did they? Damn gover'ment. Always got to do their tests on Indian land. You want a lift?"

"Yeah," I said, "Yeah, I do. Thanks."

I got in and he threw the truck in gear with a sound like a bag of cans rolling downhill. I tried to remember the last time I'd seen a gearshift on the steering column.

"My name's Big Charlie," he said.

"Travis," I said. The cab of the truck smelled like Wildroot Creme Oil, and a magazine photo of Marilyn Monroe stared at me from the open glove compartment. A rabbit's foot hung off the keys in the ignition and I had to remind myself that life was cheap in the sixties, even the lives of seals and leopards and rabbits.

A hysterical DJ on the radio was shouting, "K-Z-O-W, kay-Zow! Rockin' and rollin' Gila County with Ozzie and Harriet's favorite son . . ." The voice drowned in an ocean of reverb and out of it swam the sweet tenor of Ricky Nelson, singing "Travelin' Man."

Somehow the music made it all real and I had to look into the wind to keep the water out of my eyes. Up ahead of us in Globe was a fifteen-year-old kid who was listening to the same song, starting to get ready for his end-of-the-school-year dance. At that dance he was going to meet a girl named LeeAnn Patterson and fall in love with her. And he was never going to get over her.

Never.

Big Charlie eased the pickup off the road and found a place to cross the strip of melted glass. When the song finished the radio erupted in a flare of trumpets. "This is Saturday, May the 27th, and this is Kay-Zowzowzow NEWS!" Big Charlie turned the volume down with an automatic flip of the wrist, but I didn't care. The date was right, and I could have rattled off the headlines as well as the DJ could. Thornberg had made me do my homework.

Krushchev and Kennedy were headed for test-ban talks in Vienna. Freedom Riders were being jailed in Mississippi, and the Communists were stepping up their assault on Laos. Eichmann was on trial in Jerusalem, and Alan Shepard was still being honored for his space flight of three weeks before.

On the local scene, six teenagers were dead over in Stafford, part of the rising Memorial Day Death Toll. Rumors were going around about a strike against Kennicot Copper, whose strip mines employed about half of Globe's work force.

Eddie Sachs was going to be in the pole position when they ran the 500 on Tuesday. The Angels had taken the Tigers, and the Giants had edged the Cubs in thirteen.

A decade of peace and quiet and short hair was winding down; a time when people knew their place and stayed in it. For ten years nobody had wanted anything but a new car and a bigger TV set, but now all that was about to change. In a little over a year the Cuban missile crisis would send thousands of people into their back yards to dig bomb shelters, and the "advisors" would start pouring into Southeast Asia. In another year the president would be dead.

All that I knew. What I didn't know was why there was a huge melted scar across the desert.

Suddenly the truck's brakes squealed and I jerked back to attention. My eyes focused on the road ahead and saw a little boy straddling the white line, waving frantically.

The truck slewed to the left and stopped dead. A girl of 12 or 13 stood up from a patch of mesquite and stared at us like she wanted to run away. She had a good six years on the boy, but when he ran back to her it seemed to calm her down.

"Hey," Big Charlie shouted, leaning out his window. "What do you kids think you're doing?"

The boy was tugging on the girl's arm, saying, "It's *okay!* They're both *okay,* I'm sure, I'm really sure!"

The boy pulled her gently toward the driver's window of the truck. "Can you help us, mister?"

"What's wrong? What's the big idea of standing out there in the middle of the road like that? You could have got killed."

The boy backed away from Charlie's anger and the girl stepped in. "We . . . we were running away from home." She looked down at the boy as if she needed confirmation, and if I hadn't known before that she was lying, I knew it then. "We . . . changed our minds. Can you take us back, mister? Just as far as town? Please?"

Charlie thought it over for a minute and seemed to come up with the same answer I did. Whatever they'd done probably wasn't that serious, and they were bound to be better off in town than hitchhiking in the middle of the desert.

"In the back," he said. "And watch what you're doing!"

They scrambled over the side of the pickup, their sneakers banging on the side walls. I turned to look at them as we pulled away and they were huddled by the tailgate, arms around each other, their eyes squeezed shut.

What were they running from? I wondered. They looked like they hadn't eaten in a couple of days, and their clothes were torn and dirty.

And what in God's name had the boy meant when he said we were "okay?"

Don't worry about it, I told myself. Don't get involved. You haven't got time to get mixed up in somebody else's problems. You're not going to be here that long.

We passed Glen's Market at the foot of Skyline Drive, the one with the heavy wooden screen door that said "Rainbo is *good* bread" and the rich smells of doughnuts and bubble gum and citrus fruit.

"Where do you want off?" Big Charlie asked me.

"Downtown, anywhere." The highway had curved past Globe's three motels and now the grade school was coming up on the right. The Toastmaster Cafe, and its big Wurlitzer jukebox with the colored tube of bubbles around the side, was just across the street. Overhead was the concrete walkway used to get from one side to the other. It seemed a lot closer to the ground than it used to, even though I'd tried to prepare myself for things being smaller than I remembered.

Number 207 on the Toastmaster's Wurlitzer was "True Love Ways" by Buddy Holly.

I could almost hear those thick, syrupy violins, and the hollow moan of King Curtis' saxophone as we turned the corner and pulled up in front of Upton's.

"This okay?" Big Charlie asked.

"Fine." I was thinking about the smell of pencil shavings and the one piece of gum that was always stuck in the drain of the water fountain at the high school across the street. I got out of the truck. "I really appreciate it."

"Not to worry," Big Charlie said, and the pickup rattled away down Main Street.

The counter inside Upton's swung out in a wide U, dotted with red plastic-covered stools. The chrome and the white linoleum made it look more like an operating room than a place to eat, but it passed for atmosphere at the time.

"Help you?" said the kid behind the counter.

His name was Curtis and he lived up the street from my parents' house. He was a lot younger than I remembered him and he could have done with a shampoo. It was all I could do not to call him by name and order a Suicide. The Suicide was Curtis' own invention, and he made it by playing the chrome spiggots behind the counter like they were piano keys.

"Just coffee," I said.

Five of the tables along the south wall were occupied, two of them by clean-cut families at dinner. Dinner tonight was a hamburger or the 89¢ Daily Special: fried chicken, three vegetables, tea or coffee. The women's dresses hung to mid-calf and most of the male children had flat-top haircuts that showed a strip of close-shaven skull in the middle. Everybody seemed to be smoking.

A woman around the corner from me had bought the Jackie Kennedy look all the way, down to the red pillbox hat and the upswept hair. Two seats away from her a kid in a T-shirt and a leather jacket was flipping noisily through the metal-edged pages in the jukebox console.

I paid a nickel for a copy of the *Arizona Record* out of a wooden box by the door. There was nothing in it about melted scars in the desert, just weddings and graduations and church announcements.

When I looked up, the two kids from the highway were sitting next to me. The girl was getting some stares. Her face was streaked with dirt and her shirt was thin enough to make it obvious that she should have been wearing a training bra or something under it.

"My name's Carolyn," she said. "This is Jeremy." She put her arm around the boy, who smiled and picked at his fingernails.

"I'm Travis. Is he your brother?"

"Yes," the girl said, at the same time that the boy said, "No."

I shook my head. "This isn't going to get us anywhere."

"What do you want to know for, anyway?" the girl asked.

"I don't really care. You're following me, remember?"

Curtis was standing by the brand-new Seeburg box in the corner. He must have gotten tired of waiting for the kid in the motorcycle jacket to make up his mind. He pushed some buttons, a record dropped, and the room filled with violins. The bass thumped, a stick touched a cymbal, and Ray Charles started singing "Georgia."

"Why do you keep doing that?"

"Doing what?"

"Rubbing your hair that way. Like it feels funny."

I jerked my hand away from my ragged prison haircut. Ray was singing about his dreams. *"The road,"* he sang, *"leads back to you . . ."*

I knew he was talking to me. My road had brought me back here, to see Curtis standing in front of the jukebox, to the music hanging changeless in the air, to LeeAnn. Even if Brother Ray and Hoagy Carmichael had never imagined a road made of Thornberg's anti-particles.

"Stop that," the girl said, and for a second I thought she was talking to me. Then I saw that Jeremy was chewing on the ridge of flesh between his thumb and forefinger, staring down at the countertop. Blood was starting to trickle out of the front of his mouth. The sight of it put the music out of my head and left me scared and confused.

I hadn't looked at him closely before, but now that I did I

saw scabs all over his arms and spots of dried, chocolate-colored blood on his T-shirt. His eyes were rolling back in his head and he looked like he was going to go backwards off the stool.

Carolyn slapped him across the mouth, knocking his hand away. He started to moan, louder than the jukebox, loud enough to turn heads across the room.

"I have to get him out of here," the girl said, pulling him to his feet.

"He needs a doctor," I said. "Let me . . ."

"No," she hissed. "Stay out of it."

I flinched from the anger in her voice and she ran for the door, tugging Jeremy after her. They were halfway across the floor when the door swung open.

A man in loose slacks and a sport shirt stood in the doorway, staring at them. The little boy looked like he'd just seen the giant wasp in *Monster From Green Hell*. His jaw dropped open and started to shake. I could see the scream building from all the way across the room.

Before he could cut loose with it, Carolyn dragged him past the man and out onto the street. The man stood there for a second with a puzzled half-smile on his face, then shrugged and looked around for a seat.

When my stomach started jumping I thought at first that I was just reacting to all the confusion. Then I remembered what Thornberg had said about phase-shifting, and I knew I only had about a minute before the charge that had sent me back wore off.

I left a quarter on the counter and went to the men's room in back. The smell of the deodorant cake in the urinal almost made me sick as I leaned against the wall. I felt drunk and dizzy and there seemed to be two of everything. Then the floor went out from under me and I was falling again.

I sailed back up toward the future like a fish on the end of a line.

III

I spent two days in debriefing. Thornberg got to ask the questions, but there was always a proctor or two around, taping every sound, every gesture I made.

From Thornberg's end everything had looked fine. One second I'd been there, the next I'd just winked out. I was gone a little over an hour, then I popped back in, dizzy but conscious, and all my signs had been good.

Thornberg's excitement showed me for the first time how personally he was involved. He seemed frankly envious, and I suddenly realized that he didn't just want the experiment to work, he wanted to be able to go back himself.

I was too caught up in my own questions to worry very long about Thornberg. My common sense told me everything that had happened to me had been real, but my rational mind was still having trouble. Who were those two kids, and what were they running from? What could have torn up the highway that way?

The proctors liked it a lot less than I did. "We've been through the government files," one of them said on the second day. "No experiments on the San Carlos Reservation. Nothing even in development that could have caused it."

"So how do you explain it?" Thornberg asked.

"Hallucination," the proctor said. "The whole experience was completely subjective and internal."

"No," Thornberg said. "Out of the question. We saw his body disappear."

The proctor stood up. "I think we'd better suspend this whole thing until this is cleared up."

"No!" Thornberg got between the proctor and the door. "We've got to have more data. We have to send him back again."

The proctor shook his head. The gesture didn't put the slightest wrinkle in his maroon double-knit uniform.

"You can't stop me, you know," Thornberg said. "You'll have to get an executive order."

"I'll get it," the proctor said, and stepped around him.

When the door was closed Thornberg turned to me. "Then we send you back first. Now."

IV

I landed in the same place I'd been, leaning against the dingy walls of the rest room for support. My head cleared, and the last two days could have been no more than a fever dream caused by bad coffee on an empty stomach.

I started back into the restaurant. The jukebox was playing "Sink the Bismark" by Johnny Horton. Horton was a big local favorite and he'd died just a few months before, in a car crash in Texas.

The man in the sport shirt, the one that had scared Jeremy so badly, was sitting in a booth with a cheeseburger. I stood for a second in the shadows of the hallway and watched him. He looked ordinary to me—short, curly hair, no sideburns, no facial hair. His shirt was one of those short-sleeved African prints in muted oranges and blues that wanted to be loud but couldn't quite bring it off. Sunglasses peeked out of the shirt pocket.

He looked like a tourist. But why would there be any tourists in Globe, Arizona, in 1961?

And then I saw his fingers.

His right hand was tucked under his left elbow and the fingers were moving in short, precise gestures against his side. I'd seen hands move like that before, keying data into a computer by touch.

Cut it out, I told myself. So the guy's got a nervous habit. It's none of your business.

I picked up my copy of the newspaper from the counter and tore off the masthead, including the date. If the proctors wanted some proof, I'd try and oblige. I folded the strip of newsprint and put it in my back pocket, dropping the rest of the paper in the trash.

Once on the street I saw men all around me in short-sleeved shirts buttoned to the neck. Long, rectangular cars covered with chrome and sharp angles cruised the streets like patient sharks. TV sets blinked at me from the window of the furniture store, their screens cramped and nearly circular. I stopped and watched a toothpaste ad with an invisible shield in it and remembered the craze for secret ingredients.

That fifteen-year-old kid across town had a theory about secret ingredients. He believed they were codes, and that aliens from space were using them to take over the Earth.

GL70: Town Secure. AT-7: Send More Saucers. He dreamed at night about great domed ships gliding over the desert.

I thought about the scar in the highway and the man in the restaurant and got another chill. This one turned my whole body cold, as if my heart had started pumping ice water.

My feet carried me down the street and stopped in front of the National News Stand. The door was locked, but through the window I could see the lines of comics: *Sea Devils* and *Showcase* and *Rip Hunter, Time Master*. My father had made me stop buying *Rip Hunter* because it was ruining my sense of reality; every time Rip and his crew went back in time they found aliens there, tampering with human history.

Aliens.

A spin rack by the door was full of science-fiction paperbacks. The short, fat Ace doubles were crammed in next to the taller Ballantines with the weird, abstract covers. Right at the top, in a pocket all to itself, was Ruppelt's *Report on Unidentified Flying Objects*.

Flying Saucers.

Further back, where I could barely see it in the dimness of the store, was the rack of men's magazines. When the old man with the cigar that ran the place wasn't paying attention I used to go back and thumb through them, but I never found quite what I was looking for.

The store was like an unassembled Revell model kit of my childhood. All the pieces were there, the superheroes and the aliens and the unobtainable women, and if I could just fit them together the right way I might be able to make sense of it. In a lifetime I might have done it, but I only had another hour.

I felt too much like an aging delinquent in the T-shirt I was wearing, so I bought a fresh shirt at the dime store across the street and changed in their rest room. I thought for a second about time paradoxes as I threw the old one away, then decided to hell with it.

The dime store clock said seven-thirty and the dance should have started at seven. Enough of a crowd should have accumulated for me to become another faceless parent in the background. I started uphill toward the high school and was sweating by the time I got there. But that was okay. You could still sweat in 1961, and your clothes could still wrinkle.

All the doors to the gym were open and Japanese lanterns hung over the doors. From across the asphalt playground I could hear the heavy, thumping bass of "Little Darlin' " by the Diamonds.

I went inside. A banner across the far end of the gym read "Look for a Star" in crude, glittering letters. Across thirty years I remembered the sappy lyrics to the song that had been forced on us as our theme. Four-pointed stars, sprayed with gold paint, dangled from the girders, and the lanterns over the punch bowls had Saturn rings stapled to them.

Most of the teachers were standing in a clump. I recognized Mrs. Smith's hooked nose and long jaw; she'd cried when she found the drawing of her as a witch. Mr. Miller, next to her, was still wearing the goatee that he would be forced to shave off the next fall because it made him look "like a beatnik."

About half the kids in my class were already there. Bobby Arias, class president, and Myron Cessarini, track star and sex symbol, were quietly breaking hearts at their own end of the gym. Over by the opposite wall was Marsha Something-or-other, the one that threw up all over the floor in sixth grade, with the wings on her glasses and waxen skin.

But no sign of LeeAnn or the fifteen-year-old Travis. I went outside to get away from the heat and the close, sweat-sock smell of the place. Coals of cigarettes glowed where a few of the adults were taking advantage of the growing darkness. I sniffed the clean air and tried to think of reasons why I didn't want to stay right where I was for the rest of my life.

Lots of reasons. Racism. Sexism. People throwing trash on highways and dumping sewage in the creeks and not even knowing it was wrong. No sex. Not on TV, not in the movies, especially not in real life. Nice girls didn't. Curfews. Dress codes. Gas guzzling cars.

Still, I thought. Still . . .

Somebody was tugging at my sleeve.

"Hey, mister," said a little boy's voice. "Hey."

I winced at the sound of it. "What are you following me for? What do you want from me?"

"We need help," Carolyn said. "If they catch us they'll kill us."

"Who will?"

"Them," Jeremy said.

He wasn't pointing at anybody. Giant ants? I wondered. "I don't understand. What is it you want me to do?"

The girl shrugged and turned her face away from me. I could see the tears glistening in her eyes. Jeremy sat crosslegged on the asphalt in front of me and reached out to hold onto one of Carolyn's ankles. With my back to the wall of the gym I felt hemmed in by them, emotionally and physically.

Some obscure sense of guilt kept me asking questions. "What's wrong with Jeremy? What happened in that restaurant?"

"My father says he has some kind of eppa . . . eppa . . . ."

"Epilepsy?"

"Yeah. And he gets it whenever he gets too close to *them.*"

"Was that one of them in the restaurant?"

"Yes."

Fingers moving against his side, empty-eyed, sunglasses. Reporting on me? "Who are they?"

The girl shook her head. For a second I saw past her hollow eyes and dirty brown hair, had just a glimpse of the woman she might be if she hung on long enough. "You won't believe me," she said. "You'll think I'm crazy."

"I'm starting to think that anyway."

"What if I said they were from space? What would you say then?" In the last of the light her eyes had a hard gray sheen.

Oh God, I thought. *Invaders From Mars.* What's happening to my past?

"See?" she said. "I warned you."

"What about your parents? Can't they help you?"

"My father . . ." She stopped, swallowed, started again. "My father was all I had. They killed him. Jeremy's parents too. He's from California and they had him in one of their ships but he got away. That's where he got the . . . epilepsy. From what they did to him. My father . . . my father and me found him wandering around San Carlos and brought him back to the store."

That told me where I'd seen her before. Her father ran a rock shop out on the edge of the Apache reservation. My folks had taken me out there once to see the peridots, the green crystals that only turned up in extinct volcanic craters around San Carlos and somewhere in South America. I'd noticed her because I'd just gotten to the age where I was noticing girls, but we had shied away from actually speaking to each other.

She was wearing a big peridot ring, probably her father's, on the index finger of her right hand. "If they killed your father," I said, "why didn't you call the police?"

"I did. But when the policeman came, he was . . . one of them. Jeremy ran off into the desert and I ran after him. Now they're looking for both of us."

No matter how uncomfortable I felt, I had to believe that her story was just a fantasy. I had to make myself believe it. But even if I'd been sure she was hallucinating, what could I do for her? She needed a family and a psychiatrist and I couldn't be either one in the time I had left. I took some money out of my wallet.

"Look," I said, "here's twenty bucks. Go take a bus to Phoenix or somewhere. Call an aunt or a grandfather or somebody you know you can trust and get them to help you out. Okay?"

She knew she'd lost me. I could see it in her eyes. She wadded up the bill and held it in her fist. "They know who you are," she said.

"What?"

"They saw us with you. They'll be looking for you, now, too."

My heart slowed back to something like normal. "That's okay. I'll risk it."

I watched them until they faded into the darkness. "In the

Still of the Night'' by the Five Satins was playing in the gym
and I wanted to go in and listen to it. I wanted to forget what
the girl had told me and see what I'd come to see and get out
of there.

I took about two steps before my stomach cramped, driving
me back against the wall of the gym.

"No," I whispered. "Not yet. Not now. Please."

I was wasting my breath. In less than a minute the dizziness came over me and everything fell away.

V

The proctors weren't too happy about my coming back in a
different shirt. They didn't much care for the newspaper
masthead either, but they had their executive order and they
decided it was all academic anyhow.

They threw me in my cell and refused to let me talk to
Thornberg. This time the proctors debriefed me, and I told
them as little as I thought I could get away with. One of them
might have been the one that had threatened me after the last
trip, but I couldn't be sure. Between the uniforms and the
dark glasses they had an unnerving similarity.

Dark glasses, I thought. Sunglasses. I remembered fingers
moving against a bright sport shirt.

Cut it out, I thought. You're letting your imagination go
crazy. Don't get sucked into somebody else's fantasy.

Finally they left me alone and I wondered if the experiment
was really over. Thornberg would probably not live through
the disappointment. To have worked so hard and then lose it
all, to never get to use his own machine . . .

And what about me? I thought. To have gotten so close to
seeing LeeAnn only to miss her by a few seconds?

Memories came rushing back, out of control. The first time
we'd made love, in the back of my parents' Chevy II station
wagon with the seat folded down. Our first winter at Arizona
State, LeeAnn in a miniskirt and rag coat that hung to her
ankles, wrapped in yards of fake fur. Politics and marches,
graduation and marriage, the underground newspaper in Phoe-

nix in the late sixties. Our first house, LeeAnn's thirtieth birthday, the flowers and the cheap red wine . . .

And then the day the Proctor's Amendment passed the House. Politics and marches again, me reluctant at first, but LeeAnn outraged and dedicated, young again in the space of a few days. The first victories, Colorado voting against ratification, Texas leaning our way. People starting to wonder if the proctors really would be better than their local police, even in Houston.

And then one by one we were getting killed or crippled or lost in the basements of jails. They told me the day they arrested me that LeeAnn had died trying to construct a bomb, a bomb, for God's sake, when she had never even touched any kind of weapon . . .

I never got a trial, because the Proctors were now the Law. No charges, no lawyers, just a cell and a lot of memories.

Time moved on.

As much as I hated the proctors, I knew better than to blame them. They hadn't elected themselves; the citizens of the United States had listened to their televisions and voted them in, so it was their fault too. But mostly it was time's fault. Time had passed. Times had changed. So I sat in a jail cell and I thought about what it had been like to be fifteen years old, before I had any idea of what time could do.

That was where Thornberg found me. He needed somebody with a memory of a specific time and place that was so strong that his machines could focus on it and follow the time lines back to it. Because it was dangerous, his funding agency had sent him to the prisons to look for volunteers, and when he saw how I tested out he wanted me. I don't think the proctors had taken him seriously until the first test had worked, and once it did they seemed to panic.

What were they afraid of? What did they have to lose? Were they afraid I was going to escape through a hole in time?

Or were they afraid I was going to learn something they didn't want anybody to know?

I was still thinking about it late that night when I heard my cell door open. It was Thornberg.

"How did you get in here?" I whispered.

"Never mind. The question is, do you want to go again? Tonight? Right now?"

We headed straight for the lab and I changed into my traveling clothes. Thornberg was nervous, talking the whole time he was strapping me in.

"What I don't understand," he said, "is how you can have a past that's not the same as *my* past. Why does yours have tracks in the desert and flying saucers?"

"How should I know?" I said. "Maybe everybody's past is different. People never remember things the same way as anybody else. Maybe they *are* different. What are those waves your machine uses?"

"Retrograde probability waves."

"Retrograde because they move backwards in time, right? But couldn't they branch off, just like regular probability waves? Your machine uses my brain waves to sort through all those probabilities, so it would have to take me to whatever *I thought* the past was, right?"

Thornberg was interested. He'd gone back to his console, but he wasn't reaching for the controls. "If that's true, why is there no record of your melted track in the desert?"

"The different pasts all lead to the same place, the present. I guess there could be other pasts that lead to other presents, that 'Many Worlds' theory you were telling me about. In my past the proctors don't want any record of the mess their spaceships made, so they just covered it up. In yours, you never knew of any space-ships. But they lead to the same thing, with the proctors in power."

"You have a lot of imagination."

"Yeah. I do. Imagine this, then. Suppose I changed something? Made it so my past hooked on to a different future? Just like switching a train onto another track. You said every decision we make creates a whole new universe."

"No," Thornberg said. "Out of the question! Do you have any idea of the risk? At the end of the hour you'd be pulled back here anyway."

Or into another future, I thought, but I didn't say it. "All right. Calm down. If we're going to do this we'd better get started.''

Thornberg just stared at me for a few seconds, and I could see how frightened he was. My only question was whether he was afraid for me or afraid I'd go off into some other future and leave him stuck in this one.

I never got the answer because his hand snaked out and started pushing the buttons.

VI

Seeing myself walk into the gym was as immediate as a glance in the mirror and as distant as looking at an old photograph. I wanted to go over to myself and say, straighten up for God's sake, and turn your collar down. But even so I could see myself through my fifteen-year-old eyes and know that the slouch and the clothes and the haircut were the only ways I could say the things I didn't have words for then.

The kid had three-inch cuffs in his blue jeans, and the light jacket he wore over his T-shirt wasn't red, like James Dean's jacket in *Rebel Without A Cause,* but only because a red jacket would have been somebody else's uniform and not his own. His hair was too long for a flat top and not long enough for a DA, but five minutes didn't go by without him running a comb through it at least a couple of times.

Somebody put "Twilight Time" by the Platters on the record player. The overhead lights went out and two deep blue spots swept over the dancers. Martin and Dickie, the kid's best friends, were off to his left, talking behind their hands and bumping each other with their shoulders. The kid just stood there and stared into the crowd around the bleachers, and at the few daring couples out on the gym floor, intently, like he was trying to find somebody.

So was I.

Tony Williams sang, about falling in love all over again, *"as I did then."*

And she walked in.

For thirty years I'd been haunted by this memory. Strongly enough to get me out of prison, to send me back in Thornberg's machine, and now I was standing just across a high school gym from her, and she was just a girl. Just a fifteen-year-old girl. Skinny and shy and awkward, her first night in a new town, talked into coming to this dance by her mother and the principal of the school, both of them afraid she would go all summer without making any friends.

And then her mother said something to her that made her laugh and her head dropped down and the long red hair fell over her face and it wasn't just a girl anymore, it was LeeAnn, and I felt like somebody had just put a fist into my throat.

I turned my back on her and stood in the doorway, letting the hot night air work on my eyes until I could see again.

Something moved, just out of the range of the lanterns. Carolyn and the boy again, I thought. I didn't want to see them, didn't even want to think about them anymore. Hadn't I done enough? What more did they want from me?

I was turning back to look at LeeAnn when a flash of color across the gym distracted me. The man from Upton's, the one in the sport shirt, darted through the crowd, fingers working against his left side.

A voice behind me said, "Come outside and we'll talk." The delivery was as deep and smooth as a TV announcer's.

I turned. Two of them filled the doorway, tall, nondescript, their eyes and mouths so hard it looked like their facial nerves had been cut. They would have made terrific proctors.

Admit it, I told myself. You want to believe it. If the proctors come from *out there* somewhere, that lets you off the hook. It lets everybody off. Sure TV rots people's brains and fast food makes people fat and gives them heart attacks, but it's not our fault. We're just being manipulated by creatures of vastly superior technology.

"Outside," one of them said. "Let's go."

But suppose you really did want to take over the world. Where would you start? Level Washington with your laser cannons? Why not just take over a few ad agencies? Tell people they want to buy lots of polyester, throw your weight behind mindless situation comedies. In a few years people don't care what they watch, or what they eat, or what they wear, and after a while they don't care about anything else either. You've got everything, without having to fire a shot.

Except maybe a few in the desert, just to keep in practice.

"What do you want from me?" I asked, letting them maneuver me out onto the playground. "What's going on?"

The one in the lead showed me a pistol. It looked a lot like a squirt gun I used to have except that the end of the barrel was hollow and the thing had a heavy, chromed sense of menace about it. "The Others want to talk to you."

"Others? What Others?"

"They're waiting in the ship. Outside town."

Either this is real, I thought, or it isn't. If I could bring back a shirt and a piece of newspaper then it was probably real, or at least real enough to get me killed.

I decided to be scared.

"Fine," I said. "Let's talk. What do you want to talk about?"

"Over there," said the one with the gun.

I was just looking to see where he was pointing when a wailing noise came out of the darkness. It sounded like it had been building up inside something that wasn't strong enough to hold it and it had just blown its way free.

Jeremy.

"What's that?" hissed the one with the pistol.

"It's that kid, I think," said the other one.

"Well, shut him up, for God's sake."

The second alien disappeared into the shadows just as Jeremy screamed. The one with the gun looked around involuntarily and I went for him.

We hit the asphalt and rolled. I felt one knee tear out of my pants, just like in the old days. The alien was bigger and stronger than I was and he came out on top. He was pounding at me with his left hand, trying to get the gun around to use it on me. I grabbed his right wrist with both hands and yanked his elbow down into the pavement. The gun rattled in his grip and I slammed the elbow again. This time the gun came loose and skittered away into the darkness.

With both hands free he really opened up on me. I tried to cover up, but I didn't have enough hands, and he got a good one into my ribs. I whited out for a second and he started on my face and head.

I started to think I should have let him keep the gun. That way it would at least have been quick. In a few more seconds he was going to kill me with his bare hands anyway.

Just like they'd killed LeeAnn.

I went a little berserk, but all it got me was a knee in the gut. I was finished.

A sound whipped through the air above me. I saw a flash of pink light and then the alien fell off of me.

I rolled onto my side and pulled my knees up to my chest. I was still fighting for breath when my eyes cleared enough to see Carolyn a few feet away, still holding the gun straight out in front of her, a stunned look on her face. Jeremy sounded like pieces of his throat were coming loose, and a shadow flashed in the corner of my vision.

"Carolyn," I said, and she came unstuck, firing the pistol again. I saw the second alien fall as Jeremy's scream cut off in mid-air.

I got onto my hands and knees. In the distance, like some kind of cosmic soundtrack, I could hear Brenda Lee singing "I'm Sorry" in the gym. The music echoed flatly off the asphalt.

"You okay, mister?" Carolyn asked.

"Yeah," I said, "Okay." For once I was glad to see her.

A hand laser, I thought. A junior version of something on their ship that had cut that line through the desert. Like it or not, the aliens were as real as anything else in this version of 1961. Whether this was really my past or just some kind of metaphor, the aliens were a part of it.

Jeremy staggered over and threw his arms around Carolyn's waist. Even in the dimness of the playground I could see that her eyes were dry and clear. She looked at the gun in her hand. "This changes things," she said. "This changes everything."

The words echoed in my mind. I thought of Thornberg and

his Many Worlds. The smallest thing, he'd said, can change the entire universe. In time.

"Back at the dance," I said. "There's more of . . . *them*." I couldn't bring myself to say "aliens."

"That's okay," she said. "We'll take care of it."

"Take care of it? But you're just . . ." I tried to stand up and didn't make it.

Gently she pushed Jeremy aside and knelt down next to me. "You're hurt," she said. "There's nothing you can do to help anyway." She took the peridot ring off her index finger and slipped it onto the little finger of my left hand. "Here," she said. "This is for the twenty dollars you gave me. We'll use it to find some people to help us. To fight. To change things. They're just getting started and it's not too late. We *can* change things."

She stood up, started to walk away, and then looked back over her shoulder.

"You'll see," she said.

She was gone.

I lay there a while and looked at the stars. I hadn't seen that many stars in a night sky in a long time. When I tried to stand up again I made it, and got to the drinking fountain behind the baseball diamond.

The same piece of gum was in the drain. I smiled and cleaned myself up as best I could.

I stayed in the shadows just outside the door of the gym and watched for a while. I couldn't see the third alien.

She did it, I thought. She did it and she's going to keep on doing it. And if she's very lucky and very strong, maybe . . .

No, I told myself. Don't even think about it. Don't get your hopes up. She's just a girl and this may still turn out to be only a dream.

LeeAnn was standing at the punch bowl, talking to a kid in rolled-up jeans and a tan jacket. The record player hissed and then Buddy Holly started "True Love Ways" and the strings answered him, high and rich and infinitely sad.

The kid shuffled his feet and jerked his head at the dance floor. LeeAnn nodded and they walked into the crowd. He took her awkwardly in his arms and they slowly moved away until I couldn't see them anymore.

VII

I came back to some kind of deserted warehouse. The cage was gone. So was the jail and so were the proctors.

After the first couple of days I didn't have much trouble finding my way around. Most of my friends were still the same, and they told me they were used to my being a little quiet and disoriented. They told me I'd been that way off and on since my wife LeeAnn died in a car wreck two years before.

Thirty years were missing out of my new life, and I spent a lot of time at my computer, calling up history texts and old magazines and doing a little detective work on the side. I learned about a scientist named Thornberg at NASA, but he never answered the letter I wrote him.

The past and the future invent each other; Thornberg taught me that, and the past I invented has given me a future without LeeAnn. But somewhere in this new future of mine there should be a woman named Carolyn, born in Arizona in the late forties, maybe a year or two younger than me. I don't know exactly what I'm going to say to her when I find her, or whether she'll even believe me, but I think she'll recognize her ring.

LeeAnn is dead and Buddy Holly is dead, but people are walking the streets, free to make their own mistakes again. The sky overhead is filled with ships building a strange and wonderful future, and, in time, anything seems possible.

SAILING TO BYZANTIUM

Robert Silverberg

"Sailing to Byzantium" was purchased by Shawna Mc-Carthy and appeared in the February 1985 issue of IAsfm, with a luminous cover by Hisaki Yasuda, and interior illustrations by J. K. Potter. "Sailing to Byzantium" was an important story for the magazine; it was recognized at once as a major work, and went on to win the Nebula Award that year. It remains one of the most popular stories that IAsfm has ever published—and a story at the top even of Silverberg's high standard.

Robert Silverberg is one of the most famous SF writers of modern times, with dozens of novels, anthologies, and collections to his credit. Silverberg has won five Nebula Awards, and three Hugo Awards. His novels include Dying Inside, Downward to the Earth, The Book of Skulls, Tower of Glass, The World Inside, Shadrach in the Furnace, *and the nationwide bestseller* Lord Valentine's Castle. *His collections include* Unfamiliar Territory, Capricorn Games, The Best of Robert Silverberg, At the Conglomeroid Cocktail Party, *and* Beyond the Safe Zone. *For many years he edited the prestigious anthology series* New Dimensions, *and has recently, along with his wife, Karen Haber, taken over the editing of the* Universe *anthology series. His most recent books are the novels* Tom O'Bedlam, Star of Gypsies, *and* At Winter's End. *He lives in Oakland, California.*

———————

At dawn he arose and stepped out onto the patio for his first look at Alexandria, the one city he had not yet seen. That year the five cities were Chang-an, Asgard, New Chicago, Timbuctoo, Alexandria: the usual mix of eras, cultures, realities. He and Gioia, making the long flight from Asgard in the distant north the night before, had arrived late, well after sundown, and had gone straight to bed. Now, by the gentle apricot-hued morning light, the fierce spires and battlements of Asgard seemed merely something he had dreamed.

The rumor was that Asgard's moment was finished, anyway. In a little while, he had heard, they were going to tear it down and replace it, elsewhere, with Mohenjo-daro. Though there were never more than five cities, they changed constantly. He could remember a time when they had had Rome of the Caesars instead of Chang-an, and Rio de Janeiro rather than Alexandria. These people saw no point in keeping anything very long.

It was not easy for him to adjust to the sultry intensity of Alexandria after the frozen splendors of Asgard. The wind, coming off the water, was brisk and torrid both at once. Soft turquoise wavelets lapped at the jetties. Strong presences assailed his senses: the hot heavy sky, the stinging scent of the red lowland sand borne on the breeze, the sullen swampy aroma of the nearby sea. Everything trembled and glimmered in the early light. Their hotel was beautifully situated, high on the northern slope of the huge artificial mound known as the Paneium that was sacred to the goat-footed god. From here they had a total view of the city: the wide noble boulevards, the soaring obelisks and monuments, the palace of Hadrian just below the hill, the stately and awesome Library, the temple of Poseidon, the teeming marketplace, the royal lodge that Mark Antony had built after his defeat at Actium. And of course the Lighthouse, the wondrous many-windowed Lighthouse, the seventh wonder of the world, that immense pile of marble and limestone and reddish purple Aswan granite rising in majesty at the end of its mile-long causeway. Black smoke from the beacon-fire at its summit curled lazily into the sky. The city was awakening. Some temporaries in short white kilts appeared and began to trim the dense dark hedges that bordered the great public buildings. A few citizens wearing loose robes of vaguely Grecian style were strolling in the streets.

There were ghosts and chimeras and phantasies everywhere about. Two slim elegant centaurs, a male and a female, grazed on the hillside. A burly thick-thighed swordsman appeared on the porch of the temple of Poseidon holding a Gorgon's severed head; he waved it in a wide arc, grinning broadly. In the street below the hotel gate three small pink sphinxes, no bigger than housecats, stretched and yawned and began to prowl the curbside. A larger one, lion-sized, watched warily from an alleyway: their mother, surely. Even at this distance he could hear her loud purring.

Shading his eyes, he peered far out past the Lighthouse and across the water. He hoped to see the dim shores of Crete or Cyprus to the north, or perhaps the great dark curve of Anatolia. *Carry me toward that great Byzantium,* he thought. *Where all is ancient, singing at the oars.* But he beheld only the endless empty sea, sun-bright and blinding though the morning was just beginning. Nothing was ever where he expected it to be. The continents did not seem to be in their proper places any longer. Gioia, taking him aloft long ago in her little flitterflitter, had shown him that. The tip of South America was canted far out into the Pacific; Africa was weirdly foreshortened; a broad tongue of ocean separated Europe and Asia. Australia did not appear to exist at all.

Perhaps they had dug it up and used it for other things. There was no trace of the world he once had known. This was the fiftieth century. "The fiftieth century after *what?*" he had asked several times, but no one seemed to know, or else they did not care to say.

"Is Alexandria very beautiful?" Gioia called from within.

"Come out and see."

Naked and sleepy-looking, she padded out onto the white-tiled patio and nestled up beside him. She fit neatly under his arm. "Oh, yes, yes!" she said softly. "So very beautiful, isn't it? Look, there, the palaces, the Library, the Lighthouse! Where will we go first? The Lighthouse, I think. Yes? And then the marketplace—I want to see the Egyptian magicians—and the stadium, the races—will they be having races today, do you think? Oh, Charles, I want to see everything!"

"Everything? All on the first day?"

"All on the first day, yes," she said. "Everything."

"But we have plenty of time, Gioia."

"Do we?"

He smiled and drew her tight against his side.

"Time enough," he said gently.

He loved her for her impatience, for her bright bubbling eagerness. Gioia was not much like the rest in that regard, though she seemed identical in all other ways. She was short, supple, slender, dark-eyed, olive-skinned, narrow-hipped, with wide shoulders and flat muscles. They were all like that, each one indistinguishable from the rest, like a horde of millions of brothers and sisters—a world of small, lithe, child-like Mediterraneans, built for juggling, for bull-dancing, for sweet white wine at midday and rough red wine at night. They had the same slim bodies, the same broad mouths, the same great glossy eyes. He had never seen anyone who appeared to be younger than twelve or older than twenty. Gioia was somehow a little different, although he did not quite know how; but he knew that it was for that imperceptible but significant difference that he loved her. And probably that was why she loved him also.

He let his gaze drift from west to east, from the Gate of the

Moon down broad Canopus Street and out to the harbor, and
off to the tomb of Cleopatra at the tip of long slender Cape
Lochias. Everything was here and all of it perfect, the obelisks, the statues and marble colonnades, the courtyards and
shrines and groves, great Alexander himself in his coffin of
crystal and gold: a splendid gleaming pagan city. But there
were oddities—an unmistakable mosque near the public gardens, and what seemed to be a Christian church not far from
the Library. And those ships in the harbor, with all those red
sails and bristling masts—surely they were medieval, and
late medieval at that. He had seen such anachronisms in other
places before. Doubtless these people found them amusing.
Life was a game for them. They played at it unceasingly.
Rome, Alexandria, Timbuctoo—why not? Create an Asgard
of translucent bridges and shimmering ice-girt palaces, then
grow weary of it and take it away? Replace it with Mohenjo-
daro? Why not? It seemed to him a great pity to destroy those
lofty Nordic feasting-halls for the sake of building a squat,
brutal, sunbaked city of brown brick; but these people did not
look at things the way he did. Their cities were only temporary. Someone in Asgard had said that Timbuctoo would be
the next to go, with Byzantium rising in its place. Well, why
not? Why not? They could have anything they liked. This was
the fiftieth century, after all. The only rule was that there
could be no more than five cities at once. "Limits," Gioia
had informed him solemnly when they first began to travel
together, "are very important." But she did not know why,
or did not care to say.

He stared out once more toward the sea.

He imagined a newborn city congealing suddenly out of
mists, far across the water: shining towers, great-domed palaces, golden mosaics. That would be no great effort for them.
They could just summon it forth whole out of time, the
Emperor on his throne and the Emperor's drunken soldiery
roistering in the streets, the brazen clangor of the cathedral
gong rolling through the Grand Bazaar, dolphins leaping
beyond the shoreside pavilions. Why not? They had Timbuctoo.
They had Alexandria. Do you crave Constantinople? Then

behold Constantinople! Or Avalon, or Lyonesse, or Atlantis. They could have anything they liked. It is pure Schopenhauer here: the world as will and imagination. Yes! These slender dark-eyed people journeying tirelessly from miracle to miracle. Why not Byzantium next? Yes! Why not? *That is no country for old men,* he thought. *The young in one another's arms, the birds in the trees*—yes! Yes! Anything they liked. They even had him. Suddenly he felt frightened. Questions he had not asked for a long time burst through into his consciousness. *Who am I? Why am I here? Who is this woman beside me?*

"You're so quiet all of a sudden, Charles," said Gioia, who could not abide silence very long. "Will you talk to me? I want you to talk to me. Tell me what you're looking for out there."

He shrugged. "Nothing."

"Nothing?"

"Nothing in particular."

"I could see you seeing something."

"Byzantium," he said. "I was imagining that I could look straight across the water to Bzyantium. I was trying to get a glimpse of the walls of Constantinople."

"Oh, but you wouldn't be able to see as far as that from here. Not really."

"I know."

"And anyway, Byzantium doesn't exist."

"Not yet. But it will. Its time comes later on."

"Does it?" she said. "Do you know that for a fact?"

"On good authority. I heard it in Asgard," he told her. "But even if I hadn't, Byzantium would be inevitable, don't you think? Its time would have to come. How could we not do Byzantium, Gioia? We certainly will do Byzantium, sooner or later. I know we will. It's only a matter of time. And we have all the time in the world."

A shadow crossed her face. "Do we? Do we?"

He knew very little about himself, but he knew that he was not one of them. That he knew. He knew that his name was

Charles Phillips and that before he had come to live among these people he had lived in the year 1984, when there had been such things as computers and television sets and baseball and jet planes, and the world was full of cities, not merely five but thousands of them, New York and London and Johannesburg and Paris and Liverpool and Bangkok and San Francisco and Buenos Aires and a multitude of others, all at the same time. There had been four and a half billion people in the world then; now he doubted that there were as many as four and a half million. Nearly everything had changed beyond comprehension. The moon still seemed the same, and the sun; but at night he searched in vain for familiar constellations. He had no idea how they had brought him from then to now, or why. It did no good to ask. No one had any answers for him; no one so much as appeared to understand what it was that he was trying to learn. After a time he had stopped asking; after a time he had almost entirely ceased wanting to know.

He and Gioia were climbing the Lighthouse. She scampered ahead, in a hurry as always, and he came along behind her in his more stolid fashion. Scores of other tourists, mostly in groups of two or three, were making their way up the wide flagstone ramps, laughing, calling to one another. Some of them, seeing him, stopped a moment, stared, pointed. He was used to that. He was so much taller than any of them; he was plainly not one of them. When they pointed at him he smiled. Sometimes he nodded a little acknowledgment.

He could not find much of interest in the lowest level, a massive square structure two hundred feet high built of huge marble blocks: within its cool musty arcades were hundreds of small dark rooms, the offices of the Lighthouse's keepers and mechanics, the barracks of the garrison, the stables for the three hundred donkeys that carried the fuel to the lantern far above. None of that appeared inviting to him. He forged onward without halting until he emerged on the balcony that led to the next level. Here the Lighthouse grew narrower and became octagonal: its face, granite now and handsomely fluted, rose in a stunning sweep above him.

Gioia was waiting for him there. "This is for you," she

said, holding out a nugget of meat on a wooden skewer. "Roast lamb. Absolutely delicious. I had one while I was waiting for you." She gave him a cup of some cool green sherbet also, and darted off to buy a pomegranate. Dozens of temporaries were roaming the balcony, selling refreshments of all kinds.

He nibbled at the meat. It was charred outside, nicely pink and moist within. While he ate, one of the temporaries came up to him and peered blandly into his face. It was a stocky swarthy male wearing nothing but a strip of red and yellow cloth about its waist. "I sell meat," it said. "Very fine roast lamb, only five drachmas."

Phillips indicated the piece he was eating. "I already have some," he said.

"It is excellent meat, very tender. It has been soaked for three days in the juices of—"

"Please," Phillips said. "I don't want to buy any meat. Do you mind moving along?"

The temporaries had confused and baffled him at first, and there was still much about them that was unclear to him. They were not machines—they looked like creatures of flesh and blood—but they did not seem to be human beings, either, and no one treated them as if they were. He supposed they were artificial constructs, products of a technology so consummate that it was invisible. Some appeared to be more intelligent than others, but all of them behaved as if they had no more autonomy than characters in a play, which was essentially what they were. There were untold numbers of them in each of the five cities, playing all manner of roles: shepherds and swineherds, street-sweepers, merchants, boatmen, vendors of grilled meats and cool drinks, hagglers in the marketplace, schoolchildren, charioteers, policemen, grooms, gladiators, monks, artisans, whores and cutpurses, sailors—whatever was needed to sustain the illusion of a thriving, populous urban center. The dark-eyed people, Gioia's people, never performed work. There were not enough of them to keep a city's functions going, and in any case they were strictly tourists, wandering with the wind, moving from city to city as the whim took them, Chang-an to New Chicago, New Chicago to Timbuctoo, Timbuctoo to Asgard, Asgard to Alexandria, onward, ever onward.

The temporary would not leave him alone. Phillips walked away and it followed him, cornering him against the balcony wall. When Gioia returned a few minutes later, lips prettily stained with pomegranate juice, the temporary was still hovering about him, trying with lunatic persistence to sell him a skewer of lamb. It stood much too close to him, almost nose to nose, great sad cowlike eyes peering intently into his as it extolled with mournful mooing urgency the quality of its wares. It seemed to him that he had had trouble like this with temporaries on one or two earlier occasions. Gioia touched the creature's elbow lightly and said, in a short sharp tone Phillips had never heard her use before, "He isn't interested. Get away from him." It went at once. To Phillips she said, "You have to be firm with them."

"I was trying. It wouldn't listen to me."

"You ordered it to go away, and it refused?"

"I asked it to go away. Politely. Too politely, maybe."

"Even so," she said. "It should have obeyed a human, regardless."

"Maybe it didn't think I was human," Phillips suggested. "Because of the way I look. My height, the color of my eyes. It might have thought I was some kind of temporary myself."

"No," Gioia said, frowning, "A temporary won't solicit another temporary. But it won't ever disobey a citizen, either. There's a very clear boundary. There isn't ever any confusion. I can't understand why it went on bothering you." He was surprised at how troubled she seemed: far more so, he thought, than the incident warranted. A stupid device, perhaps miscalibrated in some way, overenthusiastically pushing its wares—what of it? What of it? Gioia, after a moment, appeared to come to the same conclusion. Shrugging, she said, "It's defective, I suppose. Probably such things are more common than we suspect, don't you think?" There was something forced about her tone that bothered him. She smiled and handed him her pomegranate. "Here. Have a bite, Charles.

It's wonderfully sweet. They used to be extinct, you know.
Shall we go on upward?''

The octagonal midsection of the Lighthouse must have
been several hundred feet in height, a grim claustrophobic
tube almost entirely filled by the two broad spiraling ramps
that wound around the huge building's central well. The
ascent was slow: a donkey team was a little way ahead of
them on the ramp, plodding along laden with bundles of
kindling for the lantern. But at last, just as Phillips was
growing winded and dizzy, he and Gioia came out onto the
second balcony, the one marking the transition between the
octagonal section and the Lighthouse's uppermost storey,
which was cylindrical and very slender.

She leaned far out over the balustrade. "Oh, Charles, look
at the view! Look at it!''

It was amazing. From one side they could see the entire
city, and swampy Lake Mareotis and the dusty Egyptian plain
beyond it, and from the other they peered far out into the gray
and choppy Mediterranean. He gestured toward the innumera-
ble reefs and shallows that infested the waters leading to the
harbor entrance. "No wonder they needed a lighthouse here,''
he said. "Without some kind of gigantic landmark they'd
never have found their way in from the open sea.''

A blast of sound, a ferocious snort, erupted just above him.
He looked up, startled. Immense statues of trumpet-wielding
Tritons jutted from the corners of the Lighthouse at this level;
that great blurting sound had come from the nearest of them.
A signal, he thought. A warning to the ships negotiating that
troubled passage. The sound was produced by some kind of
steam-powered mechanism he realized, operated by teams of
sweating temporaries clustered about bonfires at the base of
each Triton.

Once again he found himself swept by admiration for the
clever way these people carried out their reproductions of
antiquity. Or *were* they reproductions, he wondered? He still
did not understand how they brought their cities into being.
For all he knew, this place was the authentic Alexandria

itself, pulled forward out of its proper time just as he himself had been. Perhaps this was the true and original Lighthouse, and not a copy. He had no idea which was the case, nor which would be the greater miracle.

"How do we get to the top?" Gioia asked.

"Over there, I think. That doorway."

The spiraling donkey-ramps ended here. The loads of lantern fuel went higher via a dumb-waiter in the central shaft. Visitors continued by way of a cramped staircase, so narrow at its upper end that it was impossible to turn around while climbing. Gioia, tireless, sprinted ahead. He clung to the rail and labored up and up, keeping count of the tiny window-slits to ease the boredom of the ascent. The count was nearing a hundred when finally he stumbled into the vestibule of the beacon chamber. A dozen or so visitors were crowded into it. Gioia was at the far side, by the wall that was open to the sea.

It seemed to him he could feel the building swaying in the winds, up here. How high were they? Five hundred feet, six hundred, seven? The beacon chamber was tall and narrow, divided by a catwalk into upper and lower sections. Down below, relays of temporaries carried wood from the dumb-waiter and tossed it on the blazing fire. He felt its intense heat from where he stood, at the rim of the platform on which the giant mirror of polished metal was hung. Tongues of flame leaped upward and danced before the mirror, which hurled its dazzling beam far out to sea. Smoke rose through a vent. At the very top was a colossal statue of Poseidon, austere, ferocious, looming above the lantern.

Gioia sidled along the catwalk until she was at his side. "The guide was talking before you came," she said, pointing. "Do you see that place over there, under the mirror? Someone standing there and looking into the mirror gets a view of ships at sea that can't be seen from here by the naked eye. The mirror magnifies things."

"Do you believe that?"

She nodded toward the guide. "It said so. And it also told us that if you look in a certain way, you can see right across the water into the city of Constantinople."

She is like a child, he thought. They all are. He said, "You told me yourself this very morning that it isn't possible to see that far. Besides, Constantinople doesn't exist right now."

"It will," she replied. "*You* said that to me, this very morning. And when it does, it'll be reflected in the Lighthouse mirror. That's the truth. I'm absolutely certain of it." She swung about abruptly toward the entrance of the beacon chamber. "Oh, look, Charles! Here come Nissandra and Aramayne! And there's Hawk! There's Stengard!" Gioia laughed and waved and called out names. "Oh, everyone's here! *Everyone!*"

They came jostling into the room, so many newcomers that some of those who had been there were forced to scramble down the steps on the far side. Gioia moved among them, hugging, kissing. Phillips could scarcely tell one from another—it was hard for him even to tell which were the men and which were the women, dressed as they all were in the same sort of loose robes—but he recognized some of the names. These were her special friends, her set, with whom she had journeyed from city to city on an endless round of gaiety in the old days before he had come into her life. He had met a few of them before, in Asgard, in Rio, in Rome. The beacon-chamber guide, a squat wide-shouldered old temporary wearing a laurel wreath on its bald head, reappeared and began its potted speech, but no one listened to it; they were all too busy greeting one another, embracing, giggling. Some of them edged their way over to Phillips and reached up, standing on tiptoes, to touch their fingertips to his cheek in that odd hello of theirs. "Charles," they said gravely, making two syllables out of the name, as these people often did. "So good to see you again. Such a pleasure. You and Gioia—such a handsome couple. So well suited to each other."

Was that so? He supposed it was.

The chamber hummed with chatter. The guide could not be heard at all. Stengard and Nissandra had visited New Chicago for the water-dancing—Aramayne bore tales of a feast in Chang-an that had gone on for *days*—Hawk and Hekna had been to Timbuctoo to see the arrival of the salt caravan, and were going back there soon—a final party soon to celebrate the end of Asgard that absolutely should not be missed—the plans for the new city, Mohenjo-daro—we have reservations for the opening, we wouldn't pass it up for anything—and, yes, they were definitely going to do Constantinople after that, the planners were already deep into their Byzantium research—so good to see you, you look so beautiful all the time—have you been to the Library yet? The zoo? To the temple of Serapis?—

To Phillips they said, "What do you think of our Alexandria, Charles? Of course you must have known it well in your day. Does it look the way you remember it?" They were always asking things like that. They did not seem to comprehend that the Alexandria of the Lighthouse and the Library was lost and legendary by his time. To them, he suspected, all the places they had brought back into existence were more or less contemporary. Rome of the Ceasars, Alexandria of the Ptolemies, Venice of the Doges, Chang-an of the T'angs, Asgard of the Aesir, none any less real than the next nor any less unreal, each one simply a facet of the distant past, the fantastic immemorial past, a plum plucked from that dark backward and abysm of time. They had no contexts for separating one era from another. To them all the past was one borderless timeless realm. Why then should he not have seen the Lighthouse before, he who had leaped into this era from the New York of 1984? He had never been able to explain it to them. Julius Caesar and Hannibal, Helen of Troy and Charlemagne, Rome of the gladiators and New York of the Yankees and Mets, Gilgamesh and Tristan and Othello and Robin Hood and George Washington and Queen Victoria—to them, all equally real and unreal, none of them any more than bright figures moving about on a painted canvas. The past, the past, the elusive and fluid past—to them it was a single place of infinite accessibility and infinite connectivity. Of course they would think he had seen the Lighthouse before. He knew better than to try again to explain things. "No," he said simply. "This is my first time in Alexandria."

*   *   *

They stayed there all winter long, and possibly some of the spring. Alexandria was not a place where one was sharply aware of the change of seasons, nor did the passage of time itself make itself very evident when one was living one's entire life as a tourist.

During the day there was always something new to see. The zoological garden, for instance: a wondrous park, miraculously green and lush in this hot dry climate, where astounding animals roamed in enclosures so generous that they did not seem like enclosures at all. Here were camels, rhinoceroses, gazelles, ostriches, lions, wild asses; and here too, casually adjacent to those familiar African beasts, were hippogriffs, unicorns, basilisks, and fire-snorting dragons with rainbow scales. Had the original zoo of Alexandria had dragons and unicorns? Phillips doubted it. But this one did; evidently it was no harder for the backstage craftsmen to manufacture mythic beasts than it was for them to turn out camels and gazelles. To Gioia and her friends all of them were equally mythical, anyway. They were just as awed by the rhinoceros as by the hippogriff. One was no more strange—nor any less—than the other. So far as Phillips had been able to discover, none of the mammals or birds of his era had survived into this one except for a few cats and dogs, though many had been reconstructed.

And then the Library! All those lost treasures, reclaimed from the jaws of time! Stupendous columned marble walls, airy high-vaulted reading-rooms, dark coiling stacks stretching away to infinity. The ivory handles of seven hundred thousand papyrus scrolls bristling on the shelves. Scholars and librarians gliding quietly about, smiling faint scholarly smiles but plainly preoccupied with serious matters of the mind. They were all temporaries, Phillips realized. Mere props, part of the illusion. But were the scrolls illusions too? "Here we have the complete dramas of Sophocles," said the guide with a blithe wave of his hand, indicating shelf upon shelf of texts. Only seven of his hundred twenty-three plays had survived the successive burnings of the library in ancient times by Romans, Christians, Arabs: were the lost ones here, the

Triptolemus, the *Nausicaa*, the *Jason*, and all the rest? And would he find here too, miraculously restored to being, the other vanished treasures of ancient literature—the memoirs of Odysseus, Cato's history of Rome, Thucydides' life of Pericles, the missing volumes of Livy? But when he asked if he might explore the stacks, the guide smiled apologetically and said that all the librarians were busy just now. Another time, perhaps? Perhaps, said the guide. It made no difference, Phillips decided. Even if these people somehow had brought back those lost masterpieces of antiquity, how would he read them? He knew no Greek.

The life of the city buzzed and throbbed about him. It was a dazzlingly beautiful place: the vast bay thick with sails, the great avenues running rigidly east-west, north-south, the sunlight rebounding almost audibly from the bright walls of the palaces of kings and gods. They have done this very well, Phillips thought: very well indeed. In the marketplace hard-eyed traders squabbled in half a dozen mysterious languages over the price of ebony, Arabian incense, jade, panther-skins. Gioia bought a dram of pale musky Egyptian perfume in a delicate tapering glass flask. Magicians and jugglers and scribes called out stridently to passersby, begging for a few moments of attention and a handful of coins for their labor. Strapping slaves, black and tawny and some that might have been Chinese, were put up for auction, made to flex their muscles, to bare their teeth, to bare their breasts and thighs to prospective buyers. In the gymnasium naked athletes hurled javelins and discuses, and wrestled with terrifying zeal. Gioia's friend Stengard came rushing up with a gift for her, a golden necklace that would not have embarrassed Cleopatra. An hour later she had lost it, or perhaps given it away while Phillips was looking elsewhere. She bought another, even finer, the next day. Anyone could have all the money he wanted, simply by asking: it was as easy to come by as air, for these people.

Being here was much like going to the movies, Phillips told himself. A different show every day: not much plot, but the special effects were magnificent and the detail-work could hardly have been surpassed. A megamovie, a vast entertainment that went on all the time and was being played out by the whole population of Earth. And it was all so effortless, so spontaneous: just as when he had gone to a movie he had never troubled to think about the myriad technicians behind the scenes, the cameramen and the costume designers and the set-builders and the electricians and the model-makers and the boom operators, so too here he chose not to question the means by which Alexandria had been set before him. It felt real. It *was* real. When he drank the strong red wine it gave him a pleasant buzz. If he leaped from the beacon chamber of the Lighthouse he suspected he would die, though perhaps he would not stay dead for long: doubtless they had some way of restoring him as often as necessary. Death did not seem to be a factor in these people's lives.

By day they saw sights. By night he and Gioia went to parties, in their hotel, in seaside villas, in the palaces of the high nobility. The usual people were there all the time, Hawk and Hekna, Aramayne, Stengard and Shelimir, Nissandra, Asoka, Afonso, Protay. At the parties there were five or ten temporaries for every citizen, some as mere servants, others as entertainers or even surrogate guests, mingling freely and a little daringly. But everyone knew, all the time, who was a citizen and who just a temporary. Phillips began to think his own status lay somewhere between. Certainly they treated him with a courtesy that no one ever would give a temporary, and yet there was a condescension to their manner that told him not simply that he was not one of them but that he was someone or something of an altogether different order of existence. That he was Gioia's lover gave him some standing in their eyes, but not a great deal: obviously he was always going to be an outsider, a primitive, ancient and quaint. For that matter he noticed that Gioia herself, though unquestionably a member of the set, seemed to be regarded as something of an outsider, like a tradesman's great-granddaughter in a gathering of Plantagenets. She did not always find out about the best parties in time to attend; her friends did not always reciprocate her effusive greetings with the same degree of warmth; sometimes he noticed her straining to hear some bit of gossip that was not quite being shared with her. Was it because she had taken him for her lover? Or was it the other way around: that she had chosen to be his lover precisely because she was *not* a full member of their caste?

Being a primitive gave him, at least, something to talk about at their parties. "Tell us about war," they said. "Tell us about elections. About money. About disease." They wanted to know everything; though they did not seem to pay close attention: their eyes were quick to glaze. Still, they asked. He described traffic jams to them, and politics, and deodorants, and vitamin pills. He told them about cigarettes, newspapers, subways, telephone directories, credit cards, and basketball.

"Which was your city?" they asked. New York, he told them. "And when was it? The seventh century, did you say?" The twentieth, he told them. They exchanged glances and nodded. "We will have to do it," they said. "The World Trade Center, the Empire State Building, the Citicorp Center, the Cathedral of St. John the Divine: how fascinating! Yankee Stadium. The Verrazzano Bridge. We will do it all. But first must come Mohenjo-daro. And then, I think, Constantinople. Did your city have many people?" Seven million, he said. Just in the five boroughs alone. They nodded, smiling amiably, unfazed by the number.

Seven million, seventy million—it was all the same to them, he sensed. They would just bring forth the temporaries in whatever quantity was required. He wondered how well they would carry the job off. He was no real judge of Alexandrias and Asgards, after all. Here they could have unicorns and hippogriffs in the zoo, and live sphinxes prowling in the gutters, and it did not trouble him. Their fanciful Alexandria was as good as history's, or better. But how sad, how disillusioning it would be, if the New York that they conjured up had Greenwich Village uptown and Times Square in the Bronx, and the New Yorkers, gentle and polite, spoke with the honeyed accents of Savannah or New Orleans. Well, that was nothing he needed to brood about just now. Very likely they were only being courteous when they spoke of doing his New York. They had all the vastness of the past to choose from: Nineveh, Memphis of the Pharaohs, the London of Victoria or Shakespeare or Richard the Third, Florence of the Medici, the Paris of Abelard and Heloise or the Paris of Louis XIV, Moctezuma's Tenochtitlan and Atahuallpa's Cuzco; Damascus, St. Petersburg, Babylon, Troy. And then there were all the cities like New Chicago, out of time that was time yet unborn to him but ancient history to them. In such richness, such an infinity of choices, even mighty New York might have to wait a long while for its turn. Would he still be among them by the time they got around to it? By then, perhaps, they might have become bored with him and returned him to his own proper era. Or possibly he would simply have grown old and died. Even here, he supposed, he would eventually die, though no one else ever seemed to. He did not know. He realized that in fact he did not know anything.

The north wind blew all day long. Vast flocks of ibises appeared over the city, fleeing the heat of the interior, and screeched across the sky with their black necks and scrawny legs extended. The sacred birds, descending by the thousands, scuttered about in every crossroad, pouncing on spiders and beetles, on mice, on the debris of the meat-shops and the bakeries. They were beautiful but annoyingly ubiquitous, and they splashed their dung over the marble buildings; each morning squadrons of temporaries carefully washed it off. Gioia said little to him now. She seemed cool, withdrawn, depressed; and there was something almost intangible about her, as though she were gradually becoming transparent. He felt it would be an intrusion upon her privacy to ask her what was wrong. Perhaps it was only restlessness. She became religious, and presented costly offerings at the temples of Serapis, Isis, Poseidon, Pan. She went to the necropolis west of the city to lay wreaths on the tombs in the catacombs. In a single day she climbed the Lighthouse three times without any sign of fatigue. One afternoon he returned from a visit to the Library and found her naked on the patio; she had anointed herself all over with some aromatic green salve. Abruptly she said, "I think it's time to leave Alexandria, don't you?"

She wanted to go to Mohenjo-daro, but Mohenjo-daro was not yet ready for visitors. Instead they flew eastward to Chang-an, which they had not seen in years. It was Phillips' suggestion: he hoped that the cosmopolitan gaudiness of the old T'ang capital would lift her mood.

They were to be guests of the Emperor this time: an unusual privilege, which ordinarily had to be applied for far in advance, but Phillips had told some of Gioia's highly placed friends that she was unhappy, and they had quickly arranged everything. Three endlessly bowing functionaries in flowing yellow robes and purple sashes met them at the Gate of Brilliant Virtue in the city's south wall and conducted them to their pavilion, close by the imperial palace and the Forbidden Garden. It was a light, airy place, thin walls of plastered brick braced by graceful columns of some dark, aromatic wood. Fountains played on the roof of green and yellow tiles, creating an unending cool rainfall of recirculating water. The balustrades were of carved marble, the door-fittings were of gold.

There was a suite of private rooms for him, and another for her, though they would share the handsome damask-draped bedroom at the heart of the pavilion. As soon as they arrived Gioia announced that she must go to her rooms to bathe and dress. "There will be a formal reception for us at the palace tonight," she said. "They say the imperial receptions are splendid beyond anything you could imagine. I want to be at my best." The Emperor and all his ministers, she told him, would receive them in the Hall of the Supreme Ultimate; there would be a banquet for a thousand people; Persian dancers would perform, and the celebrated jugglers of Chung-nan. Afterward everyone would be conducted into the fantastic landscape of the Forbidden Garden to view the dragon-races and the fireworks.

He went to his own rooms. Two delicate little maid-servants undressed him and bathed him with fragrant sponges. The pavilion came equipped with eleven temporaries who were to be their servants: soft-voiced unobtrusive cat-like Chinese, done with perfect verisimilitude, straight black hair, glowing skin, epicanthic folds. Phillips often wondered what happened to a city's temporaries when the city's time was over. Were the towering Norse heroes of Asgard being recycled at this moment into wiry dark-skinned Dravidians for Mohenjo-daro? When Timbuctoo's day was done, would its brightly robed black warriors be converted into supple Byzantines to stock the arcades of Constantinople? Or did they simply discard the old temporaries like so many excess props, stash them in warehouses somewhere, and turn out the appropriate quantities of the new model? He did not know; and once when he had asked Gioia about it she had grown uncomfortable and vague. She did not like him to probe for information, and he suspected it was because she had very little to give. These people did not seem to question the workings of their own world; his curiosities were very twentieth-century of him, he was frequently told, in that gently patronizing way of theirs. As his two little maids patted him with their sponges he thought of asking them where they had served before Chang-an. Rio? Rome? Haroun al-Raschid's Baghdad? But these fragile girls, he knew, would only giggle and retreat if he tried to question them. Interrogating temporaries was not only improper, but pointless: it was like interrogating one's luggage.

When he was bathed and robed in rich red silks he wandered the pavilion for a little while, admiring the tinkling pendants of green jade dangling on the portico, the lustrous auburn pillars, the rainbow hues of the intricately interwoven girders and brackets that supported the roof. Then, wearying of his solitude, he approached the bamboo curtain at the entrance to Gioia'a suite. A porter and one of the maids stood just within. They indicated that he should not enter; but he scowled at them and they melted from him like snowflakes. A trail of incense led him through the pavilion to Gioia's innermost dressing-room. There he halted, just outside the door.

Gioia sat naked with her back to him at an ornate dressing-table of some rare flame-colored wood inlaid with bands of orange and green porcelain. She was studying herself intently in a mirror of polished bronze held by one of her maids: picking through her scalp with her fingernails, as a woman might do who was searching out her gray hairs.

But that seemed strange. Gray hair, on Gioia? On a citizen? A temporary might display some appearance of aging, perhaps, but surely not a citizen. Citizens remained forever young. Gioia looked like a girl. Her face was smooth and unlined, her flesh was firm, her hair was dark: that was true of all of them, every citizen he had ever seen. And yet there was no mistaking what Gioia was doing. She found a hair, frowned, drew it taut, nodded, plucked it. Another. Another. She pressed the tip of her finger to her cheek as if testing it for resilience. She tugged at the skin below her eyes, pulling it downward. Such familiar little gestures of vanity; but so odd here, he thought, in this world of the perpetually young. Gioia, worried about growing old? Had he simply failed to notice the signs of age on her? Or was it that she worked hard behind his back at concealing them? Perhaps that was it. Was he wrong about the citizens, then? Did they age even as the people of less blessed eras had always done, but simply had better ways of hiding it? How old was she, anyway? Thirty? Sixty? Three hundred?

Gioia appeared satisfied now. She waved the mirror away; she rose; she beckoned for her banquet robes. Phillips, still standing unnoticed by the door, studied her with admiration: the small round buttocks, almost but not quite boyish, the elegant line of her spine, the surprising breadth of her shoulders. No, he thought, she is not aging at all. Her body is still like a girl's. She looks as young as on the day they first had met, however long ago that was—he could not say; it was hard to keep track of time here; but he was sure some years had passed since they had come together. Those gray hairs, those wrinkles and sags for which she had searched just now with such desperate intensity, must all be imaginary, mere artifacts of vanity. Even in this remote future epoch, then, vanity was not extinct. He wondered why she was so concerned with the fear of aging. An affectation? Did all these timeless people take some perverse pleasure in fretting over the possibility that they might be growing old? Or was it some private fear of Gioia's, another symptom of the mysterious depression that had come over her in Alexandria?

Not wanting her to think that he had been spying on her, when all he had really intended was to pay her a visit, he slipped silently away to dress for the evening. She came to him an hour later, gorgeously robed, swaddled from chin to ankles in a brocade of brilliant colors shot through with threads of gold, face painted, hair drawn up tightly and fastened with ivory combs: very much the lady of the court. His servants had made him splendid also, a lustrous black surplice embroidered with gold dragons over a sweeping floor-length gown of shining white silk, a necklace and pendant of red coral, a five-cornered gray felt hat that rose in tower upon tower like a ziggurat. Gioia, grinning, touched her fingertips to his cheek. "You look marvelous!" she told him. "Like a grand mandarin!"

"And you like an empress," he said. "Of some distant land: Persia, India. Here to pay a ceremonial visit on the Son of Heaven." An excess of love suffused his spirit, and, catching her lightly by the wrist, he drew her toward him, as close as he could manage it considering how elaborate their costumes were. But as he bent forward and downward, meaning to brush his lips lightly and affectionately against the tip of her nose, he perceived an unexpected strangeness, an anomaly: the coating of white paint that was her makeup seemed oddly to magnify rather than mask the contours of her skin, highlighting and revealing details he had never observed before. He saw a pattern of lines radiating from the corners of her eyes, and the unmistakable beginning of a quirk-mark in her cheek just to the left of her mouth, and perhaps the faint indentation of frown-lines in her flawless forehead. A shiver traveled along the nape of his neck. So it was not affectation, then, that had had her studying her mirror so fiercely. Age was in truth beginning to stake its claim on her, despite all that he had come to believe about these people's agelessness. But a moment later he was not so sure. Gioia turned and slid gently half a step back from him—she must have found his stare disturbing—and the lines he had thought he had seen were gone. He searched for them and saw only girlish smoothness once again. A trick of the light? A figment of an overwrought imagination? He was baffled.

"Come," she said. "We mustn't keep the Emperor waiting."

Five mustachioed warriors in armor of white quilting and seven musicians playing cymbals and pipes escorted them to the Hall of the Supreme Ultimate. There they found the full court arrayed: princes and ministers, high officials, yellow-robed monks, a swarm of imperial concubines. In a place of honor to the right of the royal thrones, which rose like gilded scaffolds high above all else, was a little group of stern-faced men in foreign costumes, the ambassadors of Rome and Byzantium, of Arabia and Syria, of Korea, Japan, Tibet, Turkestan. Incense smouldered in enameled braziers. A poet sang a delicate twanging melody, accompanying himself on a small harp. Then the Emperor and Empress entered: two tiny aged people, like waxen images, moving with infinite slowness, taking steps no greater than a child's. There was the sound of trumpets as they ascended their thrones. When the little Emperor was seated—he looked like a doll up there, ancient, faded, shrunken, yet still somehow a figure of extraordinary power—he stretched forth both his hands, and enormous gongs began to sound. It was a scene of astonishing splendor, grand and overpowering.

These are all temporaries, Phillips realized suddenly. He saw only a handful of citizens—eight, ten, possibly as many as a dozen—scattered here and there about the vast room. He knew them by their eyes, dark, liquid, knowing. They were watching not only the imperial spectacle but also Gioia and him; and Gioia, smiling secretly, nodding almost imperceptibly to them, was acknowledging their presence and their interest. But those few were the only ones in here who where autonomous living beings. All the rest—the entire splendid court, the great mandarins and paladins, the officials, the giggling concubines, the haughty and resplendent ambassadors, the aged Emperor and Empress themselves—were simply part of the scenery. Had the world even seen entertainment on so grand a scale before? All this pomp, all this pageantry, conjured up each night for the amusement of a dozen or so viewers?

At the banquet the little group of citizens sat together at a table apart, a round onyx slab draped with translucent green silk. There turned out to be seventeen of them in all, including Gioia; Gioia appeared to know all of them, though none, so far as he could tell, was a member of her set that he had met before. She did not attempt introductions. Nor was conversation at all possible during the meal: there was a constant astounding roaring din in the room. Three orchestras played at once and there were troupes of strolling musicians also, and a steady stream of monks and their attendants marched back and forth between the tables loudly chanting sutras and waving censers to the deafening accompaniment of drums and gongs. The Emperor did not descend from his throne to join the banquet; he seemed to be asleep, though now and then he waved his hands in time to the music. Gigantic half-naked brown slaves with broad cheekbones and mouths like gaping pockets brought forth the food, peacock tongues and breast of phoenix heaped on mounds of glowing saffron-colored rice, served on frail alabaster plates. For chopsticks they were given slender rods of dark jade. The wine, served in glistening crystal beakers, was thick and sweet, with an aftertaste of raisins, and no beaker was allowed to remain empty for more than a moment.

Phillips felt himself growing dizzy: when the Persian dancers emerged he could not tell whether there were five of them or fifty, and as they performed their intricate whirling routines it seemed to him that their slender muslin-veiled forms were blurring and merging one into another. He felt frightened by their proficiency, and wanted to look away, but he could not. The Chung-nan jugglers that followed them were equally skillful, equally alarming, filling the air with scythes, flaming torches, live animals, rare porcelain vases, pink jade hatchets, silver bells, gilded cups, wagon-wheels, bronze vessels, and never missing a catch. The citizens applauded politely but did not seem impressed. After the jugglers, the dancers returned, performing this time on stilts; the waiters brought platters of steaming meat of a pale lavender color, unfamiliar in taste and texture: filet of camel, perhaps, or haunch of hippopotamus, or possibly some choice chop from a young dragon. There was more wine. Feebly Phillips tried to wave it away, but the servitors were implacable. This was a drier sort, greenish gold, austere, sharp on the tongue. With it came a silver dish, chilled to a polar coldness, that held shaved ice flavored with some potent smoky-flavored brandy. The jugglers were doing a second turn, he noticed. He thought he was going to be ill. He looked helplessly toward Gioia, who seemed sober but fiercely animated, almost manic, her eyes blazing like rubies. She touched his cheek fondly.

A cool draft blew through the hall: they had opened one entire wall, revealing the garden, the night, the stars. Just outside was a colossal wheel of oiled paper stretched on wooden struts. They must have erected it in the past hour: it stood a hundred fifty feet high or even more, and on it hung lanterns by the thousands, glimmering like giant fireflies. The guests began to leave the hall. Phillips let himself be swept along into the garden, where under a yellow moon strange crook-armed trees with dense black needles loomed ominously. Gioia slipped her arm through his. They went down to a lake of bubbling crimson fluid and watched scarlet flamingo-like birds ten feet tall fastidiously spearing angry-eyed turquoise eels. They stood in awe before a fat-bellied Buddha of gleaming blue tilework, seventy feet high. A horse with a golden mane came prancing by, striking showers of brilliant red sparks wherever its hooves touched the ground. In a grove of lemon trees that seemed to have the power to wave their slender limbs about, Phillips came upon the Emperor, standing by himself and rocking gently back and forth. The old man seized Phillips by the hand and pressed something into his palm, closing his fingers tight about it; when he opened his fist a few moments later he found his palm full of

gray irregular pearls. Gioia took them from him and cast them
into the air, and they burst like exploding firecrackers, giving
off splashes of colored light. A little later, Phillips realized
that he was no longer wearing his surplice or his white silken
undergown. Gioia was naked too, and she drew him gently
down into a carpet of moist blue moss, where they made love
until dawn, fiercely at first, then slowly, languidly, dreamily.
At sunrise he looked at her tenderly and saw that something
was wrong.

"Gioia?" he said doubtfully.

She smiled. "Ah, no. Gioia is with Fenimon tonight. I am
Belilala."

"With—Fenimon?"

"They are old friends. She had not seen him in years."

"Ah. I see. And you are—?"

"Belilala," she said again, touching her fingertips to his
cheek.

It was not unusual, Belilala said. It happened all the time.
Couples formed, traveled together for a while, drifted apart,
eventually reunited. It did not mean that Gioia had left him
forever. It meant only that just now she chose to be with
Fenimon. Gioia would return. In the meanwhile he would not
be alone. "You and I met in New Chicago," Belilala told
him. "And then we saw each other again in Timbuctoo. Have
you forgotten? Oh, yes, I see that you have forgotten!" She
laughed prettily; she did not seem at all offended.

She looked enough like Gioia to be her sister. But, then, all
the citizens looked more or less alike to him. And apart from
their physical resemblance, so he quickly came to realize,
Belilala and Gioia were not really very similar. There was a
calmness, a deep reservoir of serenity, in Belilala that Gioia,
eager and volatile and ever impatient, did not seem to have.
Strolling the swarming streets of Chang-an with Belilala, he
did not perceive in her any of Gioia's restless feverish need
always to know what lay beyond, and beyond, and beyond
even that. When they toured the Hsing-ch'ing Palace, Belilala
did not after five minutes begin—as Gioia surely would have

done—to seek directions to the Fountain of Hsuan-tsung or the Wild Goose Pagoda. Curiosity did not consume Belilala as it did Gioia. Plainly she believed that there would always be enough time for her to see everything she cared to see. There were some days when Belilala chose not to go out at all, but was content merely to remain at their pavilion playing a solitary game with flat porcelain counters, or viewing the flowers of the garden.

He found, oddly, that he enjoyed the respite from Gioia's intense world-swallowing appetites; and yet he longed for her to return. Belilala—beautiful, gentle, tranquil, patient—was too perfect for him. She seemed unreal in her gleaming impeccability, much like one of those Sung celadon vases that appear too flawless to have been thrown and glazed by human hands. There was something a little soulless about her: an immaculate finish outside, emptiness within. Belilala might almost have been a temporary, he thought, though he knew she was not. He could explore the pavilions and palaces of Chang-an with her, he could make graceful conversation with her while they dined, he could certainly enjoy coupling with her; but he could not love her or even contemplate the possibility. It was hard to imagine Belilala worriedly studying herself in a mirror for wrinkles and gray hairs. Belilala would never be any older than she was at this moment; nor could Belilala ever have been any younger. Perfection does not move along an axis of time. But the perfection of Belilala's glossy surface made her inner being impenetrable to him. Gioia was more vulnerable, more obviously flawed—her restlessness, her moodiness, her vanity, her fears—and therefore she was more accessible to his own highly imperfect twentieth-century sensibility.

Occasionally he saw Gioia as he roamed the city, or thought he did. He had a glimpse of her among the miracle-vendors in the Persian Bazaar, and outside the Zoroastrian temple, and again by the goldfish pond in the Serpentine Park. But he was never quite sure that the woman he saw was really Gioia, and he never could get close enough to her to be certain: she had a way of vanishing as he approached, like some mysterious

Lorelei luring him onward and onward in a hopeless chase. After a while he came to realize that he was not going to find her until she was ready to be found.

He lost track of time. Weeks, months, years? He had no idea. In this city of exotic luxury, mystery, and magic all was in constant flux and transition and the days had a fitful, unstable quality. Buildings and even whole streets were torn down of an afternoon and re-erected, within days, far away. Grand new pagodas sprouted like toadstools in the night. Citizens came in from Asgard, Alexandria, Timbuctoo, New Chicago, stayed for a time, disappeared, returned. There was a constant round of court receptions, banquets, theatrical events, each one much like the one before. The festivals in honor of past emperors and empresses might have given some form to the year, but they seemed to occur in a random way, the ceremony marking the death of T'ai Tsung coming around twice the same year, so it seemed to him, once in a season of snow and again in high summer, and the one honoring the ascension of the Empress Wu being held twice in a single season. Perhaps he had misunderstood something. But he knew it was no use asking anyone.

One day Belilala said unexpectedly, "Shall we go to Mohenjo-daro?"

"I didn't know it was ready for visitors," he replied.

"Oh, yes. For quite some time now."

He hesitated. This had caught him unprepared. Cautiously he said, "Gioia and I were going to go there together, you know."

Belilala smiled amiably, as though the topic under discussion were nothing more than the choice of that evening's restaurant.

"Were you?" she asked.

"It was all arranged while we were still in Alexandria. To go with you instead—I don't know what to tell you, Belilala." Phillips sensed that he was growing terribly flustered. "You know that I'd like to go. With you. But on the other hand I can't help feeling that I shouldn't go there until I'm back with

Gioia again. If I ever am." How foolish this sounds, he thought. How clumsy, how adolescent. He found that he was having trouble looking straight at her. Uneasily he said, with a kind of desperation in his voice. "I did promise her—there was a commitment, you understand—a firm agreement that we would go to Mohenjo-daro together—"

"Oh, but Gioia's already there!" said Belilala in the most casual way.

He gaped as though she had punched him.

"What?"

"She was the first to go, after it opened. Months and months ago. You didn't know?" she asked, sounding surprised, but not very. "You really didn't know?"

That astonished him. He felt bewildered, betrayed, furious. His cheeks grew hot, his mouth gaped. He shook his head again and again, trying to clear it of confusion. It was a moment before he could speak. "Already there?" he said at last. "Without waiting for me? After we had talked about going there together—after we had agreed—"

Belilala laughed. "But how could she resist seeing the newest city? You know how impatient Gioia is!"

"Yes. Yes."

He was stunned. He could barely think.

"Just like all short-timers," Belilala said. "She rushes here, she rushes there. She must have it all, now, now, right away, at once, instantly. You ought never expect her to wait for you for anything for very long: the fit seizes her, and off she goes. Surely you must know that about her by now."

"A short-timer?" He had not heard that term before.

"Yes. You knew that. You must have known that." Belilala flashed her sweetest smile. She showed no sign of comprehending his distress. With a brisk wave of her hand she said, "Well, then, shall we go, you and I? To Mohenjo-daro?"

"Of course," Phillips said bleakly.

"When would you like to leave?"

"Tonight," he said. He paused a moment. "What's a short-timer, Belilala?"

Color came to her cheeks. "Isn't it obvious?" she asked.

* * *

Had there ever been a more hideous place on the face of the earth than the city of Mohenjo-daro? Phillips found it difficult to imagine one. Nor could he understand why, out of all the cities that had ever been, these people had chosen to restore this one to existence. More than ever they seemed alien to him, unfathomable, incomprehensible.

From the terrace atop the many-towered citadel he peered down into grim claustrophobic Mohenjo-daro and shivered. The stark, bleak city looked like nothing so much as some prehistoric prison colony. In the manner of an uneasy tortoise it huddled, squat and compact, against the gray monotonous Indus River plain: miles of dark burnt-brick walls enclosing miles of terrifyingly orderly streets, laid out in an awesome, monstrous gridiron pattern of maniacal rigidity. The houses themselves were dismal and forbidding too, clusters of brick cells gathered about small airless courtyards. There were no windows, only small doors that opened not onto the main boulevards but onto the tiny mysterious lanes that ran between the buildings. Who had designed this horrifying metropolis? What harsh, sour souls they must have had, these frightening and frightened folk, creating for themselves in the lush fertile plains of India such a Supreme Soviet of a city!

"How lovely it is," Belilala murmured. "How fascinating!"

He stared at her in amazement.

"Fascinating? Yes," he said. "I suppose so. The same way that the smile of a cobra is fascinating."

"What's a cobra?"

"Poisonous predatory serpent," Phillips told her. "Probably extinct. Or formerly extinct, more likely. It wouldn't surprise me if you people had re-created a few and turned them loose in Mohenjo to make things livelier."

"You sound angry, Charles."

"Do I? That's not how I feel."

"How do you feel, then?"

"I don't know," he said after a long moment's pause. He shrugged. "Lost, I suppose. Very far from home."

"Poor Charles."

"Standing here in this ghastly barracks of a city, listening to you tell me how beautiful it is, I've never felt more alone in my life."

"You miss Gioia very much, don't you?"

He gave her another startled look.

"Gioia has nothing to do with it. She's probably been having ecstasies over the loveliness of Mohenjo just like you. Just like all of you. I suppose I'm the only one who can't find the beauty, the charm. I'm the only one who looks out there and sees only horror, and then wonders why nobody else sees it, why in fact people would set up a place like this for *entertainment*, for pleasure—"

Her eyes were gleaming. "Oh, you are angry! You really are!"

"Does that fascinate you too?" he snapped. "A demonstration of genuine primitive emotion? A typical quaint twentieth-century outburst?" He paced the rampart in short quick anguished steps. "Ah. Ah. I think I understand it now, Belilala. Of course: I'm part of your circus, the star of the sideshow. I'm the first experiment in setting up the next stage of it, in fact." Her eyes were wide. The sudden harshness and violence in his voice seemed to be alarming and exciting her at the same time. That angered him even more. Fiercely he went on, "Bringing whole cities back out of time was fun for a while, but it lacks a certain authenticity, eh? For some reason you couldn't bring the inhabitants too; you couldn't just grab a few million prehistorics out of Egypt or Greece or India and dump them down in this era, I suppose because you might have too much trouble controlling them, or because you'd have the problem of disposing of them once you were bored with them. So you had to settle for creating temporaries to populate your ancient cities. But now you've got me. I'm something more real than a temporary, and that's a terrific novelty for you, and novelty is the thing you people crave more than anything else: maybe the *only* thing you crave. And here I am, complicated, unpredictable, edgy, capable of anger, fear, sadness, love, and all those other formerly extinct things. Why settle for picturesque architecture when you can observe picturesqe emotion, too? What fun I must be for all of you! And if you decide that I was really interesting, maybe you'll ship me back where I came from and check out a few other ancient types—a Roman gladiator, maybe, or a Renaissance pope, or even a Neanderthal or two—''

"Charles," she said tenderly. "Oh, Charles, Charles, Charles, how lonely you must be, how lost, how troubled! Will you ever forgive me? Will you ever forgive us all?''

Once more he was astounded by her. She sounded entirely sincere, altogether sympathetic. Was she? Was she, really? He was not sure he had ever had a sign of genuine caring from any of them before, not even Gioia. Nor could he bring himself to trust Belilala now. He was afraid of her, afraid of all of them, of their brittleness, their slyness, their elegance. He wished he could go to her and have her take him in her arms; but he felt too much the shaggy prehistoric just now to be able to risk asking that comfort of her.

He turned away and began to walk around the rim of the citadel's massive wall.

"Charles?"

"Let me alone for a little while," he said.

He walked on. His forehead throbbed and there was a pounding in his chest. All stress systems going full blast, he thought: secret glands dumping gallons of inflammatory substances into his bloodstream. The heat, the inner confusion, the repellent look of this place—

Try to understand, he thought. Relax. Look about you. Try to enjoy your holiday in Mohenjo-daro.

He leaned warily outward, over the edge of the wall. He had never seen a wall like this; it must be forty feet thick at the base, he guessed, perhaps even more, and every brick perfectly shaped, meticulously set. Beyond the great rampart, marshes ran almost to the edge of the city, although close by the wall the swamps had been dammed and drained for agriculture. He saw lithe brown farmers down there, busy with their wheat and barley and peas. Cattle and buffaloes grazed a little farther out. The air was heavy, dank, humid. All was still. From somewhere close at hand came the sound of a droning, whining stringed instrument and a steady insistent chanting.

Gradually a sort of peace pervaded him. His anger subsided. He felt himself beginning to grow calm again. He looked back at the city, the rigid interlocking streets, the maze of inner lanes, the millions of courses of precise brickwork.

It is a miracle, he told himself, that this city is here in this place and at this time. And it is a miracle that I am here to see it.

Caught for a moment by the magic within the bleakness, he thought he began to understand Belilala's awe and delight, and he wished now that he had not spoken to her so sharply. The city was alive. Whether it was the actual Mohenjo-daro of thousands upon thousands of years ago, ripped from the past by some wondrous hook, or simply a cunning reproduction, did not matter at all. Real or not, this was the true Mohenjo-daro. It had been dead and now, for the moment, it was alive again. These people, these *citizens*, might be trivial, but reconstructing Mohenjo-daro was no trivial achievement. And that the city that had been reconstructed was oppressive and sinister-looking was unimportant. No one was compelled to live in Mohenjo-daro any more. Its time had come and gone, long ago; those little dark-skinned peasants and craftsmen and merchants down there were mere temporaries, mere inanimate things, conjured up like zombies to enhance the illusion. They did not need his pity. Nor did he need to pity himself. He knew that he should be grateful for the chance to behold these things. Some day, when this dream had ended and his hosts had returned him to the world of subways and computers and income tax and television networks, he would think of Mohenjo-daro as he had once beheld it, lofty walls of tightly woven dark brick under a heavy sky, and he would remember only its beauty.

Glancing back, he searched for Belilala and could not for a moment find her. Then he caught sight of her carefully descending a narrow staircase that angled down the inner face of the citadel wall.

"Belilala!" he called.

She paused and looked his way, shading her eyes from the sun with her hand. "Are you all right?"

"Where are you going?"

"To the baths," she said. "Do you want to come?"

He nodded. "Yes. Wait for me, will you? I'll be right there." He began to run toward her along the top of the wall.

The baths were attached to the citadel: a great open tank the size of a large swimming pool, lined with bricks set on edge in gypsum mortar and waterproofed with asphalt, and eight smaller tanks just north of it in a kind of covered arcade. He supposed that in ancient times the whole complex had had some ritual purpose, the large tank used by common folk and the small chambers set aside for the private ablutions of priests or nobles. Now the baths were maintained, it seemed, entirely for the pleasure of visiting citizens. As Phillips came up the passageway that led to the main bath he saw fifteen or twenty of them lolling in the water or padding languidly about, while temporaries of the dark-skinned Mohenjo-daro type served them drinks and pungent little morsels of spiced meat as though this were some sort of luxury resort. Which was, he realized, exactly what it was. The temporaries wore white cotton loincloths; the citizens were naked. In his former life he had encountered that sort of casual public nudity a few times on visits to California and the south of France, and it had made him mildly uneasy. But he was growing accustomed to it here.

The changing-rooms were tiny brick cubicles connected by rows of closely placed steps to the courtyard that surrounded the central tank. They entered one and Belilala swiftly slipped out of the loose cotton robe that she had worn since their arrival that morning. With arms folded she stood leaning against the wall, waiting for him. After a moment he dropped his own robe and followed her outside. He felt a little giddy, sauntering around naked in the open like this.

On the way to the main bathing area they passed the private baths. None of them seemed to be occupied. They were elegantly constructed chambers, with finely jointed brick floors and carefully designed runnels to drain excess water into the passageway that led to the primary drain. Phillips was struck with admiration for the cleverness of the prehistoric engineers. He peered into this chamber and that to see how the conduits and ventilating ducts were arranged, and when he came to the last room in the sequence he was surprised and embarrassed to discover that it was in use. A brawny grinning man, big-muscled, deep-chested, with exuberantly flowing shoulder-length red hair and a flamboyant, sharply tapering beard, was thrashing about merrily with two women in the small tank. Phillips had a quick glimpse of a lively tangle of arms, legs, breasts, buttocks.

"Sorry," he muttered. His cheeks reddened. Quickly he ducked out, blurting apologies as he went. "Didn't realize the room was occupied—no wish to intrude—"

Belilala had proceeded on down the passageway. Phillips hurried after her. From behind him came peals of cheerful raucous booming laughter and high-pitched giggling and the sound of splashing water. Probably they had not even noticed him.

He paused a moment, puzzled, playing back in his mind that one startling glimpse. Something was not right. Those women, he was fairly sure, were citizens: little slender elfin dark-haired girlish creatures, the standard model. But the man? That great curling sweep of red hair? Not a citizen. Citizens did not affect shoulder-length hair. And *red*? Nor had he ever seen a citizen so burly, so powerfully muscular. Or one with a beard. But he could hardly be a temporary, either. Phillips could conceive no reason why there would be so Anglo-Saxon-looking a temporary at Mohenjo-daro; and it was unthinkable for a temporary to be frolicking like that with citizens, anyway.

"Charles?"

He looked up ahead. Belilala stood at the end of the passageway, outlined in a nimbus of brilliant sunlight. "Charles?" she said again. "Did you lose your way?"

"I'm right here behind you," he said. "I'm coming."

"Who did you meet in there?"

"A man with a beard."

"With a what?"

"A beard," he said. "Red hair growing on his face. I wonder who he is."

"Nobody I know," said Belilala. "The only one I know with hair on his face is you. And yours is black, and you shave it off every day." She laughed. "Come along, now! I see some friends by the pool!"

He caught up with her and they went hand in hand out into the courtyard. Immediately a waiter glided up to them, an obsequious little temporary with a tray of drinks. Phillips waved it away and headed for the pool. He felt terribly exposed: he imagined that the citizens disporting themselves here were staring intently at him, studying his hairy primitive body as though he were some mythical creature, a Minotaur, a werewolf, summoned up for their amusement. Belilala drifted off to talk to someone and he slipped into the water, grateful for the concealment it offered. It was deep, warm, comforting. With swift powerful strokes he breast-stroked from one end to the other.

A citizen perched elegantly on the pool's rim smiled at him. "Ah, so you've come at last, Charles!" Char-less. Two syllables. Someone from Gioia's set: Stengard, Hawk, Aramayne? He could not remember which one. They were all so much alike.

Phillips returned the man's smile in a halfhearted, tentative way. He searched for something to say and finally asked, "Have you been here long?"

"Weeks. Perhaps months. What a splendid achievement this city is, eh, Charles? Such utter unity of mood—such a total statement of a uniquely single-minded esthetic—"

"Yes. Single-minded is the word," Phillips said drily.

"Gioia's word, actually. Gioia's phrase. I was merely quoting."

Gioia. He felt as if he had been stabbed.

"You've spoken to Gioia lately?" he said.

"Actually, no. It was Hekna who saw her. You do remember Hekna, eh?'' He nodded toward two naked women standing on the brick platform that bordered the pool, chatting, delicately nibbling morsels of meat. They could have been twins. ''There is Hekna, with your Belilala.'' Hekna, yes. So this must be Hawk, Phillips thought, unless there has been some recent shift of couples. ''How sweet she is, your Belilala,'' Hawk said. ''Gioia chose very wisely when she picked her for you.''

Another stab: a much deeper one. ''Is that how it was?'' he said. ''Gioia *picked* Belilala for me?''

''Why, of course!'' Hawk seemed surprised. It went without saying, evidently. ''What do you think? That Gioia would merely go off and leave you to fend for yourself?''

''Hardly. Not Gioia.''

''She's very tender, very gentle, isn't she?''

''You mean Belilala? Yes, very,'' said Phillips carefully. ''A dear woman, a wonderful woman. But of course I hope to get together with Gioia again soon.'' He paused. ''They say she's been in Mohenjo-daro almost since it opened.''

''She was here, yes.''

''Was?''

''Oh, you know Gioia,'' Hawk said lightly. ''She's moved along by now, naturally.''

Phillips leaned forward. ''Naturally,'' he said. Tension thickened his voice. ''Where has she gone this time?''

''Timbuctoo, I think. Or New Chicago. I forget which one it was. She was telling us that she hoped to be in Timbuctoo for the closing-down party. But then Fenimon had some pressing reason for going to New Chicago. I can't remember what they decided to do.'' Hawk gestured sadly. ''Either way, a pity that she left Mohenjo before the new visitor came. She had such a rewarding time with you, after all: I'm sure she'd have found much to learn from him also.''

The unfamiliar term twanged an alarm deep in Phillips' consciousness. *''Visitor?''* he said, angling his head sharply toward Hawk. ''What visitor do you mean?''

''You haven't met him yet? Oh, of course, you've only just arrived.''

Phillips moistened his lips. "I think I may have seen him. Long red hair? Beard like this?"

"That's the one! Willoughby, he's called. He's—what?—a Viking, a pirate, something like that. Tremendous vigor and force. Remarkable person. We should have many more visitors, I think. They're far superior to temporaries, everyone agrees. Talking with a temporary is a little like talking to one's self, wouldn't you say? They give you no significant illumination. But a visitor—someone like this Willoughby—or like you, Charles—a visitor can be truly enlightening, a visitor can transform one's view of reality—"

"Excuse me," Phillips said. A throbbing began behind his forehead. "Perhaps we can continue this conversation later, yes?" He put the flats of his hands against the hot brick of the platform and hoisted himself swiftly from the pool. "At dinner, maybe—or afterward—yes? All right?" He set off at a quick half-trot back toward the passageway that led to the private baths.

As he entered the roofed part of the structure his throat grew dry, his breath suddenly came short. He padded quickly up the hall and peered into the little bath-chamber. The bearded man was still there, sitting up in the tank, breast-high above the water, with one arm around each of the women. His eyes gleamed with fiery intensity in the dimness. He was grinning in marvelous self-satisfaction; he seemed to brim with intensity, confidence, gusto.

Let him be what I think he is, Phillips prayed. I have been alone among these people long enough.

"May I come in?" he asked.

"Aye, fellow!" cried the man in the tub thunderously. "By my troth, come ye in, and bring your lass as well! God's teeth, I wot there's room aplenty for more folk in this tub than we!"

At that great uproarious outcry Phillips felt a powerful surge of joy. What a joyous rowdy voice! How rich, how lusty, how totally uncitizen-like!

And those oddly archaic words! *God's teeth? By my troth?*

What sort of talk was that? What else but the good pure sonorous Elizabethan diction! Certainly it had something of the roll and fervor of Shakespeare about it. And spoken with—an Irish brogue, was it? No, not quite: it was English, but English spoken in no manner Phillips had ever heard.

Citizens did not speak that way. But a *visitor* might.

So it was true. Relief flooded Phillips' soul. Not alone, then! Another relict of a former age—another wanderer—a companion in chaos, a brother in adversity—a fellow voyager, tossed even farther than he had been by the tempests of time—

The bearded man grinned heartily and beckoned to Phillips with a toss of his head. "Well, join us, join us, man! 'Tis good to see an English face again, amidst all these Moors and rogue Portugals! But what have ye done with thy lass? One can never have enough wenches, d'ye not agree?"

The force and vigor of him were extraordinary: almost too much so. He roared, he bellowed, he boomed. He was so very much what he ought to be that he seemed more a character out of some old pirate movie than anything else, so blustering, so real, that he seemed unreal. A stage-Elizabethan, larger than life, a boisterous young Falstaff without the belly.

Hoarsely, Phillips said, "Who are you?"

"Why, Ned Willoughby's son Francis am I, of Plymouth. Late of the service of Her Most Protestant Majesty, but most foully abducted by the powers of darkness and cast away among these blackamoor Hindus, or whatever they be. And thyself?"

"Charles Phillips." After a moment's uncertainty he added, "I'm from New York."

"*New* York? What place is that? In faith, man, I know it not!"

"A city in America."

"A city in America, forsooth! What a fine fancy that is! In America, you say, and not on the Moon, or perchance underneath the sea?" To the women Willoughby said, "D'ye hear him? He comes from a city in America! With the face of an Englishman, though not the manner of one, and not quite the proper sort of speech. A city in America! A *city*. God's blood, what will I hear next?"

Phillips trembled. Awe was beginning to take hold of him. This man had walked the streets of Shakespeare's London, perhaps. He had clinked canisters with Marlowe or Essex or Walter Raleigh; he had watched the ships of the Armada wallowing in the Channel. It strained Phillips' spirit to think of it. This strange dream in which he found himself was compounding its strangeness now. He felt like a weary swimmer assailed by heavy surf, winded, dazed. The hot close atmosphere of the baths was driving him toward vertigo. There could be no doubt of it any longer. He was not the only primitive—the only *visitor*—who was wandering loose in this fiftieth century. They were conducting other experiments as well. He gripped the sides of the door to steady himself and said, "When you speak of Her Most Protestant Majesty, it's Elizabeth the First you mean, is that not so?"

"Elizabeth, aye! As to the First, that is true enough, but why trouble to name her thus? There is but one. First and Last, I do trow, and God save her, there is no other!"

Phillips studied the other man warily. He knew that he must proceed with care. A misstep at this point and he would forfeit any chance that Willoughby would take him seriously. How much metaphysical bewilderment, after all, could this man absorb? What did he know, what had anyone of his time known, of past and present and future and the notion that one might somehow move from one to the other as readily as one would go from Surrey to Kent? That was a twentieth-century idea, late nineteenth at best, a fantastical speculation that very likely no one had ever considered before Wells had sent his time traveler off to stare at the reddened sun of the Earth's last twilight. Willoughby's world was a world of Protestants and Catholics, of kings and queens, of tiny sailing vessels, of swords at the hip and ox-carts on the road: that world seemed to Phillips far more alien and distant than was this world of citizens and temporaries. The risk that Willoughby would not begin to understand him was great.

But this man and he were natural allies against a world they had never made. Phillips chose to take the risk.

"Elizabeth the First is the queen you serve," he said. "There will be another of her name in England, in due time. Has already been, in fact."

Willoughby shook his head like a puzzled lion. "Another Elizabeth, d'ye say?"

"A second one, and not much like the first. Long after your Virgin Queen, this one. She will reign in what you think of as the days to come. That I know without doubt."

The Englishman peered at him and frowned. "You see the future? Are you a soothsayer, then? A necromancer, mayhap? One of the very demons that brought me to this place?"

"Not at all," Phillips said gently. "Only a lost soul, like yourself." He stepped into the little room and crouched by the side of the tank. The two citizen-women were staring at him in bland fascination. He ignored them. To Willoughby he said, "Do you have any idea where you are?"

The Englishman had guessed, rightly enough, that he was in India: "I do believe that these little brown Moorish folk are of the Hindu sort," he said. But that was as far as his comprehension of what had befallen him could go.

It had not occurred to him that he was no longer living in the sixteenth century. And of course he did not begin to suspect that this strange and somber brick city in which he found himself was a wanderer out of an era even more remote than his own. Was there any way, Phillips wondered, of explaining that to him?

He had been here only three days. He thought it was devils that had carried him off. "While I slept did they come for me," he said. "Mephistophilis Sathanas his henchmen seized me—God alone can say why—and swept me in a moment out to this torrid realm from England, where I had reposed among friends and family. For I was between one voyage and the next, you must understand, awaiting Drake and his ship—you know Drake, the glorious Francis? God's blood, there's a mariner for ye! We were to go to the Main again, he and I,

but instead here I be in this other place—'' Willoughby
leaned close and said, ''I ask you, soothsayer, how can it be,
that a man go to sleep in Plymouth and wake up in India? It is
passing strange, is it not?''

''That it is,'' Phillips said.

''Be he that is in the dance must needs dance on, though he
do but hop, eh? So do I believe.'' He gestured toward the two
citizen-women. ''And therefore to console myself in this
pagan land I have found me some sport among these little
Portugal women—''

''Portugal?'' said Phillips.

''Why, what else can they be, but Portugals? Is it not the
Portugals who control all these coasts of India? See,
the people are of two sorts here, the blackamoors and the
others, the fair-skinned ones, the lords and masters who lie
here in these baths. If they be not Hindus, and I think they
are not, then Portugals is what they must be.'' He laughed
and pulled the women against himself and rubbed his hands
over their breasts as though they were fruits on a vine.
''Is that not what you are, you little naked shameless Papist
wenches? A pair of Portugals, eh?''

They giggled, but did not answer.

''No,'' Phillips said ''This is India, but not the India you
think you know. And these women are not Portuguese.''

''Not Portuguese?'' Willoughby said, baffled.

''No more so than you. I'm quite certain of that.''

Willoughby stroked his beard. ''I do admit I found them
very odd, for Portugals. I have heard not a syllable of their
Portugee speech on their lips. And it is strange also that they
run naked as Adam and Eve in these baths, and allow me free
plunder of their women, which is not the way of Portugals at
home, God wot. But I thought me, this is India, they choose
to live in another fashion here—''

''No,'' Phillips said. ''I tell you, these are not Portuguese,
nor any other people of Europe who are known to you.''

''Prithee, who are they, then?''

Do it delicately, now, Phillips warned himself. *Delicately*.
He said, ''It is not far wrong to think of them as spirits of

some kind—demons, even. Or sorcerers who have magicked us out of our proper places in the world." He paused, groping for some means to share with Willoughby, in a way that Willoughby might grasp, this mystery that had enfolded them. He drew a deep breath. "They've taken us not only across the sea," he said, "but across the years as well. We have both been hauled, you and I, into the days that are to come."

Willoughby gave him a look of blank bewilderment.

"Days that are to come? Times yet unborn, d'ye mean? Why, I comprehend none of that!"

"Try to understand. We're both castaways in the same boat, man! But there's no way we can help each other if I can't make you see—"

Shaking his head, Willoughby muttered, "In faith, good friend, I find your words the merest folly. Today is today, and tomorrow is tomorrow, and how can a man step from one to t'other until tomorrow be turned into today?"

"I have no idea," said Phillips. Struggle was apparent on Willoughby's face; but plainly he could perceive no more than the haziest outline of what Phillips was driving at, if that much. "But this I know," he went on, "that your world and all that was in it is dead and gone. And so is mine, though I was born four hundred years after you, in the time of the second Elizabeth."

Willoughby snorted scornfully. "Four hundred—"

"You must believe me!"

"Nay! Nay!"

"It's the truth. Your time is only history to me. And mine and yours are history to *them*—ancient history. They call us visitors, but what we are is captives." Phillips felt himself quivering in the intensity of his effort. He was aware how insane this must sound to Willoughby. It was beginning to sound insane to him. "They've stolen us out of our proper times—seizing us like gypsies in the night—"

"Fie, man! You rave with lunacy!"

Phillips shook his head. He reached out and seized Willoughby tightly by the wrist. "I beg you, listen to me!" The citizen-women were watching closely, whispering to one another behind their hands, laughing. "Ask them!" Phillips cried. "Make them tell you what century this is! The sixteenth, do you think? Ask them!"

"What century could it be, but the sixteenth of our Lord?"

"They will tell you it is the fiftieth."

Willoughby looked at him pityingly. "Man, man, what a sorry thing thou art! The fiftieth, indeed!" He laughed. "Fellow, listen to me, now. There is but one Elizabeth, safe upon her throne in Westminster. This is India. The year is Anno 1591. Come, let us you and I steal a ship from these Portugals, and make our way back to England, and peradventure you may get from there to your America—"

"There is no England."

"Ah, can you say that and not be mad?"

"The cities and nations we knew are gone. These people live like magicians, Francis." There was no use holding anything back now, Phillips thought leadenly. He knew that he had lost. "They conjure up places of long ago, and build them here and there to suit their fancy, and when they are bored with them they destroy them, and start anew. There is no England. Europe is empty, featureless, void. Do you know what cities there are? There are only five in all the world. There is Alexandria of Egypt. There is Timbuctoo in Africa. There is New Chicago in America. There is a great city in China—in Cathay, I suppose you would say. And there is this place, which they call Mohenjo-daro, and which is far more ancient than Greece, than Rome, than Babylon."

Quietly Willoughby said, "Nay. This is mere absurdity. You say we are in some far tomorrow, and then you tell me we are dwelling in some city of long ago."

"A conjuration, only," Phillips said in desperation. "A likeness of that city. Which these folks have fashioned somehow for their own amusement. Just as we are here, you and I: to amuse them. Only to amuse them."

"You are completely mad."

"Come with me, then. Talk with the citizens by the great pool. Ask them what year this is; ask them about England; ask them how you come to be here." Once again Phillips grasped Willoughby's wrist. "We should be allies. If we work together, perhaps we can discover some way to get ourselves out of this place, and—"

"Let me be, fellow."

"Please—"

"Let me be!" roared Willoughby, and pulled his arm free. His eyes were stark with rage. Rising in the tank, he looked about furiously as though searching for a weapon. The citizen-women shrank back away from him, though at the same time they seemed captivated by the big man's fierce outburst. "Go to, get you to Bedlam! Let me be, madman! Let me be!"

Dismally Phillips roamed the dusty unpaved streets of Mohenjo-daro alone for hours. His failure with Willoughby had left him bleak-spirited and somber: he had hoped to stand back to back with the Elizabethan against the citizens, but he saw now that that was not to be. He had bungled things; or, more likely, it had been impossible ever to bring Willoughby to see the truth of their predicament.

In the stifling heat he went at random through the confusing congested lanes of flat-roofed, windowless houses and blank, featureless walls until he emerged into a broad market-place. The life of the city swirled madly around him: the pseudo-life, rather, the intricate interactions of the thousands of temporaries who were nothing more than wind-up dolls set in motion to provide the illusion that pre-Vedic India was still a going concern. Here vendors sold beautiful little carved stone seals portraying tigers and monkeys and strange humped cattle, and women bargained vociferously with craftsmen for ornaments of ivory, gold, copper, and bronze. Weary-looking women squatted behind immense mounds of newly made pottery, pinkish red with black designs. No one paid any attention to him. He was the outsider here, neither citizen nor temporary. They belonged.

He went on, passing the huge granaries where workmen ceaselessly unloaded carts of wheat and others pounded grain on great circular brick platforms. He drifted into a public restaurant thronging with joyless silent people standing elbow to elbow at small brick counter, and was given a flat round piece of bread, a sort of tortilla or chapatti, in which was stuffed some spiced mincemeat that stung his lips like fire. Then he moved onward, down a wide, shallow, timbered staircase into the lower part of the city, where the peasantry lived in cell-like rooms packed together as though in hives.

It was an oppressive city, but not a squalid one. The intensity for the concern with sanitation amazed him: wells and fountains and public privies everywhere, and brick drains running from each building, leading to covered cesspools. There was none of the open sewage and pestilent gutters that he knew still could be found in the India of his own time. He wondered whether ancient Mohenjo-daro had in truth been so fastidious. Perhaps the citizens had redesigned the city to suit their own ideals of cleanliness. No: most likely what he saw was authentic, he decided, a function of the same obsessive discipline that had given the city its rigidity of form. If Mohenjo-daro had been a verminous filthy hole, the citizens probably would have re-created it in just that way, and loved it for its fascinating, reeking filth.

Not that he had ever noticed an excessive concern with authenticity on the part of the citizens; and Mohenjo-daro, like all the other restored cities he had visited, was full of the usual casual anachronisms. Phillips saw images of Shiva and Krishna here and there on the walls of buildings he took to be temples, and the benign face of the mother-goddess Kali loomed in the plazas. Surely those deities had arisen in India long after the collapse of the Mohenjo-daro civilization. Were the citizens indifferent to such matters of chronology? Or did they take a certain naughty pleasure in mixing the eras—a mosque and a church in Greek Alexandria, Hindu gods in prehistoric Mohenjo-daro? Perhaps their records of the past had become contaminated with errors over the thousands of years. He would not have been surprised to see banners bearing portraits of Gandhi and Nehru being carried in procession through the streets. And there were phantasms and chimeras at large here again too, as if the citizens were untroubled by the boundary between history and myth: little fat elephant-headed Ganeshas blithely plunging their trunks into water-fountains, a six-armed, three-headed woman sunning herself on a brick terrace. Why not? Surely that was the motto of these people: *Why not, why not, why not?* They could do as they pleased, and they did. Yet Gioia had said to him, long ago, "Limits are very important." In what, Phillips wondered, did they limit themselves, other than the number of their cities? Was there a quota, perhaps, on the number of "visitors" they allowed themselves to kidnap from the past? Until today he had thought he was the only one; now he knew there was at least one other; possibly there were more elsewhere, a step or two ahead or behind him, making the circuit with the citizens who traveled endlessly from New Chicago to Chang-an to Alexandria. We should join forces, he thought, and compel them to send us back to our rightful eras. *Compel?* How? File a class-action suit, maybe? Demonstrate in the streets? Sadly he thought of his failure to make common cause with Willoughby. We are natural allies, he thought. Together perhaps we might have won some compassion from these people. But to Willoughby it must be literally unthinkable that Good Queen Bess and her subjects were sealed away on the far side of a barrier hundreds of centuries thick. He would prefer to believe that England was just a few months' voyage away around the Cape of Good Hope, and that all he need do was commandeer a ship and set sail for home. Poor Willoughby: probably he would never see his home again.

The thought came to Phillips suddenly:

Neither will you.

And then, after it:

If you could go home, would you really want to?

One of the first things he had realized here was that he knew almost nothing substantial about his former existence. His mind was well stocked with details on life in twentieth-century New York, to be sure; but of himself he could not say much more than that he was Charles Phillips and had come from 1984. Profession? Age? Parents' names? Did he have a wife? Children? A cat, a dog, hobbies? No data: none. Possibly the citizens had stripped such things from him when they brought him here, to spare him from the pain of separation. They might be capable of that kindness. Knowing so little of what he had lost, could he truly say that he yearned for it? Willoughby seemed to remember much more of his former life, and longed for it all the more. He was spared that. Why not stay here, and go on and on from city to city, sightseeing all of time past as the citizens conjured it back into being? Why not? Why not? The chances were that he had no choice about it, anyway.

He made his way back up toward the citadel and to the baths once more. He felt a little like a ghost, haunting a city of ghosts.

Belilala seemed unaware that he had been gone for most of the day. She sat by herself on the terrace of the baths, placidly sipping some thick milky beverage that had been sprinkled with a dark spice. He shook his head when she offered him some.

"Do you remember I mentioned that I saw a man with red hair and a beard this morning?" Phillips said. "He's a visitor. Hawk told me that."

"Is he?" Belilala asked.

"From a time about four hundred years before mine. I talked with him. He thinks he was brought here by demons." Phillips gave her a searching look. "I'm a visitor too, isn't that so?"

"Of course, love."

"And how was *I* brought here? By demons also?"

Belilala smiled indifferently. "You'd have to ask someone else. Hawk, perhaps. I haven't looked into these things very deeply."

"I see. Are there many visitors here, do you know?"

A languid shrug. "Not many, no, not really. I've only heard of three or four besides you. There may be others by now, I suppose." She rested her hand lightly on his. "Are you having a good time in Mohenjo, Charles?"

He let her question pass as though he had not heard it.

"I asked Hawk about Gioia," he said.

"Oh?"

"He told me that she's no longer here, that she's gone on to Timbuctoo or New Chicago, he wasn't sure which."

"That's quite likely. As everybody knows, Gioia rarely stays in the same place very long."

Phillips nodded. "You said the other day that Gioia is a short-timer. That means she's going to grow old and die, doesn't it?"

"I thought you understood that, Charles."

"Whereas you will not age? Nor Hawk, nor Stengard, nor any of the rest of your set?"

"We will live as long as we wish," she said. "But we will not age, no."

"What makes a person a short-timer?"

"They're born that way, I think. Some missing gene, some extra gene—I don't actually know. It's extremely uncommon. Nothing can be done to help them. It's very slow, the aging. But it can't be halted."

Phillips nodded. "That must be very disagreeable," he said. "To find yourself one of the few people growing old in a world where everyone stays young. No wonder Gioia is so impatient. No wonder she runs around from place to place. No wonder she attached herself so quickly to the barbaric hairy visitor from the twentieth century, who comes from a time when *everybody* was a short-timer. She and I have something in common, wouldn't you say?"

"In a manner of speaking, yes."

"We understand aging. We understand death. Tell me: is Gioia likely to die very soon, Belilala?"

"Soon? Soon?" She gave him a wide-eyed childlike stare. "What is soon? How can I say? What you think of as soon and what I think of as soon are not the same things, Charles." Then her manner changed: she seemed to be hearing what he was saying for the first time. Softly she said, "No, no, Charles. I don't think she will die very soon."

"When she left me in Chang-an, was it because she had become bored with me?"

Belilala shook her head. "She was simply restless. It had nothing to do with you. She was never bored with you."

"Then I'm going to look for her. Wherever she may be, Timbuctoo, New Chicago, I'll find her. Gioia and I belong together."

"Perhaps you do," said Belilala. "Yes. Yes, I think you really do." She sounded altogether unperturbed, unrejected, unbereft. "By all means, Charles. Go to her. Follow her. Find her. Wherever she may be."

They had already begun dismantling Timbuctoo when Phillips got there. While he was still high overhead, his flitterflitter hovering above the dusty tawny plain where the River Niger met the sands of the Sahara, a surge of keen excitement rose in him as he looked down at the square gray flat-roofed mud brick buildings of the great desert capital. But when he landed he found gleaming metal-skinned robots swarming everywhere, a horde of them scuttling about like giant shining insects, pulling the place apart.

He had not known about the robots before. So that was how all these miracles were carried out, Phillips realized: an army of obliging machines. He imagined them bustling up out of the earth whenever their services were needed, emerging from some sterile subterranean storehouse to put together Venice or Thebes or Knossos or Houston or whatever place was required, down to the finest detail, and then at some later time returning to undo everything that they had fashioned. He watched them now, diligently pulling down the adobe walls, demolishing the heavy metal-studded gates, bulldozing the amazing labyrinth of alleyways and thoroughfares, sweeping away the market. On his last visit to Timbuctoo that market had been crowded with a horde of veiled Tuaregs and swaggering Moors, black Sudanese, shrewd-faced Syrian traders, all of them busily dickering for camels, horses, donkeys, slabs of salt, huge green melons, silver bracelets, splendid vellum Korans. They were all gone now, that picturesque crowd of swarthy temporaries. Nor were there any citizens to be seen. The dust of destruction choked the air. One of the robots came up to Phillips and said in a dry crackling insect-voice, "You ought not to be here. This city is closed."

He stared at the flashing, buzzing band of scanners and sensors across the creature's glittering tapered snout. "I'm trying to find someone, a citizen who may have been here recently. Her name is—"

"The city is closed," the robot repeated inexorably.

They would not let him stay as much as an hour. There is no food here, the robot said, no water, no shelter. This is not a place any longer. You may not stay. You may not stay. You may not stay.

This is not a place any longer.

Perhaps he could find her in New Chicago, then. He took to the air again, soaring northward and westward over the vast emptiness. The land below him curved away into the hazy horizon, bare, sterile. What had they done with the vestiges of the world that had gone before? Had they turned their gleaming metal beetles loose to clean everything away? Were there no ruins of genuine antiquity anywhere? No scrap of Rome, no shard of Jerusalem, no stump of Fifth Avenue? It was all so barren down there: an empty stage, waiting for its next set to be built. He flew on a great arc across the jutting hump of Africa and on into what he supposed was southern Europe: the little vehicle did all the work, leaving him to doze or stare as he wished. Now and again he saw another flitterflitter pass by, far away, a dark distant winged teardrop outlined against the hard clarity of the sky. He wished there was some way of making radio contact with them, but he had no idea how to go about it. Not that he had anything he wanted to say; he wanted only to hear a human voice. He was utterly isolated. He might just as well have been the last living man on Earth. He closed his eyes and thought of Gioia.

"Like this?" Phillips asked. In an ivory-paneled oval room sixty stories above the softly glowing streets of New Chicago he touched a small cool plastic canister to his upper lip and pressed the stud at its base. He heard a foaming sound; and then blue vapor rose to his nostrils.

"Yes," Cantilena said. "That's right."

He detected a faint aroma of cinnamon, cloves, and something that might almost have been broiled lobster. Then a spasm of dizziness hit him and visions rushed through his head: Gothic cathedrals, the Pyramids, Central Park under fresh snow, the harsh brick warrens of Mohenjo-daro, and fifty thousand other places all at once, a wild roller-coaster ride through space and time. It seemed to go on for centuries. But finally his head cleared and he looked about, blinking, realizing that the whole thing had taken only a moment. Cantilena still stood at his elbow. The other citizens in the room—fifteen, twenty of them—had scarcely moved. The strange little man with the celadon skin over by the far wall continued to stare at him.

"Well?" Cantilena asked. "What did you think?"

"Incredible."

"And very authentic. It's an actual New Chicagoan drug. The exact formula. Would you like another?"

"Not just yet," Phillips said uneasily. He swayed and had to struggle for his balance. Sniffing that stuff might not have been such a wise idea, he thought.

He had been in New Chicago a week, or perhaps it was two, and he was still suffering from the peculiar disorientation that that city always aroused in him. This was the fourth time that he had come here, and it had been the same every time. New Chicago was the only one of the reconstructed cities of this world that in its original incarnation had existed *after* his own era. To him it was an outpost of the incomprehensible future; to the citizens it was a quaint simulacrum of the archaeological past. That paradox left him aswirl with impossible confusions and tensions.

What had happened to *old* Chicago was of course impossible for him to discover. Vanished without a trace, that was clear: no Water Tower, no Marina City, no Hancock Center, no Tribune building, not a fragment, not an atom. But it was hopeless to ask any of the million-plus inhabitants of New

Chicago about their city's predecessor. They were only temporaries; they knew no more than they had to know, and all that they had to know was how to go through the motions of whatever it was they did by way of creating the illusion that this was a real city. They had no need of knowing ancient history.

Nor was he likely to find out anything from a citizen, of course. Citizens did not seem to bother much about scholarly matters. Phillips had no reason to think that the world was anything other than an amusement park to them. Somewhere, certainly, there had to be those who specialized in the serious study of the lost civilizations of the past—for how, otherwise, would these uncanny reconstructed cities be brought into being? "The planners," he had once heard Nissandra or Aramayne say, "are already deep into their Byzantium research." But who were the planners? He had no idea. For all he knew, they were the robots. Perhaps the robots were the real masters of this whole era, who created the cities not primarily for the sake of amusing the citizens but in their own diligent attempt to comprehend the life of the world that had passed away. A wild speculation, yes; but not without some plausibility, he thought.

He felt oppressed by the party gaiety all about him. "I need some air," he said to Cantilena, and headed toward the window. It was the merest crescent, but a breeze came through. He looked out at the strange city below.

New Chicago had nothing in common with the old one but its name. They had built it, at least, along the western shore of a large inland lake that might even be Lake Michigan, although when he had flown over it had seemed broader and less elongated than the lake he remembered. The city itself was a lacy fantasy of slender pastel-hued buildings rising at odd angles and linked by a webwork of gently undulating aerial bridges. The streets were long parentheses that touched the lake at their northern and southern ends and arched gracefully westward in the middle. Between each of the great boulevards ran a track for public transportation—sleek aquamarine bubble-vehicles gliding on soundless wheels—and flanking each of the tracks were lush strips of park. It was beautiful, astonishingly so, but insubstantial. The whole thing seemed to have been contrived from sunbeams and silk.

A soft voice beside him said, "Are you becoming ill?"

Phillips glanced around. The celadon man stood beside him: a compact, precise person, vaguely Oriental in appearance. His skin was of a curious gray-green hue like no skin Phillips had ever seen, and it was extraordinarily smooth in texture, as though he were made of fine porcelain.

He shook his head. "Just a little queasy," he said. "This city always scrambles me."

"I suppose it can be disconcerting," the little man replied. His tone was furry and veiled, the inflection strange. There was something feline about him. He seemed sinewy, unyielding, almost menacing. "Visitor, are you?"

Phillips studied him a moment. "Yes," he said.

"So am I, of course."

"Are you?"

"Indeed." The little man smiled. "What's your locus? Twentieth century? Twenty-first at the latest, I'd say."

"I'm from 1984. 1984 A.D."

Another smile, a self-satisfied one. "Not a bad guess, then." A brisk tilt of the head. "Y'ang-Yeovil."

"Pardon me?" Phillips said.

"Y'ang-Yeovil. It is my name. Formerly Colonel Y'ang-Yeovil of the Third Septentriad."

"Is that on some other planet?" asked Phillips, feeling a bit dazed.

"Oh, no, not at all," Y'ang-Yeovil said pleasantly. "This very world, I assure you. I am quite of human origin. Citizen of the Republic of Upper Han, native of the city of Port Ssu. And you—forgive me—your name—?"

"I'm sorry. Phillips. Charles Phillips. From New York City, once upon a time."

"Ah, New York!" Y'ang-Yeovil's face lit with a glimmer of recognition that quickly faded. "New York—New York—it was very famous, that I know—"

This is very strange, Phillips thought. He felt greater compassion for poor bewildered Francis Willoughby now. This man comes from a time so far beyond my own that he barely knows of New York—he must be a contemporary of the real New Chicago, in fact; I wonder whether he finds this version authentic—and yet to the citizens this Y'ang-Yeovil too is just a primitive, a curio out of antiquity—

"New York was the largest city of the United States of America," Phillips said.

"Of course. Yes. Very famous."

"But virtually forgotten by the time the Republic of Upper Han came into existence, I gather."

Y'ang-Yeovil said, looking uncomfortable, "There were disturbances between your time and mine. But by no means should you take from my words the impression that your city was—"

Sudden laughter resounded across the room. Five or six newcomers had arrived at the party. Phillips stared, gasped, gaped. Surely that was Stengard—and Aramayne beside him— and that other woman, half-hidden behind them—

"If you'll pardon me a moment—" Phillips said, turning abruptly away from Y'ang-Yeovil. "Please excuse me. Someone just coming in—a person I've been trying to find ever since—"

He hurried toward her.

"Gioia?" he called. "Gioia, it's me! Wait! Wait!"

Stengard was in the way. Aramayne, turning to take a handful of the little vapor-sniffers from Cantilena, blocked him also. Phillips pushed through them as though they were not there. Gioia, halfway out the door, halted and looked toward him like a frightened deer.

"Don't go," he said. He took her hand in his.

He was startled by her appearance. How long had it been since their strange parting on that night of mysteries in Chang-an? A year? A year and a half? So he believed. Or had he lost all track of time? Were his perceptions of the passing for him here as in a dream, and he had never known it. She looked strained, faded, worn. Out of a thinner and strangely altered face her eyes blazed at him almost defiantly, as though saying, *See? See how ugly I have become?*

He said, "I've been hunting for you for—I don't know how long it's been, Gioia. In Mohenjo, in Timbuctoo, now here. I want to be with you again."

"It isn't possible."

"Belilala explained everything to me in Mohenjo. I know that you're a short-timer—I know what that means, Gioia. But what of it? So you're beginning to age a little. So what? So you'll only have three or four hundred years, instead of forever. Don't you think I know what it means to be a short-timer? I'm just a simple ancient man of the twentieth century, remember? Sixty, seventy, eighty years is all we would get. You and I suffer from the same malady, Gioia. That's what drew you to me in the first place. I'm certain of that. That's why we belong with each other now. However much time we have, we can spend the rest of it together, don't you see?"

"You're the one who doesn't see, Charles," she said softly.

"Maybe. Maybe I still don't understand a damned thing about this place. Except that you and I—that I love you—that I think you love me—"

"I love you, yes. But you don't understand. It's precisely because I love you that you and I—you and I can't—"

With a despairing sigh she slid her hand free of his grasp. He reached for her again, but she shook him off and backed up quickly into the corridor.

"Gioia?"

"Please," she said. "No. I would never have come here if I knew you were here. Don't come after me. Please. Please."

She turned and fled.

He stood looking after her for a long moment. Cantilena and Aramayne appeared, and smiled at him as if nothing at all had happened. Cantilena offered him a vial of some sparkling amber fluid. He refused with a brusque gesture. Where do I go now, he wondered? What do I do? He wandered back into the party.

Y'ang-Yeovil glided to his side. "You are in great distress," the little man murmured.

Phillips glared. "Let me be."

"Perhaps I could be of some help."

"There's no help possible," said Phillips. He swung about and plucked one of the vials from a tray and gulped its contents. It made him feel as if there were two of him, standing on either side of Y'ang-Yeovil. He gulped another. Now there were four of him. "I'm in love with a citizen," he blurted. It seemed to him that he was speaking in chorus.

"Love. Ah. And does she love you?"

"So I thought. So I think. But she's a short-timer. Do you know what that means? She's not immortal like the others. She ages. She's beginning to look old. And so she's been running away from me. She doesn't want me to see her changing. She thinks it'll disgust me, I suppose. I tried to remind her just now that I'm not immortal either, that she and I could grow old together, but she—"

"Oh, no," Y'ang-Yeovil said quietly. "Why do you think you will age? Have you grown any older in all the time you have been here?"

Phillips was nonplussed. "Of course I have. I—I—"

"Have you?" Y'ang-Yeovil smiled. "Here. Look at yourself." He did something intricate with his fingers and a shimmering zone of mirror-like light appeared between them. Phillips stared at his reflection. A youthful face stared back at him. It was true, then. He had simply not thought about it. How many years had he spent in this world? The time had simply slipped by: a great deal of time, though he could not calculate how much. They did not seem to keep close count of it here, nor had he. But it must have been many years, he thought. All that endless travel up and down the globe—so many cities had come and gone—Rio, Rome, Asgard, those were the first three that came to mind—and there were others; he could hardly remember every one. Years. His face had not changed at all. Time had worked its harshness on Gioia, yes, but not on him.

"I don't understand," he said. "Why am I not aging?"

"Because you are not real," said Y'ang-Yeovil. "Are you unaware of that?"

Phillips blinked. "Not—real?"

"Did you think you were lifted bodily out of your own time?" the little man asked. "Ah, no, no, there is no way for them to do such a thing. We are not actual time travelers: not you, not I, not any of the visitors. I thought you were aware of that. But perhaps your era is too early for a proper understanding of these things. We are very cleverly done, my friend. We are ingenious constructs, marvelously stuffed with the thoughts and attitudes and events of our own times. We are their finest achievement, you know: far more complex even than one of these cities. We are a step beyond the temporaries—more than a step, a great deal more. They do only what they are instructed to do, and their range is very narrow. They are nothing but machines, really. Whereas we are autonomous. We move about by our own will; we think, we talk, we even, so it seems, fall in love. But we will not age. How could we age? We are not real. We are mere artificial webworks of mental responses. We are mere illusions, done so well that we deceive even ourselves. You did not know that? Indeed, you did not know?"

He was airborne, touching destination buttons at random. Somehow he found himself heading back toward Timbuctoo. *This city is closed. This is not a place any longer.* It did not matter to him. Why should anything matter?

Fury and a choking sense of despair rose within him. I am software, Phillips thought. I am nothing but software.

Not real. Very cleverly done. An ingenious construct. A mere illusion.

No trace of Timbuctoo was visible from the air. He landed anyway. The gray sandy earth was smooth, unturned, as though there had never been anything there. A few robots were still about, handling whatever final chores were required in the shutting-down of a city. Two of them scuttled up to him. Huge bland gleaming silver-skinned insects, not friendly.

"There is no city here," they said. "This is not a permissible place."

"Permissible by whom?"

"There is no reason for you to be here."

"There is no reason for me to be anywhere," Phillips said. The robots stirred, made uneasy humming sounds and ominous clicks, waved their antennae about. They seem troubled, he thought. They seem to dislike my attitude. Perhaps I run some risk of being taken off to the home for unruly software for debugging. "I am leaving now," he told them. "Thank you. Thank you very much." He backed away from them and climbed into his flitterflitter. He touched more destination buttons.

We move about by our own will. We think, we talk, we even fall in love.

He landed in Chang-an. This time there was no reception committee waiting for him at the Gate of Brilliant Virtue. The city seemed larger and more resplendent: new pagodas, new palaces. It felt like winter: a chilly cutting wind was blowing. The sky was cloudless and dazzlingly bright. At the steps of the Silver Terrace he encountered Francis Willoughby, a great hulking figure in magnificent brocaded robes, with two dainty little temporaries, pretty as jade statuettes, engulfed in his arms. "Miracles and wonders! The silly lunatic fellow is here too!" Willoughby roared. "Look, look, we are come to far Cathay, you and I!"

We are nowhere, Phillips thought. *We are mere illusions, done so well that we deceive even ourselves.*

To Willoughby he said, "You look like an emperor in those robes, Francis."

"Aye, like Prester John!" Willoughby cried. "Like Tamburlaine himself! Aye, am I not majestic?" He slapped Phillips gaily on the shoulder, a rough playful poke that spun him halfway about, coughing and wheezing. "We flew in the air, as the eagles do, as the demons do, as the angels do! Soared like angles! Like angels!" He came close, looming over Phillips. "I would have gone to England, but the wench Belilala said there was an enchantment on me that would keep me from England just now; and so we voyaged to Cathay. Tell me this, fellow, will you go witness for me when we see England again? Swear that all that has befallen us did in truth befall? For I fear they will say I am as mad as Marco Polo, when I tell them of flying to Cathay.''

"One madman backing another?'' Phillips asked. "What can I tell you? You still think you'll reach England, do you?'' Rage rose to the surface in him, bubbling hot. "Ah, Francis, Francis, do you know your Shakespeare? Did you go to the plays? We aren't real. *We aren't real.* We are such stuff as dreams are made on, the two of us. That's all we are. O brave new world! What England? Where? There's no England. There's no Francis Willoughby. There's no Charles Phillips. What we are is—''

"Let him be, Charles,'' a cool voice cut in.

He turned. Belilala, in the robes of an empress, coming down the steps of the Silver Terrace.

"I know the truth,'' he said bitterly. "Y'ang-Yeovil told me. The visitor from the twenty-fifth century. I saw him in New Chicago.''

"Did you see Gioia there too?'' Belilala asked.

"Briefly. She looks much older.''

"Yes. I know. She was here recently.''

"And has gone on, I suppose?''

"To Mohenjo again, yes. Go after her, Charles. Leave poor Francis alone. I told her to wait for you. I told her that she needs you, and you need her.''

"Very kind of you. But what good is it, Belilala? I don't even exist. And she's going to die.''

"You exist. How can you doubt that you exist? You feel, don't you? You suffer. You love. You love Gioia: is that not so? And you are loved by Gioia. Would Gioia love what is not real?''

"You think she loves me?''

"I know she does. Go to her, Charles. Go. I told her to wait for you in Mohenjo.''

Phillips nodded numbly. What was there to lose?

"Go to her,'' said Belilala again. "Now.''

"Yes," Phillips said. "I'll go now." He turned to Willoughby. "If ever we meet in London, friend, I'll testify for you. Fear nothing. All will be well, Francis."

He left them and set his course for Mohenjo-daro, half expecting to find the robots already tearing it down. Mohenjo-daro was still there, no lovelier than before. He went to the baths, thinking he might find Gioia there. She was not; but he came upon Nissandra, Stengard, Fenimon. "She has gone to Alexandria," Fenimon told him. "She wants to see it one last time, before they close it."

"They're almost ready to open Constantinople," Stengard explained. "The capital of Byzantium, you know, the great city by the Golden Horn. They'll take Alexandria away, you understand, when Byzantium opens. They say it's going to be marvelous. We'll see you there for the opening, naturally?"

"Naturally," Phillips said.

He flew to Alexandria. He felt lost and weary. All this is hopeless folly, he told himself. I am nothing but a puppet jerking about on its strings. But somewhere above the shining breast of the Arabian Sea the deeper implications of something that Belilala had said to him started to sink in, and he felt his bitterness, his rage, his despair, all suddenly beginning to leave him. *You exist. How can you doubt that you exist? Would Gioia love what is not real?* Of course. Of course. Y'ang-Yeovil had been wrong: visitors were more than mere illusions. Indeed Y'ang-Yeovil had voiced the truth of their condition without understanding what he was really saying: *We think, we talk, we fall in love.* Yes. That was the heart of the situation. The visitors might be artificial, but they were not unreal. Belilala had been trying to tell him that just the other night. *You suffer. You love. You love Gioia. Would Gioia love what is not real?* Surely he was real, or at any rate real enough. What he was was something strange, something that would probably have been all but incomprehensible to the twentieth-century people whom he had been designed to simulate. But that did not mean that he was unreal. Did one have to be of woman born to be real? No. No. No. His kind of reality was a sufficient reality. He had no need to be ashamed of it. And, understanding that, he understood that Gioia did not need to grow old and die. There was a way by which she could be saved, if only she would embrace it. If only she would.

When he landed in Alexandria he went immediately to the hotel on the slopes of the Paneium where they had stayed on their first visit, so very long ago; and there she was, sitting quietly on a patio with a view of the harbor and the Lighthouse. There was something calm and resigned about the way she sat. She had given up. She did not even have the strength to flee from him any longer.

"Gioia," he said gently.

She looked older than she had in New Chicago. Her face was drawn and sallow and her eyes seemed sunken; and she was not even bothering these days to deal with the white strands that stood out in stark contrast against the darkness of her hair. He sat down beside her and put his hand over hers, and looked toward the obelisks, the palaces, the temples, the Lighthouse. At length he said, "I know what I really am, now."

"Do you, Charles?" She sounded very far away.

"In my era we called it software. All I am is a set of commands, responses, cross-references, operating some sort of artificial body. It's infinitely better software than we could have imagined. But we were only just beginning to learn how, after all. They pumped me full of twentieth-century reflexes. The right moods, the right appetites, the right irrationalities, the right sort of combativeness. Somebody knows a lot about what it was like to be a twentieth-century man. They did a good job with Willoughby, too, all that Elizabethan rhetoric and swagger. And I suppose they got Y'ang-Yeovil right. *He* seems to think so: who better to judge? The twenty-fifth century, the Republic of Upper Han, people with gray-green skin, half Chinese and half Martian for all I know. *Somebody* knows. Somebody here is very good at programming, Gioia."

She was not looking at him.

"I feel frightened, Charles," she said in the same distant way.

"Of me? Of the things I'm saying?"

"No, not of you. Don't you see what has happened to me?"

"I see you. There are changes."

"I lived a long time wondering when the changes would begin. I thought maybe they wouldn't, not really. Who wants to believe they'll get old? But it started when we were in Alexandria that first time. In Chang-an it got much worse. And now—now—"

He said abruptly, "Stengard tells me they'll be opening Constantinople very soon."

"So?"

"Don't you want to be there when it opens?"

"I'm becoming old and ugly, Charles."

"We'll go to Constantinople together. We'll leave tomorrow, eh? What do you say? We'll charter a boat. It's a quick little hop, right across the Mediterranean. Sailing to Byzantium! There was a poem, you know, in my time. Not forgotten, I guess, because they've programmed it into me. All these thousands of years, and someone still remembers old Yeats. *The young in one another's arms, birds in the trees.* Come with me to Byzantium, Gioia."

She shrugged. "Looking like this? Getting more hideous every hour? While *they* stay young forever? While *you*—" She faltered; her voice cracked; she fell silent.

"Finish the sentence, Gioia."

"Please. Let me alone."

"You were going to say, 'While *you* stay young forever too, Charles,' isn't that it? You knew all along that I was never going to change. I didn't know that, but you did."

"Yes. I knew. I pretended that it wasn't true—that as I aged, you'd age too. It was very foolish of me. In Chang-an, when I first began to see the real signs of it—that was when I realized I couldn't stay with you any longer. Because I'd look at you, always young, always remaining the same age, and I'd look at myself, and—" She gestured, palms upward. "So I gave you to Belilala and ran away."

"All so unnecessary, Gioia."

"I didn't think it was."

"But you don't have to grow old. Not if you don't want to!"

"Don't be cruel, Charles," she said tonelessly. "There's no way of escaping what I have."

"But there is," he said.

"You know nothing about these things."

"Not very much, no," he said. "But I see how it can be done. Maybe it's a primitive simple-minded twentieth-century sort of solution, but I think it ought to work. I've been playing with the idea ever since I left Mohenjo. Tell me this, Gioia: Why can't you go to them, to the programmers, to the artificers, the planners, whoever they are, the ones who create the cities and the temporaries and the visitors. And have yourself made into something like me!"

She looked up, startled. "What are you saying?"

"They can cobble up a twentieth-century man out of nothing more than fragmentary records and make him plausible, can't they? Or an Elizabethan, or anyone else of any era at all, and he's authentic, he's convincing. So why couldn't they do an even better job with you? Produce a Gioia so real that even Gioia can't tell the difference? But a Gioia that will never age—a Gioia-construct, a Gioia-program, a visitor-Gioia! Why not? Tell me why not, Gioia."

She was trembling. "I've never heard of doing any such thing!"

"But don't you think it's possible?"

"How would I know?"

"Of course it's possible. If they can create visitors, they can take a citizen and duplicate her in such a way that—"

"It's never been done. I'm sure of it. I can't imagine any citizen agreeing to any such thing. To give up the body—to let yourself be turned into—into—"

She shook her head, but it seemed to be a gesture of astonishment as much as of negation.

He said, "Sure. To give up the body. Your natural body, your aging, shrinking, deteriorating short-timer body. What's so awful about that?"

She was very pale. "This is craziness, Charles. I don't want to talk about it any more."

"It doesn't sound crazy to me."

"You can't possibly understand."

"Can't I? I can certainly understand being afraid to die. I don't have a lot of trouble understanding what it's like to be one of the few aging people in a world where nobody grows old. What I can't understand is why you aren't even willing to consider the possibility that—"

"No," she said. "I tell you, it's crazy. They'd laugh at me."

"Who?"

"All of my friends. Hawk, Stengard, Aramayne—" Once again she would not look at him. "They can be very cruel, without even realizing it. They despise anything that seems ungraceful to them, anything sweaty and desperate and cowardly. Citizens don't do sweaty things, Charles. And that's how this will seem. Assuming it can be done at all. They'll be terribly patronizing. Oh, they'll be sweet to me, yes, dear Gioia, how wonderful for you, Gioia, but when I turn my back they'll laugh. They'll say the most wicked things about me. I couldn't bear that."

"They can afford to laugh," Phillips said. "It's easy to be brave and cool about dying when you know you're going to live forever. How very fine for them; but why should you be the only one to grow old and die? And they won't laugh, anyway. They're not as cruel as you think. Shallow, maybe, but not cruel. They'll be glad that you've found a way to save yourself. At the very least, they won't have to feel guilty about you any longer, and that's bound to please them. You can—"

"Stop it," she said.

She rose, walked to the railing of the patio, stared out toward the sea. He came up behind her. Red sails in the harbor, sunlight glittering along the sides of the Lighthouse, the palaces of the Ptolemies stark white against the sky. Lightly he rested his hand on her shoulder. She twitched as if to pull away from him, but remained where she was.

"Then I have another idea," he said quietly. "If you won't go to the planners, *I* will. Reprogram me, I'll say. Fix things so that I start to age at the same rate you do. It'll be more authentic, anyway, if I'm supposed to be playing the part of a twentieth-century man. Over the years I'll very gradually get some lines in my face, my hair will turn gray, I'll walk a little more slowly—we'll grow old together, Gioia. To hell with your lovely immortal friends. We'll have each other. We won't need them."

She swung around. Her eyes were wide with horror.

"Are you serious, Charles?"

"Of course."

"No," she murmured. "No. Everything you've said to me today is monstrous nonsense. Don't you realize that?"

He reached for her hand and enclosed her fingertips in his. "All I'm trying to do is find some way for you and me to—"

"Don't say any more," she said. "Please." Quickly, as though drawing back from a suddenly flaring flame, she tugged her fingers free of his and put her hand behind her. Though his face was just inches from hers he felt an immense chasm opening between them. They stared at one another for a moment; then she moved deftly to his left, darted around him, and ran from the patio.

Stunned, he watched her go, down the long marble corridor and out of sight. It was folly to give pursuit, he thought. She was lost to him: that was clear, that was beyond any question. She was terrified of him. Why cause her even more anguish? But somehow he found himself running through the halls of the hotel, along the winding garden path, into the cool green groves of the Paneium. He thought he saw her on the portico of Hadrian's palace, but when he got there the echoing stone halls were empty. To a temporary that was sweeping the steps he said, "Did you see a woman come this way?" A blank sullen stare was his only answer.

Phillips cursed and turned away.

"Gioia?" he called. "Wait! Come back!"

Was that her, going into the Library? He rushed past the startled mumbling librarians and sped through the stacks, peering beyond the mounds of double-handled scrolls into the shadowy corridors. "Gioia? *Gioia!*" It was a desecration, bellowing like that in this quiet place. He scarcely cared.

Emerging by a side door, he loped down to the harbor. The Lighthouse! Terror enfolded him. She might already be a hundred steps up that ramp, heading for the parapet from which she meant to fling herself into the sea. Scattering citizens and temporaries as if they were straws, he ran within. Up he went, never pausing for breath, though his synthetic lungs were screaming for respite, his ingeniously designed heart was desperately pounding. On the first balcony he imagined he caught a glimpse of her, but he circled it without finding her. Onward, upward. He went to the top, to the beacon chamber itself: no Gioia. Had she jumped? Had she gone down one ramp while he was ascending the other? He clung to the rim and looked down, searching the base of the Lighthouse, the rocks offshore, the causeway. No Gioia. I will find her somewhere, he thought. I will keep going until I find her. He went running down the ramp, calling her name. He reached ground level and sprinted back toward the center of town. Where next? The temple of Poseidon? The tomb of Cleopatra?

He paused in the middle of Canopus Street, groggy and dazed.

"Charles?" she said.

"Where are you?"

"Right here. Beside you." She seemed to materialize from the air. Her face was unflushed, her robe bore no trace of perspiration. Had he been chasing a phantom through the city? She came to him and took his hand, and said, softly, tenderly, "Were you really serious, about having them make you age?"

"If there's no other way, yes."

"The other way is so frightening, Charles."

"Is it?"

"You can't understand how much."

"More frightening than growing old? Than dying?"

"I don't know," she said. "I suppose not. The only thing I'm sure of is that I don't want you to get old, Charles."

"But I won't have to. Will I?" He stared at her.

"No," she said. "You won't have to. Neither of us will."

Phillips smiled. "We should get away from here," he said after a while. "Let's go across to Byzantium, yes, Gioia? We'll show up in Constantinople for the opening. Your friends will be there. We'll tell them what you've decided to do. They'll know how to arrange it. Someone will."

"It sounds so strange," said Gioia. "To turn myself into— into a visitor? A visitor in my own world?"

"That's what you've always been, though."

"I suppose. In a way. But at least I've been *real* up to now."

"Whereas I'm not?"

"Are you, Charles?"

"Yes. Just as real as you. I was angry at first, when I found out the truth about myself. But I came to accept it. Somewhere between Mohenjo and here, I came to see that it was all right to be what I am: that I perceive things, I form ideas, I draw conclusions. I am very well designed, Gioia. I can't tell the difference between being what I am and being completely alive, and to me that's being real enough. I think, I feel, I experience joy and pain. I'm as real as I need to be. And you will be too. You'll never stop being Gioia, you know. It's only your body that you'll cast away, the body that played such a terrible joke on you anyway." He brushed her cheek with his hand. "It was said for us before, long ago:

> *Once out of nature I shall never take*
> *My bodily form from any natural thing,*
> *But such a form as Grecian goldsmiths make*
> *Of hammered gold and gold enamelling*
> *To keep a drowsy Emperor awake—*"

"Is that the same poem?" she asked.

"The same poem, yes. The ancient poem that isn't quite forgotten yet."

"Finish it, Charles."

 —*"Or set upon a golden bough to sing*
 To lords and ladies of Byzantium
 Of what is past, or passing, or to come."

"How beautiful. What does it mean?"

"That is isn't necessary to be mortal. That we can allow ourselves to be gathered into the artifice of eternity, that we can be transformed, that we can move on beyond the flesh. Yeats didn't mean it in quite the way I do—he wouldn't have begun to comprehend what we're talking about, not a word of it—and yet, and yet—the underlying truth is the same. Live, Gioia! With me!" He turned to her and saw color coming into her pallid cheeks. "It does make sense, what I'm suggesting, doesn't it? You'll attempt it, won't you? Whoever makes the visitors can be induced to remake you. Right? What do you think: can they, Gioia?"

She nodded in a barely perceptible way. "I think so," she said faintly. "It's very strange. But I think it ought to be possible. Why not, Charles? Why not?"

"Yes," he said. "Why not?"

In the morning they hired a vessel in the harbor, a low sleek pirogue with a blood-red sail, skippered by a rascally-looking temporary whose smile was irresistible. Phillips shaded his eyes and peered northward across the sea. He thought he could almost make out the shape of the great city sprawling on its seven hills, Constantine's New Rome beside the Golden Horn, the mighty dome of Hagia Sophia, the somber walls of the citadel, the palaces and churches, the Hippodrome, Christ in glory rising above all else in brilliant mosaic streaming with light.

"Byzantium," Phillips said. "Take us there the shortest and quickest way."

"It is my pleasure," said the boatman with unexpected grace.

Gioia smiled. He had not seen her looking so vibrantly alive since the night of the imperial feast in Chang-an. He reached for her hand—her slender fingers were quivering lightly—and helped her into the boat.

GHOST LECTURER

Ian Watson

"Ghost Lecturer" was purchased by Shawna McCarthy, and appeared in the March 1984 issue of IAsfm, with an interior illustration by Jim Odbert. Watson is known for his vivid and highly-original conceptualization, and "Ghost Lecturer" was no exception; in one of the oddest stories ever published in IAsfm, Watson brings a visitor from the distant past to the present, and thereby changes—quite literally—the way we see the world.

Ian Watson sold his first story in 1969, and first attracted widespread critical attention in 1973 with his first novel, The Embedding. *His novel* The Jonah Kit *won the British Science Fiction Award and the British Science Fiction Association Award in 1976 and 1977, respectively. Watson's other books include the novels* Alien Embassy, Miracle Visitors, The Book of the River, The Book of the Stars, The Book of Being, Gardens of Delight, *and* The Martian Inca, *and the collections* The Very Slow Time Machine, Sunstroke, *and* Slow Birds. *His most recent books are the novel*

Queenmagic, Kingmagic, *and the collection* Evil Water.
*Watson lives with his wife and daughter in a small
village in Northhamptonshire, in England.*

As soon as Lucretius materialized, stark naked, at the focus
of the Roseberry Field, one of the Institute technicians rushed
to drape a bathrobe round him. Another technician furnished
our ancient Roman with a pair of sandals.

It seems a genuine toga took at least half an hour to don; so
a bathrobe was the next best thing.

Then Jim Roseberry advanced to greet our honored guest
and explain the setup, in Latin. Jim really radiated benevolence—
you felt you could trust him. with those twinkling blue eyes,
that shambling gait, that wild halo of grizzling hair, he looked
like a friendly bear whose only wish was to hug you.

"Magister," he declared, "welcome! We of the future
salute you, who are about to die. With our science we have
plucked you from your deathbed, to honor your wisdom
. . ." And so on.

Titus Lucretius Carus stood listening, his head cocked. He
was a short skinny fellow with a crimped, tiered hairstyle
surmounting a large, lined forehead. His nose was long and
thin; lively brown eyes were encased in lugubrious lids.

He didn't *look* on the point of death, but of course Jim had
already explained to me the night before that in snatching a
dying man from the continuum and prolonging his dying
moment into seven days' life in the present, the Roseberry
Effect revitalized its subject thoroughly, for as long as he
remained with us.

Me, I'd originally suspected that the resurrectees weren't
real people at all but were more like a sort of ectoplasm, like
ghosts at séances. No, Jim had assured me; real flesh and
blood. And if I was a continuum topologist like him, I'd
understand why.

Real flesh and blood: that gave me an idea or two for livening things up. Because of course the problem facing us a the Network was that Roseberry's Memorial Laureate Lectures were simply *not* prime TV material. Naturally the first announcement of the Roseberry Effect and the fantastic piece of science behind it had been a sensation. But following it up was the problem. Charles Darwin was simply *not entertaining*, and as for the second resurrectee, Galileo . . . well, computer translating in that monotonous synthesized machine-speech is a real bromide, and we couldn't expect millions of viewers to rent hypno-teach equipment to learn medieval Italian. It was only the rumor that Jim was thinking of resurrecting Jesus Christ which persuaded us to buy TV rights to Lucretius, in order to get an option on subsequent resurrections. I mean, who cared about Lucretius or what he had to tell the world?

So here was I burdened with directing the show. We just *had* to concentrate on the personal angle: the week this old Roman would spend after his lecture, *en famille* with the Roseberry family. And already I knew it would be up to me to personalize his visit.

Once the initial shock was over, Lucretius approached this whole business of his resurrection with admirable composure—though from my point of view it wouldn't be so admirable if he kept his cool all week long.

So presently we all adjourned from the resurrection room with its power cables, continuum-matrix-engine and other doodahs, next door for a buffet of canapés, cookies, and cola prior to the guest lecture itself. . . .

. . . Which Muhammed and Carl dutifully filmed and recorded, while Lucretius held forth from the podium to an invited audience in Latin on Atomic theory and the nature of the universe. Obviously we would have to edit 99 or 100 percent of this out. My thoughts drifted to Tony, who was away at the Roseberry home elsewhere in the Institute grounds, fitting it up with auto-mini-cams and snoopy-mikes as per the checklist I'd handed him.

After a while I began watching Jim Roseberry; and noted

how slyly he smiled from time to time during the lecture, how knowingly he nodded.

It occurred to me that something wasn't quite kosher about Jim . . . .

Afterwards, when the audience of Nobel laureates and whatnot had departed, we walked back through the rhodo-dendrons towards the Roseberry residence, leaving the mirror-glass and concrete of the Institute behind: Jim and Lucretius and me. With Carl and Muhammed pacing us assiduously, taping every golden moment.

Lucretius mustn't have been used to our modern toe-grip style of sandal—or else delayed shock caught up with him—since we hadn't gone far before he stumbled and collided with me. I took the opportunity to slip my arm through his.

"Is it true you were driven mad by a love-potion?" I whispered. (This was something my researcher Karen had turned up, cheering me considerably. Our Roman reportedly had died raving mad, crazed by aphrodisiacs. Too, he had always been a manic depressive, forever flipping from ecstasy at the beauties of the world to gloomy horror at all the carnage in it. Though he had tried very hard to maintain a philosophical detachment.)

Jim overheard. "For God's sake!"

Lucretius eyed Jim with a pained expression. "Do you *still* believe in gods?"

Me, he continued to clutch. I guess my knee-boots, micro-shorts and halter must have turned him on. Goodness knows what he thought Muhammed was up to, bobbing about with his mini-cam. A black slave, fanning us?

Invited to dinner that first evening were two people from the afternoon audience: tubby Max Stein the astrophysicist, and particle physicist Ingrid Langholm wearing a full-length orange gown with organdy insets showing flesh discreetly. Our hostess, Martha Roseberry, was definitely a Rubens woman: portly and pink and powdered. Daughter Harmony Roseberry, an adolescent know-it-all, was plump too, and spotty, thanks to her addiction to greasy doughnuts. Mother and daughter both obviously regarded Jim as the next best thing to God.

Muhammed and Carl had gone off to the local motel; Tony was relegated to the kitchen, whence Machiko, the Japanese maid, served drinks and the products of the family's Filipino cook. Whenever Machiko came into the dining room, Lucretius inspected her oriental features in puzzlement. Finally, in the midst of the smoked salmon and asparagus, he enquired whether she was Egyptian—which sent Jim rushing off to his study, to return with a globe of the world: one more modern marvel to amaze our Roman with, to add to electric light, TV, and flush toilets.

And as I listened to Jim explain how we had explored and mapped every last inch of the earth, and even gone to the Moon, I began to understand what wasn't quite kosher about him.

It was like this: Jim's great scientific breakthrough was to yank past geniuses out of time, supposedly to honor them so they would know their lives had been worthwhile in the eyes of the future. But then he would go on to tell them—oh so kindly—where they had gone wrong or fallen short of the mark. And how much more we knew nowadays. "You almost got it right, boy! You were on the right track, and no mistake. Bravo! *But* . . ."

That was why he chose scientists to resurrect and host. An artist like Mozart or Shakespeare could never be upstaged; but a scientist could be—by superior knowledge. Thus Jim Roseberry became superior to Darwin, Galileo, and whoever else.

True, Lucretius was a poet, but he only wrote poetry in order to explain science. He was sort of the Carl Sagan of ancient Rome.

Beef Stroganoff with pilau rice was next. Max Stein devoured second and third helpings; but Lucretius only toyed with his food.

"How do you find your meal, Magister Lucretius?" Martha asked in Latin. (We had all spent a night with the hypno equipment, of course.)

"Bitter," he replied. "Sour."

She passed the salt cellar. Harmony demonstrated its use. Lucretius tasted and grimaced.

"Do the rough atoms tear your tongue?" asked Jim with a twinkle in his eye.

The Burgundy was a success, though.

During the dessert (lemon mousse—and a doughnut for Harmony) conversation turned to electrons and quarks, and the Big Bang. Ingrid Langholm proved rather ingenious at coining Latin words to explain what happens when you split the unsplittable. Coffee and Cognac followed; and Lucretius began to frown and ask for more Cognac. He was still keeping his cool; but for how long? I was next to him; I rubbed my bare leg against his bathrobe, innocently. (Tonight was too soon. Perhaps the next night . . .)

That was when I heard thunder. Jim jumped up and went to part the drapes. Outside the night was black and moonless, and no stars showed. A wind seemed to be rising. "Dirty weather brewing," he told Max and Ingrid.

Max consulted his watch and sprang up. "I'd better be going!" He stuck his hand out at Lucretius. "A real pleasure to talk with you, Magister!"

"Me too," said Ingrid, also rising.

Lucretius stared at Max's offered hand. "That's all right. I don't wish to go outside to vomit."

"Goodness!" exclaimed Martha.

"Roman feasts were so gutsy, Mom," said Harmony, "the diners usually had to vomit between courses."

"Was this a feast?" asked Lucretius. "I admired its moderation, if not its flavor."

"Well, I never!" Martha said.

And so the party broke up.

I spent a scary night in one of the guest rooms. That storm kept circling round and waking me. Every hour or so, fresh bouts of thunder erupted and lightning flashes squeezed through the drapes. Most of the time, a real banshee of a wind howled. Occasionally I thought I heard a cry or owl-screech. I felt *edgy,* and burrowed deep under the duvet, even if it over-heated me.

When I got up the next morning, the wind was still wild. Enormous cloud galleons scudded through the sky, sail piled on sail high up to the stratosphere.

My bedroom window looked on to woodland which hid us from the highway. Amidst the general gray-green I noticed something brightly orange.

Suddenly it seemed as if the area of trees I was staring at, well, *threw* itself at me—shucking off veil after veil which flew towards me. I felt the impact of each thin copy of the scene like a physical blow upon my eyes. What I was looking at was *radiating* its surface at me. For a moment I thought I was having a flashback to an acid trip, years ago. But then I focussed on that orange patch.

It was Ingrid Langholm, and she was halfway up a tree!

Was this a hallucination? It didn't seem to be.

I dressed quickly, and went to rouse Tony and Jim Roseberry too. If Ingrid had spent the whole night up in a tree in a storm, she must have had a damn good reason.

When we got back to the house, supporting a bedraggled, worn-out particle physicist, Martha Roseberry was outdoors too, in her housecoat, ignoring the wild weather. Lucretius had also emerged, in his bathrobe.

"Whatever happened?" squawked Martha.

"Front wheel gave out," gasped Ingrid. "I had a flat."

"Her chariot wheel gave out," Jim said in Latin, mindful of his duties as host.

"No flashlight with me . . . So I started walking back . . . and a goddam *lion*—"

"A lion chased her up a tree. It kept prowling about."

"Lions fear the cry of a cockerel," remarked Lucretius, sagely.

"Eh?" from Martha.

"So it would flee at dawn. Pigs shun perfume and marjoram, lions fear a rooster." Lucretius regarded poor Ingrid with dour satisfaction. Her gown was torn and sodden. Her makeup had all run. Her hair was in rats' tails. She looked a bleary ragbag.

Just then, Ingrid's face detached itself and flew at mine— time and again. It was as if she wore an infinity of masks, which each peeled off in turn and flew through the air, without in any way diminishing her. Martha, too, rubbed her eyes in disbelief.

But Jim was too busy staring up at the wild and roiling sky. He pointed shakily. A giant face was grinning down at us from the side of the cloud. It became a snarling lion's head, then dissolved, dripping like wax.

"Did you see *that?*"

"Flimsy films of vision sometimes generate themselves spontaneously in the sky," Lucretius said helpfully.

As though this wasn't bad enough, at that moment two neighboring Douglas firs suddenly burst into flames. Jim rounded on Lucretius.

"Oh, and what's the reason for *that,* then?"

"Why, wind rubs the trees together. Friction enflames them."

By now the steady rain of blows from the wind was dislodging the atoms of my mind and body from their station so fast that I felt I hadn't slept at all the night before. I'd lost a lot of density and I needed food to fill the cracks. (And part of me asked another part, "What the hell am I thinking? Blows? Dislodged atoms? Loss of density?") My limbs tottered. I didn't notice the snake sneaking through the grass till Tony shouted, "Look out!"

Hastily I jogged my vital spirit, to get it to jog my body aside. (I did . . . *what?*) Lucretius spat casually at the snake. Instantly the serpent writhed around and bit its own tail, stinging itself to death.

Lucretius clucked in satisfaction. "Luckily it's one of those which human spittle poisons."

I was reeling. And in the furnace of colliding clouds, seeds of fire were being crammed together. A thunderbolt burst forth and smashed into the ground quite near us.

"What the hell's going on?" cried Tony.

"I need some breakfast urgently," I told Martha. "Please! I've lost too many atoms. My vital spirit will quit."

"Are you into some new kind of therapy?" Martha asked, baffled.

"We'd better get inside fast," advised Jim.

We breakfasted on waffles with maple syrup; the smoothly trickling particles of syrup seemed to please Lucretius's palate. Soon the storm was on the wane.

Jim gazed across the table at me balefully. "What's happening? I'll tell you what's happening. Those 'films' you see flying off surfaces and hitting your eyes—that's how our friend here thought vision worked. And now we're seeing it happen, as though it's true. All the crazy rest of it, too! His world-view is affecting us. Somehow it's . . . projecting itself. And I'll tell you why. It's because you sexed him up! On account of how you're dressed. Or undressed!"

"So what's wrong with shorts and a halter? I'm not exactly nude with body paint!"

"I watched you at dinner. You caused the onset of a love-frenzy."

"A what?" asked Harmony.

Martha said mildly, "Do you think we should be discussing this in front of our guest?"

"Aw, the hell with that."

I spoke from the depths of me. I cut sounds into words with my tongue and molded them with my lips. (At least that's what it felt like.) "The hell with my costume and morals, too! *How* is this happening to us?"

"It's his world-view taken literally—and taken to extremes . . . . This must be an aspect of the Roseberry Effect I hadn't taken into account. With Darwin and even Galileo we were on the same general wavelength. The modern scientific world-view," Jim mumbled.

I just had to laugh. "So instead of *you* wising Lucretius up, he's changing things to suit his own half-baked ancient notions? Oh, that's too rich!"

Jim went white. "I'm going to make some phone calls. Excuse me."

Harmony looked daggers at me, then rushed out of the room after him. I hoped the mini-cams and snoopy-mikes were working okay, getting all this taped.

While Jim was away, Ingrid, wrapped in a spare bathrobe, drank a lot of hot coffee. After a while Lucretius coughed, to clear his throat of sticky atoms, I suppose.

"Indeed I must confess that I felt love-frenzy coming over me. Will we never reach a state of equanimity? Will we never heed the Master's word?"

"The Master?" asked Ingrid.

"Epicurus."

"Oh."

"And yet . . . if one concentrates on the defects of a woman, however fair at first she seems . . ." He looked steadfastly at Ingrid, who resembled a drowned rat after her night out; and I realized to my chagrin that Lucretius had been more excited by *her* than by me.

Maybe that was just as well! Otherwise I might have been the one who was trashed. Still, the snake had been heading for me . . . I could almost imagine myself swelling up and raving, the black flux pouring from my bowels . . . . Where were such notions coming from? I *must not* think along those lines!

Presently Jim returned, followed by Harmony. "The phone's okay. Those little atoms still rush along the wires. The effect's quite local." He sat down, though he wouldn't meet my eyes at first—because I had seen through him. "I've been thinking."

"So have I," said Ingrid. "If Jesus Christ were here instead of Lucretius—if this were *His* Second Coming—then we could experience joy and peace and true love. For a while. In one little corner of the world."

Oh beautiful! thought I. Bless you, Ingrid. Press that button again. I'd been trying to get on to the business of resurrecting Jesus, but whenever I broached the subject Jim had neatly evaded it—till I suspected that maybe he had begun the rumor himself, just to get hold of a fancy chunk of TV money for the Institute.

Ingrid blushed. "I guess I was praying a bit last night. Old habit, long forgotten. It kept me company."

And maybe it wouldn't be so beautiful, after all! Lucretius was an unreligious man. Would we want real archangels flying about . . . and Satan knocking on the door in person?

"As I say," resumed Jim, "this is a local problem. Reality has become a little unhinged in our friend's vicinity. And definitely more plastic. His imagination is molding it—and he always had a strong imagination! As to *why* exactly, it's too soon to say. We'll have to put our heads together at the Institute. But for my money I'd say it's a function of how far we've gone into the past this time. Apparently the further back we pluck a fellow from, the more we loosen the continuum. Don't worry, it'll bounce back afterwards."

"After he goes home," said Harmony, rather grimly.

"Meanwhile we'll have to watch our step. Avoid exciting him too much."

"Who," asked Lucretius, "is Jesus Christ?"

"Ah. Um. Long story, that," said Jim. "I guess you could call him a teacher. Like Epicurus."

"He was the Son of God," said Ingrid, with eyes downcast.

"A god?" cried Lucretius irritably. "Then maybe *I'm* a god, if I can produce storms and thunderbolts? But I have already pointed out in persuasive verse that this is nonsense. Lightning strikes where it wills! Do you mock me?"

"No, no," Jim hastily assured him. "It's just that reality is a bit more complicated than you thought. . . . Look," he said, with an effort at bonhomie, "it's brightening. Let's all go for a walk on the grounds. That'll clear our heads." He switched to English briefly. "I'll fetch my hunting rifle. Just in case. I'll pretend it's a walking stick." And in Latin: "We won't meet any more lions, will we, Magister?"

Lucretius was offended. "*I'm* not responsible for hallucinations. Wild beasts are sometimes seen when none are there, because the mind is constantly beset by images; and if a person happens to be afraid, and thinking of wild beasts—

perhaps because her chariot has broken down at night—then from these images the mind selects . . ."

"Sure, sure," said Jim. "We won't think of lions, will we? Not any of us! We'll think of nice things: like flowers, and poetry. We'll walk down by the lake. Feed the geese. That's always soothing. Fetch some doughnuts for the birds," he told Harmony.

Jim hustled us outdoors rapidly, so that I hadn't any time to summon Carl and Muhammed from the motel; though Tony came along, with a mini-cam hastily mounted on one shoulder and a snoopy-mike fixed to the other. Ingrid had flaked out by now and was being put to bed by Martha. So five of us set out: me, Tony, Lucretius, Jim, and his daughter.

The wind had dropped. Clouds were evaporating quickly. As we stepped out of the house, suddenly the sun shone forth. Unfortunately I glanced up at it—and a film of solar disc hit my face with force. Particles of fire scorched my eyeballs. "The sun!" I yelped. "Don't anyone look at it!" It was a whole minute before I regained my vision, and even then my eyes remained untrustworthy; they kept watering and unfocusing. Tony helped me along for a while, but I shook him off. I wanted him filming, not guiding me as once Antigone led blind Oedipus.

On our way to the lake we passed through woods, which were moist and warm. The sunlight dappling down was genial, here.

What I took at first to be a giant puffball sprouting from the loam suddenly split open as we drew abreast of it—to disgorge a bleating baby goat. The young kid tottered to a nearby bump on the ground, from which white liquid began leaking. Splay-legged, the kid grabbed hold of this bump with its mouth and sucked greedily. Yes indeed, suckling milk from a breast of the earth!

The bump just had to be a nipple. Which meant that the puffball, now collapsed, must have been . . . not a fungus but a rooted womb!

We stared in amazement as a kid grew apace. Soon it was

grazing contentedly on poisonous hellebore which had sprung up nearby.

Lucretius frowned, and tutted.

"How odd. In the late, decaying state of the world nowadays, only worms and animalcules should be generated spontaneously from the soil. This is exceptional."

"Isn't it just?" snapped Jim.

"And if goats can get born from the soil," broke in Harmony, "why not lions as well? Gee, Dad, *anything* could pop up. This is scary." Oddly, though, the prospect didn't seem to scare her, so much—how can I put it?—as to encourage her.

Lucretius shook his head. "I still maintain the lion must have been a hallucination. One must always select the most *reasonable* explanation of phenomena. Though in this case—"

"Oh, shut up," Jim growled softly. Yet just then (when I thought back on it) he too looked oddly content.

And we carried on.

The lake was circled by lawns. Our group was still in treeshade, but all before us the sunlight was blazing down. (I took care not to look anywhere near the sun again, but one thing I remembered about it was that it had seemed to be only a few miles away—and no larger than it looked.) The rainfall of the night before was steaming off the grass. At that moment I could see quite clearly.

A flock of Canada geese came winging in towards the water. One moment they were flying blithely along; the next they were tumbling out of the sky. Falling like rocks on to the lawn. Thump, thump. Dead as ducks.

For one mad instant I thought Jim must have shouldered his gun and zapped the geese in an incredible—and silent—display of marksmanship. But no; he was still tapping the ground with the rifle butt, like the old man in the riddle of the Sphinx.

"And *what*, Magister," Jim asked icily, "is the cause of that? I *liked* those birds."

"Ah . . ." Lucretius scratched his chin. "A vacuum must have formed, you see. The ground has been rotted by unseasonable rain, and now it is pelted with sunbeams. Consequently a foul effluence rises, expelling all the air above."

"Of course! How stupid of me! What other explanation could there be?"

Lucretius regarded the phenomenon equably. "We must believe the evidence of our senses, as interpreted by Reason. I have a question, though."

"Ask away."

Thump, thump. A trio of mallards slapped on to the lawn.

"By use of Reason, I discovered the causes of pestilence: pestiferous clouds of atoms uncongenial to us, which fly about. Yet different air in different lands breeds characteristic diseases. Thus elephantiasis is only found in Egypt, while gout is native to Attica. Tell me, what is the characteristic disease of this land, America?"

"Cancer and heart disease mostly," remarked Tony, who was otherwise occupied with the occasional tumbling bird.

"Jesus, what did you tell him that for? Magister, disease is *not* caused by atoms in the air. Well, usually it isn't. . . ."

"Maybe it is, around this neck of the woods." Tony pointed. "Here come more kamikaze birdies."

At this point my eyes blurred, as if they had just been attacked by cataract-causing atoms. I heard Harmony scream, "A monster!" I heard the bang of the rifle. Then a thump.

"Holy Moses," I head Tony cry. "You've shot him."

My vision swam back to normal. Jim was standing with his rifle at the slope. Harmony had her hands over her mouth in a theatrical show of shock; she had dropped all the doughnuts. Lucretius lay sprawled on his back, looking very dead.

"Did you *see* that monster?" babbled Harmony. "It was breathing *fire!* My Daddy saved us!"

"What do you mean, *saved?*" said Tony. "The bullet hit Mr. Lucretius."

"What a terrible accident," said Jim. "Oh, this is awful. I hope you got it all on film."

"Of course I didn't! I was looking over there. I didn't see any monster."

"It was like a lion," said Harmony. "But worse. It breathed fire. Now it's gone."

"Did *you* see anything?" Tony asked me. I shook my head.

But I had the gravest suspicions that Jim Rosenberry had just killed Titus Lucretius Carus deliberately. Out of almighty pique at how he, Jim, had been upstaged.

He must have thought this was was the perfect murder, too. For how can you be guilty of murder when your victim already died two thousand years ago?

Well, there was quite some fuss then. We rushed back to the house, where Jim monopolized the phone for a while. Soon as I could, I called Carl and Muhammed at the motel; and a bit later a police captain and a lieutenant arrived in a Buick, all lit up and screaming—just beating the Network minibus by a short head.

However, Jim must already have been calling in a favor or two before he even called the police to report the fatality, since the two officers were so respectful and apologetic; and what's more, even as we were all heading back down to the lakeside, they were already deciding that the matter was right outside their jurisdiction.

And Jim was nodding so concernedly and saying that on scientific grounds the body *would* really have to be rushed back to the Institute for dematerialization; though he had felt it his duty as a citizen, et cetera.

When we got to the lake, Institute staff were already standing by with a stretcher. After asking the bare minimum of questions, the captain and lieutenant waved the body on its way; and departed.

Dead Lucretius departed too. To return to his own time. Back where he was already on the point of death. So nobody back in ancient times would notice any real difference; except maybe that Lucretius now had a hole in his chest. If he had indeed stabbed himself to death, crazed by a love-potion, this mightn't look too odd. Or maybe the murder, up in our present day, was what *caused* the tale of suicide? Even if nobody back in the past could locate a knife—since there wasn't one. . . .

Very neat, Jim!

Except, it wasn't neat at all.

As I was the first to notice, while we headed for the Institute in the wake of the corpse, when Jim's face suddenly unpeeled and flew at my eyes several times.

"Hey!" cried Carl, staring at *my* face in alarm.

I tapped Jim on the arm. "Notice something?"

"You mean, the effect still continuing. Hmm, I thought it would fade as soon as he died—"

"Did you just?"

He flushed. "So instead, it'll go away when we get rid of the body. Be *very* careful what you imply."

"Oh, I will be careful, don't you worry."

And so we all saw Lucretius off, six days early, from the resurrection room accompanied by crackling air and sparks and a little sonic boom. And our show had gone down the drain, thought I.

But on our way back through the rhododendrons afterwards, to the Roseberry house, I thought I heard the distant roar of a lion.

"Just thunder," Jim said dismissively, and scanned the sky.

He froze, ashen. For up on the side of the nearest cloud hung a familiar face. The cloud-mouth of Lucretius opened and dripped red blood like a sunset, before dissolving.

So the effect hadn't gone away, after all. It stayed, and I could guess why. It was because Lucretius died here in the present. His vital spirit had already flavored the environment in a most exaggerated manner, courtesy of the Roseberry Effect and its derangement of space-time. Him being killed here, this feature was locked in. All that Jim sent back to ancient times was a lump of meat.

The grounds of the Institute were haunted now. Meteorologically, optically, psychologically *haunted*.

Storms broke out. Trees burst into flames. Birds plunged from the sky from time to time. Phantom images flew about. Faces appeared on clouds. Love-frenzies possessed people.

One thing was for sure: the reputation of Lucretius endured in the modern world. Jim had seen to that. A couple of square miles were definitely Lucretian.

Ironically enough, Lucretius himself always poured scorn on the idea of life after death. As I discovered when I read *The Nature of the Universe* not long after.

I also discovered that our Roman never believed in fire-breathing monsters. "If fire burns all known animals, even lions," he argued, very rationally, "then no animal can ever breathe fire." Harmony went right over the top there. Which only proves how she conspired, hastily, with her daddy. They must have loved it when they saw that kid goat born from the puffball womb.

And at one point the Lucretius Zone overlapped the grounds a bit, and slopped over a stretch of state highway. Since nobody can drive safely when images might zap their eyes, this effectively rendered the highway unusable. And some real estate was hexed, too. So Jim was in trouble.

Not trouble as a murderer, of course. As I said, you can't murder a dead man. But soon he would be hit by suits for damages from neighboring residents whose property values had crashed; not to mention the highway authority, who were going to have to build a very costly detour.

Those members of the Institute who hadn't fled were busy studying the new Roseberry Effect—of disordered reality. One thing they quickly found was that the old Roseberry Effect was blocked by the haunting. So there would be no more resurrections at the Institute.

One morning Jim phoned me at the Network. He sounded stressed.

"It occurs to me," he said, "that you could shoot a damn fine horror movie here in the Roseberry Zone." (He didn't, of course, refer to it as the Lucretius Zone.) "I mean, we have a genuine *phenomenon* here."

"Do you really think anyone would want to act in *there*, when they could catch instant plague or be smeared by thunderbolts?"

"So do your location shooting here—build your script around the phenomena. Then find somewhere else that's similar-looking, but safe, for the actors." He was almost pleading.

"Do I hear the rattle of an almost empty money box?"

"Look, it'll stir up a lot more interest than laureate lectures. Or even a real live sermon by Jesus, and seeing how he uses the bathroom."

"Ah, but we can't host Jesus now. Not any longer. And frankly I wouldn't want to. In fact, I'd personally whip up a real campaign to block any such proposal. *No*, Jim. But let me give you a bit of advice, out of the pure kindness of my heart. Get out of there fast."

"What?"

"Take to your heels. I know that you murdered Lucretius—and his zone knows it, too. It's just biding its time."

Oh yes. Pretty soon it would trap Jim Roseberry in a nasty doom. Worse than any lawsuits. Perhaps that doom would be such as overwhelmed the Athenians with loathsome ulcers and malignant fluxes of foul blood, descending to the groin, so that some men only saved their lives by self-castration, while other victims completely forgot who they were. As Lucretius reveals in the gory and psychotic climax to *The Nature of the Universe*.

"You're out of your mind," said Jim.

"No, you're *into his* mind. Slap in the midst of all his cockeyed ideas, exaggerated and made real."

Of course, Jim wouldn't listen. Was he not the custodian of a profound natural mystery?

Really, all that poor old Lucretius ever wanted out of life was peace and quiet. So resurrecting him had been a fairly unkind cut. But resurrecting him, then murdering him had been the unkindest cut of all. No wonder Lucretius died raving mad—mad at Jim.

A week after that, a snake bit Harmony—though she did recover, away from the Zone in intensive care.

A fortnight subsequent, the Roseberry house was struck by a thunderbolt and burned down. So Jim moved into the Institute, to camp out.

Just yesterday I heard how Jim has caught, yes, plague. And a Lucretian plague isn't very pleasant. But you can't say I didn't warn him.

HAUNTINGS

Kim Antieau

*"Hauntings" was purchased by Shawna McCarthy,
and appeared in the February 1985 issue of* IAsfm,
*with an interior illustration by Janet Aulisio. Lyrical
and—dare I say—haunting, "Hauntings" marked the
debut of a talented new writer, and also gave us a
fascinating new perspective on the classical ghost
story.*

New writer Kim Antieau has sold to The Twilight
Zone Magazine, *and* Shadows, *in addition to* IAsfm.
*She is at work on her first novel, and lives in Tucson,
Arizona.*

Kate awakened to the sound of her name being whispered in
her ear, to the feel of warm breath on her cheek. She let the
dream ebb away, taking with it the sound and warmth before
she opened her eyes to darkness.

"Kate," the whisperer said again, sighing, settling and creaking as all houses do in the quiet of night.

Still not fully awake, Kate switched on the light over her bed. Eerie shadows gave way to reveal her ordinary bedroom: faded peach wallpaper, painted ceramic light fixtures, jeans and shirt strewn on a chair, a black and white television set. The sound was gone.

She took a drink of water from the glass that was always on the night stand. She drank a great deal of water now, as if it could wash her clean if she drank enough of it. She yawned and settled back against her pillow. The whispering didn't frighten her. She had grown accustomed to the occasional noises in the two weeks she had lived in the nineteenth-century farmhouse. They were almost company to her.

Except now they were disturbing her sleep even more than usual. She liked her time in her dreams. In them, she was usually well, whole; no one had taken a knife to her, no one had injected poisons into her.

She turned the light off. In the morning, she supposed, she'd have to find out why the house talked to her.

"Can I help you find anything, Mrs. Hein?" the librarian asked. Kate looked up and smiled. Everyone in Canyons insisted on calling her Mrs. even though her last name was different from her husband's. All they knew was that she was married, so she was Mrs. Hein to them.

"Call me Kate, please," Kate said, closing the book in front of her. "Maybe you can help. Do you know anything about the Nelson farmhouse?"

"You mean the house you bought?" he asked, sitting down next to her. On this sunny Monday afternoon, the library was empty except for Kate and the librarian. "It's been researched extensively by our historical society—of which I am a member. It hasn't been declared a historical landmark or anything—not architecturally unique enough—but it is one of our older homes. The society has pictures of it and of the people who lived in it. Their office is just across the courtyard."

"Before I bought it had the Nelsons always owned it?"

He shook his head. "It was built by a family from back East in the 1890s. They had money and decided to come here and get back to nature."

"People were doing that back then, too, eh?" Kate said, laughing. One of the reasons she had moved to Canyons was because there was no industry, no waste dumps, and plenty of land to grow her own food.

"I can't remember their names, something simple though," he said. "They owned it for about fifty years. Then they sold it to a distant cousin and moved back to New York. This cousin married a Nelson and it was kept in their family after that. They overfarmed the land, though, and they couldn't make any money, so they finally left. It was up for sale two years before you bought it."

"Any rumors of unusual happenings?" Kate asked.

The librarian glanced at her books *Poltergeists* and *Hauntings*.

"Nary a word," he said, "and I would have heard. It seems it was quite a happy home."

"Any Indian burial grounds nearby?"

The librarian laughed and stood up. "Nope. We didn't have Indians in that area. You're going to have to settle with just your run-of-the-mill ordinary house."

"Thanks." She turned back to her stack of books and magazines and he went back to the check-out counter. Leafing through one of the magazines, the headline "Laetrile: Hope of the Future" caught her attention. She quickly turned the page. She never wanted to see another cancer article. When she had first found out she had cancer, she had read them all—after the initial frightened vomiting ended and the terrified night sweats lessened in frequency. For a time, she had thought about going the "natural" route, healing with foods and state of mind. In the end, she decided she couldn't trust her mind not to make the disease worse, so she had allowed surgery and chemotherapy.

She pushed away from the table and quickly left the library. Anger whirled around her as she stepped into the sunshine; the anger swelled in her and turned into fear. They said she was free of cancer now. What did they know? In twenty years when she was just over fifty, she would probably get cancer from the chemo and have to go through it all over again. She shivered and pulled the sweater closer to her. The house. She had to concentrate on the house. She crossed the courtyard and went toward the historical society office.

"Can I come for a visit soon?" Jeff asked over the phone. "It's been two weeks, Katie. I miss you."

"I thought you had an assignment," Kate said. She pulled the long telephone cord around with her as she walked from one end of the huge farm kitchen to the other. It was an uneconomical space, but the painted blue walls and the Dutch ceramic tiles made her feel cozy. The white cupboards stretched to the ceiling and Kate envisioned shelf upon shelf of Kerr canning jars filled with peaches, apples, tomatoes.

"Winter has set in there early this year," Jeff said, "so they canceled it until spring."

"Spring?" Kate said, taking the tea kettle off the burner. The piercing whistle slowly hiccoughed to a stop. "That's six months."

"Yeah," he said. "Maybe by then you'll want to come back to work. Hint, hint."

Kate stopped moving. "I'm through, Jeff. Period. I like it here." There was silence on the other end. "Whatsamatter, don't you like your new partner?" she joked.

"He's not fun to cuddle with and he's not my partner," he said. "You and I are still under contract."

That much was true; they owed their publisher three books. She had been writing the texts and Jeff had been taking the photographs for their travel books since before they left college. They had just started branching out into more naturalistic settings (versus tourist spots) when Kate had gotten sick.

"I love you," he said. He sighed. "If you still need time alone, I understand."

She bit the inside of her cheek so she wouldn't cry. They had never been apart for this long, and even though it was her choice and it was temporary, she missed him.

"Come this weekend," she said.

*   *   *

Kate liked the house. In some ways it reminded her of her childhood—though when she really thought about it, she knew it was her father's childhood it reminded her of. She didn't want to think about her own past. What she had believed had been an idyllic child's life now seemed tainted with all the things that should have been done: her parents should have fed her better foods, they shouldn't have put her through the stress of a custody battle when she was a teenager, and they should have known they lived two miles from the most toxic waste dump in the state. She leaned back in the chair, stretching her legs across the table. It made her too angry, the past, because there was not a thing she could do about it. It was just a compilation of "ifs."

The house shifted, and Kate let all thoughts of her past slip away. It was the house's past she was interested in now. The library and the historical society had not given her any clues as to why the house made noises; perhaps the house itself could.

"The attic," she said, dropping her feet from the coffee table and standing up. She glanced out the window at the fading light, wondering if she wanted to go into the attic at night, especially the attic of a haunted house. Heroines of horror novels were often doing things just like this and she'd always thought they were a bit stupid. She laughed; the sound vibrated around her, as if the walls were enjoying the sound. Kate was not afraid of the house; and she was not a heroine.

The attic was brightly lit by a line of fluorescent lights a previous owner had installed. Except for a worktable and several boxes strewn in different corners, the room was empty. What little there was of Kate's things was still downstairs. Between buying the house and maintaining an apartment in the city, they had had little money left over for her to buy furnishings.

Kate knelt on the floor and began examining the boxes. Two of them were filled with moth-eaten clothes. Another box contained homemade Christmas decorations.

"Bingo," Kate said as she opened the last box and began

taking out papers. Twenty-year-old grocery and utility bills. She dug deeper and found several letters. All were newsy, chatty letters from relatives asking the Nelsons about their rural life. At the bottom of the box were three letters written by Agatha Nelson to Aunt Betty Carens which had never been mailed: "The new calf is doing better. . . . We need rain. . . . The cows got loose in the alfalfa patch and gorged themselves." Folded in with Agatha's third letter was a faded page written in someone else's hand: ". . . Look what I found in the attic," Agatha had written. "Nellie Smith was one of the original owners. Please return this to me. . . ."

Smiths and Nelsons. The all-American farmhouse. Nellie Smith's letter was like a piece of a diary, addressed to no one in particular. She described the farm and then the house: "The house is completed now, and we are settled in. I love it here away from the city. It is still in this house as if there is no past or future, just now—or as if it were all one time and what happened or will does not matter . . ."

Kate smiled and tucked the letter into her pocket to show to Jeff later. Perhaps one day she would develop Nellie's philosophy and none of it would matter to her either. She switched off the lights and went down the stairs.

"You're too ordinary," Kate said. "Maybe that's why you're haunted."

She brought herbal tea and peanut butter cookies up to her bedroom and turned on a romantic comedy from the fifties. She skimmed through the book on hauntings. It told her nothing new. Dead people haunted houses. Period.

She snapped the book shut and opened the one on poltergeists. They were usually short-term phenomena revolving around one person, often a troubled adolescent. It had not occurred to her that she could be causing the sounds, that perhaps it was all in her head. She was not a troubled teenager, but she was not a particularly happy adult.

When Kate awakened that night, the only noise she heard was coming from the marsh pond over her back hill. She sat up and drank from her glass. The clock read 2:45.

Feeling irritable, Kate got out of bed and went downstairs. She had not slept through an entire night in nearly two years.

She took an orange from the refrigerator and went into the living room and sank into her chair. Through the open curtains, she could see the back yard, touched with a bit of fairyland by the moonlight.

"Kate," the room whispered.

Kate sat up straight and looked around the room. It was bathed in a white glow—moonlight—and something else in the middle of the room.

Shimmering half there and half not was a woman. Kate blinked. The woman appeared to be sitting, her arms outstretched, her hands flat against something. Her image wavered, and Kate thought she saw someone else sitting next to her. The image faded and was gone.

Kate sat very still for a long while. When the clock chimed four, she went back upstairs.

The next morning, Kate was still not frightened, and it puzzled her. Normal everyday Janes did not see ghosts. Perhaps the chemo had fried her brain a bit, or it had opened it up for new experiences. She took a long walk on her property and then spent the rest of the day putting the house into order. She could hardly wait until it was dark.

After supper, she read a book to put her to sleep and was not surprised to come awake just before 3:00.

She hurried downstairs and sat in her chair, waiting for the woman in white, concentrating only on seeing her. Then, as if it were quite natural, the woman was there again. This time, as she came into view, Kate saw she really wasn't wearing white, there was just a glow around her body. The image wavered and solidified. Five people sat around a table, their hands joined. She didn't recognize any of them from the photos she'd seen of the Smiths and Nelsons.

"Kate? Are you there?" the whisperer said. The woman looked up, her head moving as if in slow motion, the white glow shaking and then becoming still when she stopped.

They looked as though they were having a seance. Kate remembered holding seances on overnight camping trips when she'd been a Girl Scout. It had been an excuse to giggle and scream. These people looked quite serious. And they were calling her? It couldn't be. They were the ghosts; she was alive. It had to be another Kate.

Hesitating, Kate got up from her chair and moved closer.

"I can feel something," one of them whispered, the words floating through the house like a breeze through autumn-dried leaves.

"Kate, if you're there, give us a sign," the dark-haired woman said.

Kate giggled, a Girl Scout again.

"I am here," she said.

The woman nodded, as if she'd expected it all along.

"How are you, Kate Hein?" the woman asked.

Startled, Kate stopped walking around the circle.

"What? How?"

"Don't be frightened," the woman said.

"Ask her about Jenny. Have you seen my daughter Jenny? She's been dead three weeks," said another woman.

"Let me—" the dark-haired woman tried to interrupt.

"Can you tell us what it's like? Being dead?" a man asked.

Kate backed up and crashed into a table. Five heads turned toward her. "Look, there she is."

Someone screamed. The clock began chiming. The image faded away.

Kate breathed deeply, listening to her heart. The house's silence pounded at her ears. Her cotton night shirt felt soft against her skin. Her mouth was dry. And she felt the floor firmly beneath her. She saw the moon outside. She had to be alive. She pinched her arm; it hurt.

What was happening? Had she died on the operating table and this was hell? No, it was too pleasant. Maybe heaven. This was what it was like to die and you never found out unless someone summoned you via a seance.

She ran to the phone and dialed her apartment.

"Jeff? It's Kate. Jeff, you've got to tell me. Did I die when I was operated on?"

"What?" he asked sleepily. "What are you talking about? Are you all right? Of course you didn't die."

"How do you know?" she asked, and then realized he wouldn't know if he was part of it all. This was crazy. Impossible. There had to be another reason.

"I'll leave now, Kate, and be there tomorrow night," he said.

She didn't object. She told him to drive carefully and hung up the phone. Sitting in the kitchen, she listened to the birds come awake one by one.

She didn't want to work anymore. She had told Jeff that during the treatments.

"I want to live in the country and enjoy life," she said. "All I'll need is food, and I'll grow my own."

"Why can't we live in the country and work, too?" Jeff had asked.

"I didn't say we," she said. "I'm not going to make you live in the country. You'd hate it."

"How can you know that when I don't?"

One thing about her past she wouldn't change was Jeff. He had always been there when she needed him, always supportive. When she had gotten sick, she found herself moving away from him, half angry with him all the time.

Now she wished he would get there. She looked out the window again. It would be dark soon, and she didn't want to be alone, didn't want to think she was dead.

There had to be another explanation. She thought of the dark-haired ghost woman and her companions, trying to remember everything: perhaps details would help her. The woman asking after Jennifer had worn a red smock that matched her bright red hair; the dark-haired woman had on jeans and a sweater; one man looked as if he had on a robe. She couldn't see their faces clearly enough to describe them. The table had a shiny surface, perhaps glass, reflecting the light of a single candle. Were they people from another part of the world, their thoughts linked with hers?

That did not explain why they thought she was dead.

Jeff's car rolled across the gravel driveway. Looking concerned, he got out of the car and ran toward the house. She
opened the door, and they embraced. He smelled of Jeff, a
warm musky smell that made her hold him tighter.

"I missed you," she said.

He pulled away and looked down at her.

"Are you all right?" he asked.

"Come on in. I'll tell you all about it."

She related her experiences while they sipped tea and ate
brightly colored salad, losing some of her fear as she talked.
Jeff took the story at face value, just as she knew he would.

"So you thought you were dead?"

She grimaced and then smiled. "I never overreact, do I?"

"Oh no," he said. "When you found out you were sick,
you called to have your tombstone made the next day."

"Luckily I decided not to tempt fate," she said, laughing.
"Let's come downstairs tonight and see if you can figure out
what is going on. Are you up to it?"

"I'll go to sleep after I eat, and you can wake me when it's
time."

Kate put Jeff to bed, tucking him in as if he were a child.

"I left some things in the car," he murmured before
drifting off.

Kate put on the floodlight and went outside. Inside the car
were all of their plants, three suitcases, and Lockheart, their
cat, asleep on a pile of clothes. She opened her eyes, meowed
and stretched. Kate shook her head and picked the cat up. She
protested at first; she was fond of the car, but she soon
realized Kate was warmer.

Kate had not wanted the cat or the plants, and she felt a
twinge of anger as she unloaded the car. They all required
responsibility. Plants needed water; cats had to be fed. And
people got sick and died. Of course, Jeff could not have
called neighbors up at 3:00 A.M. and asked them to cat- and
plant-sit.

Once inside, Lockheart sniffed at her litter box and food

and then padded upstairs to sleep with Jeff. Just like home, Kate thought.

When she grew tired, Kate went to bed, curling herself around Jeff and the cat. At 2:30, she shook Jeff awake. They shut the door behind them and went down to the living room where they sat in the dark until it was almost three. Kate began to wonder if it would happen at all; perhaps she had made it up. Then the woman shimmered into view.

"Kate Hein, come back to us. We didn't mean to frighten you," the woman said. The others joined her.

"Do you see them?" Kate whispered. She was relieved when Jeff nodded; she hadn't made it all up.

Kate stood and went to them. Tonight she could see more details: a counter behind the table, a beauty mark on the man's left cheek, a window—her window.

"Give us a sign," the woman said.

Reaching into the light, Kate picked up a cup from the counter. She couldn't feel it, but it moved and crashed to the floor. They all jumped.

Kate pulled her hand back. The clock chimed. She looked at Jeff, and the picture faded.

Jeff fumbled with the light and then sat down.

"Let me sit for a minute," he said.

Kate heard the cat crying upstairs. She went up and let her out.

"They looked different," Jeff said as she came down. "Didn't they? Their clothes. That room. It was like this one only a bit different."

"I know. The clothes weren't old-fashioned," Kate said. She smiled. "Not like I would have expected from ghosts."

"They did call to you," he said. "Maybe there's another Kate Hein somewhere."

"They're calling to her in this house? Doubtful," she said. "Why would they be in this room, in this house, calling me? Why do they think I'm dead? I'm not!"

"You will be someday in the future," he said, "in the far, far future."

"I'll be dead in the future. Yes, that's right," she said,

suddenly excited. "I'm not dead now but I will be in the future, Jeff, so *they* could be from the future. Instead of holding a seance and getting the dead me, they get the past, with me in it."

"A kind of time travel?"

"I suppose," she answered, pacing the room. "Maybe in the future this house is haunted—strange noises in the night, things like that. Maybe I grow old and die here. They think I'm the one who is haunting the house, so they call me. To me the house is haunted, too, but it's haunted by the future! A window which goes both ways."

She laughed. "Think of it! Maybe many of the so-called haunted houses are really time windows—pieces of the future or past flickering back and forth with no one ever suspecting because both ends believe it's the nether regions."

"That's a better explanation than your first one," Jeff said.

Lockheart jumped onto Jeff's lap and he stroked her.

"I wish there was one of these windows in the house I grew up in," Kate said, stopping to gaze across the yard.

Jeff sighed. "Why? So you could tell little Katie to eat right and move away from the dump? What would that have accomplished? Your parents would have taken you to a shrink and you would have grown up terrified of this woman who told you you would get cancer," Jeff said. "You can't change the past."

She walked across the room and dropped down on her knees in front of his chair. "But maybe I can change the future. Those people know who I am, for some reason; and in their time I'm dead. They could tell me why and how. I would know." She grabbed his hands. "I could stop being afraid. No more ifs."

"Katie," he said, cupping her face in his hands. "What does it matter? You can't live the future or the past. What if you find out I die in two years or you die a pauper or you win the Pulitzer or you live to be a hundred? Would you want to know any of those things ahead of time, really?"

She moved away from him.

"How can you understand? How can you sit there and

pretend you do? You don't have a timebomb inside of you!''

"Is that why you've been so angry with me?" he asked. "Because I didn't get sick? Well, how do you know I don't have a 'timebomb' inside of me?" He started to leave the room. She reached for his arm.

"Don't you see? That's what I'm afraid of."

The house seemed even more warm and alive the next morning. Lockheart climbed along the counters while Jeff fixed breakfast.

"I tried the tractor again the other day," Kate said as they ate. "It still works. I wish it were spring so I could plant. All organic. I'll have complete control."

"I? Aren't you going to let me help?"

"It's something I want to do by myself," she answered. "Besides, I doubt you'll be here much of the time, will you? What would you do out here?"

"Eat what you grow," he said. "This is an interesting part of the state. We could do a back to nature book. I married you for better or worse. Don't the vows hold for both of us?"

"That's not nice," Kate said.

"I don't feel nice, Katie," he said. "I want to be with you, but only in the here and now, not with you angry about the past and worrying about the future."

Kate looked at her food and wished the night would come.

She moved slowly out of bed, trying not to disturb the cat or Jeff.

"Don't tell me," Jeff whispered. "Whatever you learn, I don't want to know."

She started to answer him, but instead she tiptoed out of the room and went downstairs. She sat in the chair waiting for her future and thinking about her past.

What she didn't like about the past was that she had no control of it: she had trusted the world to let her grow up unharmed, and it had failed her. Her doctor had told her she shouldn't blame her illness on any one thing: it was a combi-

nation of factors, nothing she could do now, but soon she
would know her future and she would be prepared.

But would that give her more choices? Or would she just
feel as if she were a puppet or actor playing out a role?

Was Jeff a part of her future? Jeff, the cat, and the plants
the cat was always eating? She smiled. She liked the house
better with them all in it.

The woman came into being in a milky glow, followed by
the others.

"Are you there, Kate Hein?" the woman whispered.

"I'm here," Kate answered.

The people looked at each other and then warily about the
room.

"Ask her," the other woman said.

"Kate, Mrs. Packard wants to know if you've had contact
with her daughter Jennifer. Jenny passed away a short time
ago."

Kate looked around the room. The plants made pointed
silhouettes in the dark. Upstairs she heard Lockheart scratching at the door. She rubbed her stomach where she was still
warm from Jeff's body pressed against hers as they slept.

"Tell Mrs. Packard that Jennifer is here with us, and she
sends her love."

The clock struck three, and the window closed.

KLEIN'S MACHINE

Andrew Weiner

"Klein's Machine" was purchased by Shawna McCarthy, and appeared in the April 1985 issue of IAsfm, *with an illustration by J. K. Potter. Weiner has a reputation for ingenuity and unorthodox perspectives, and in "Klein's Machine" he gives us one of the most bizarre scenarios in the whole body of time-travel tales—and one of the most affecting human stories.*

Andrew Weiner is one of science fiction's fastest rising young professionals. In recent years, he has become one of IAsfm's *most frequent contributors, and also appears regularly in* The Magazine of Fantasy & Science Fiction, Interzone, Amazing, *and elsewhere. In 1987, he published his first novel,* Station Gehenna. *Weiner lives in Toronto, Canada.*

1.

They took him off the bus in Mt. Vernon, Ohio. His eyes were blank, and he had been sobbing quietly to himself for the past fifty miles. He was holding the crushed remains of a bright green flower in his left hand.

The driver turned him over to the ticket clerk, who called the local police. He was unresponsive to their questions. He had no identification, and no possessions except a one-way ticket to San Francisco and a crumpled $20 bill.

They threw the flower in the garbage and took him to the emergency ward of the local hospital.

"He's spaced out," one of the police officers told the intern. "Flying high."

Subsequent blood and urine analysis, however, showed no trace of drugs.

2.

"Could be a travel psychosis," said the senior psychiatrist. "Haven't seen one in years."

"Travel psychosis?" asked the intern.

"During the war," the psychiatrist said, "they would send soldiers cross-country by bus, transferring from base to base. Some of them would just disintegrate. The monotony got to them, you see. They had nowhere to look except inside. And they realized that they didn't know who they were. Of course, these were people who never had a very good grip in the first place."

He turned to the blank-eyed patient.

"Been travelling far, kid?"

The patient spoke for the first time.

"Oh yes," he said. "Very far."

3.

The patient was identified on the basis of his fingerprints. He had a minor criminal record in New York State, having been picked up several times at political demonstrations for disturbing the peace. He also had an active file at the FBI, documenting his involvement with several fringe leftist groups, although there were no recent entries.

The patient's name was Philip Herbert Klein. He was a resident of New York City. He had been reported missing three weeks before by his mother, Mrs. Alice Klein.

4.

Klein was transferred to a state mental hospital, and given anti-psychotic medication.

Within a few days he was able to converse normally, although he appeared fatigued and withdrawn. He claimed to have no memory of leaving New York City, nor of how he had come to be on a cross-country bus.

The duty psychiatrist modified the diagnosis from psychosis to hysterical reaction, dissociative type, and arranged for his immediate discharge.

"Amnesia," he told the patient's mother, when she came to take him home.

"Like on *Another World*?" she asked.

"Something like that," he said. "Although in this case he doesn't seem to have hit his head."

"But where has he been?" she asked. "Where has he been all this time?"

"Maybe it will come back to him," the duty psychiatrist said.

5.

On his return to New York City, Mrs. Klein, on the recommendation of the duty psychiatrist, arranged for a home visit by a psychiatric social worker.

While Klein sat on the couch watching a *Star Trek* rerun, Mrs. Klein explained the situation.

"He never did anything like this before," she told the social worker. "He was always a good boy. A little nervous, maybe. High strung. Perhaps a bit over-imaginative. But always such a good boy."

After taking a family history, the social worker asked to speak with Klein in private.

6.

Report of the psychiatric social worker
Philip Herbert Klein

I interviewed the client on the morning of July 24th, three days after his return from Ohio. I also interviewed the client's mother, Mrs. Alice Klein.

The client is 23 years old. He has never lived outside his family's home, and continues to reside with his widowed mother in a rent-controlled apartment on the Upper West Side. He has never held regular employment. He failed to complete his studies in accountancy at the City University, dropping out at the end of the first year. He told me that he had wished to study physics, but had been urged by his mother towards a more "practical" field.

Neither the client nor his mother were forthcoming as to the circumstances surrounding him leaving university, although Mrs. Klein noted on several occasions that her son was troubled at times by "nerves" and was "highly strung."

The family has never sought psychiatric assistance for the client, although he was treated briefly for enuresis by a pediatrician at the age of nine, soon after his father's death.

The client and his mother subsist on a modest income from the estate of the late Mr. Harry Klein, a clothing manufacturer. The client is the only child. Mr. Klein was a refugee from eastern Europe, considerably older and rather less educated than his wife. Mrs. Klein recalls that her parents felt she had married "beneath" her, a verdict which she only superficially disclaims. Mrs. Klein came from a family with some pretensions to social standing, although little wealth after setbacks in the market.

At the time of their marriage, Mr. Klein was quite successful in his business, but later he suffered considerable reverses. This change in their fortunes, in some way a repetition of Mrs. Klein's own childhood experiences, coincided with the birth of their son. It seems that the client grew up in an atmosphere of some tension and economic insecurity, and that these conflicts between the parents were transmitted to him.

Philip himself claims to recall little about his father, who

worked long hours and was rarely home. He does recall that
Mr. Klein spoke with a marked accent, and had no knowledge of or interest in popular sports such as baseball, which
caused him some embarrassment with his peer group. He
"does not remember" how he felt when his father died,
although his mother says that he "took it badly." As already
noted, his enuresis first became severe at that time.

The mother, in any case, has apparently always been the
dominant figure within this family constellation. Currently,
she appears less concerned about her son's condition *per se* as
with the fact that he was outside her surveillance and control
for so lengthy a period.

Mrs. Klein suggested, in fact, that Philip might have been
"kidnapped" and "brainwashed" by some radical group,
although she was quite unable to suggest any motive for such
an action. She has, apparently, warned her son repeatedly of
the dangers of mixing with "bad company."

The boy (it is very difficult to think of him as a man) has
little social life, and rarely leaves the apartment. For some
period of time he was involved with peripheral socialist groups,
but left following a disagreement he appears to have gone out
of his way to engineer. He has no close friends of either sex,
although he is a prolific letter-writer. He spends much of his
time tinkering with fantastic and apparently useless machinery,
styling himself an "inventor." (His mother recalls that in his
teens he attempted to obtain a patent for a "space drive," an
incident she found enormously comical.)

His other great interest is reading popular fiction, specifically science fiction. His room is littered with paperbacks of
this description. His interest in this literature goes back to
early adolescence, and at one time he himself produced an
amateur journal of criticism and discussion for circulation to
similarly anomic and obsessive individuals.

"There is nothing like (these books)," he told me. "Nothing in the world."

The client has been diagnosed as suffering a classical
dissociative reaction, of amnesia coupled with fugue state. On
the occasion of the home visit, the client still claimed to be

unable to recall any details of his experiences during his absence from home. He did, however, offer a hypothetical explanation of his disappearance, one so bizarre as to raise the question of a more severe pathology. The client told me that he believed that he had been "travelling in time." He attempted to substantiate this claim through reference to his personal journal.

I have referred the client for further psychiatric treatment on an out-patient basis.

7.

Excerpts from the journal of Philip Herbert Klein
February 7, 198-

Freezing cold today, arse-freezing cold, highest wind chill factor for the day in eleven years, got to be a screw-up in the sunspot cycle. Almost died of exposure getting over to Claude's place for the Progressive League meeting. Big argument with Ma before I left, why am I wasting my life hanging around with commie creeps, why am I doing this to her, and etc. You just can't win. Last year it was, get out of the house, find an interest, make new friends.

Lousy attendance at the meeting, not even the whole Central Committee. Claude is a lousy speaker, and "Capital Movements in West Africa" is not exactly a crowd-puller. I could have done without it myself. All his usual stuff about the Rockefellers and the Chase-Manhattan and the Trilateral Commission. No facts, just speculation. Claude has always been flipped-out on the Rockefellers. Always has to *personalize* everything.

"Come on," I said, when I couldn't take it anymore. "We have to be scientific, here. We're supposed to be *scientific* socialists, aren't we?"

"What do you know about science?" Claude asked.

"More than you," I said.

He didn't like that at all.

I've got to admit I'm getting sick of all these personality conflicts. How are we ever going to establish socialism in this country when we can't even agree on when to take a coffee break? They say every personality conflict is really a political conflict, but I'm starting to wonder.

I haven't told anyone in the League about my project. I've got to have some concrete proof first. Otherwise, they're going to laugh in my face.

February 24th, 198-

Long letter from Sam Gold, replying to a letter of comment I wrote about an article on Heinlein which appeared in *Space Potatoes*. It's so long since I wrote the letter I can't even remember what I said, but I guess I was attacking Sam for attacking Heinlein's *Time Enough for Love*, which I still think is a great book. I guess Sam is on a literary kick these days.

Sam also asked if I was ever going to put out another issue of *Kleinlight*. The truth of it is, ever since Ma smashed my Gestetner, I've sort of lost the urge. Also, I really don't have the time anymore. Maybe that's what growing up is all about.

March 2nd, 198-

Leafletted with Penny outside the local supermarket, in support of the union local. It rained the whole time, I'm probably going to get pneumonia. I was almost glad when the union goons chased us away, although you'd think they would know who their friends are. I've had it up to here with leafletting, anyway. There's got to be a faster way to make a revolution.

Coffee with Penny afterwards; she was wearing a green blouse, looked very pretty. She told me I should go back to college, maybe study pol-sci. That's what she's doing at Columbia. I guess she thinks I just fritter away most of my time. I almost told her about my machine, but then I got worried about what she would think.

I thought about asking her to a movie, but I decided to go home and work on my project instead. There'll be more time later. All the time in the world.

March 7th 198-

The hamster didn't come back. I sat and watched the cage

for two hours straight, and it didn't come back. Then I
crashed out, and when I woke up it was past noon, and still
no hamster. Now I have to figure out where it went.

March 10th, 198-

Another big blow-up with Ma. We're back on my reading
habits of all things. The stuff I read is ruining my mind,
driving me crazy, making me blind, and like that. She should
know how crazy. I almost felt like walking out of the house
and never coming back. But I'm too close to success now to
have to worry about finding a place to live, and a job and all
that stuff.

Why do I have to put up with this shit? I'm *twenty-three
years old.*

March 18th, 198-

League meeting. Dick presented his paper on "Technology
in a Socialist Society." Against capital-intensive energy re-
sources, in favor of small, localized power units and an
overall reduction in energy consumption. The usual hippy-
dippy stuff.

What kind of future, I asked, are we going to have with
less energy?

Nearly got kicked out on my ear.

Walking to the subway, Penny told me that my position in
the League is insecure, and urged me to keep quiet for
awhile. Apparently Claude is looking to start a schism. Wants
to expel me and a few others who have crossed him. I'm not
even sure that I care, although I'm glad that she seems to.

March 26th, 198-

The hamster is back. Also my wristwatch, which I strapped
on its back. The watch appears to have stopped at the moment
the field was induced. The hamster seems fine, though a bit
sleepy. Have begun follow-up observations.

April 2nd, 198-

Well, I got expelled from the League. Deviationism. Big

surprise. I guess I'm more relieved than anything else. In fact I should have quit first. I'm only sorry because I think I was starting to get close to Penny, and now she can't be seen consorting with a deviationist.

Of course, this changes everything concerning the project. I was almost ready to make my pitch, lay it all out for the League.

"We *can* change the future," I was going to tell them. "And fast."

Maybe I should have tried it anyway. Probably they would have dumped all over it, but I could have tried.

Maybe I'm not such a principled type after all. Maybe I wanted to keep all this to myself all along. But now I really do have to think things through, decide where I go from here.

April 3rd, 198-

Went out to pick up some magazines, and when I came back I found that Ma had poisoned the hamster. Said she couldn't stand the smell.

Thomas Alva Edison never had to put up with this shit!

Post-test follow-up incomplete. Should repeat the whole performance, make sure the hamster wouldn't have eventually dropped dead. But I'm not sure I can wait that long.

8.

"So you built a time machine," said the psychiatrist, whose name was Dr. Lawrence Segal.

"That's right," Klein said.

"Where is this machine?"

"In my apartment," Klein said. "But it doesn't work anymore."

"Why not?"

"I don't know," Klein said. "Maybe Ma tampered with it. Maybe something burned out. I can't make it work anymore."

"But it did work at least once?"

"Twice. Once for the hamster, and once for me."

"Tell me, Philip, what made you want to travel in time?"

"I don't know," Klein said. "It's something I thought

about for years. I used to daydream about it, even back in high school. It came from reading all those stories about people travelling in time, into the future, into the past. People changing history. I used to wish I could do that too. Not change history, exactly. Just a few details here and there."

"What sort of details?"

"I don't know. It's like people always say, *if I could do it all again*. Go back before things went wrong and make them right. Things I said and wished I hadn't. Places I went to when I wanted to stay home, or go someplace else. Dumb, embarrassing scenes with girls. Like that. Go back and short-circuit all the pain.

"And then I started to thinking about bigger things. Like maybe going back to Dallas and saving Kennedy. I used to think that the world would have been a much better place if only Kennedy had lived.

"That was naive, of course. Saving Kennedy wouldn't really have changed anything. That was something I realized when I got into being a socialist. It would all have been the same. The same misery, the same wars, same everything. Only the names of the presidents would have been different.

"And then I thought about something my mother said. She used to point to this picture of Franklin Roosevelt, we always had a picture of him on the wall, and she would say, 'Without that man, there would have been a revolution in this country.' She thought that was great, of course, that old FDR stuck his finger in the dike. But I could see how Roosevelt had really been an obstacle to genuine social progress in this country.

"So that was my plan. To build a time machine, and get the League to knock off Roosevelt. And if that didn't help, we would try knocking off somebody else.

"I don't know if I was serious about all this. I don't know if I could actually bring myself to kill anyone, let alone FDR, who was always revered in my family as something approaching a goddam saint. And I never even tried to win over the League. So I don't know if I was ever really serious about all this political stuff. I think probably it was always personal, really.

"So in the end, I decided to go forward rather than back. To try and find a place for myself somewhere in the future. Because I wasn't happy here, that was for sure, and I don't think that even a revolution would have changed that much.

"I suppose my mother thought I was just beating off in there, all those months. But that was what I was doing. Building a time machine. And I did it. I really did it. I travelled in time."

"Except," Dr. Segal said, "that you don't remember a thing about it."

9.

With Philip Klein's consent, Dr. Segal scheduled a session using sodium pentathol in an attempt to bring back his lost memory and lead him through and beyond whatever traumatic event or events might have precipitated his fugue.

"Philip," Dr. Segal said, once the drug had taken hold. "I want you to think back to the night of July 5th. Do you remember that night?"

"Of course," Philip said. "Tonight's the night. The night I test my machine."

"How do you feel?"

"Good," Philip said. "Excited. I can hardly wait. Should have done this months ago. I was nervous, I guess. And then I wanted to wait for July 4th. For the fireworks. I always did like the fireworks."

"Where are you, Philip?"

"I'm at home. In my room. I'm inducing the field."

"And then what?"

"I'm . . . travelling. Into the future."

"Tell me about it. Tell me about the future."

Klein appeared agitated. He shifted in his seat.

"What's happening, Philip?"

"I don't know. I don't remember . . ."

"Go with it, Philip. Don't fight it. You remember the future. You're there now. In the future now . . ."

"The walls are high . . ."

"Yes?"

"Very high. And white, sheer white. Dazzling in the sun. The swollen sun. I see no one, no one at all. The air . . . the air is hard to breathe. Thin. Harsh." Klein's breathing became labored. "There's something wrong with the air."

"Easy, Philip. Take it easy."

Klein's expression changed. He became alert, jerked his head back.

"I see something in the sky. Some kind of flying machine. It makes no noise, no noise at all. The shape is strange, I can't describe the shape. The machine is getting closer. The machine is firing at me. Firing some sort of ray . . ."

"And?"

"Now I'm inside the machine. The walls are smooth. Dark. There is no one else inside the flying machine. I can see out the window. We are flying above the city. The city of the future. Glass, concrete. Stripped, massed, streamlined. Overhead roads link the towers. The golden towers. But the city is empty."

"Empty?"

"There is no one, no sign of life."

"Then who guides the flying machine?"

"Machines guide the flying machine. Nothing but machines. I am taken to the Hall of the Central Computer. The Computer speaks to me. It tells me that the people have gone now, all gone away to other worlds circling other stars. But the people will return. They have promised that they will return."

"And then?"

"I move on. Onwards into the future. I travel on."

"And what do you see?"

"I see the sun explode. The wind burns my skin. My hair is matted with a fine ash. I move back. I watch the children swim in the decaying flower gardens. I stoop down to smell the sweet green flowers. I pick a flower, I hold it in my hand. . . . I move on, to visit the golden city. The buildings are crystal, so very high. And the people fly! Faces are yellow this year, this wonderful year." Tears welled up in his eyes. "The ice! I see and will remember the ice! And the fire. I will not forget the fire."

10.

"It was amazing the way it all came back," Klein told Dr. Segal at the next session. "All came flooding back. In no coherent order. No pattern. But the future. The actual future!"

Dr. Segal's expression was noncommittal.

"You think it's a delusion, don't you?" Klein asked. "A hallucination. From your perspective, that's all it could be. You think this is some private fantasy. Like the guy in *The Fifty-Minute Hour*. The one who thought he travelled in time and space."

Dr. Segal raised his eyebrows.

"You've read Lindner?"

"Oh sure. And Freud, and Rogers, and Skinner. I liked Lindner's book. But you know, I couldn't help thinking. What if the guy was right?"

11.

Excerpt from the notebook of Dr. Lawrence Segal

I had asked Philip Klein to bring in a selection of his favorite science fiction books, and have now spent the better part of a weekend in reading them. Most of the authors were unknown to me, although I had heard of, if not actually read, Kurt Vonnegut, Jr. Somehow I am always suspicious of a man who calls himself "Jr.," but it is hardly surprising that he should be so much better known than his contemporaries. He can, at least, manipulate the language.

Leaving aside the question of literary quality, I was both fascinated and repelled by these materials. This is, in many ways, a literature steeped in pathology, and there would surely be an article here if I could find the time.

Behind the veneer of reasoned "scientific" speculation, sometimes tiresomely detailed, more often as thin and perfunctory as the plot of some pornographic movie, one finds, almost inevitably, an enormous and overweening narcissism, luxuriating in the most joyously infantile fantasies of limit-lessness and omnipotence.

Machines are everywhere in this literature. Phallic and magical machines, powered only by our most secret wishes and fears, penetrating the thin webs of space and time.

The most central and repetitious vision is one of escape, of mobility without limit, of a freedom never defined except by the absence of all civilized constraints. Characters rip them-selves free of their proper place in the social and familial framework to achieve a personal transcendence.

It should go without saying that this is a profoundly oedipal literature, although typically these yearnings are at least some-what masked. The parent or parent-figure is merely vilified, escaped, left behind.

But, almost an embarrassment of riches, there are actually stories in which we see a complete return of the repressed. The incest drive itself breaks surface, like some great white whale billowing water. Here a spaceman who travels to far stars and returns to make love to his own great-granddaughter. And there, yes, a time traveller who goes back to kill the hated father figure, to seduce his unsuspecting mother, even to become his own father.

Confronted even with such explicit material, Klein demon-strates absolutely no insight into his attachment to this literature.

"It's not a question of being for or against incest," he told me, in reference to one such story. "It's only a *speculation*. To provoke thought about the socio-cultural taboos surround-ing the incest taboo."

"To provoke thought?" I said. "I see."

Klein places great importance on having his thoughts pro-voked. Contrary to the report of the psychiatric social worker, he is actually exceptionally well-read. He has been a vora-cious consumer of organized knowledge, has set himself upon a course of relentless self-education, seeking to understand intellectually a world in which he has always felt out of place. He has read physics, chemistry, biology, history, even psy-chology. On several occasions he has attempted to draw me into a discussion of Pepper's critique of psychoanalysis. Yet

his reading has been without discrimination, mixing relativity
theory and kaballah, Mendel and the mail-order wisdom of
the Rosicrucians.

His idol is the English polymath and socialist H. G. Wells,
perhaps best known as an early writer of these scientific
romances. Klein, too, claims to be a "socialist," despite a
profound aversion for his fellow man. But essentially his
philosophy is one of self-improvement. Not only must man
evolve as a species, but each one of us must evolve as a
person. "There must be progress," he told me. "There must
be."

Socially awkward, distanced from his peers, dominated
always by his mother, Klein has set out deliberately to expand
his mind the way that others might expand their muscle
tissue, through exercise, training, and rigor. He has kept
journals of his every waking thought, scraps of time and
broken insights hoarded to chew over again and again, playing
constantly with his own ideas, not so much stimulating his
imagination as masturbating it.

He is, in fact, exactly the sort of alienated individual to
whom this literature of science fiction would most powerfully
appeal. Passive and detached, he seeks refuge from the storm
of life in these Faustian fantasies of superiority, of an understanding which transcends normal understanding. In reality,
of course, Klein is only dizzied and intoxicated by these
restless, pointless dreams.

"What did you think the future would be like?" I asked
him.

"I don't know," he said. "Different. I thought things
would be different. Like California, maybe. Only better."

He rambled on, then, about a world in which abundance
has replaced scarcity, automation has removed the need to
work, love has replaced greed, where individuals live their
lives only to create. No doubt all this came from his reading
of these utopian tales of magic kingdoms at the end of the
warp, where one floats in sweetness and light, where genera-
tions merge and smear themselves immortally across all space
and time and even death itself is defeated.

And yet one must be careful not to accept these surface notions, these relatively simple and obvious yearnings of a desperately alienated individual, at face value. Far more real and urgent wishes, however unacknowledged, lay behind the construction of his supposed machine. His desire to travel forward in time, then, screens out his shameful and inexpressible wish to travel backwards in time and re-unite with his own narcissistic vision of the pre-Oedipal mother. He toys with various rationalizations that might justify this voyage back, but in the end is unable to sustain them, for they bring him too close to recognizing his real desires. His fantasy of saving Kennedy, for example, shields his repressed wish to kill Kennedy, kill the primal father. Later, disguised as a "scientific socialist" he actually permits himself partial expression of these aggressive impulses, in his extraordinary scheme for the assassination of Franklin Roosevelt. But this plan, too, is quickly repressed, discarded, thrown away.

It is a truism, of course, that time does not exist in the unconscious. We may travel back there, at will, back to infancy, back to our primal paradise of infantile omnipotence, of unlimited control and unqualified love. Klein's longing to return is not in itself unusual. Yet typically such wishes are displaced upon the social environment. The effort to recover lost infancy is channeled into the drive for economic or social transcendence, or else dissipated in nostalgic and romantic illusion. Klein, however, has become fixated on this matter of changing the very flow of time.

12.

"You picked a flower, Philip. Do you remember the flower?"

"It was green," Klein said. "Amazingly green. I held it in my hand."

"What happened to it?"

"I don't know," Klein said. "I don't know."

13.

"The machine, Philip. How is your machine?"

"It doesn't work, anymore."

"Where is it? Is it still in your apartment?"

"It's here."

"Where?"

"Here. I am the machine. The time machine. I am it."

14.

On the advice of his psychiatrist, Philip Klein moved out of his mother's apartment.

He got a furnished room, and supported himself through a job in a bookstore.

He began taking night school classes in Business Administration.

He read very little science fiction.

He began dating.

His therapy continued, but they no longer spoke of Klein's machine. They explored his childhood, and his current relationships with the world.

He was, according to Dr. Segal, developing good insight into himself and his world.

15.

The garbage from the Mt. Vernon bus station found its way, eventually, to the city dump.

Strange green flowers bloomed there briefly, then withered away, before being covered under new loads of garbage.

16.

"The Earth is all gone now, all gone away," Klein said. *He was deep under the drug now, breathing very slowly. "And the Sun, the Sun is a long time gone. And yet the light is still bright, brighter than you could imagine. But soft, so it doesn't hurt my eyes. And I'm floating, floating inside the light. Floating on some fixed path. Moving through the space and the time. And now the light is pulsing. It's breaking down. There's darkness in between the light. And the lights are shrinking, moving away from me. Slowly. Very slowly. All going away now. All."*

THE PURE PRODUCT

John Kessel

"The Pure Product" was purchased by Gardner Dozois, and appeared in the March 1986 issue of IAsfm, *with an illustration by J. K. Potter. Taut, hard-edged, casually and cold-bloodedly horrifying, it was one of the most powerful stories to appear in* IAsfm *that year. It remains Kessel's best story to date, in my opinion—and one of the most adroit and chilling examinations of this theme ever to appear anywhere.*

John Kessel is one of the major new talents to enter SF in recent years. He made his first sale in 1975, and since has become a frequent contributor to IAsfm, *as well as to almost all of the other major SF magazines and anthologies. Kessel won a Nebula Award in 1983 for his novella "Another Orphan." His most recent book is the novel* Freedom Beach, *written with frequent collaborator James Patrick Kelly. He is currently at work on a new novel, entitled* Good News from Outer Space. *Born in Buffalo, New York, Kessel now lives with his wife, Sue Hall, in Raleigh, North Carolina, where he is an associate professor of American litera-*

ture and creative writing at North Carolina State University.

———————

I arrived in Kansas City at one o'clock on the afternoon of the thirteenth of August. A Tuesday. I was driving the beige 1983 Chevrolet Citation that I had stolen two days earlier in Pocatello, Idaho. The Kansas plates on the car I'd taken from a different car in a parking lot in Salt Lake City. Salt Lake City was founded by the Mormons, whose God tells them that in the future Jesus Christ will come again.

I drove through Kansas City with the windows open and the sun beating down through the windshield. The car had no air conditioning and my shirt was stuck to my back from seven hours behind the wheel. Finally I found a hardware store, "Hector's" on Wornall. I pulled into the lot. The Citation's engine dieseled after I turned off the ignition; I pumped the accelerator once and it coughed and died. The heat was like syrup. The sun drove shadows deep into corners, left them flattened at the feet of the people on the sidewalk. It made the plate glass of the store window into a dark negative of the positive print that was Wornall Avenue. August.

The man behind the counter in the hardware store I took to be Hector himself. He looked like Hector, slain in vengeance beneath the walls of paintbrushes—the kind of semi-friendly, publicly optimistic man who would tell you about his good wife and his ten-penny nails. I bought a gallon of kerosene and a plastic paint funnel, put them into the trunk of the Citation, then walked down the block to the Mark Twain Bank. Mark Twain died at the age of seventy-five with a heart full of bitter accusations against the Calvinist god and no hope for the future of humanity. Inside the bank I went to one of the desks, at which sat a Nice Young Lady. I asked about starting a business checking account. She gave me a form to fill out, then sent me to the office of Mr. Graves.

Mr. Graves wielded a formidable handshake. "What can I do for you, Mr. . . . ?"

"Tillotsen. Gerald Tillotsen," I said. Gerald Tillotsen, of Tacoma, Washington, died of diphtheria at the age of four weeks—on September 24, 1938. I have a copy of his birth certificate.

"I'm new to Kansas City. I'd like to open a business account here, and perhaps take out a loan. I trust this is a reputable bank? What's your exposure in Brazil?" I looked around the office as if Graves were hiding a woman behind the hatstand, then flashed him my most ingratiating smile.

Mr. Graves did his best. He tried smiling back, then looked as if he had decided to ignore my little joke. "We're very sound, Mr. Tillotsen."

I continued smiling.

"What kind of business do you own?"

"I'm in insurance. Mutual Assurance of Hartford. Our regional office is in Oklahoma City, and I'm setting up an agency here, at 103rd and State Line." Just off the interstate.

He examined the form I had given him. His absorption was too tempting.

"Maybe I can fix you up with a life policy? You look like dead meat."

Graves' head snapped up, his mouth half open. He closed it and watched me guardedly. The dullness of it all! How I tire. He was like some cow, like most of the rest of you in this silly age, unwilling to break the rules in order to take offense. "Did he really say that?" he was thinking. "If he did say that, was that his idea of a joke? What is he after? He looks normal enough." I did look normal, exactly like an insurance agent. I was the right kind of person, and I could do anything. If at times I grate, if at times I fall a little short of or go a little beyond convention, there is not one of you who can call me to account.

Mr. Graves was coming around. All business.

"Ah—yes, Mr. Tillotsen. If you'll wait a moment, I'm

sure we can take care of this checking account. As for the loan. . .''

"Forget it."

That should have stopped him. He should have asked after my credentials, he should have done a dozen things. He looked at me, and I stared calmly back at him. And I knew that, looking into my honest blue eyes, he could not think of a thing.

"I'll just start the checking account now with this money order," I said, reaching into my pocket. "That will be acceptable, won't it?"

"It will be fine," he said. He took the completed form and the order over to one of the secretaries while I sat at the desk. I lit a cigar and blew some smoke rings. The money order had been purchased the day before in a post office in Denver. It was for thirty dollars. I didn't intend to use the account very long. Graves returned with my sample checks, shook hands earnestly, and wished me a good day. Have a *good* day, he said. I *will*, I said.

Outside, the heat was still stifling. I took off my sportcoat. I was sweating so much I had to check my hair in the sideview mirror of my car. I walked down the street to a liquor store and bought a bottle of chardonnay and a bottle of Chivas Regal. I got some paper cups from a nearby grocery. One final errand, then I could relax for a few hours.

In the shopping center I had told Graves would be the location for my nonexistent insurance office, there was a sporting goods store. It was about three o'clock when I parked in the lot and ambled into the shop. I looked at various golf clubs: irons, woods, even one set with fiberglass shafts. Finally I selected a set of eight Spaulding irons with matching woods, a large bag, and several boxes of Topflites. The salesman, who had been occupied with another customer at the rear of the store, hustled up, his eyes full of commission money. I gave him little time to think. The total cost was $612.32. I paid with a check drawn on my new account, cordially thanked the man, and had him carry all the equipment out to the trunk of the car.

I drove to a park near the bank; Loose Park, they called it. I felt loose. Cut loose, drifting free, like one of the kites people were flying in the park that had broken its string and was ascending into the sun. Beneath the trees it was still hot, though the sunlight was reduced to a shuffling of light and shadow on the brown grass. Kids ran, jumped, swung on playground equipment. I uncorked my bottle of wine, filled one of the paper cups, and lay down beneath a tree, enjoying the children, watching young men and women walking along the paths of the park.

A girl approached along the path. She did not look any older than seventeen. She was short and slender, with clean blonde hair cut to her shoulders. Her shorts were very tight. I watched her unabashedly; she saw me watching her and left the path to come over to me. She stopped a few feet away, her hands on her hips. "What are you looking at?" she asked.

"Your legs," I said. "Would you like some wine?"

"No thanks. My mother told me never to accept wine from strangers." She looked right through me.

"I take whatever I can get from strangers," I said. "Because I'm a stranger, too."

I guess she liked that. She was different. She sat down and we chatted for a while. There was something wrong about her imitation of a seventeen-year-old; I began to wonder whether hookers worked the park. She crossed her legs and her shorts got tighter. "Where are you from?" she asked.

"San Francisco. But I've just moved here to stay. I have a part interest in the sporting goods store at the Eastridge Plaza."

"You live near here?"

"On West 89th." I had driven down 89th on my way to the bank.

"I live on 89th! We're neighbors."

An edge of fear sliced through me. A slip? It was exactly what one of my own might have said to test me. I took a drink of wine and changed the subject. "Would you like to visit San Francisco someday?"

She brushed her hair back behind one ear. She pursed her lips, showing off her fine cheekbones. "Have you got something going?" she asked, in queerly accented English.

"Excuse me?"

"I said, have you got something going," she repeated, still with the accent—the accent of my own time.

I took another sip. "A bottle of wine," I replied in good Midwestern 1980s.

She wasn't having any of it. "No artwork, please. I don't like artwork."

I had to laugh: my life was devoted to artwork. I had not met anyone real in a long time. At the beginning I hadn't wanted to and in the ensuing years I had given up expecting it. If there's anything more boring than you people it's us people. But that was an old attitude. When she came to me in K.C. I was lonely and she was something new.

"Okay," I said. "It's not much, but you can come for the ride. Do you want to?"

She smiled and said yes.

As we walked to my car, she brushed her hip against my leg. I switched the bottle to my left hand and put my arm around her shoulders in a fatherly way. We got into the front seat, beneath the trees on a street at the edge of the park. It was quiet. I reached over, grabbed her hair at the nape of her neck and jerked her face toward me, covering her little mouth with mine. Surprise: she threw her arms around my neck, sliding across the seat and awkwardly onto my lap. We did not talk. I yanked at the shorts; she thrust her hand into my pants. St. Augustine asked the lord for chastity, but not right away.

At the end she slipped off me, calmly buttoned her blouse, brushed her hair back from her forehead. "How about a push?" she asked. She had a nailfile out and was filing her index fingernail to a point.

I shook my head, and looked at her. She resembled my grandmother. I had never run into my grandmother but she had a hellish reputation. "No thanks. What's your name?"

"Call me Ruth." She scratched the inside of her left elbow

with her nail. She leaned back in her seat, sighed deeply. Her eyes became a very bright, very hard blue.

While she was aloft I got out, opened the trunk, emptied the rest of the chardonnay into the gutter and used the funnel to fill the bottle with kerosene. I plugged it with part of the cork and a kerosene-soaked rag. Afternoon was sliding into evening as I started the car and cruised down one of the residential streets. The houses were like those of any city or town of that era of the midwest USA: white frame, forty or fifty years old, with large porches and small front yards. Dying elm trees hung over the street. Shadows stretched across the sidewalks. Ruth's nose wrinkled; she turned her face lazily toward me, saw the kerosene bottle, and smiled.

Ahead on the left-hand sidewalk I saw a man walking leisurely. He was an average sort of man, middle-aged, probably just returning from work, enjoying the quiet pause dusk was bringing to the hot day. It might have been Hector; it might have been Graves. It might have been any one of you. I punched the cigarette lighter, readied the bottle in my right hand, steering with my leg as the car moved slowly forward. "Let me help," Ruth said. She reached out and steadied the wheel with her slender fingertips. The lighter popped out. I touched it to the rag; it smoldered and caught. Greasy smoke stung my eyes. By now the man had noticed us. I hung my arm, holding the bottle, out the window. As we passed him, I tossed the bottle at the sidewalk like a newsboy tossing a rolled-up newspaper. The rag flamed brighter as it whipped through the air; the bottle landed at his feet and exploded, dousing him with burning kerosene. I floored the accelerator; the motor coughed, then roared, the tires and Ruth both squealing in delight. I could see the flaming man in the rearview mirror as we sped away.

On the Great American Plains, the summer nights are not silent. The fields sing the summer songs of insects—not individual sounds, but a high-pitched drone of locusts, cicadas, small chirping things for which I have no names. You drive along the superhighway and that sound blends with the sound of wind rushing through your opened windows, hiding the thrum of the automobile, conveying the impression of incredible velocity. Wheels vibrate, tires beat against the pavement, the steering wheel shudders, alive in your hands, droning insects alive in your ears. Reflecting posts at the roadside leap from the darkness with metronomic regularity, glowing amber in the headlights, only to vanish abruptly into the ready night when you pass. You lose track of time, how long you have been on the road, where you are going. The fields scream in your ears like a thousand lost, mechanical souls, and you press your foot to the accelerator, hurrying away.

When we left Kansas City that evening we were indeed hurrying. Our direction was in one sense precise: Interstate 70, more or less due east, through Missouri in a dream. They might remember me in Kansas City, at the same time wondering who and why. Mr. Graves checks the morning paper over his grapefruit: "Man Burned by Gasoline Bomb." The clerk wonders why he ever accepted an unverified check, a check without even a name or address printed on it, for 600 dollars. The check bounces. They discover it was a bottle of chardonnay. The story is pieced together. They would eventually figure out how—I wouldn't lie to myself about that—I never lie to myself—but the why would always escape them. Organized crime, they would say. A plot that misfired.

Of course, they still might have caught me. The car became more of a liability the longer I held onto it. But Ruth, humming to herself, did not seem to care, and neither did I. You have to improvise those things; that's what gives them whatever interest they have.

Just shy of Columbia, Missouri, Ruth stopped humming and asked me, "Do you know why Helen Keller can't have any children?"

"No."

"Because she's dead."

I rolled up the window so I could hear her better. "That's pretty funny," I said.

"Yes. I overheard it in a restaurant." After a minute she asked, "Who's Helen Keller?"

"A dead woman." An insect splattered itself against the

windshield. The lights of the oncoming cars glinted against the smear it left.

"She must be famous," said Ruth. "I like famous people. Have you met any? Was that man you burned famous?"

"Probably not. I don't care about famous people anymore." The last time I had anything to do, even peripherally, with anyone famous was when I changed the direction of the tape over the lock in the Watergate so Frank Wills would see it. Ruth did not look like the kind who would know about that. "I was there for the Kennedy assassination," I said, "but I had nothing to do with it."

"Who was Kennedy?"

That made me smile. "How long have you been here?" I pointed at her tiny purse. "That's all you've got with you?"

She slid across the seat and leaned her head against my shoulder. "I don't need anything else."

"No clothes?"

"I left them in Kansas City. We can get more."

"Sure," I said.

She opened the purse and took out a plastic Bayer aspirin case. From it she selected two blue-and-yellow caps. She shoved her sweaty palm up under my nose. "Serometh?"

"No thanks."

She put one of the caps back into the box and popped the other under her nose. She sighed and snuggled tighter against me. We had reached Columbia and I was hungry. When I pulled in at a McDonald's she ran across the lot into the shopping mall before I could stop her. I was a little nervous about the car and sat watching it as I ate (Big Mac, small Dr. Pepper). She did not come back. I crossed the lot to the mall, found a drugstore and bought some cigars. When I strolled back to the car she was waiting for me, hopping from one foot to another and tugging at the door handle. Serometh makes you impatient. She was wearing a pair of shiny black pants, pink and white checked sneakers and a hot pink blouse. " 's go!" she hissed at me.

I moved even slower. She looked like she was about to wet herself, biting her soft lower lip with a line of perfect white teeth. I dawdled over my keys. A security guard and a young man in a shirt and tie hurried out of the mall entrance and scanned the lot. "Nice outfit," I said. "Must have cost you something."

She looked over her shoulder, saw the security guard, who saw her. "Hey!" he called, running toward us. I slid into the car, opened the passenger door. Ruth had snapped open her purse and pulled out a small gun. I grabbed her arm and yanked her into the car; she squawked and her shot went wide. The guard fell down anyway, scared shitless. For the second time that day I tested the Citation's acceleration; Ruth's door slammed shut and we were gone.

"You scut," she said as we hit the entrance ramp of the interstate. "You're a scut-pumping Conservative. You made me miss." But she was smiling, running her hand up the inside of my thigh. I could tell she hadn't ever had so much fun in the twentieth century.

For some reason I was shaking. "Give me one of those seromeths," I said.

Around midnight we stopped in St. Louis at a Holiday Inn. We registered as Mr. and Mrs. Gerald Bruno (an old acquaintance) and paid in advance. No one remarked on the apparent difference in our ages. So discreet. I bought a copy of the *Post-Dispatch* and we went to the room. Ruth flopped down on the bed, looking bored, but thanks to her gunplay I had a few more things to take care of. I poured myself a glass of Chivas, went into the bathroom, removed the toupee and flushed it down the toilet, showered, put a new blade in my old razor and shaved the rest of the hair from my head. The Lex Luthor look. I cut my scalp. That got me laughing, and I could not stop. Ruth peeked through the doorway to find me dabbing the crown of my head with a bloody kleenex.

"You're a wreck," she said.

I almost fell off the toilet laughing. She was absolutely right. Between giggles I managed to say, "You must not stay anywhere too long, if you're as careless as you were tonight."

She shrugged. "I bet I've been at it longer than you." She stripped and got into the shower. I got into bed.

The room enfolded me in its gold-carpet, green-bedspread mediocrity. Sometimes it's hard to remember that things were ever different. In 1596 I rode to court with Essex; I slept in a chamber of supreme garishness (gilt escutcheons in the corners of the ceiling, pink cupids romping on the walls), in a bed warmed by any of the trollops of the city I might want. And there in the Holiday Inn I sat with my drink, in my pastel blue pajama bottoms, reading a late-twentieth century newspaper, smoking a cigar. An earthquake in Peru estimated to have killed 8,000 in Lima alone. Nope. A steelworker in Gary, Indiana, discovered to be the murderer of six pre-pubescent children, bodies found buried in his basement. Perhaps. The President refuses to enforce the ruling of his Supreme Court because it "subverts the will of the American people." Probably not.

We are everywhere. But not everywhere.

Ruth came out of the bathroom, saw me, did a double take. "You look—perfect!" she said. She slid in the bed beside me, naked, and sniffed at my glass of Chivas. Her lip curled. She looked over my shoulder at the paper. "You can understand that stuff?"

"Don't kid me. Reading is a survival skill. You couldn't last here without it."

"Wrong."

I drained the scotch. Took a puff of the cigar. Dropped the paper to the floor beside the bed. I looked her over. Even relaxed, the muscles in her arms and along the tops of her thighs were well-defined.

"You even smell like one of them," she said.

"How did you get the clothes past their store security? They have those beeper tags clipped to them."

"Easy. I tried on the shoes and walked out when they weren't looking. In the second store I took the pants into a dressing room, cut off the bottoms, along with the alarm tag, and put them on. I held the alarm tag that was clipped to the blouse in my armpit and walked out of that store,too. I put the blouse on in the mall women's room.''

"If you can't read, how did you know which was the women's room?"

"There's a picture on the door."

I felt very tired and very old. Ruth moved close. She rubbed her foot up my leg, drawing the pajama leg up with it. Her thigh slid across my groin. I started to get hard. "Cut it out," I said. She licked my nipple.

I could not stand it. I got off the bed. "I don't like you."

She looked at me with true innocence. "I don't like you either."

Although he was repulsed by the human body, Jonathan Swift was passionately in love with a woman named Esther Johnson. "What you did at the mall was stupid," I said. "You would have killed that guard."

"Which would have made us even for the day."

"Kansas City was different."

"We should ask the cops there what they think."

"You don't understand. That had some grace to it. But what you did was inelegant. Worst of all it was not gratuitous. You stole those clothes for yourself, and I hate that." I was shaking.

"Who made all these laws?"

"I did."

She looked at me with amazement. "You're not just a Conservative. You've gone native!"

I wanted her so much I ached. "No I haven't," I said, but even to me, my voice sounded frightened.

Ruth got out of the bed. She glided over, reached one hand around to the small of my back, pulled herself close. She looked up at me with a face that held nothing but avidity. "You can do whatever you want," she whispered. With a feeling that I was losing everything, I kissed her. You don't need to know what happened then.

I woke when she displaced herself: there was a sound like the sweep of an arm across fabric, a stirring of air to fill the place where she had been. I looked around the still brightly lit room. It was not yet morning. The chain was across the door; her clothes lay on the dresser. She had left the aspirin box beside my bottle of scotch.

She was gone. Good, I thought, now I can go on. But I found I could not sleep, could not keep from thinking. Ruth must be very good at that, or perhaps her thought is a different kind of thought from mine. I got out of the bed, resolved to try again but still fearing the inevitable. I filled the tub with hot water. I got in, breathing heavily. I took the blade from my razor. Holding my arm just beneath the surface of the water, hesitating only a moment, I cut deeply one, two, three times along the veins in my left wrist. The shock was still there, as great as ever. With blood streaming from me I cut the right wrist. Quickly, smoothly. My heart beat fast and light, the blood flowed frighteningly; already the water was stained. I felt faint—yes—it was going to work this time, yes. My vision began to fade—but in the last moments before consciousness fell away I saw, with sick despair, the futile wounds closing themselves once again, as they had so many times before. For in the future the practice of medicine may progress to the point where men need have no fear of death.

The dawn's rosy fingers found me still unconscious. I came to myself about eleven, my head throbbing, so weak I could hardly rise from the cold, bloody water. There were no scars. I stumbled into the other room and washed down one of Ruth's megamphetamines with two fingers of scotch. I felt better immediately. It's funny how that works sometimes, isn't it? The maid knocked as I was cleaning the bathroom. I shouted for her to come back later, finished as quickly as possible and left the motel immediately. I ate shredded wheat with milk and strawberries for breakfast. I was full of ideas. A phone book gave me the location of a likely country club.

The Oak Hill Country Club of Florissant, Missouri, is not a spectacularly wealthy institution, or at least it does not give that impression. I'll bet you that the membership is not as purely white as the stucco clubhouse. That was all right with me. I parked the Citation in the mostly empty parking lot, hauled my new equipment from the trunk, and set off for the locker room, trying hard to look like a dentist. I successfully ran the gauntlet of the pro shop, where the proprietor was busy telling a bored caddy why the Cardinals would fade in the stretch. I could hear running water from the shower as I shuffled into the locker room and slung the bag into a corner. Someone was singing the "Ode to Joy," abominably.

I began to rifle through the lockers, hoping to find an open one with someone's clothes in it. I would take the keys from my benefactor's pocket and proceed along my merry way. Ruth would have accused me of self-interest; there was a moment in which I accused myself. Such hesitation is the seed of failure: as I paused before a locker containing a likely set of clothes, another golfer entered the room along with the locker room attendant. I immediately began undressing, lowering my head so that the locker door would obscure my face. The golfer was soon gone, but the attendant sat down and began to leaf through a worn copy of *Penthouse*. I could come up with no better plan than to strip and enter the showers. Amphetamine daze. Perhaps the kid would develop a hard-on and go to the john to take care of it.

There was only one other man in the shower, the operatic soloist, a somewhat portly gentleman who mercifully shut up as soon as I entered. He worked hard at ignoring me. I ignored him in return: neither of us was much to look at. I waited a long five minutes after he left; two more men came into the showers and I walked out with what composure I could muster. The locker room boy was stacking towels on a table. I fished a five from my jacket in the locker and walked up behind him. Casually I took a towel.

"Son, get me a pack of Marlboros, will you?"

He took the money and left.

In the second locker I found a pair of pants that contained the keys to some sort of Audi. I was not choosy. Dressed in record time, I left the new clubs beside the rifled locker. My note read, "The pure products of America go crazy." There were three eligible cars in the lot, two 4000s and a Fox. The key would not open the door of the Fox. I was jumpy, but almost home free, coming around the front of a big Chrysler. . .

"Hey!"

My knee gave way and I ran into the fender of the car. The keys slipped out of my hand and skittered across the hood to the ground, jingling. Grimacing, I hopped toward them, plucked them up, glancing over my shoulder at my pursuer as I stooped. It was the locker room attendant.

"Your cigarettes." He was looking at me the way a sixteen-year-old looks at his father, that is, with bored skepticism. All our gods in the end become pitiful. It was time for me to be abruptly friendly. As it was he would remember me too well.

"Thanks," I said. I limped over, put the pack into my shirt pocket. He started to go, but I couldn't help myself. "What about my change?"

Oh, such an insolent silence! I wonder what you told them when they asked you about me, boy. He handed over the money. I tipped him a quarter, gave him a piece of Mr. Graves' professional smile. He studied me. I turned and inserted the key into the lock of the Audi. A fifty-percent chance. Had I been the praying kind I might have prayed to one of those pitiful gods. The key turned without resistance; the door opened. The kid slouched back toward the club-house, pissed at me and his lackey's job. Or perhaps he found it in his heart to smile. Laughter—the Best Medicine.

A bit of a racing shift, then back to Interstate 70. My hip twinged all the way across Illinois.

I had originally intended to work my way east to Buffalo, New York, but after the Oak Hill business I wanted to cut it short. If I stayed on the interstate I was sure to get caught; I had been lucky to get as far as I had. Just outside of Indianapolis I turned onto Route 37 north to Ft. Wayne and Detroit.

I was not, however, entirely cowed. Twenty-five years in one time had given me the right instincts, and with the coming of evening and the friendly insects to sing me along, the boredom of the road became a new recklessness. Hadn't I already been seen by too many people in those twenty-five years? Thousands had looked into my honest face—and where were they? Ruth had reminded me that I was not stuck here. I would soon make an end to this latest adventure one way or another, and once I had done so, there would be no reason in god's green world to suspect me.

And so: north of Ft. Wayne, on Highway 6 east, a deserted country road (what was he doing there?), I pulled over to pick up a young hitchhiker. He wore a battered black leather jacket. His hair was short on the sides, stuck up in spikes on top, hung over his collar in back; one side was carrot-orange, the other brown with a white streak. His sign, pinned to a knapsack, said "?" He threw the pack into the back seat and climbed into the front.

"Thanks for picking me up." He did not sound like he meant it. "Where you going?"

"Flint. How about you?"

"Flint's as good as anywhere."

"Suit yourself." We got up to speed. I was completely calm. "You should fasten your seat belt," I said.

"Why?"

The surly type. "It's not just a good idea. It's the Law."

"How about turning on the light." He pulled a crossword puzzle book and a pencil from his jacket pocket. I flicked on the domelight for him.

"I like to see a young man improve himself," I said.

His look was an almost audible sigh. "What's a five-letter word for 'the lowest point?'"

"Nadir," I replied.

"That's right. How about 'widespread'; four letters."

"Rife."

"You're pretty good." He stared at the crossword for a minute, then suddenly rolled down his window and threw the book, and the pencil, out of the car. He rolled up the window and stared at his reflection in it, his back to me. I couldn't let him get off that easily. I turned off the interior light and the darkness leapt inside.

"What's your name, son? What are you so mad about?"

"Milo. Look, are you queer? If you are, it doesn't matter to me but it will cost you . . . if you want to do anything about it."

I smiled and adjusted the rearview mirror so I could watch him—and he could watch me. "No, I'm not queer. The name's Loki." I extended my right hand, keeping my eyes on the road.

He looked at the hand. "Loki?"

As good a name as any. "Yes. Same as the Norse god."

He laughed. "Sure, Loki. Anything you like. Fuck you."

Such a musical voice. "Now there you go. Seems to me, Milo—if you don't mind my giving you my unsolicited opinion—that you have something of an attitude problem." I punched the cigarette lighter, reached back and pulled a cigar from my jacket on the back seat, in the process weaving the car all over Highway 6. I bit the end off the cigar and spat it out the window, stoked it up. My insects wailed. I cannot explain to you how good I felt.

"Take for instance this crossword puzzle book. Why did you throw it out the window?"

I could see Milo watching me in the mirror, wondering whether he should take me seriously. The headlights fanned out ahead of us, the white lines at the center of the road pulsing by like a rapid heartbeat. Take a chance, Milo. What have you got to lose?

"I was pissed," he said. "It's a waste of time. I don't care about stupid games."

"Exactly. It's just a game, a way to pass the time. Nobody ever really learns anything from a crossword puzzle. Corporation lawyers don't get their Porsches by building their word power with crosswords, right?"

"I don't care about Porsches."

"Neither do I, Milo. I drive an Audi."

Milo sighed.

"I know, Milo. That's not the point. The point is that it's all a game, crosswords or corporate law. Some people devote their lives to Jesus; some devote their lives to artwork. It all comes to pretty much the same thing. You get old. You die."

"Tell me something I don't already know."

"Why do you think I picked you up, Milo? I saw your question mark and it spoke to me. You probably think I'm some pervert out to take advantage of you. I have a funny name. I don't talk like your average middle-aged business-man. Forget about that." The old excitement was upon me; I was talking louder and louder, leaning on the accelerator. The car sped along. "I think you're as troubled by the materialism and cant of life in America as I am. Young people like you, with orange hair, are trying to find some values in a world that offers them nothing but crap for ideas. But too many of you are turning to extremes in response. Drugs, violence, religious fanaticism, hedonism. Some, like you I suspect, to suicide. Don't do it, Milo. Your life is too valuable." The speedometer touched eighty, eighty-five. Milo fumbled for his seat-belt but couldn't find it.

I waved my hand, holding the cigar, at him. "What's the matter, Milo? Can't find the belt?" Ninety now. A pickup went by us going the other way, the wind of its passing beating at my head and shoulder. Ninety-five.

"Think, Milo! If you're upset with the present, with your parents and the schools, think about the future. What will the future be like if this trend toward valuelessness continues in the next hundred years? Think of the impact of new tech-nologies! Gene splicing, gerontological research, artificial in-telligence, space exploration, biological weapons, nuclear proliferation! All accelerating this process! Think of the vio-lent reactionary movements that could arise—are arising al-ready, Milo, as we speak—from people's efforts to find something to hold onto. Paint yourself a picture, *Milo*, of the kind of man or woman another hundred years of this process might produce!"

"What are you talking about?" He was terrified.

"I'm talking about the survival of values in America! Simply that." Cigar smoke swirled in front of the dashboard lights, and my voice had reached a shout. Milo was gripping the sides of his seat. The speedometer read 105. "And you, *Milo*, are at the heart of this process! If people continue to think the way you do, *Milo*, throwing their crossword puzzle books out the windows of their Audis across America, *the future will be full of absolutely valueless people!* Right, MILO?'' I leaned over, taking my eyes off the road, and blew smoke into his face, screaming, ''ARE YOU LISTENING, MILO? MARK MY WORDS!''

''Y—yes.''

''GOO, GOO, GA-GA-GAA.''

I put my foot all the way to the floor. The wind howled through the window; the gray highway flew beneath us.

''Mark my words, Milo,'' I whispered. He never heard me. ''Twenty-five across. Eight letters. N-i-h-i-l—.''

My pulse roared in my ears, there joining the drowned choir of the fields and the roar of the engine. My body was slimy with sweat, my fingers clenched through the cigar, fists clamped on the wheel, smoke stinging my eyes. I slammed on the brakes, downshifting immediately, sending the transmission into a painful whine as the car slewed and skidded off the pavement, clipping a reflecting marker and throwing Milo against the windshield. The car stopped with a jerk in the gravel at the side of the road, just shy of a sign announcing, ''Welcome to Ohio.''

There were no other lights on the road; I shut off my own and sat behind the wheel, trembling, the night air cool on my skin. The insects wailed. The boy was slumped against the dashboard. There was a star fracture in the glass above his head, and warm blood came away on my fingers when I touched his hair. I got out of the car, circled around to the passenger's side, and dragged him from the seat into the field adjoining the road. He was surprisingly light. I left him there, in a field of Ohio soybeans on the evening of a summer's day.

The city of Detroit was founded by the French adventurer Antoine de la Mothe Cadillac, a supporter of Comte de Pontchartrain, minister of state to the Sun King, Louis XIV. All of these men worshipped the Roman Catholic god, protected their political positions, and let the future go hang.

Cadillac, after whom an American automobile was named, was seeking a favorable location to advance his own economic interests. He came ashore on July 24, 1701, with fifty soldiers, an equal number of settlers, and about one hundred friendly Indians near the present site of the Veterans Memorial Building, within easy walking distance of the Greyhound Bus Terminal.

The car had not run well after the accident, developing a reluctance to go into fourth, but I did not care. The encounter with Milo had gone exactly as such things should go, and was especially pleasing because it had been totally unplanned. An accident—no order, one would guess—but exactly as if I had laid it all out beforehand. I came into Detroit late at night via Route 12, which eventually turned into Michigan Avenue. The air was hot and sticky. I remember driving past the Cadillac Plant; multitudes of red, yellow, and green lights glinting off dull masonry and the smell of auto exhaust along the city streets. The sort of neighborhood I wanted was not far from Tiger Stadium: pawnshops, an all-night deli, laundromats, dimly lit bars with red Stroh's signs in the windows. Men on street corners walked casually from noplace to noplace.

I parked on a side street just around the corner from a 7-Eleven. I left the motor running. In the store I dawdled over a magazine rack until at last I heard the racing of an engine and saw the Audi flash by the window. I bought a copy of *Time* and caught a downtown bus at the corner. At the Greyhound station I purchased a ticket for the next bus to Toronto and sat reading my magazine until departure time.

We got onto the bus. Across the river we stopped at customs and got off again. "Name?" they asked me.

"Gerald Spotsworth."

"Place of birth?"

"Calgary." I gave them my credentials. The passport photo showed me with hair. They looked me over. They let me go.

I work in the library of the University of Toronto. I am well-read, a student of history, a solid Canadian citizen. There I lead a sedentary life. The subways are clean, the people are friendly, the restaurants are excellent. The sky is blue. The cat is on the mat.

We got back on the bus. There were few other passengers, and most of them were soon asleep; the only light in the darkened interior was that which shone above my head. I was very tired, but I did not want to sleep. Then I remembered that I had Ruth's pills in my jacket pocket. I smiled, thinking of the customs people. All that was left in the box were a couple of tiny pink tabs. I did not know what they were, but I broke one down the middle with my fingernail and took it anyway. It perked me up immediately. Everything I could see seemed sharply defined. The dark green plastic of the seats. The rubber mat in the aisle. My fingernails. All details were separate and distinct, all interdependent. I must have been focused on the threads in the weave of my pants leg for ten minutes when I was surprised by someone sitting down next to me. It was Ruth. "You're back!" I exclaimed.

"We're all back," she said. I looked around and it was true: on the opposite side of the aisle, two seats ahead, Milo sat watching me over his shoulder, a trickle of blood running down his forehead. One corner of his mouth pulled tighter in a rueful smile. Mr. Graves came back from the front seat and shook my hand. I saw the fat singer from the country club, still naked. The locker room boy. A flickering light from the back of the bus: when I turned around there stood the burning man, his eye sockets two dark hollows behind the wavering flames. The shopping mall guard. Hector from the hardware store. They all looked at me.

"What are you doing here?" I asked Ruth.

"We couldn't let you go on thinking like you do. You act like I'm some monster. I'm just a person."

"A rather nice-looking young lady," Graves added.

"People are monsters," I said.

"Like you, huh?" Ruth said. "But they can be saints, too."

That made me laugh. "Don't feed me platitudes. You can't even read."

"You make such a big deal out of reading. Yeah, well, times change. I get along fine, don't I?"

The mall guard broke in. "Actually, miss, the reason we caught on to you is that someone saw you go into the men's room." He looked embarrassed.

"But you didn't catch me, did you?" Ruth snapped back. She turned to me. "You're afraid of change. No wonder you live back here."

"This is all in my imagination," I said. "It's because of your drugs."

"It is all in your imagination," the burning man repeated. His voice was a whisper. "What you see in the future is what you are able to see. You have no faith in God or your fellow man."

"He's right," said Ruth.

"Bull. Psychobabble."

"Speaking of babble," Milo said, "I figured out where you got that goo-goo-goo stuff. Talk—"

"Never mind that," Ruth broke in. "Here's the truth. The future is just a place. The people there are just people. They live differently. So what. People make what they want of the world. You can't escape human failings by running into the past." She rested her hand on my leg. "I'll tell you what you'll find when you get to Toronto," she said. "Another city full of human beings."

This was crazy. I knew it was crazy, I knew it was all unreal, but somehow I was getting more and more afraid. "So the future is just the present writ large," I said bitterly. "More bull."

"You tell her, pal," the locker room boy said.

Hector, who had been listening quietly, broke in, "For a man from the future, you talk a lot like a native."

"You're the king of bullshit, man," Milo said. " 'Some people devote themselves to artwork!' Jesus!"

I felt dizzy. "Scut down, Milo. That means 'Fuck you too.' " I shook my head to try to make them go away. That was a mistake: the bus began to pitch like a sailboat. I grabbed for Ruth's arm but missed. "Who's driving this thing?" I asked, trying to get out of the seat.

"Don't worry," said Graves. "He knows what he's doing."

"He's brain-dead," Milo said.

"You couldn't do any better," said Ruth, pulling me back down.

"No one is driving," said the burning man.

"We'll crash!" I was so dizzy now that I could hardly keep from vomiting. I closed my eyes and swallowed. That seemed to help. A long time passed; eventually I must have fallen asleep.

When I woke it was late morning and we were entering the city, cruising down Eglinton Avenue. The bus had a driver after all—a slender black man with neatly trimmed sideburns who wore his uniform hat at a rakish angle. A sign above the windshield said, "Your driver—safe, courteous," and below that, on the slide-in name plate, "Wilbert Caul." I felt like I was coming out of a nightmare. I felt happy. I stretched some of the knots out of my back. A young soldier seated across the aisle from me looked my way; I smiled, and he returned it briefly.

"You were mumbling to yourself in your sleep last night," he said.

"Sorry. Sometimes I have bad dreams."

"It's okay. I do too, sometimes." He had a round, open face, an apologetic grin. He was twenty, maybe. Who knew where his dreams came from? We chatted until the bus reached the station; he shook my hand and said he was pleased to meet me. He called me "sir."

I was not due back at the library until Monday, so I walked over to Yonge Street. The stores were busy, the tourists were out in droves, the adult theaters were doing a brisk business. Policemen in sharply creased trousers, white gloves, sauntered along among the pedestrians. It was a bright, cloudless day, but the breeze coming up the street from the lake was cool. I stood on the sidewalk outside one of the strip joints and watched the videotaped come-on over the closed circuit. The Princess Laya. Sondra Nieve, the Human Operator. Technology replaces the traditional barker, but the bodies are more or less the same. The persistence of your faith in sex and machines is evidence of your capacity to hope.

Francis Bacon, in his masterwork *The New Atlantis*, foresaw the utopian world that would arise through the application of experimental science to social problems. Bacon, however, could not solve the problems of his own time and was eventually accused of accepting bribes, fined £40,000, and imprisoned in the Tower of London. He made no appeal to God, but instead applied himself to the development of the virtues of patience and acceptance. Eventually he was freed. Soon after, on a freezing day in late March, we were driving near Highgate when I suggested to him that cold might delay the process of decay. He was excited by the idea. On impulse he stopped the carriage, purchased a hen, wrung its neck and stuffed it with snow. He eagerly looked forward to the results of his experiment. Unfortunately, in haggling with the street vendor he had exposed himself thoroughly to the cold and was seized with a chill which rapidly led to pneumonia, of which he died on April 9, 1626.

There's no way to predict these things.

When the videotape started repeating itself I got bored, crossed the street, and lost myself in the crowd.

AYMARA

Lucius Shepard

*"Aymara" was purchased by Gardner Dozois, and
appeared in the August 1986 issue of* IAsfm. *with a
striking cover and interior illustration by Terry Lee. A
complex and passionate tale of wild romance, time
travel, and revolutionary politics, all played out against
a lush tropical setting, "Aymara" was one of the most
popular stories of the year, and an important one for
the magazine, showing up on that year's award ballots.
It helped to further solidify Shepard's reputation as one
of the best short-story writers to enter the field in
decades—and as one of the mainstays of* IAsfm.

*Lucius Shepard began publishing in 1983, and in a
very short time has become one of the most popular and
prolific writers to come along in many years. In 1985,
Shepard won the John W. Campbell Award as the
year's best new writer, as well as being on the Nebula
Award final ballot an unprecedented three times in
three separate categories. Since then, he has turned up
several more times on the final Nebula ballot, as well
as being a finalist for the Hugo Award, the British*

Fantasy Award, the John W. Campbell Memorial Award, the Philip K. Dick Award, and the World Fantasy Award. In 1987, he finally picked up his first though probably not his last award, winning the Nebula for his landmark novella "R&R," another IAsfm *story. His acclaimed first novel,* Green Eyes, *was published in 1984. His most recent books are the novel* Life During Wartime *and the collection* The Jaguar Hunter. *Born in Lynchburg, Virginia, Shepard now lives somewhere in the wilds of Nantucket.*

———————

My name is William Page Corson, and I am the black sheep of the Buckingham County Corsons of Virginia. How I came to earn such disrepute relates to several months I spent in Honduras during the spring and summer of 1978, while doing research for a novel to be based on the exploits of an American mercenary who had played a major role in regional politics. That novel was never written, partly because I was of an age (twenty-one) at which one's concentration often proves unequal to lengthy projects, but mainly due to reasons that will be made clear—or if not made clear, then at least brought somewhat into focus—in the following pages.

One day while leafing through an old travel book, *A Honduran Adventure* by William Wells, I ran across the photograph of a blandly handsome young man with blond hair and mustache, carrying a saber and wearing an ostrich plume in his hat. The caption identified him as General Lee Christmas, and the text disclosed that he had been a railroad engineer in Louisiana until 1901, when—after three consecutive days on the job—he had fallen asleep at the wheel and wrecked his train. To avoid prosecution he had fled to Honduras, there securing employment on a fruit company railroad. One year later, soldiers of the revolution led by General Manuel Bonilla had seized his train, and rather than merely surrendering, he had showed his captors how to armor the flatcars with sheet iron; thus protected, the soldiers had gained control of the entire north coast, and for his part in the proceedings, Christmas had been awarded the rank of general.

From other sources I learned that Christmas had taken a fine house in Tegucigalpa after the successful conclusion of the revolution, and had spent most of his time hunting in Olancho, a wilderness region bordering Nicaragua. By all accounts, he had been the prototypical good ol' boy, content with the cushy lot that had befallen him; but in 1904 something must have happened to change his basic attitudes, for it had been then that he entered the employ of the United Fruit Company, becoming in effect the company enforcer. Whenever one country or another would balk at company policy, Christmas would foment a rebellion and set a more malleable government in office; through this process, United Fruit had come to dominate Central American politics earning the sobriquet El Pulpo (The Octopus) by virtue of its grasping tactics.

These materials fired my imagination and inflamed my leftist sensibility, and I traveled to Honduras in hopes of fleshing out the story. I soon unearthed a wealth of anecdotal detail, much of it testifying to Christmas' irrational courage: he had, for instance, once blown up a building atop which he was standing to prevent the armory it contained from falling into counter-revolutionary hands. But nowhere could I discover what event had precipitated the transformation of an affable, easygoing man into a ruthless mercenary, and an understanding of Christmas' motivations was, I believed, of central importance to my book. Six weeks went by, no new knowledge came to light, and I had more or less decided to create a fictive cause for Christmas' transformation, when I heard that some of the men who had fought alongside him in 1902 might still be alive on the island of Guanoja Menor.

From the window of the ancient DC-3 that conveyed me to Guanoja, the island resembled the cover of a travel brochure, with green hills and white beaches fringed by graceful palms; but at ground level it was revealed to be the outpost of an unrelenting poverty. Derelict shacks were tucked into the folds of the hills, animal wastes fouled the beaches, and the harbors were choked with sewage. The capital, Meachem's Landing, consisted of a few dirt streets lined with weatherbeaten shanties set on pilings, and beneath them lay a carpet of coconut litter and broken glass and crab shells. Black men wearing rags glared at me as I hiked in from the airport, and their hostility convinced me that even the act of walking was an insult to the lethargic temper of the place.

I checked into the Hotel Captain Henry—a ramshackle wooden building, painted pink, with a rust-scabbed roof and an electric pole lashed to its second-story balcony—and slept until nightfall. Then I set out to investigate a lead provided by the hotel's owner: he had told me of a man in his nineties, Fred Welcomes, who lived on the road to Flowers Bay and might have knowledge of Christmas. I had not gone more than a half mile when I came upon a little graveyard confined by a fence of corroded ironwork and overgrown with weeds from which the tops of the tombstones bulged like toadstools. Many of the stones dated from the turn of the century, and realizing that the man I was soon to interview had been a contemporary of these long-dead people, I had a sense of foreboding, of standing on the verge of a supernatural threshold. Dozens of times in the years to follow, I was to have similar apprehensions, a notion that everything I did was governed by unfathomable forces; but never was it stronger than on that night. The wind was driving glowing clouds across the moon, intermittently allowing it to shine through, causing the landscape to pulse dark to bright with the rhythm of a failing circuit, and I could feel ghosts blowing about me, hear windy voices whispering words of warning.

Welcomes' shanty sat amid a banana grove, its orange-lit windows flickering like spirits in a dark water. As I drew near, its rickety shape appeared to assemble the way details are filled in during a dream, acquiring a roof and door and pilings whenever I noticed that it seemed to lack such, until at last it stood complete, looking every bit as dilapidated as I supposed its owner to be. I hesitated before approaching, startled by a banging shutter. Glints of moonlit silver coursed along the warp of the tin roof, and the plastic curtains twitched like the eyelids of a sleeping cat. At last I climbed the steps, knocked, and a decrepit voice responded, asking who was there. I introduced myself, explained that I was interested in Lee Christmas, and—after a considerable pause—was invited to enter.

The old man was sitting in a room lit by a kerosene lantern, and on first glance he seemed a giant; even after I had more realistically estimated his height to be about six-five, his massive hands and the great width of his shoulders supported the idea that he was larger than anyone had a right to be. It may be that this impression was due to the fact that I had expected him to be shriveled with age; but though his coal-black skin was seamed and wrinkled, he was still well-muscled: I would have guessed him to be a hale man in his early seventies. He wore a white cotton shirt, gray trousers, and a baseball cap from which the emblem had been ripped. His face was solemn and long-jawed, all its features so prominent that it looked to be a mask carved of black bone; his eyes were clouded over with milky smears, and from his lack of reaction to my movements, I came to realize he was blind.

"Well, boy," he said, apparently having gauged my youth from the timbre of my voice. "What fah you want to know 'bout Lee Christmas? You want to be a warrior?"

I switched on my pocket tape recorder and glanced around. The furniture—two chairs and a table—was rough-hewn; the bed was a pallet with some clothes folded atop it. An outdated calendar hung from the door, and mounted on the wall opposite Welcomes was a small cross of black coral: in the orange flux of the lantern light, it looked like a complex incision in the boards.

I told him about my book, and when I had done he said, "I 'spect I can help you some. I were wit' Lee from the Battle of La Ceiba 'til the peace at Comayagua, and fah a while after dat."

He began to ramble on in a direction that did not interest me, and I cut in, saying, "I've heard there was no love lost between the islanders and the Spanish. Why did they join Bonilla's revolution?"

"Dat were Lee's doin'," he said. "He promise dat dis Bonilla goin' to give us our freedom, and so he have no trouble raisin' a company. And he tell us that we ain't goin' to have no difficulty wit' de Sponnish, 'cause dey can't shoot straight.'' He gave an amused grunt. ''Nowadays dey better at shootin', lemme tell you. But in de back-time de men of de island were by far de superior marksmen, and Lee figure if he have us wit' him, den he be able to defeat the garrison at La Ceiba. Dat were a tall order. De leader of de garrison, General Carrillo, were a man wit' magic powers. He ride a white mule and carry a golden sword, and it were said no bullet can bring him down. Many of de boys were leery; but Lee gather us on the dock and make us a speech. 'Boys,' he say, 'you done break your mothers' hearts, but you no be breakin' mine. We goin' to come down on de Sponnish like buzzards on a sick steer, and when we through, dey goin' to be showin' to de bone.' And by de time he finish, we everyone of us was spittin' fire.''

As evidenced by this recall of a speech made seventy-five years before, Welcomes' memory was phenomenal, and the longer he spoke, the more fluent and vital his narrative became. Everything I had learned about Christmas—his age (twenty-seven in 1902), his short stature, his background—all that was knitted into a whole cloth, and I began to see him as he must have been: an ignorant, cocky man whose courage stemmed from a belief that his life had been ruined and so he might as well throw what remained of it away on this joke of a revolution. And yet he had not been without hope of redemption. Like many of his countrymen, he adhered to the notion that through the application of American knowhow, the inferior peoples of Central America could be brought forward into a Star-Spangled future and civilized; I believe he nurtured the hope that he could play a part in this process.

When Welcomes reached a stopping point, I took the opportunity to ask if he knew what had motivated Christmas to enter the service of United Fruit. He mulled the question over a second or two and finally answered with a single word: ''Aymara.''

So, Aymara, it was then I first heard your name.

Perhaps it is passionate experience that colors my memory,

but I recall now that the word had the sound of a charm the old man had pronounced, one that caused the wind to gust hard against the shanty, keening in the cracks, fluttering the pages of the calendar on the door as if it, too, were a creature playing with time. But it was only a name, that of a woman whom Christmas and Welcomes had met while on a hunting trip to Olancho in 1904; specifically, a trip to the site of the ruined city of Olancho Viejo, a place founded by the Spanish in 1589 and destroyed by a mysterious explosion not fifty years thereafter. Since that day, Welcomes said, the vegetation there had grown stunted and malformed, and all manner of evil legend had attached to the area, the most notable being that a beautiful woman had been seen walking in the flames that swept over the valley. Though the city had not been rebuilt, this apparition had continued to be sighted by travelers and Indians, always in the vicinity of a cave that had been blasted into the top of one of the surrounding hills by the explosion. Christmas and Welcomes had arrived at this very hilltop during a furious storm and . . . Well, I will let the old man's words (edited for the sake of readability) describe what happened, for it is his story, not mine, that lies at the core of these complex events.

That wind can blow, Lord, that wind can blow! Howlin', rippin' branches off the trees, and drivin' slants of gray rain. Seem like it 'bout to blow everything back to the beginnin' and start all over with creation. Me and Lee was leadin' the horses along the rim of the valley, lookin' for shelter and fearin' for our lives, 'cause the footin' treacherous and the drop severe. And then I spot the cave. Not for a second did I think this the cave whereof the legend speak, but when I pass through the entrance, that legend come back to me. The walls, y'see, they smooth as glass, and there were a tremble in the air like you'd get from a machine runnin' close by . . . 'cept there ain't no sound. The horses took to snortin' and balkin', and Lee pressed hisself flat against the wall and pointed his pistol at the dark. His hair were drippin' wet, plastered to his brow, and his eyes was big and starin'. "Fred," he says, "this here ain't no natural place."

"You no have to be tellin' me," I say, and I reckon the shiver in my voice were plain, 'cause he grins and say, "What's the matter, Fred? Ain't you got no sand?" That were Lee's way, you understand—another man's fear always be the tonic for his own.

Just then I spy a light growin' deeper in the cave. A white light, and brighter than any star. Before I could point it out to Lee, that light shooted from the dark and pass right through me with a flash of cold. Then come another light, and another yet. Each one colder and brighter than the one previous, and comin' faster and faster, 'til it 'pears the cave brightly lit and the lights they flickerin' a little. It were so damn cold that the rainwater have froze in my hair, and I were half-blinded on top of that, but I could have swore I seen somethin' inside the light. And when the cold begin to heaten up, the light to dwindle, I made out the shape of a woman . . . just her shape at first, then her particulars. Slim and black-haired, she were. More than pretty, with both Spanish and Indian breedin' showin' in her face. And she wearin' a garment such as I never seen before, but what in later years I come to recognize as a jump-suit. There were blood on her mouth and a fearful expression on her face. The light gathered 'round her in a cloud and dwindle further, fadin' and shrinkin', and right when it 'bout to fade away complete, she take a step toward us and slump to the ground.

For a moment the cave were pitch-dark, with only the wind and the vexed sounds of the horses, but directly I hear a clatter and a spark flares and I see that Lee have got one of the lanterns goin'. He kneel beside the woman and make to touch her, and I tell him, "Man, I wouldn't be doin' that. She some kinda duppy."

"Horseshit!" he say. "Ain't no such thing."

"You just seen her come a'whirlin' outta nowhere," I say. "That's the duppy way."

'Bout then the woman give out with a moan and her eyelids they flutter open. When she spot Lee bendin' to her, the

muscles in her face start strainin' and she try to speak, but all
that come out were this creaky noise. Finally she muster her
strength and say, "Lee . . . Lee Christmas?" Like she ain't
quite sure he's who she thinks.

Lee 'pears dumbstruck by the fact she know his name and
he can't say nothin'. He glance up to me, bewildered.

"It *is* you," she say. "Thank God . . . thank God." And
she reach out to him, clawin' at his hand. Lee flinched some,
and I expected him to go a'whirlin' off with her into white
light. But nothin' happen.

"Who are you?" Lee asks, and the question seem to amuse
her, 'cause she laugh, and the laugh turn into a fit of coughin'
that bring up more blood to her lips. "Aymara," she say after
the fit pass. "My name is Aymara." Her eyes look to go
blank for a second or two, and then she clutch at Lee's hand,
desperate-like, and say, "You have to listen to me! You have
to!"

Lee look a little desperate himself. I can tell he at sea with
this whole business. But he say, "Go easy, now. I'll listen."
And that calm her some. She lie back, breathin' deep, eyes
closed, and Lee's starin' at her, fixated. Suddenly he give
himself a shake and say, "We got to get you some doctorin',"
and try to lift her. But she fend him off. "Naw," she say.
"Can't no doctor help me. I'm dyin'." She open her eyes
wide as if she just realize this fact. "Listen," she say. "You
know where I come from?" And Lee say, No, but he's been
a'wonderin'. "The future," she tell him. "Almost a hundred
years from now. And I come all that way to see you, Lee
Christmas."

Well sir, me and Lee exchange looks, and it's clear to me
that he thinks whatever happened to this here lady done
'fected her brain.

"You don't believe me!" she say in a panic. "You got
to!" And she hold up her wrist and show Lee her watch.
"See that? You ain't got watches like that in 1904!" I peer
close and see that this watch ain't got no hands, just numbers
made up of dots that flicker and change as they toll off the
seconds. But it don't convince me of nothin'—I figure it's

just some foreign thing. She must can tell we still don't believe her, 'cause she pull out a coupla other items to make her case. I know what them items was now—a ballpoint pen and a calculator—but at the time they was new to me. I still ain't convinced. Her bein' from the future were a hard truth to swallow, no matter the manner of her arrival in the cave. She start gettin' desperate again, beggin' Lee to believe her, and then her features they firm up and she say, "If I ain't from the future, then how come I know you been talkin' to United Fruit 'bout doin' some soldierin' for 'em."

This were the first I hear 'bout Lee and United Fruit, and I were surprised, 'cause Lee didn't have no use for them people. "How the hell you know that?" he asks, and she say, "I told you how. It's in the history books. And that ain't all I know." She take to reelin' off a list of names that weren't familiar to me, but—from the dumbstruck expression on Lee's face—must have meant plenty to him. I recall she mention Jacob Wettstein and Andrew Colby and Machine Gun Guy Maloney, who were to become Lee's second-in-command. And then she reel off another list, this one of battles and dates. When she finish, she clutch his hand again. "You gotta 'cept their offer, Lee. If you don't, the world gonna suffer for it."

I could tell Lee have found reason to believe from what she said, but that the idea of workin' with United Fruit didn't set well with him. "Couldn't nothin' good come of that," he say. "Them boys at the fruit company ain't got much in mind but fillin' their pockets."

"It's true," she say. "The company they villains, but sometimes you gotta do the wrong thing for to 'chieve the right result. And that's what *you* gotta do. 'Less you help 'em, 'less America takes charge down here, the world's gonna wind up in a war that might just be the end of it."

I know this strike a chord in Lee, what with him always carryin' on 'bout good ol' American ingenuity bein' the salvation of the world. But he don't say nothin'.

"You gotta trust me," she say. "Everything depends 'pon you trustin' me and doin' what I say. I come all this way, knowin' I were bound to die of it, just to tell you this, to make sure you'd do what's necessary. You think I'd do that to tell you a lie?''

"Naw," he says. "I s'pose not." But I can see he still havin' his doubts.

She sigh and look worried and then she start explainin' to us that the machine what brought her have gone haywire and set her swayin' back and forth through time like a pendulum. Back to the days of the Conquistador and into the future an equal ways. She tell us 'bout watchin' the valley explode and the old city crumblin' and finally she say, "I only have a glimpse of the future, of what's ahead of my time, and I won't lie, it were too quick for me to have much sense of it. But I have a feelin' from it, a feelin' of peace and beauty . . . like a perfume the world's givin' off. When I 'cepted this duty, I thought it were just to make sure things wouldn't work out worse than they has, but now I know somethin' glorious is goin' to come, somethin' you never would 'spect to come of all the bloodshed and terror of history.''

It were the 'spression on her face at that moment—like she's still havin' that feelin' of peace—that's what put my doubts to rest. It weren't nothin' she coulda faked. Lee he seemed moved by it, but maybe he's stuck with thinkin' that she's addled, 'cause he say, "If you from the future, you tell me some more 'bout my life.''

A shudder pass through her, and for a second I think we gonna lose her then and there. But she gather herself and say, "You gonna marry a woman named Anna and have two daughters, one by her and one by another woman.''

Not many knew Lee were in love with Anna Towers, the daughter of an indigo grower in Truxillo, and even less knew 'bout his illegitimate daughter. Far as I concerned, this sealed the matter, but Aymara didn't understand the weight of what she'd said and kept goin'.

"You gonna die of a fever in Puerto Cortez," she says, "in the year . . .''

"No!" Lee held up his hand. "I don't wanna hear that.''

"Then you believe me.''

"Yes," he say. "I do."

For a while there weren't no sound 'cept the keenin' of the wind from the cave mouth. Lee were downcast, studyin' the backs of his hands like he were readin' there some sorry truth, and Aymara were glum herself, like she were sad he did believe her. "Will you do it?" she asks.

Lee give a shrug. "Do I got a choice?"

"Maybe not," she tell him. "Maybe this how it have to be. One of the men who . . . who help send me here, he claim the course of time can't be changed. But I couldn't take the chance he were wrong." She wince and swallow hard. "Will you do it?"

"Hell," he say after mullin' it over. "Guess I ain't got no better thing to do. Might as well go soldierin' awhile."

She search his face to see if he lyin' . . . 'least that's how it look to me. "Swear to it," she say, takin' his hand. "Swear you'll do it."

"All right," he say. "I swear. Now you rest easy."

He try doctorin' her some, wettin' down her brow and such, but nothin' come of it. Somethin' 'bout the manner of travel, she say, have tore up her insides, and there's no fixin' 'em. It 'pear to me she just been hangin' on to drag that vow outta Lee, and now he done it, she let go and start slippin' away. Once she make a rally, and she tell us more' 'bout her journey, sayin' the strange feelin's that sweep over her come close to drivin' her mad. I think Lee's doubtin' her again, 'cause he ask another question or two 'bout the future. But it seem she answer to his satisfaction. Toward the end she take to talkin' crazy to someone who ain't there, callin' him Darlin' and sayin' how she sorry. Then she grab hold of Lee and beg him not to go back on his word.

"I won't," he say. But I think she never hear him, 'cause as he speak blood come gushin' from her mouth and she sag and look to be gazin' into nowhere.

Lee don't hardly say nothin' for a long time, and then it's only after the storm have passed and he concerned with makin' a grave. We put her down near the verge of the old city, and once she under the earth, Lee ask me to say a little somethin' over her. So I utter up a prayer. It were strange tryin' to talk to God with the ruined tower of the cathedral loomin' above, all ivied and crumblin', like a sign that no prayers would be answered.

"What you gonna do?" I ask Lee as he saddlin' up.

He shake his head and tighten the cinch. "What would you do, Fred?"

"I guess I wouldn't want to be messin' with them fruit company boys," I say. "They takes things more serious than I likes."

"Ain't that the truth," he say. He look over to me, and it seem all the hollows in his face has deepened. "But maybe I ain't been takin' things serious enough." He worry his lip. "You really think she from the future?" He ask this like he wantin' to have me say, No.

"I think she from somewhere damn strange," I say. "The future sound 'bout as good as anything."

He scuff the ground with his heel. "Pretty woman," he say. "I guess it ain't reasonable she just throw her life away for nothin'."

I reckoned he were right.

"Jesus Christ!" He smack his saddle. "I wish I could just forget all 'bout her."

"Well, maybe you can," I tell him. "A man can forget 'bout most anything with enough time."

I never should have say that, 'cause it provide Lee with somethin' to act contrary to, with a reason to show off his pride, and it could be that little thing I say have tipped the scales of his judgment.

"Maybe *you* can forget it," he say testily. "But not me. I ain't 'bout to forget I give her my word." He swing hisself up into the saddle and set his horse prancin' with a jerk of the reins. Then he grin. "Goddamn it, Fred! Let's go! If we gotta win the world for ol' United Fruit, we better get us a move on!"

And with that, we ride up from the valley and into the wild and away from Aymara's grave, and far as I know, Lee never

did take a backward glance from that day forth, so busy he
were with his work of forgin' the future.

I asked questions, attempting to clarify certain points, the
exact date of the encounter among other things, but of course
I did not believe Welcomes. Despite his aura of folksy integ-
rity, I knew that Guanoja was rife with storytellers, men who
would stretch the truth to any dimension for a price, and I
assumed Welcomes to be one of these. Yet I was intrigued by
what I perceived as the pathos surrounding the story's invention. Here was the citizen of a country long oppressed by the
economic policies of the United States, who—in order to earn
a tip from an American tourist (I had given him twenty
lempira upon the conclusion of his tale)—had created a fable
that exonerated the United States from guilt and laid the
blame for much of Central America's brutal history upon the
shoulders of a mystical woman from the future. On returning
to my hotel, I typed up sections of the story and seeded them
throughout a longer piece that documented various of Christmas' crimes along with others committed by his successors. I
entitled the piece "Aymara," and the following day I sent it
off to *Mother Jones*, having no real expectations that it would
see print.

But "Aymara" *was* published, as was my next piece, and
the next . . . And so began a journalistic career that has
lasted these sixteen years.

During those years, my espousal of left-wing causes and
the ensuing notoriety inspired my family to break off all
connections with me. (They preferred not to acknowledge that
I also lent my support to populist rebellions against Soviet-
sponsored regimes.) I was not offended by their action; in
fact, I took it for a confirmation of the rightness of my
course, since—with their stock portfolios and mausoleum-like
homes and born-again conservatism—they were as nasty a
pack of capitalist rats as one could meet. I traveled to Argen-
tina, South Africa, The Phillipines, to any country that offered the scenario of a superpower-backed dictatorship and
masses of the oppressed, and I wired back stories that sought

to undermine the Commie-hating mentality engendered by the
Reagan years. I admit that my zeal was occasionally mis-
placed, that I was used at times by corrupt men who passed
themselves off as populist leaders. And I will further admit
that in some cases I was motivated less by passionate concern
than by a desire to increase my own legend. I had, you see,
become a media figure. My photograph was featured on the
covers of national magazines concomitant with such headings
as ''William Corson and the New Journalism''; my books
made the best-seller lists; talk shows pestered my agent. But
despite the glitter, I truly cared about the causes I espoused.
Perhaps I cared too much. Perhaps—like Lee Christmas—I
made the mistaken assumption that my American citizenship
was a guarantee of wisdom superior to that of the peoples
whom I tried to help. In retrospect, I can see that the impulses
that provoked my writing of ''Aymara'' were no less ingenu-
ous, no more informed, than those that inspired his career;
but this is an irony I do not choose to dwell upon.

In January of 1994, I returned to Guanoja. The purpose of
the trip was partly for a vacation, my first in many years, and
also to satisfy a nostalgic whim to visit the place where my
career had begun. The years had brought little change to
Meachem's Landing. True, there was now a jetport outside of
town, and a few of the shanty bars had been replaced by more
pricey watering holes of concrete block; but it remained
essentially the same confluence of dirt streets lined with
weathered shacks and populated by raggedly dressed blacks.
The most salient differences were the gaggle of lower-echelon
Honduran civil servants who spent each day hunched over
their typewriters on the second-story verandah of the Hotel
Captain Henry, churning out reams of officialese, and the
alarming number of CIA agents: cold-eyed, patently anony-
mous men who could be seen sitting in the bars, gazing
moodily toward Nicaragua and the Red Menace. War was in
the offing, its onset as inevitable as the approach of a season,
and this, too, was a factor in my choice of a vacation spot. I
had received word of a mysterious military installation on the
Honduran mainland, and—after having nosed around Wash-

ington for several weeks—I had been invited to inspect this installation. The Pentagon apparently wanted to assure me of its harmlessness and thus prevent their benign policies from being besmirched by more of my yellow journalism.

After checking into the hotel, I walked out past the town to the weedy little graveyard, where I expected I would find a stone marking the remains of Fred Welcomes. There was, indeed, such a stone, and I was startled to learn that he had survived until 1990, dying at the age of 106. I had assumed that he could not have lived much past the date of my interview with him, and the fact that he had roused my guilt. All my good fortune was founded upon his eloquent lie, and I could have done a great deal to ease his decline. I leaned against the rusted fence, thinking that I was no better than the businessmen whose exploitative practices I had long decried, that I had mined gold from the old man's imagination and given him a pittance in return. I was made so morose that later the same night, unable to achieve peace of mind, I set out on a drunk . . . at least this was my intent.

Across the street from the hotel was a two-story building of white stucco with faded lettering above the door that read Maud Price's Golden Dream. I remembered Maud from my previous trip—a fat, black woman who had kept an enormous turtle in a tin washtub and would entertain herself by feeding it chicken necks and watching it eat—and I was saddened to discover that she, too, had passed away. Her daughter was now the proprietor, and I was pleased to find that she had maintained Maud's inimitable decor. Strung across the ceiling were dozens upon dozens of man-shaped paper dolls, colored red and black, and these cast magical-looking shadows on the walls by the light of two flickering lanterns. Six wooden tables, a bar atop which rested a venerable stereo that was grinding out listless reggae, and a number of framed photographs whose glass was too flyspecked to permit easy observation of the subject matter. I ordered a beer, a Salvavida, and was preparing for a bout of drunken self-abnegation, when I noticed a young woman staring at me from the rear table. On meeting my eyes, she showed no sign of embarrassment and held her gaze steady for a long moment before turning back to the magazine she had been reading. Even in that dim light, I could see she was beautiful. Slim, long-limbed, with a honeyed complexion. Curls of black hair hung over the front of her white blouse, their shapes as elegant as the tailfeathers of exotic birds. Her face . . . I could tell you that she had large dark eyes and high cheekbones, that her features had an impassive Indian cast. But that does nothing more than to define her by type and illuminates her not at all. This was a woman with whom I was soon to be in love, if I was not somewhat in love with her already, and the most difficult thing in the world to describe is the face of your lover, because though it is familiar in every detail, it tends to become a mirror of your devotion, to reflect the ideals of passion, and thus is less a human face than the face of love itself.

I continued to watch her, and after a while she looked up again and smiled. There was no way I could ignore this contact. I walked over, introduced myself (in Spanish, which I assumed to be her native tongue), and asked if I could join her. "Why not?" she replied in English, and after I had taken a seat, she pushed her magazine toward me, pointing to an inset photograph of me, one snapped some years before when I had worn a mustache. "I thought it was you," she said. "You look much more handsome clean-shaven."

Her name, she told me, was Ivie Solis. She was employed by a travel agency in La Ceiba and was on a working vaca-tion, having arrived the day before. We talked of this and that, nothing of consequence, but the air between us seemed to crackle. Everything about her, everything she did, struck a chord within me, and I was mesmerized by her movements, entranced, as if she were a magician who might at any moment loose a flight of birds from her fingertips.

Eventually the conversation turned to my work, of which she had read the lion's share, and she told me that her favorite piece was my first, "Aymara." I expressed surprise that she had seen it—it had never been reprinted—and she explained that her parents had run a small hotel catering to American tourists, and the magazine had been left in one of the rooms. "It had the feel of being part of a puzzle," she said. "Or the answer to a riddle."

"It seems fairly straightforward to me," I said.

She tucked a curl behind her ear, a gesture I was coming to recognize as characteristic. "That's because you didn't believe the old man's story."

"And you did?"

"I didn't leap to disbelief as you did." She settled back in her chair, picking at the label of her beer bottle. "I guess I just like thinking about what motivated the woman."

"Obviously," I said, "according to the logic of the story, she came from a world worse off than this one and was hoping to initiate a course of events that would improve it."

"I thought that myself at first," she said. "But it *doesn't* fit the logic of the story. Don't you remember? She knew what would happen to Christmas. His military career, his triumphs. If she'd come from a world in which those things hadn't occurred, she wouldn't have had knowledge of them."

"So—" I began.

"I think," she cut in, "that if she did exist, she came from this world. That she knew she would have to sacrifice herself in order to ensure that Christmas did as he did. It may be that your article was the agency that informed her of her duty."

"Even if that's the case," I said, "why would she have tried to inspire Christmas' crimes? Why wouldn't she have tried to make him effect good works? Perhaps she could have destroyed United Fruit."

"That would be the last thing she'd want. Don't you see? If her actions were politically motivated, she would understand that before real change could occur, the circumstances, the conditions of life under American rule, would have to be so oppressive that violent change would become a viable option. Revolution. She'd realize that Christmas' violences were necessary. They set the tone for American policies and licensed subsequent violence. She'd be afraid that if Christmas didn't work for United Fruit, the process of history that set the stage for revolution might be slowed down or negated. Perhaps the

American stranglehold might be achieved with such subtlety that change would be forever impossible.''

She spoke these words with marked intensity, and I believe I realized then that there was more to Ivie than met the eye. Her logic was the logic of terrorism, the justification of bloodshed in terms of its consciousness-raising effects. But I was so intent upon her as a woman, I scarcely noticed the implication of what she had said.

''Well,'' I said, ''given that your scenario is accurate, it still doesn't make sense. The idea of time travel, of tinkering with the past . . . it's absurd. Too many paradoxes are involved. What you're supposing isn't a chain of events wherein one action predicates another. It's a loop, a metaphysical knot tied in reality, linking my article and some woman and a man years dead. There's no end, no beginning. Things don't work that way.''

''They don't?'' She lowered her eyes and traced a design in the moisture on the table. ''It seems to me that life *is* paradox. Things occur without apparent reason between nations.'' She looked up at me. ''Between people. Perhaps there are reasons, but they're impossible to unravel or define. And dealing with such an unreasonable quantity as time, I wouldn't expect it to be anything other than paradoxical.''

We moved on to other topics, and shortly afterward we left the bar and walked along the road to Flowers Bay. A few hundred yards past the last shanty, at a point where the road meandered close to the shore and the sea lay calm beneath a sheen of starlight, visible through a labyrinthine fringe of mangrove, there I kissed her. It was the kind of kiss that holds a lifetime of promise, tentative, then growing more assured and involving as the contact surpasses all your expectations. I had thought kisses like that existed solely in the province of romance novels, and on discovering this was not so, all my cynicism was dissolved and I fell wholly in love with Ivie Solis.

I do not propose to detail our affair, the evolution of our feelings. While these things seemed to me remarkable, I doubt they were more so than the interactions of any other pair of lovers, and they are pertinent to my story only in the volatility that attached to our moments together. Despite Ivie's thesis that love—like time—was an inexplicable mystery, I sought to explain it to myself and decided that because I had never had any slack in my life, because I had never allowed myself the luxury of deep emotional involvement, I had therefore been ripe for the picking. I might, I told myself, have fallen in love with anyone. Ivie had simply been the first acceptable candidate to happen along. All I knew of her aside from her work and place of birth were a few bits and pieces: that she was twenty-seven; that she had attended the University of Miami; that—like most Hondurans—she resented the American presence in her country; that she had a passion for coconut candy and enjoyed the works of Manuel Puig. How, I wondered, could I be obsessed with someone about whose background I was almost completely ignorant. And yet perhaps my depth of feeling was enhanced by this lack of real knowledge. Things are often most alluring when they are not quite real, when your contact with them is brief and intense, and in the light of the mind they acquire the vividity and artfulness of a dream.

We spent nearly every moment of every day in each other's company, and most of this in making love. My room, our clothing, smelled of sex, and we became such a joke to the old woman who cleaned the hotel that whenever she saw us she would let loose with gales of laughter. The only times we were apart were an hour or so each afternoon when Ivie would have to perform her function as a travel agent, securing— she said—cheap group rates from various resorts that would be offered by her firm to American skin-divers. On most of these occasions I would pace back and forth, impatient for her return. But then, ten days after we had initiated the affair, thinking I might as well make some use of the interval, I rented a car and drove to Spanish Harbor, a small town up the coast where there had lately been several outbreaks of racial violence, highly untypical for Guanoja; I was interested in determining whether or not these incidents were related to the martial atmosphere that had been gathering about the island.

By the time I arrived in the town, which differed from Meachem's Landing hardly at all, having a larger harbor and perhaps a half a dozen more streets, I was thirsty, and I stopped in a tourist restaurant for a beer. This particular restaurant, The Treasure Chest, consisted of a small room done up in pirate decor that was fronted by a cement deck where patrons sat beneath striped umbrellas. Standing at the bar, I had a clear view of the deck, and as I sipped my beer, wondering how best to pursue my subject, I spotted Ivie sitting at a table near the railing. With her was a man wearing a gray business suit. I assumed him to be a resort owner, but when he turned to signal a waiter, I recognized him by his hawkish features and fringe of salt-and-pepper beard to be Abimael Sotomayor, the leader of *Sangre y Verdad* (Blood and Truth), one of the most extreme of Latin American terrorist groups. I had twice interviewed him and I knew him for a charismatic and scary man, a poet who excelled at torture, whose followers performed quasi-mystical blood rituals in his name prior to each engagement. The sight of him with Ivie numbed me, and I began to construct rationalizations that would explain her presence in innocent terms. But none of my rationalizations held water.

I left the restaurant and drove full-tilt back to Meachem's Landing, where I bribed the cleaning woman into admitting me to Ivie's room. It was identical to mine, with gray boards and a metal cot and a night table covered in plastic and a single window that opened onto the second-story verandah. I began by searching the closet, but found only shoes and clothing, apparel quite in keeping with her purported job. Her overnight case contained makeup, and the rest of her luggage was empty . . . or so it appeared. But as I hefted one of the suitcases, preparing to stow it beneath the cot, I realized it was heavier than it should have been. I laid it on the cot and before long I located the catch that opened a false bottom; inside was a machine pistol.

I sat staring at the gun. It was an emblem of Ivie's complicity with an organization so violent that even I, who sympathized with their cause, was repelled by their actions. Yet despite this, I found I loved her no less; I only feared that she did not love me, that she was using me. And, too, I feared for her: the fact that she was at the least an associate of *Sangre y Verdad* offered little hope of a happy ending for the two of us. Finally I replaced the false bottom, restored the suitcase to its original spot beneath the cot and went to my room to wait for Ivie.

That night I said nothing about the gun, rather I tested Ivie in a variety of ways, trying to learn whether or not her affections for me were fraudulent. Not only did she pass every test, but I came to understand much about her that had been puzzling me. I realized that her distracted silences, her deferential attitude concerning the future, her vague references to "responsibilities," all these were symptomatic of the difficulty our relationship was causing her, the contrary pulls exerted by her two passions. Throughout the night, I kept thinking of horror stories I had heard about *Sangre y Verdad*, but I loved Ivie too much to judge her. How could I—a citizen of the country which had created the conditions that bred organizations like Sotomayor's—ever hope to fathom the pressures that had brought her to this pass?

For the next three days, knowing that our time together was likely to be brief, I tried to put politics from mind. Those days were nearly perfect. We swam, we danced, we rented a dory and rowed out past the reef and threw out lines and caught silkfish, satinfish, fish that gleamed iridescent red and blue and yellow, like talismans of our own brilliance. Yet despite our playfulness, our happiness, I was constantly aware that the end could not be far off.

Four days after her meeting with Sotomayor, Ivie told me she had an appointment that evening, one that might last two or three hours; her nervous manner informed me that something important was in the works. At eight o'clock she drove off along the road to Flowers Bay, and I tailed her in my rented car, maintaining a discreet distance, my headlights dark. She parked by the side of the road about a mile past Welcomes' shanty, and seeing this, I pulled my car into a thicket and continued on foot.

●

It was a moonless night, but the stars were thick, their light revealing every shadowy rut, silhouetting the palms and mangrove. Mosquitoes whined in my ear; the sound of waves on the reef came as a faint hiss. A couple of hundred feet beyond Ivie's car stood a largish shanty set among a stand of cocals. Several cars were parked out front, and two men were lounging by the door, obviously on sentry duty. Orange light flickered in the window. I eased through the brush, making my way toward the rear of the shanty, and after ascertaining that no guards were posted there, I duckwalked across a patch of open ground and flattened against the wall. I could hear many voices speaking at once, none of them intelligible. I inched along the wall to the window whose shutter was cracked open. Through the gap I spotted Sotomayor sitting atop a table, and beside him, a thin, agitated looking man of thirty-five or so, with prematurely gray hair. I could see none of the others, but judging by their voices, I guessed there to be at least a dozen men and women present.

With a peremptory gesture, Sotomayor signaled for quiet. "I would much have preferred to use my organization alone," he said. "But Doctor Dobler"—he acknowledged the gray-haired man with a nod—"insisted that the entire spectrum of the left be included and I had no choice but to agree. However, in the interests of security, I wish to limit participation in this operation to those in this room. And, since some of you are unknown to the rest, I suggest that we not increase our intimacy by an exchange of names. Let us choose false names. Simple ones, if you please." He smoothed back his hair, glancing around at his audience. "As I am to lead, I will take a military rank for my name." He smiled. "And as I am not overly ambitious, you may refer to me as the Sergeant." Laughter. "Perhaps if we are successful, I will receive a promotion."

Each of the men and women—there were fourteen in all—selected a name, and I heard Ivie say, "Aymara."

The hairs on the back of my neck prickled to hear it, but knowing her fascination with my article, I did not think it an unexpected choice.

"Very well," said Sotomayor, all business now. "The matter under consideration is the American military project known as Longshot."

I was startled—Longshot was the code name of the installation I was soon to inspect.

"For some months," Sotomayor went on, "we have been hearing rumors concerning Longshot, none likely to inspire confidence in our neighbors to the north. We have been unable to substantiate the rumors, but this situation has changed. Doctor Dobler was until recently one of the coordinators of the project. He has come to us at great personal risk, because he believes there is terrible danger associated with Longshot, and because, with our lack of bureaucratic impediments, he believes we may be the only ones capable of acting swiftly enough to forestall disaster. I will let him explain the rest."

Sotomayor stepped out of view, leaving the floor to Dobler, who looked terrified. Thinking what it must have taken for him to venture forth from his ivory tower and out among the bad dogs, I awarded him high marks for guts. He cleared his throat. "Project Longshot is essentially an experiment in temporal displacement . . . that is to say, time travel."

This sparked a babble, and Sotomayor called for quiet. I wished I could have seen Ivie's face, wanting to know if she were as stunned and frightened as I was.

"The initial test is to be conducted twenty-three days from now," said Dobler. "We have every reason to believe it will succeed, because evidence exists in the past . . ." He broke off, appearing confused. "There's so much to . . ." His eyes darted left to right. "I'm sorry. I . . ."

"Please be calm," advised Sotomayor. "You're among friends."

Dobler squared his shoulders. "I'm all right," he said, and drew a deep breath. "The site of the project is a hill overlooking the ruins of Olancho Viejo, a colonial city destroyed in 1623 by an explosion. I say 'explosion,' but I believe I can safely state that it was not an explosion in the typical sense of the word. For one thing, eyewitness accounts testify that while, indeed, some of the buildings were blown apart, others appeared to crumble, to collapse into powder and chunks of rotten stone, the result of being washed over by a wave of blinding white radiance. Of course these accounts were written by superstitious men—mainly priests—and are thus suspect. Some tell of a beautiful woman walking in the midst of the light, but I think we can attribute that to the Catholic propensity for seeing the Virgin in moments of stress.'' This elicited a few chuckles, and Dobler was braced by the response. ''However, allied with readings we have taken, with other anomalies we've discovered on and near the site, it's evident that the destruction of Olancho Viejo was a direct result of our experiment. Though our target date is in the 1920s, it seems that the displacement will create a kind of shockwave that will produce dire effects three hundred and sixty years in the past.''

''How does that affect us?'' someone asked.

''I'll get to that in a minute,'' said Dobler. He was warming to his task, becoming the model of an enthused lecturer. ''First it's important you understand that although the initial experiment will merely consist of the displacement of a few laboratory animals and some mineral specimens, plant life, and so forth, the target purpose of the project is the manipulation of the past through assassination and other means.''

Expressions of outrage from the gathering.

''Wait!'' said Dobler. ''That's not what you should be worried about, because I don't think it's possible.''

''Why not?'' A woman's voice.

''I really don't think I could explain it to you,'' said Dobler. ''The mathematics are too complex . . . and my conclusions, I admit, are arguable. Several of my colleagues are in complete disagreement; they believe the past *can* be altered. But I'm convinced otherwise. Time, according to my mathematical model, has a fixed shape. It is not simply a process that affects physical objects; it has its own physicality, or—better said—the process of time involves its own spectrum of physical events, all on the particulate level, and it is the isolation of this spectrum that will allow us to displace objects into the past.'' He must have been the focus of

bewildered stares, for he threw up his hands in helplessness.
"The language isn't capable of conveying an accurate explanation. Suffice it to say, that in my opinion, any attempt to alter the course of history will fail, because the physical potentials of time will compensate for that alteration.

"It sounds to me," said Sotomayor, "as if you're embracing the doctrine of predestination."

"That's a rather murky analogue," said Dobler. "But, yes, I suppose I am."

"Then why are you asking us to stop something which, according to you, cannot be stopped? If evidence exists that the experiment was carried out, we can do nothing . . . at least if we are to accept your logic."

"As I stated, I may be wrong in this," said Dobler. "In which case, an attack on the project might succeed. But even if time does prove to be unalterable, what is unalterable in this circumstance is the destruction of Olancho Viejo. It's possible that our experiment can be stopped, and the malleability of time will enlist some other causal agent."

"There's something I don't understand." Ivie's voice. "If you are correct about the unalterability of time, what do we have to fear?"

"For every action," said Dobler, "there must be a reaction. The action will be the experiment. One small part of the reaction can be observed in what happened three centuries ago. But my figures show that the greater part of the reaction will occur in the present. I've gone over and over the equations, and there's no error." Dobler paused, summoning thought. "I've no idea what form this end of the reaction will take. It may be similar to the explosion in 1623; it may be entirely different. We know nothing about the forces involved . . . except how to trigger them and how to perform a few simple tricks. But I'm sure of one thing. The reaction will affect matter on the subatomic levels and it will be on the order of a billion times more extensive than what happened in 1623. I doubt anything will survive it."

A silence ensued, broken at last by Sotomayor. "Have you shown these equations to your colleagues?"

"Of course." Dobler gave a despairing laugh. "They believe they've solved the problem by constructing a containment chamber. It's a solution comparable to wrapping a blanket around a nuclear device."

"How can we discount their opinion?" someone asked.

"Look," said Dobler, peeved. "Unless you can understand the mathematics involved, there's no way I can prove my case. I believe my colleagues are too excited about the project to accept the fact that it's potentially disastrous. But what does it mean for me to tell you that? The best evidence I can give you is the fact that I am here, that I have in effect thrown away my career in order to warn you." He looked down at the floor. "Though perhaps I can offer one further proof."

They began to bombard him with questions, most of them challenging in tone, and—concerned that the meeting might suddenly break up and my car be discovered—I slipped away from the window and headed back toward town.

It is a measure, I believe, of the foolishness of love that I was less worried about the fate of the world than about Ivie's possible involvement in the events of Welcomes' story, a story I was now hard put to disbelieve; it seemed I was operating under the assumption that if Ivie and I could work things out, everything else would fall into place around us. I drove back to the hotel, waited a while, and then, deciding that I wanted to talk to her somewhere more private, somewhere an argument—I thought one likely—would not be overheard, I left a note asking her to meet me on the far side of the island, at an abandoned construction site a short ways up the beach from St. Mark's Key—the skeleton of a large house belonging to the estate of an American who had died shortly after work had begun. This site was of special moment for Ivie and me. It was set back from the shore, hidden from prying eyes by dense growths of palms and sea grape and cashew trees, and we had made love there on several occasions. By the time I reached it, the moon had risen and the unfinished house—with its gapped walls and skewed beams and free-standing doorways—had the look of a surreal maze of silver light and shadow. Sitting inside it on the ground floor, I felt it was an apt metaphor for the labyrinthine complexity of the situation.

Until that moment, I had not brought my concentration to bear on this complexity, and now, trying to unravel the problem, I found I could not do so. The circumstances of Welcomes' story, of Dobler's, Ivie's, and my own . . . all this smacked of magical serendipity and was proof against logic. Time, which had always been for me a commodity, something to be saved and expended, seemed to have been revealed as a vast fabulous presence cloaked in mystery and capable of miracles, and I had as little hope of comprehending its processes as I would those of a star winking overhead. Less, actually. I attempted to narrow my focus, to consider separate pieces of the puzzle, beginning with what Welcomes had told me. Assuming it was true, I saw how it explained much I had not previously given thought to. Christmas' courage, for instance. Knowing that he would die of a fever would have made him immune to fear in battle. All the pieces fit together with the same irrational perfection. It was only the whole, the image they comprised, that was inexplicable.

At last I gave it up and sat staring at the white combers piling in over the reef, listening to the scattery hiss of lizards running in the beach grass, watching the colored lights of the resort on St. Mark's Key flicker as palm fronds were blown across them by the salt breeze. I must have sat this way an hour before I heard a car engine; a minute later, Aymara—so I had been thinking of her—walked through the frame of the front door and sat beside me. "Let's not stay here," she said, and kissed me on the cheek. "I'd like a drink." In the moonlight her face looked to have been carved more finely, and her eyes were aswim with silvery reflections.

I could not think how to begin. Finally, settling on directness, I said, "Did you know what Dobler was going to tell you? Is that why you chose the name Aymara?"

She pulled back from me, consternation written on her

features. "How . . ." she said; and then: "You followed me. You shouldn't have done that."

"Why the hell not?" Anger over her betrayal, her subterfuge, suddenly took precedence over my concern for her. "How else am I going to keep track of who's who in the revolution these days?"

"You could have been killed,'" she said flatly.

"Right!" I said, refusing to let her lack of emotionality subdue me. "God knows, Sotomayor might have had you drink my blood for a nightcap! What the hell possessed you to get involved with him?"

"I'm not involved with him!" she said, her own temper surfacing.

"You're not with *Sangre y Verdad*?"

"No, the FDLM."

I was relieved—the FDLM was the most populist and thus the most legitimate element of the Honduran left. "You haven't answered my first question," I said. "Why did you choose that name?"

"I was thinking of you. That's all it was. But now . . . I don't know."

"You're going to do it, aren't you? Play out the story?" I slugged my thigh in frustration. "Jesus Christ! Sotomayor will kill you if he finds out! And Dobler, he might be a crazy! A CIA plant! Right now he's—"

"You didn't stay until the end?" she cut in.

"No."

"He's dead," she said. "He told us that if we attacked, we should destroy all the computers and records, anyone who had knowledge of the process. He said that when he was younger, he would have supported any evil whose goal was the increase of knowledge, but now he had uncovered knowledge that he couldn't control and he couldn't live with that. He said he hoped what he intended to do would prove something to us. Then he went onto the porch and shot himself."

I sat stunned, picturing that nervous little man and his moment of truth.

"I believe him," she said. "Everyone did. I doubt we would have otherwise."

"Sotomayor would have believed him no matter what," I said. "He yearns for disaster. He'd find the end of the world an erotic experience."

"I shouldn't have to explain to you what produces men like Abimael," she said stiffly. She reached behind her to—I assumed—adjust the waistband of her skirt. "Are you going to inform on us?"

Her voice was tremulous, her expression strained, and she continued holding her hand behind her back; it was an awkward posture, and I began to suspect her reasons for maintaining it. "What have you got there?" I asked, knowing the answer.

A car passed on the beach, its headlights throwing tattered leaf shadows over the beams.

"What if I said I *was* going to inform on you?"

She lowered her eyes, sighed and brought forth a small-caliber automatic; after a second, she let it fall to the floor. She studied it despondently, as if it were a failed something for which she had entertained high hopes. "I'm sorry," she said. "I'm . . . " She put her hand to her brow, covering her eyes.

The gun showed a negative black against the planking, an ugly brand marring the smooth grain. I picked it up. Its cold weight fueled my anger, and I heaved it into the shadows.

"I love you." She trailed her fingers across my arm, but I refused to speak or turn to her. "Please, believe me! It's just I don't know what to do anymore." Her voice broke, and it seemed I could smell her tears.

"It's all right." My voice was harsh, burred with anger.

We sat in silence. The crunch of waves on the reef built louder, the wind seethed in the palm crowns, and faint music from the resort added a fractured tinkling—I felt that the things of nature were losing definition, blending into a dissolute melodic rush. Finally I asked her what she intended to do, and she said, "I doubt my intentions matter. I don't think I can avoid going back."

"To 1902? Is that what you mean?" I said this helplessly, sensing the gravity of events sweeping toward us like a huge dark fist. "How can you even consider it? You heard Dobler, you know the dangers."

"I don't believe it's dangerous. Only inevitable."

I turned to her then, ready with protests, arguments. Christ, she was beautiful! It was as if tears had washed her clean of a film, exposed a new depth of beauty. The words caught in my throat.

"Just before Dobler killed himself," she said, "I asked him what he thought time was. He'd been talking about it as a mathematical entity, but I had the idea he wasn't saying what he really felt, and I wanted to know everything he did . . . because I was afraid. It seemed something magical was happening, that I was being drawn into some incomprehensible scheme." She brushed a strand of hair from her eyes. "Dobler said that when he had begun to develop his equations, he'd had a feeling like mine. 'An apprehension of the mystical,' he called it. There was something hypnotic about the equations . . . they reminded him of mantras the way they affected him. The further his work progressed, the more he came to think of time—its event spectrum—as evidence of divinity. Its basic operation, its mechanics. Abimael laughed at this and asked if he was talking about God. And Dobler said that if by God he meant a stable energy system governing the actions of all matter on a subatomic level, then Yes, that's exactly what he was talking about."

I wanted to refute this, but it was so similar to my own thoughts concerning the nature of time, I could not muster a contrary word.

"You feel it, too," she said. "Don't you?"

I took her by the shoulders. "Let's leave here. Tonight. We can hire a boat to run us over to La Ceiba, and by tomorrow—"

She put a finger to my lips, then kissed me. The kiss deepened, and from that point on I lost track of what happened. One moment we were sitting on the floor of that skeleton house, and the next—our clothes magicked away—we were lying in the grass behind the house, in a tiny clearing bordered by banana trees. The way Ivie's hair was fanned out around her head, its color merging with the dark grass, she looked to be a pale female bloom sprouting from the sandy soil, and her skin felt like the moonlight, smooth, coated with a cool emulsion. I thought I could taste the moonlight on the tips of her breasts. She guided me between her legs, her expression grave, focused on the act, and as I entered her she arched her neck, staring up into the banana leaves, and cried, "Oh, God!" as if she saw there some enrapturing presence. But I knew to whom she was really crying out. To that sensation of heat and weakness that enveloped us, sheltered us. To that sublimation of hope and fear into a pour of pure desiring. To that strange thoughtless and self-adoring creature we became, all hip and mouth and heart. *That* was God.

Afterward as we dressed, among the sibilant noises and wind and sea, I heard a sharper noise, a click. But before I could categorize it, I put it from mind. My head was full of plans. I would knock Ivie out, drug her, carry her off to the States. I would allow the guerrillas to destroy the project, and at the last moment come swinging out of nowhere and snatch her to safety. I envisioned even more improbable heroics. Strong with love, all these plans seemed workable to me.

We walked around the side of the house, hand in hand, and I did not notice the figure standing in the shadow of a cashew tree until it spoke, saying, "Aymara!" Ivie gave a shriek of alarm, and I stepped in front of her, shielding her. The figure moved forward, and I saw it was Sotomayor, his sharp features set in a grim expression, his neatly trimmed beard looking fake in the moonlight. He stopped about six feet away, training a pistol on us, and fixed Ivie with a contemptuous stare. *"Puta!"* he said. He pulled something from his pocket and flung it at our feet. A folded piece of paper with writing on it. "You should be more discreet in your correspondence," he said to me.

"Listen . . ." I began.

He swung the pistol to cover my forehead. "You may have

value as a hostage,'' he said. "But I wouldn't rely on that. I don't like being betrayed, and I'm not in the best of moods.''

"I haven't betrayed you!" Ivie stepped from behind me. "You don't understand."

The muscles of Sotomayor's face worked as if he were repressing a scream of rage.

"He's on our side," said Ivie. "You know that. He's always supported the cause."

Sotomayor smiled—a vicious, predator's smile—and leveled the pistol at her. "Did you enjoy your last fuck, bitch? I could hear you squealing down on the beach."

The muscles of his forearms bunched, preparing for the kick, and I dove for him. Too late. The pistol went off an instant before I knocked him over, the report blending with Ivie's cry, and we rolled in the grass and sand, clawing, grappling. Sotomayor was strong, but I was fighting out of sheer desperation, and he was no match for me. I tore the pistol from his grasp and brought the butt down on his temple. Brought it down a second time. He sagged, his head lolling. I crawled to where Ivie had fallen. Her legs were kicking in spasms, and when I touched her hair, I found it mired with blood. The bullet had entered through the side of her head and lodged in the brain. She must have been clinically dead already, but obeying some dumb reflex, she was trying to speak. Each time her mouth opened, blood jetted forth. She was bleeding from the eyes, the nostrils. Her entire face was slick with blood, and still her mouth kept opening and closing, making glutinous choking sounds. I wanted to touch her, to heal her with a touch, but there was so much broken, I could not decide where to lay my hands. They fluttered above her like stupid animals, and I heard myself screaming for it to stop, for her to stop. Her arms began to flop around, her hips to thrash, convulsing. A broken, bloody doll. I aimed the pistol at her chest, but could not bring myself to pull the trigger. Finally I covered her with my body, and, sobbing, held her until all movement ceased.

I came to my feet, staggered over to Sotomayor. He had not yet regained consciousness. Tears streaming down my cheeks, I pointed the pistol at him. But it did not seem sufficient that he merely die. I kneeled beside him, then straddled his chest.

A voice called out from behind me. "What goin' on dere, mon?"

Visible as shadows, two men were standing at the water's edge.

"Man killed somebody!" I answered.

"You call de police?"

"No!"

"Den I'll be goin' to de Key, ax 'em to spark up dere radio!"

I waved acknowledgment, watched the men sprint away. Once they were out of sight, I pried Sotomayor's mouth open and inserted the pistol barrel. "Wake up!" I shouted. I spat in his face, slapped him. Repeated the process. His eyelids twitched, and he let out a muffled groan. "Wake up, you son of a bitch!" He gazed at me blearily, and I wiggled the pistol to make him aware of it. His eyes widened. He tried to speak, his eyebrows arching comically with the effort. I cocked the pistol, and he froze.

"I should turn you in," I said. "Let the police torture your ass. But I don't trust you to be a hero, man. Maybe you'd talk. Maybe you know something worth trading for your life."

He gurgled something unintelligible.

"Can't hear you," I said. "Sorry."

Using the pistol as a lever, I began turning his head from side to side. He tried to keep his eyes on mine. Sweat popped out on his brow, and he was having trouble swallowing.

"Here it comes," I said.

He tensed and shut his eyes.

"Just kidding," I told him. I waited a few seconds, then shouted, "Here it comes!"

He flinched.

I started sobbing again. "Did you see what you did to her, man? Did you see? You fucking son of a bitch! Did you see!'' The pistol was shaking, and Sotomayor bit the barrel to keep it still.

For a minute or thereabouts I was crying so hard, I was blinded. At last I managed to gain control. I wiped away the tears. "Here it comes," I said.

He blinked.

"Here it comes!"

Another blink.

"Here it fucking comes!"

His stare was mad and full of hate. But his hatred was nothing compared to mine. I was dizzy with it. The stars seemed very near, wheeling about my head. I wanted to sit astride him forever and cause him pain.

I dug the fingers of my left hand in back of his Adam's apple, forcing his jaws apart, and I battered his teeth with the barrel, breaking a couple. Blood filmed over his lower lip, trickled down into his beard. He gagged, choking on the fragments.

"Like that?" I asked him. "How about this?"

I broke his nose with the heel of my hand. Tears squeezed from his eyes, bloody saliva and mucous came from his nose. His breath made a sucking noise.

Shouts from the direction of St. Mark's Key.

I leaned close to Sotomayor, my face inches away, the blood-slimed barrel sheathed in his mouth.

"Here it comes," I whispered. "Here. It. Comes."

I know he believed me, but he was mesmerized by my proximity, by whatever he saw in my eyes, and could not look away. I screamed at him and met his terrified gaze as I fired.

Perhaps I would have been charged with murder in the States, but in Honduras, where politics and passion license all manner of violence, I was a hero.

I was a hero, and insane . . . for grief possessed me as powerfully as had love.

Now that Ivie was dead, it seemed only just that the others join her on the pyre. I told the police everything I knew. The island was sealed off, the guerrillas rounded up. The press acclaimed me; the President of the United States called to commend my actions; my fellow journalists beseiged the Hotel Captain Henry, seeking to interview me but usually settling for interviews with the cleaning woman and the owner. I was in no mood to play the hero. I drank, I wept, I wandered. I gazed into nowhere, seeing Ivie's face. Aymara's face. In memoriam, I accorded her that name. Brave-sounding and lyrical, it suited her. And I wished she could have died wearing that name in 1902—that, I realized, should have been her destiny. Whenever I saw a dark-haired young woman, I would have the urge to follow her, to spy on her, to discover who her friends were, what made her laugh, what movies she liked, how she made love, thinking that knowing these details would help me regain the definition that Aymara had brought to my life. Yet even had this not been a fantasy, I could not have acted upon it. Grief had immobilized me. Grief . . . and guilt. It had been my meddling that had precipitated her death, hadn't it? I was a dummy moving on a track between these two emotions, stopping now and again to stare at something that had caught my eye, some curiosity that would for a moment reduce my self-awareness.

Several days after her death, the regional director of the CIA paid me a call. My visit to Project Longshot had originally been scheduled for two weeks prior to the initial test, but he now told me that since I knew about "our little secret down here," the President had authorized my presence at the test. This exclusive was to be my reward for patriotism. I accepted his invitation and came close to telling him that I would be delighted to stand at ground zero during the end of the world.

I had been too self-absorbed to give much thought to Dobler's warnings, but now I decided I wanted the world to end. What was the point in trying to save it? We had been heading toward destruction for years, and as far as I was concerned the time was ripe. A few days before I might have raised a mighty protest against the project, but my political conscience—and perhaps my moral one—had died with

Aymara, and I was angry at the world, at its hollow promise and mock virtues and fallacious judgments. Anger made my grief more endurable, and I nourished it, picturing it to be a tiny golden snake with ruby eyes. A familiar. It would feed on tears, transform them into venom. It would be my secret, coiled and ready to strike. It would fit perfectly inside my heart.

On the day prior to the test, I was flown by small plane to a military base on the mainland, and from there by helicopter to the project site, passing over the valley in which lay the ruined city of Olancho Viejo, with its creeper-hung cathedral tower sticking up like an eroded green fang. Three buildings of white concrete crowned a massive jungled hill overlooking the valley, and on the hillside facing away from the valley were other buildings—living quarters and storage rooms and sentry posts. The administrator, a middle-aged balding man named Morrel, briefed me on the test; but I cut this short, informing him that I had heard most of what he was telling me from Dobler. His only reaction was to cluck his tongue and say, "Poor fellow."

Afterward, Morrel led me downhill to the commissary and introduced me to the rest of the personnel. Ostensibly this was a joint US-Honduran project, but there were only two Hondurans among the twenty-eight scientists—an elderly man clearly past his prime, and a dark-haired young woman who tried to duck out the door when I approached. Morrel urged her forward and said, "Mister Corson, this is *Señorita* Aymara Luján."

I was nearly too stunned to accept her handshake. She refused to meet my eyes, and her hand was trembling. I could not believe that this was mere coincidence. Though to my mind she was not as lovely as my Aymara, she was undeniably beautiful and of a type with my dead love. Slim and large-eyed, her features displaying more than a trace of Indian blood. I had a mental image of a long line of beautiful dark-haired women stretching across the country, each prepared to step forward should an accident befall her sisters.

"I'm pleased to meet you," this one said. "I've always

admired your work.'' She glanced around in apparent alarm as if she had said something indiscreet; then, recovering her poise, she added, ''Perhaps we'll have a chance to talk at dinner.''

She placed an unnatural stress on these last words, making it plain that this was a message sent. ''I'd like that,'' I said.

For the remainder of the day I was shown a variety of equipment and instrumentation to which I paid little attention. The appearance of this new Aymara undermined my anger somewhat, and Dobler's thesis concerning the inalterability of time, its capacity to compensate for change, seemed to embody the menace of prophecy. But I made no move to reveal what I suspected. This development had brought my insanity to a peak, and I was gripped by a fatalistic malaise. Who the hell was I to trifle with fate, I reasoned. And besides, it was unlikely that any action I took would have an effect. Maybe it *was* coincidence. I retreated from the problem into an almost puritanical stance, as if dealing with the matter was somehow vile, beneath me, and when the dinner hour arrived, deciding it would be best to avoid the woman, I pled weariness and retired to my quarters.

My room was a white cubicle furnished with a bed, a desk and chair, and a word processor. The window provided a view of the jungle that swept away toward Nicaragua, and I sat by it, watching sunset resolve into a slate-colored dusk, and then into a darkness figured by stars and a half-moon. With no one about to engage my interest, grief closed in around me.

A few minutes after eight o'clock, small-arms fire began to crackle on the hilltop. I went to the door and peered out. Muzzle flashes were probing the darkness higher up. I had an impulse to run, but my inertia prevailed and I went back to the chair. Soon thereafter, the door opened and the woman who called herself Aymara entered. She wore a white project jumpsuit that glowed in the moonlight, and she carried an automatic rifle, which she kept at the ready but aimed at a point to my right.

Neither of us spoke for several seconds, and then I said,

"What's going on?" and laughed at the banal tone that comment struck.

Another burst of fire from above.

"It's almost over," she said.

I allowed several more seconds to elapse before saying, "How did you pull it off? Security looked pretty tight."

"Most of them died at dinner." She tossed her head, shaking hair from her eyes. "Poison."

"Oh." Again I laughed. "Sorry I couldn't make it."

"I didn't want to kill you," she said with urgency. "You've . . . been a friend to my country. But after what you did on Guanoja . . ."

"What I did there was execute a murderer! An animal!"

She studied me a moment. "I believe you. Sotomayor was an evil man."

"Evil!" I made a disparaging noise. "And what force for good do you represent? The EDP? The FDLM?"

"We acted independently . . . I and a few friends."

Silence, then a single gunshot.

"Is that really your name?" I asked. "Aymara?"

She nodded. "I've often wondered how much influence your article has had on me. On everything. Because of it, I've always felt I was involved in—"

"Something mystical, right? Magical. I know all about it."

"How could you?"

"How could I have written the article in the first place? I don't have any answers." I turned back to the window. "I suppose you're going to try to contact Christmas."

"I don't have a choice," she said defiantly. "I feel—"

"Believe me," I cut in. "I understand why. When did you decide to do this?"

"I'd been considering it for some time, but I wasn't sure. Then the news came about Sotomayor. . . ."

"Jesus God!" I leaned forward, burying my face in my hands.

"What's wrong?"

"Get out!" I said. "Kill me, do whatever you have to . . . just get out of here."

"I'm not going to kill you."

I sensed her moving close, and through my fingers saw her lay some papers on the desk.

"I'm giving you a map," she said. "At the foot of the hill, next to the sentry post, there's a trail leading east. It's well-traveled, and even in the dark it won't be difficult to follow. Less than a day's walk from here, you'll come to a river. You'll find villages. Boats that'll take you to the coast."

I said nothing.

"We won't be able to go operational until dawn," she went on. "You have about ten hours. Things might not be so bad once you're out of the immediate area."

"Go away," I told her.

"I . . ." She faltered. "I think we . . ."

"What the hell do you want from me?" Angry, I spun around. But on seeing her, my anger evaporated. The moonlight seemed to have erased all distinction between her and my Aymara—she might have been my lover reborn, her spirit returned. "What do you want?" I said weakly.

"I don't know. But I do want something from you. For so long I've felt we were linked. Involved." She reached out as if to touch me, then jerked back her hand. "I don't know. Maybe I just want your blessing."

I could smell her scent of soap and perfume, sharp and clean in that musty little room, and I felt a stirring of sexual attraction. In my mind's eye I saw again that endless line of dark-haired women, and I suddenly believed that love was the scheme that had enforced our intricate union, that—truly or potentially—we were all lovers, I and a thousand Aymaras, all tuned to the same mystical pitch. I got to my feet, rested my hands on her hips. Pulled her close. Her lips grazed my cheek as she settled into the embrace. Her heart beat rapidly against my chest. Then she drew back, her face tilted up to receive a kiss. I tasted her mouth, and her warmth spread through me, melting the cold partition I had erected between myself and life. At last she pushed me away and—averting her eyes—walked to the door.

"Goodbye." She said it in Spanish—"*Adios*"—a word that translates literally as "to God."

I heard her footsteps running up the hill.

I was tempted to go after her, and to resist this temptation, not to save myself, I took her map and set out walking the trail east. Yet as I went, my desire to survive grew stronger, and I increased my pace, beating my way through thickets and plaited vines, stumbling down rocky defiles. Had I been alone in the jungle at any other time, I would have been terrified, for the night sounds were ominous, the shadows eerie; but all my fear was focused upon those white buildings on the hilltop, and I paid no mind to the threat of jaguars and snakes. Toward dawn, I stopped in a weedy clearing bordered by ceibas and giant figs, their crowns towering high above the rest of the canopy. I was bruised, covered with scratches, exhausted, and I saw no reason to continue. I sat down, my back propped against a ceiba trunk, and watched the sky fading to gray.

I had thought brightness would fan across the heavens as with the detonation of a nuclear bomb, but this was not the case. I felt a disturbance in the air, a vibration, and then it was as if everything—trees, the earth, even my own flesh—were yielding up some brilliant white essence, blinding yet gradually growing less intense, until it seemed I was in the midst of a thick white fog through which I could just make out the phantom shapes of the jungle. Accompanying the whiteness was a bone-chilling cold; this, however, dissipated quickly, whereas it turned out that the fog lingered for hours, dwindling to a fine haze before at last becoming imperceptible. At first I was full of dread, anticipating death in one form or another; but soon I began to experience a perverse disappointment. The world had suffered a cold flash, a spot of vagueness, like the symptoms of a mild fever, and the idea that my lover had died for this made me more heartsick than ever.

I waited the better part of an hour for death to take me. Then, disconsolate, thinking I might as well push on, I glanced at my watch to estimate how much farther I had to travel, and found that not only had it stopped but that it could not be rewound. Curious, I thought. As I brushed against a bush at the edge of the clearing, its leaves crumbled to dust; its twigs remained intact, but when I snapped one off, a greenish fluid welled from the cortex. I tasted it, and within seconds I felt a burst of energy and well-being. Continuing on, I observed other changes. An intricate spiderweb whose strands I could not break, though I exerted all my strength; a whirling column of dust and light that looked to be emanating from the site of the project; and in the reflecting waters of a pond I discovered that my hair had gone pure white. Perhaps the most profound change was in the atmosphere of the jungle. Birds twittered, monkeys screeched. All as usual. Yet I sensed a vibrancy, a vitality, that had not been in evidence before.

By the time I reached the river, the fog had cleared. I walked along the bank for half an hour and came to a village of thatched huts, a miserable place littered with feces and mango rinds, hemmed in by brush and stands of bamboo. It appeared deserted, but moored to the bank, floating in the murky water, was a dilapidated boat that—except for the fact it was painted bright blue, decorated with crosses and bearded, haloed faces—might have been the twin of the scow in *The African Queen*. As I drew near, a man popped out of the cabin and waved. An old, old man wearing a gray robe. His hair was white and ragged, his face tanned and wrinkled, and his eyes showed as blue as the painted hull.

"Praise the Lord!" he yelled. "Where the hell you been?"

I glanced behind me to make sure he was not talking to someone else. "Hey," I said. "Where is everybody?"

"Gone. Fled. Scared to death, they were. But now they'll believe me, won't they?" He beckoned impatiently. "Hurry up! You think I got all day. Souls are wastin' for want of Jerome's good news." He tapped his chest. "That's me. Jerome."

I introduced myself.

Again he signaled his impatience. "Got all eternity to learn your name. Let's get a move on." He leaned on the railing, squinting at me. "You're the one sent, ain'tcha?"

"I don't think so."

" 'Course you are!" He clasped his hands prayerfully. "And, lo, I fell asleep in the white light of the Rapture and the Lord spake, sayin', 'Jerome, there will come a man of dour countenance bearin' My holy sign, and he will aid your toil and lend ballast to your joy.' Well, here you are, and here I am, and if that hair of your'n ain't a sign, I don't know what is. Come on!" He patted the railing. "Help me push 'er out into the current."

"Why don't you use the engine?"

"It don't work." He cackled, delighted. "Nothin' works. Not the radio, not the generator. None of the Devil's tools. Ain't it wonderful?" He scowled. "Now come on! That's enough talk. You gonna aid my toil or not?"

"Where are you headed?"

"Down the Fundamental Stream to the Source and back again. Ain't no other place to go now the Lord is come."

"To the coast?" I insisted, not in the least taken with this looney.

"Yeah, yeah!" Jerome put his hands on his hips and regarded me with displeasure. "You gotta lighten up some, boy. Don't know as I'm gonna be needin' all this much ballast to my joy."

I have been a month on the river with Jerome, and I expect I will remain with him a while longer, for I have no desire to return to civilization until its breakdown is complete—the world, it seems, has ended, though not in the manner I would have thought. I am convinced Jerome is crazy, the victim of long solitudes and an overdose of religious tracts; yet he has no doubt I am the crazy one, and who is to say which of us is right. At every village we stop to allow him to proclaim the Rapture, the advent of the Age of Miracles . . . and, indeed, miracles abound. I have seen a mestizo boy call fish into his net by playing a flute; I have witnessed healings performed by a matronly Indian woman; I have watched an old German expatriate set fires with his stare. As for myself, I have acquired the gift of clairvoyance, which has permitted me to see something of the world that is aborning. Jerome attributes all this to an increase in the wattage of the Holy Spirit; whereas I believe that Project Longshot caused a waning of certain principles—especially those pertaining to anything mechanical or electrical—and a waxing of certain others—in particular those applying to ESP and related phenomena. The two ideas are not opposed. I can easily imagine some long-dead psychic perceiving a whiteness at the end of time and assigning it Godlike significance. Yet I have no faith that a messiah will appear. It strikes me that this new world holds greater promise than the old (though perhaps the old world merely milked its promise dry), a stronger hope of survival, and a wider spectrum of possibility; but God, to my way of thinking, darts among the quarks and neutrinos, an eternal signal harrying them to order, a resource capable of being tapped by magic or by science, and it may be that love is both the seminal impulse of this signal and the ultimate distillation of this resource.

We argue these matters constantly, Jerome and I, to pass green nights along the river. But upon one point we agree. All arguments lapse before the mystery and coincidence of our lives. All systems fail, all logics prove to zero.

So, Aymara, we have worked our spell, you and I and time. Now I must seek my own salvation. Jerome tells me time heals all wounds, but can it—I wonder—heal a wound that it has caused. Though we had only a few weeks, they were the central moments of my life, and their tragic culmination, the sudden elimination of their virtues, has left me irresolute and weak. The freshness and optimism of the world has made your loss more poignant, and I am not ashamed to admit that—like the most cliched of grievers—I see your face in clouds, hear your voice in the articulations of the wind, and feel your warmth in the shafts of light piercing the canopy. Often I feel that I am breaking inside, that my heart is turning in my chest like a haywire compass, trying to fix upon some familiar pole and detecting none, and I know I will never be done with weeping.

Buck up, Jerome tells me. You can't live in the past, you gotta look to the future and be strong.

I reply that I am far less at home in the fabulous present than I am in the past. As to the future, well . . . I have envisioned myself walking the high country, a place of mountains and rivers without end, of snow fields and temples with bronze doors, and I sense I am searching for something. Could it be you, Aymara? Could that white ray of science pouring from the magical green hill have somewhere resurrected you or your likeness? Perhaps I will someday find the strength to leave the river and find answers to these questions; perhaps finding that strength is an answer in itself. That hope alone sustains me. For without you, Aymara, even among miracles I am forlorn.

WELCOME TO
ISAAC ASIMOV'S
ROBOT CITY

A wondrous world of robots opened up for the first time to today's most talented science fiction writers. Each author takes on the challenge of wrestling with the mystery of Robot City. Laden with traps and dazzling adventure, each book in the series integrates Asimov's "Laws of Humanics" with his famous "Laws of Robotics."